Stones, Echoes, & Altars

By Octavia J. Riley

Copyright © 2022 by Octavia J. Riley

Stones, Echoes, & Altars (Coven Chronicles, book 6)

First edition October 2022

Book design by Poisoned Apple Publishing, L.L.C.
Editing by Poisoned Apple Publishing, L.L.C.

ISBN: 978-1-955222-05-1

Published by Poisoned Apple Publishing, L.L.C.
www.poisonedapplepublishing.com

Printed in the United States

Dedicated

To myself.

You hadn't written a book in years, and now look at you. You've finished an entire series and an amazing one at that. You battled depression, you started going to school full-time, you set high goals for yourself, and you reached them. Yes, you fell many times. You thought about giving up a lot. But don't ever forget it was you who put pen to paper and finished what you started.

And a special thank you to Nia Rose. Thank you for inspiring me and pushing me when I dug my heels in. Without all your hard work, we would not be where we are today. This world is as much yours as it is mine, and I adore everything we've come to create. Coming together to do what we've done is not for the faint of heart, but if given the choice, I would do it all over again.

I love you.

DESERT TEMPLE
GAYGHA PESHTPENHVET I ESTVETSYT' AYNNIRUV
HEAVEN'S HAND
RED TIPPED MOUNTAINS
DRAGON'S MOUTH
HELL'S H
MOUN TEMP
THE GOLDEN SEA
SILVER THREAD
TOLVAD
KORV
BANSHEE BOG
TEMPLE RUINS
JEWELED CA

'S HAND
UNTAIN
TEMPLE
FOREST TEMPLE
SATVIRIYA
THE CURSED MIRROR
THE BLACK FOREST
WEMBESE LAKE
HALF HEART BAY
WADE
THE GENTLE TITAN
RVO LAKE
THE DEVIL'S PITCHFORK
UINS
CANOPY
AERISTRIA

Chapter One

Birds of a Feather

She was floating. A dismal fog enveloped her, caressing her in soft whispers and cool, glancing touches. Her limbs were numb, her body weightless. Her eyes felt heavy in their sockets. So, so heavy. She could feel the brush of her lashes across her cheeks as she struggled to keep them open.

When she did, glassy irises of burnt orange stared back at her. Ancient. Timeless. Knowledge, known and unknown by the world, rested within those eyes.

Why wasn't she afraid?

Her eyelids drooped against her will, and the vision was lost to darkness. She fought to open them back up, but those strange eyes were gone when she did.

Rustling sounded in her ears. Wings flapped in the distance, and the noise echoed around her like deafening claps of thunder and the hushed flutter of dandelion seeds all at once.

She blinked, the action slow and sluggish. Around her, feathers now drifted in the air. Black, glossy. Catching the light and shifting in an array of brilliant colors. Hundreds and hundreds more floated down, showering her in a plethora of gothic rainbow hues.

The feathers vanished, and her vision was filled with the full moon, soaked through in deep crimson and bleeding off into a blackened sky. Words, muffled or underwater or behind clasped

fingers, swarmed her ears like bees buzzing in her brain. Eyes stared back at her, but now they were drowning in insanity, and they were countless in number. They were the same eyes that gleamed in the blood-soaked light of the fires that swept through the borough as she pointed her weapon at Rafe. They were everywhere, surrounding her on all sides.

Hands reached out with long, chipped nails. The noises grew louder, sharper, swelling in her ears until she felt they might pop. The cackling laughter pierced the veil, and then it was chaos.

Fingers grabbed her, pulling and yanking her in hundreds of directions. She tried to scream, tried to thrash out of their hold on her, but she couldn't. Paralyzed, helpless. Her lungs burned. The faces grew closer. The sounds were ear-splitting.

Everything was red.

Red glow of the moon.

Red stains on teeth in too-wide grins.

Red blood trailing down her arms.

Red fire sweeping through the borough.

Red.

Red.

Red!

"Thea!"

Thea gasped, and her eyes flew open. Rafe was below her, shoved down flat on a white cot. At his neck, a dagger was poised just above his flesh.

It took her a moment to register that it was *her* fingers wrapped around the handle. She jerked back and flung the object away from him, uncaring of where it landed. She heard the metal clatter against the floor. She stared down at him in shock, then at the hands that had nearly harmed him. Her fingers began to tremble, and shivers wracked her body.

Rafe began to move and sit up slowly, and it was then she realized she was sitting on his legs—dressed only in a hospital gown.

She scrambled off him and hastily set a good distance away from the cot. The tile was cold under her bare feet, and more shivers danced their way up her arms. She couldn't meet Rafe's gaze, so her eyes skittered along the floor until they rested on the knife several feet away. That was *her* weapon.

Water sloshed somewhere off to the side, and Thea whirled around to find the source of the noise. She found the stupefied gazes of Namara and Mokana. The kelpie was half-submerged in a metal tub, but after a moment of stunned silence, she clambered out and leaped into Thea's arms. The breath was nearly knocked out of her from the impact, but she managed to stay upright and shakily return the embrace. She closed her eyes and let go of a long, deep sigh. Her heart slowed its frantic pace as the minutes ticked by, and her senses, dulled by her initial panic, came back to her.

Wet.

Her clothes were becoming soaked. Her fingers brushed against sopping tresses. Her nose was filled with the scents of salt, brine, and evergreen trees. She could hear Namara's breathing, could hear her own breathing. All these things calmed her. She was safe. She was home. She was with her trusted partners.

The cot behind her squeaked as Rafe moved, and a warm hand gently clasped her shoulder. She pulled back, easing out of the hug, and turned toward Rafe.

"I—" Her voice cracked and crumbled around the dry words wanting to come out. She tried clearing her throat, tried swallowing, but the muscles in her neck refused to work.

"Here," Mokana spoke and handed her a glass of water.

She gratefully took the cup and downed its chilled contents, hissing at the ice that flooded her chest. When she was done, she couldn't find it within herself to meet anyone's eyes.

What had she done? She had attacked Rafe. *Rafe.* Her fingers bit into the glass as she eyed the weapon lying forgotten on the floor.

"Thea, it's okay," she heard him say as he shuffled closer.

"It's not," she quickly bit out, and her words halted the man from coming any closer. "I didn't ... I don't ..." She grasped her head and let out a harsh breath. What was she even trying to say? Sorry? She hadn't meant to attack him?

The grip on her shoulder flexed, reminding her of its presence. "It is. I know you, T. I know you would never intentionally wield a weapon at me. Not unless you're sparring with me. That's when I'm actually scared."

Her lips quirked up at the corners despite herself. She glanced up and caught his blue-green gaze.

"How do you feel?" Namara asked, pulling Thea's attention away.

She blinked and peered down at herself. Aside from the damp hospital gown keeping her somewhat modest, nothing stuck out to her. She stretched her arms out, rotated her shoulders, and flexed her fingers and toes.

"I feel fantastic," she said after a few moments. It was hard to believe.

Rafe nodded. "You should after having a few drops of wyvern blood."

Thea froze. *The cure. The battle. Blythe. Rafe sacrificing himself to the blood mages.*

She jerked her gaze back to him, and her eyes flashed as anger coursed through her and combatted the chill from the hospital room. "Don't you *ever* do something stupid like that again!"

Rafe, taken aback by her sudden burst of anger, took a moment to respond. Then his eyes narrowed, and he placed his hands on his belt pouches. "So, you're the only one who can do something stupid or reckless?"

Thea crossed her arms stiffly over her chest, her own glare intensifying. "And who lectures me to death when I do something stupid or reckless?" she yelled.

Rafe scoffed. "There wasn't anything else I could do. They were closing in on all sides—"

"Uh-uh, no. I could have fought by your side—I *did* fight by your side."

"And you could have died—you almost *did* die!"

"You *would* have died if I hadn't jumped in!"

"Better me than you—"

"No!" Thea shouted, silencing the Summoner. The entire room descended into an uncomfortable stillness. She closed her eyes and took a large, calming breath. Anger still churned hotly within her, but she wouldn't let it burn those she cared about. She wasn't going to let it consume her. Her tone remained stern, but the fire in her had fizzled. "*Never* say that to me again. Am I clear?" She didn't wait for his response. "Don't you dare assume my feelings are any less than yours. What you would feel if I died, I would feel if you died. You aren't allowed to throw yourself into suicidal situations any more than I am. You have to hold yourself to the same standards you hold me to."

Rafe's mouth bobbed open and closed as he floundered for words. "I … I didn't—" But a soft knock on the door interrupted him before he could finish.

All four heads jerked to the entrance and watched as Savanna Snow emerged from the other side, surrounded by tiny red imps. From the doorway, they looked as if they were standing on top of one another to see into the room.

"Good, you're awake. We can discuss your health later, seeing as there's nothing physically wrong with you. The Council has ordered an emergency meeting as soon as you wake up."

Thea blinked, head suddenly swimming as she was brought back to the matter at hand. Right. The tablet. The Council.

They probably want to discuss the fight in Herbon as well.

She swiveled her head back to Rafe. He was regarding her with a cool gaze, eyes frosting into a chilling blue. Whether his mood had turned for the worse because of her, their interruption, or the fact that they now had to go before the Council was unclear. Regardless, "We'll talk about this later." Then, to everyone else, "I'll be out in a minute. I need to get changed."

Chapter Two

Positions of Power

Thea stood before the Council dressed in all black. Her slate-gray cloak was laid over her arm, useless in the toasty room. Her hair had been a mess of wild curls and frizz, but Mokana had tried to help her tame it by pulling her hair back into a thick braid. Namara had picked out her outfit for her while she'd been comatose, and she was most thankful to be out of the hospital garb. The cheap material made her feel like she'd break out into rashes if she kept it on long enough.

In the room with her and standing before the High Priests and Celestial were Rafe and Dr. Snow. Namara and Mokana had not been invited as they had not been a part of the mission, and no one had needed to tell Savanna twice to keep her seven mini devils out. Thea's eyes had shifted and darted around the Council room to see if any damage from the now infamous "battle of the blue cloaks" remained. None could be found.

Her eyes drifted back to the High Priests, specifically to the new faces she saw there. Upon stepping into the chamber, Thea had done well to mask her surprise at the most recent additions to the Council. The same could not have been said for Rafe.

Two people now took up one of the thirteen seats—the Remes twins. The high-backed chair they sat in had been modified to accommodate them both.

In Tolvade, twins were not that rare—they were about as common as those born without magic. What *was* rare were twins gifted with equally strong magic. Both parents could be powerful casters, but twins usually always came out with just enough magic to make a crystal ball call. Rafe's siblings had mostly fortune-telling level of magic at best, except for the one who had been born singularly like him.

It was theorized that the magic inherited by the parents of twins was split between the two embryos. Support to back this claim came from all accounts of twins—regardless of their level of magic—having near telepathic links with one another. Somewhere along the line, the belief that twins were two facets of the same soul became concrete throughout society.

Lilith and Leto sharing one seat on the Council was nothing to bat an eye at, though Thea did wonder what would happen if they should come to a disagreement on something. Their individual magic was strong enough to land them Summoner positions, and combined with a semi-telepathic link, it was no wonder they had been chosen for the open High Priest position.

Another Summoner had been promoted directly to High Priest, but the woman's name was currently slipping her mind. Rafe would know, but from eyeing the man beside her, she noticed his eyes hadn't left the twins' knowing smirks.

"I believe we're still missing someone," the Celestial spoke up with a murmur. It was hard staring directly at the being, but Thea thought she detected a note of amusement in their voice.

Lilith's simper transformed into something much more lighthearted, but a quiet huff left the other twin. "I apologize, High One," he said and glared over the tops of Thea and Rafe's heads at the large double doors. "I was explicitly clear on the time she needed to be here."

Thea glanced at Rafe, eyebrow ticking high in question. She received a small shrug from the man, who then peered curiously over his shoulder as if the doors to the Council room would announce just who was supposed to breach them.

Thea cleared her throat, and immediately all eyes shifted to her. How she loathed the attention, the cold blanket of anxiety wrapping heavily around her chest, the tight grasp of fingers around her throat that made it hard to swallow, but she steeled her spine and reminded herself she had stared down a dragon, ghosts, and crazed blood mages all in one day. She could look to the leaders of her country with confidence. "Who are we waiting on exactly?"

The Celestial aimed a gentle smile at her, but it was the strained lines around their mouth and eyes that made Thea all the more nervous. Before the High One could speak, though, the double doors behind them flung open. Thea, Rafe, and Dr. Snow pivoted to see who the mystery person was that they were waiting on.

A woman with a blood-red, long-bobbed hairstyle stumbled in. She was huffing as if she'd just run from wherever she'd come from, and a wide grin stretched her lips. She flipped her hair out of her dark eyes and strode forward, unapologetically confident in the wake of the

Council's scrutiny. Thea eyed the woman's gait and noted that, although indiscernible to the untrained eye, this woman favored her left leg. Either a weapon was attached to her ankle and was hidden under her pants, she was injured and on the mend, or one leg was slightly longer than the other.

"Isabel?" Rafe queried with a look of astonishment.

Thea couldn't even be surprised that Rafe knew the woman. Who didn't he know at this point? Isabel's head whipped to the side, and her wide smile grew as recognition bloomed in her gaze. She strode over and slapped the man on the back with a laugh. "Yo, Big 'Bain, what's up? Ah, man, are you the one I'm goin' with?"

Thea, having grimaced at the nickname, grew suddenly curious. "You're going somewhere?" She threw at Rafe, but the Summoner was just as confused, with his brow furrowed and blue eyes flicking from Isabel to Thea and then back to Isabel.

"Isabel, please calm yourself before you cause any more confusion," Leto called from his seat. Isabel made a show of zipping her mouth shut and tossing away the key, and Leto let go of another quiet sigh. Traces of amusement still lingered in his dark eyes.

Thea was trying to draw together the connection. Rafe obviously knew her, and Leto and Lilith both seemed fond of her. Was she a member of their team? She hadn't been present the day they saved her from the rainforest. Her dark green cloak also wasn't pinned with the symbol of the phoenix, but she hadn't given Thea the impression that she was well-organized or put together. The emblem could have been left sitting on the woman's kitchen table for all she knew.

The Celestial clapped softly and gained everyone's attention. "Now that we are all here," their smile was also fond as they glanced at Isabel, "it is time we hear the story of your latest mission, Summoner MacBain and Spellweaver Bauer."

Rafe stepped forward, and Thea let him take the reins. He was used to dealing with the High Priests more than she was, and she was not at all jealous of their undivided attention currently aimed at him. It gave her time to analyze Isabel, who was whispering something to Savanna that had the young doctor struggling to keep her chuckles down. It was a new experience to see the usually cordial but straight-faced doctor cutting up. It seemed everyone was friendly with the redhead.

Said redhead came up to Thea's chin in terms of height, and her arms and legs were toned and carried scars that could have easily been healed with magic. They ran along her hands and what was visible of her neck and chest. She wore her cloak—much thinner and shorter than either Thea's or Rafe's—over a loose tunic shirt. Her cargo pants had more pockets than Thea's belts. They were tucked into the woman's tall boots and were thick with tread and laced up tightly with long shoestrings that wrapped around her ankles. The belt slung over her hips was not full of powders, magic trinkets, or objects for spells. Strapped to her person instead were knives with different ends, hooks, a rolled-up ball of thick twine, and a stained, leatherbound journal with yellowing pages.

It clicked.

Isabel was a researcher.

As Rafe droned on about their struggles in the desert and the wyvern that took them to the forgotten temple, Thea thought back to what Isabel had said earlier. If she were indeed a researcher, that meant she was going out on an expedition, and someone in this room was going with her.

Researchers weren't part of the Coven, but their expeditions were Coven-funded. They would come before the Council and plead their cases to run off in the search for discovery, and the blue cloaks would confer with one another on whether the request should be approved or not. It was the researchers who expanded Tolvade's borders by scouting out habitable areas in the surrounding districts, advanced medicine with their discoveries of new plants, and furthered knowledge of the world they all lived in, not just for the Coven but for all of Tolvade. Their research filled the library downstairs as well as the public ones in town.

Researchers also didn't have to abide by the same rules she, Rafe, Savanna, and anyone else with a phoenix insignia had to abide by—hence why her showing up late without so much as an apology hadn't ended with a verbal lashing and threats of demotion. Once researchers were approved for an expedition, the Coven stepped back and let them do whatever they felt they needed to do. If the Council was to Coven members the strict, overbearing parents, to researchers, they were the disinterested babysitters children took full advantage of.

"Spellweaver Bauer," someone spoke her name.

"Yes?" she replied automatically, looking up and finding the face to the voice.

It had been Caden. The man had a square jaw and graying stubble with long ringlet tresses that fell to his elbows in a mass of dark hair that he pulled back in a respectable half-plait. His eyes were severe, the color of evergreens highlighted by the sunset, and they stared down at Thea with an air of authority and—despite his grave depictions—sympathy. "I spoke to you just now about your encounter in Herbon."

The gazes of everyone in the room fell on her once again. "I apologize, Councilman Wallace. My mind was … elsewhere."

Caden nodded sagely, no anger detected in those evergreen eyes. "Do not apologize. I understand how difficult it has been for you in the past few days. If the matter weren't so urgent, you would have been given ample time for rest. As it stands, however, the Coven has just been handed something very important. Summoner MacBain has us under the impression you and he are well aware of its significance."

"The tablet and the blood of the wyvern, yes. If I was not convinced of their power in the desert, I was when they were used to destroy the blood mages in Herbon and heal all my injuries."

Caden shared a glance with the rest of the High Priests. Thea chanced a look at Torro to see if she was still under his scrutiny, but the man had shuttered his thoughts to the world and looked upon her with a blank expression. Her eyes darted to Lilith and Leto. Just about a week ago, she had met them on somewhat level grounds. Summoners didn't go around barking orders unless it was important or mission-related, but now the twins were staring down at her from their throne-like chair, embellished in cloaks as blue as polished cobalt. Their gazes were appraising, almost proud, but that was surely a trick of the light.

"Taking on a horde of blood mages and surviving is a feat in itself and should be praised," Caden continued, peering down at both Summoner and Spellweaver. "Your mission was successful. Not only did you accomplish your goal of finding a cure that will surely eradicate such a nasty disease, but you have brought back part of a long-forgotten relic that will save our world. We, as decreed by the Council, would like to reward you both for your contributions."

Thea forgot her professionalism for a moment and barely managed to catch her jaw from clattering on the floor. Reward them? Sure, they'd nearly killed themselves on this mission, and they had brought back a piece of the Wild Hunt spell, but when had the Coven started handing out rewards for things that were expected of them?

Rafe seemed similarly confused. "You are going to reward us?"

It was the Celestial who spoke next. "While I had my doubts on your capabilities in consideration of the mission preceding this one," they paused for effect, and both Thea and Rafe felt that effect down to their bones, "you two went above and beyond the call of duty to ensure the survival of not only our people but for magic itself. With that in mind, I give Councilmen Lilith and Leto Remes the floor."

"Thank you, High One," the twins said in perfect unison. Lilith stood and, with a booming voice, decreed, "On this day, the Council celebrates Rafe MacBain, of Summoner status, who led Dark Market raids to gather information and mitigate the flow of dark artifacts spreading into the city, who patrolled and safeguarded the outer districts, and who aided in the summoning and tethering of feral demons while maintaining the upmost control. It is here I offer you to shed these responsibilities as Summoner for the position of Second Chosen. Do you accept?"

Thea couldn't stop her jaw from dropping a second time. She turned toward Rafe. His eyes had blown wide, and his lips had parted in his shock. What Thea would liken to panic formed in his gaze, and he sputtered aloud, "Uh, I don't—I couldn't—Wha—"

Something in Lilith's expression stopped his nonsensical drivel. Something that screamed *you owe me*. And he did. Without the twins' help, Thea would never have been found, and their acceptance of Rafe's secret—the secret that got them all into this mess in the first place—was a debt that was just now being paid.

"I … accept," he said finally, exasperation but not total displeasure evident in his tone.

Lilith nodded and took her seat. Leto stood next and continued. "The inauguration will begin in one week. You may change your mind during the deliberation period, however, once you accept for the final time, you will not go back down to Summoner status. Violation of Coven conduct will not end in suspension or demotion but termination. Do you accept these terms?"

Rafe had straightened his spine. This promotion was a serious one to consider. Thea hadn't heard these terms before, but in wake of the recent betrayal of blue cloaks and the distinct separation of Second Chosens becoming their own rank, the responsibility placed on his shoulders would double if not triple. There would be no room for error, no slap on the wrist if he stepped out of line. The severity of termination would ensure everyone did as they were assigned.

"I do," he stated. Leto nodded and took his seat.

The Celestial's head swiveled back to the front, and the light from the high windows made the iridescent eyes glint as they gazed down at Thea. "Now onto you," they said softly. "On this day, the Council celebrates Thea Bauer, of Spellweaver status, who has advanced her skills of combat and spellcasting, developed the quick-thinking abilities necessary for survival, and volunteered to take on missions so perilous in these trying times. It is here I offer you to shed these responsibilities as Spellweaver for the position of Summoner. Do you accept?"

Chapter Three

Same Old, Same Old. Another Mission, Another Dragon—Wait a Second …

It was Thea's turn to have the spotlight shining on her. Shed her responsibilities as Spellweaver? Before she'd joined the Coven, her goal was to become a Spellweaver. That was it. Nothing higher. Field work excited her—not that Summoners didn't do some field work—but she would have to tack on the extra responsibilities that came with being a Summoner. Right now, she didn't have to worry about her concentration skills, she didn't have to worry about advancing her magic to take on Summoner-level spells, and she didn't have to worry about ever going to the Dark Market. *Again.*

Being a Summoner just seemed so confusing as well. There may as well have been different ranks for the types of Summoners one could be. Some mainly focused on field work with occasional summonings, paperwork, and the rare Dark Market raid. Some focused primarily on summoning, had more paperwork to do, and only took high-level mission scrolls, or did what Rafe did and took on Dark Market raids only. The others were practically Second Chosens in training. Lots of paperwork, only took high-class mission scrolls like going undercover, and maybe, every once in a while, summoned a demon.

She took a deep breath. Her decision would alter her entire career. She didn't think she was ready, but the Celestial was waiting for an answer. Everyone in the room was waiting for an answer.

After a long, brooding moment, she finally asked, "May I have some time to think on it?"

Several of the blue cloaks appeared surprised, but the Celestial's calm expression remained unfazed. "Of course, Spellweaver Bauer. If you would like, you may come to a decision after your next mission."

Next mission?

"We on the Council understand that while your physical injuries have healed, your mental and emotional well-being is just as important. We urge you to take the rest of today to gather yourself. Tomorrow, you will be headed to the mountains with Isabel, a prominent researcher for the Coven and Tolvade. We feel you are most capable for the job as you understand what it is you will be looking for. We would also like to keep the information about this mission as discreet as possible."

Thea blinked. Her wide eyes caught the excited stare of Isabel before it registered what the High One had said. The mountains. Where the legendary dragons that walked Aeristria thousands of years ago supposedly resided.

"But I don't understand what it is I'll be looking for."

"Ah," the Celestial made a noise of realization. "You were unconscious when we were alerted to what happened to the Great Orb."

Thea's eyebrows shot up. "What happened to the orb?"

"It was down until about an hour ago. It's barely operable as of right now," Mina cut in. Her soft gaze was weary, exhaustion over the recent events eating away at her, but she pressed on with quiet determination. "Just before you awoke, we were informed of the source of the viewing orb's shutdown. Five points of incredible magic power had reacted all at once."

"One point came from within the Black Forest," Ronan announced. "Another came from the Red Tipped Mountains, and the third came from the Borlimane district—which we thought odd until we realized it was the tablets activating that caused such power to be released."

So, does that mean Blythe activated the tablets?

Thea wasn't about to bring Blythe into the equation in front of the blue cloaks. They would most likely want to speak to her, and … Thea didn't think it was the best time. She felt the sharp pang of guilt strike through her chest, but she ignored it and focused on the present. "And the last two?"

Ronan sighed and sat back in his chair. "One came from the Jeweled Canopy, and the other came from the Adalith district. Though they were not as strong as the other three."

Torro suddenly cleared his throat from the far end of the line of chairs, and dread settled in the pit of Thea's stomach. "We cannot be sure if the tablet is in the Jeweled Canopy because of this. That is why we assigned you the task of finding the tablet in the mountain temple."

Thea nodded once in understanding. She wasn't about to question the order given to her, but she would have been tempted to try had they made her the one to go into the rainforest. She wanted to mention the potential issues of the time warping magic, but the twins had known about it even before they'd gotten involved with her rescue mission. She'd let them brief whoever was assigned the dangers to expect.

"So, my mission is to head into the Red Tipped Mountains and retrieve the tablet?"

"You are correct," the Celestial agreed. "Time is of the essence, but exploring uncharted territory escalates the possibilities of discoveries that could be beneficial to Tolvade as a whole. While you are tasked with retrieving the tablet, Isabel will accompany you and research the area."

Thea eyed Isabel once again, and the palpable excitement swirling off the redhead hadn't dissipated in the least. Great, another dangerous, possibly death-defying mission with an overzealous person to take care of.

"Will I also be responsible for her survival?"

Isabel gave an unladylike snort of laughter, and the twins also found amusement in her question. Thea didn't dare narrow her eyes at her new bosses, but she felt a twitch in her features from her annoyance.

"Do not fret," the Celestial grinned. "Isabel is a very successful researcher. She will be able to handle herself on this journey, of that the Council has no doubts."

"Understood." She didn't really understand how Isabel had managed to gain everyone on the Council's trust so thoroughly, but she wasn't going to question that either. "What about the supplies I am allowed to bring?"

Again, Isabel snorted a laugh, and again Thea felt her face twitch. *What is so funny?*

"You will be allowed to keep your second Coven-issued weapon, and your tethered demonic companion will be able to accompany you as well. I understand she was not able to do so when your mission took you out into the desert."

"Understood."

The Celestial nodded before their iridescent gaze flitted to the doctor. "Dr. Snow, how has your team's research progressed?"

Savanna cleared her throat and stepped forward. She pulled a clipboard away from her chest, and a charming smirk split her face in two. "We couldn't have hoped for a better specimen. Not only has it cured all the symptoms of Medusa's Kiss in our patients, but we have yet to see regrowth in the malignant cells produced by the disease. Also, there is a significant amount of transformation in the bone marrow that Medusa's Kiss attacks. Per the blood tests we've conducted, the regrowth of platelets and red and white blood cells has quadrupled their natural development. This regrowth has boosted patient immune systems. Further analysis will have to be done to see if this will build immunity for Medusa's Kiss in the future. But, for now, nothing is conclusive." She gave the clipboard a fleeting glance before she returned her gaze to the Celestial. "The lab team is already working on experimentation with droplets of the specimen. We realize the risks involved in wasting what limited supply we have, but we are hoping to clone the cells' reconstructive properties so that—when we do run out—we will have a perfect copy to continue using in treatments."

"Excellent," the Celestial said with a satisfied smile.

"Furthermore, if patients continue to react similarly, and if we are capable of recreating the specimen, we would eventually like to apply this method in reversing the spread of Gargoylism."

Soft gasps filled the room, and the Celestial looked pleasantly surprised. "And you would have a ready supply of antidote available should this method fail?"

Savanna nodded. "Of course, High One. However, if this method succeeds with Gargoylism, it will eliminate the need for the antidotal venom and the process of extracting it in the first place."

The Celestial nodded. "We eagerly await your results." Then they turned and found Rafe's gaze. "Everyone may be dismissed with the exception of Summoner MacBain. Please stay so that you may be briefed on your new position."

Thea found herself hesitating to leave, sharing one last look with Rafe before she forced her feet to start moving, lest she be told a second time to vacate the room. She left with Isabel and Dr. Snow on her heels, and, while the two women behind her giggled on—thick as thieves it seemed like—her head was crammed with thoughts.

As the imposing double doors shut behind her, Thea was thankful she had been given the rest of the day to "gather herself." She was going to need it.

Chapter Four

At the End of the Rainbow

Her mind was strangely calm as she trudged down the spiral staircase and stepped onto the marble of HQ's main floor. She knew hundreds of buzzing thoughts were just waiting to be fired off in her head, but for now, she had pulled a curtain to the wave of questions she'd soon have to answer. Her limbs moved like a golem's under orders, and she was halfway through the Coven's lobby when a voice snapped her out of her musings.

"Hey! Wait up, uh—what was your name? … Oh! Thea! Wait up, Thea!"

Thea blinked the haze from her eyes and turned around to find the redhead from earlier storming down the stairwell and rushing through the crowd of Coven members and various demon pets until she stood before the witch with a broad grin on her freckled face. She wasn't even out of breath after weaving her lithe body through a circus of sorted beings.

Her honey-brown eyes were bright with excitement, freckled cheeks dimpled as she bared her teeth in an exuberant smile. "Are you ready to head out? Where's your—" The smile vanished, replaced with pursed lips as her hand twirled in the air and the wheels in her head tried to spin. "Your uh, buddy? Your demon horse thing. Uh …" Her hand continued to twirl about as the skin between her eyebrows pinched.

Thea's own brows raised high on her forehead. This was who she was supposed to traverse up the mountain with? She was doomed. As crazy as Blythe often seemed, at least she knew where she had been going when she led them through the desert.

"My kelpie?" she supplied helpfully. That was a good question, though. Where was Namara? Was she still in the infirmary ward?

"Aha!" Isabel shouted, startling Thea with her volume. "Yes, that's what she is. Where is she? We got places to be."

"Okay, wait a moment." Thea brought a hand up to massage her temples that were starting to throb. The curtain holding back all the thoughts in her mind was threatening to bulge, tear, and rip apart from all the overwhelming feelings coursing through her. "Where do we need to go, and why do I need to come with you?" When she pulled her hand down and opened her eyes, Isabel's mind had wandered and was now attached to a little notebook she held up. Her tongue was poking out as she scribbled something down.

"Huh?" She looked up and quickly shoved the notebook into her belt pouch. "What did you say?" Thea was about to repeat her question, but the words hadn't even left her mouth yet before Isabel began answering. "Oh! Right. Well, we're leaving super early tomorrow, so we need to have everything taken care of before we head out. Since your partner just got promoted and everything, that means we gotta buddy up."

Thea already wanted to be done with this conversation, go home, curl up in bed, and sleep the rest of the day away.

"That really only applies to Coven members, seeing as we're trained in combat and defense skills, and we have demonic partners to protect—"

"Psh, the Council makes exceptions with me," Isabel said with a dismissive wave. "I went through the same training as Hattie. She's a Summoner, by the way. And 'sides, I got this little guy to do all the protectin' I need." She flung around the bag on her shoulder and pulled the flap off. Nestled inside, a brown field mouse blinked drowsily up at them. Thea glanced from the bag to Isabel and then to the bag again.

"A mouse."

The redhead snorted. "Not just *any* mouse. Agni here is a rakshasa demon."

Thea's eyes widened. A rakshasa? That was nearly on par with the blasted ogre Rafe helped summon. Rakshasas could shapeshift into almost any creature and could spew flames from their palms (not hellfire, thankfully, and that was why they were technically below a guardian ogre in rank). Still, though, they were serious contenders in the demon underworld in terms of battling capabilities.

Banish a banshee, how on Raen did she manage to get her hands on a rakshasa? She obviously didn't acquire him through a summoning.

Her thoughts must have scrolled themselves onto her face, for Isabel was chuckling her amusement as she put Agni away. "He's been around a while. Found him around the assimilated housing development when I was a kid. Came up to me as a cat. I didn't know no better, so there I was for all of ten plus years thinkin' this thing's a cat until I come home with news of my research career and Agni transforms in the middle of my living room to tell me he wants to come with me. Like, how are you just going to pull the rug out from under me like that, and *that's* the first thing you say? I changed in front of him for years, thinkin' he was just a cat. At least I never caught him looking at me in all my glory … What were we talking about again?"

Thea stared at her. Oh, this was going to be a *long* mission.

"Thea!"

The Spellweaver was thankfully saved from answering. She turned toward the west wing, where her name had been called, to find Namara striding toward her with Mokana in tow. Water dripped off her body as if she'd just dunked herself in the tub, but that was normal. What wasn't normal was the magic mop that had been spelled to follow after the demon wherever she went.

Have more water-based demons been summoned, or was this something put in place specifically for Namara? She bit her thumb to stifle her smirk the thought conjured and decided not to bring it up. "Were you waiting in the infirmary?"

Namara nodded, sliding up to her owner. Her dark, bottomless eyes were watchful and full of concern. Thea ignored the look lest it be the straw that broke the oxcart. "Dr. Snow came back and gave us the rundown." Her voice hardened suddenly as she said, "You better not be thinking of going on this mission without me."

"Don't worry. This time you get to come along for the ride." Thea found herself smirking. "Well, I'll be the one riding."

The kelpie rolled her eyes. Mokana sighed and scratched at her scalp with her long, sharp talons. "Lucky. I have a feeling I won't get to see much in the field anymore because of Rafe's new title."

"Depends. Winona was certainly snooping around a lot."

"With good reason," Namara snapped.

The rusalka ignored them both. "Are you guys heading out now?"

Thea glanced at Isabel, who was staring off in the direction of Ell's desk with her thumbs in her pockets. The receptionist must have fallen (again) and was now cleaning up her mess and fending off helping hands with an embarrassed expression.

"Where are we going exactly, Isabel?"

Isabel didn't even bat an eye.

Thea waited for a few moments, seeing as the last time she went to repeat herself the researcher's lagging mind had caught up. Then she cleared her throat. Nothing.

"Isabel."

The redhead was completely zoned out.

"*Isabel!*" she hissed finally.

The woman jumped and whirled around, brown eyes in a daze. "Huh? What?"

Thea suppressed an exasperated sigh. "Where are we going exactly?"

"Oh!" Isabel's gaze cleared up, and she snapped her finger. "Right. Yes. Um, so …" She cleared her throat, and Thea heard Namara and Mokana giggle beside her. "We need to go by the bank."

Thea's brow pinched. "Raen and Bows? Why?"

Isabel was nodding her head. "Yep yep. The one and only. Well, never mind, there's two of them — but does that count if it's just a separate branch? Anyway!" She slapped her palms together, and the loud clap startled the Spellweaver. "I need to make a large withdrawal. So, let's get going." Then she was marching out the door.

Thea was left staring at the researcher's retreating back until the doors closed and cut off her vision. She shut her eyes briefly and inhaled deeply, letting out her breath in a large sigh. She flicked her gaze over to Namara, who was biting her seaweed-green lips to keep from laughing at her owner.

She glared halfheartedly at the kelpie as she shook her cloak off her arm and pulled the thick material over her shoulders. "Let's go before we get left behind. See ya, Mokana."

A snicker escaped Namara, and the demoness waved at her companion in parting. "Bye, Moka!"

Mokana stood waving at the entrance as the two set off after Isabel. They both missed how the demoness's face fell when the doors behind them closed.

The morning was bright, cold, and windy. Thea's cloak billowed around her legs, and the breeze sliced at the skin of her face until she pulled her black facemask up over the bridge of her nose. She began trudging off in the direction of Raen & Bows' main branch. Namara kept up the pace easily with her long legs, despite pausing to splash through sloshy piles of half-melted snow just how an unruly child would. Up ahead and not too far away was Isabel, having gotten distracted by a street vendor.

They had managed to get caught up with the redhead by the time she was done paying for a shiny stone necklace inlaid with a silver, swirling design. She turned to flash Thea a wide smile as she tied the dark cord around her neck. "Was wonderin' what was taking you so long. Don't go gettin' too distracted now." Then she turned and strode off again, leaving a baffled Thea and giggling Namara in her wake.

"This is going to be—"

"Don't even say it," Thea gritted out and started after her newfound partner. Namara's lips thinned, but they wobbled in their attempt to keep her laughter contained.

The street was fairly quiet today. Only a few of the braver—or desperate—vendors had set up their carts, tents, and stalls. Half of the city had no doubt heard the commotion from last night, and not many had dared leave their homes to see which side had prevailed. Morning would come and shed light on the situation, but it was still early, and beings were still timid to uncover the truth just yet.

The major establishments were forced to open regardless of their fears. Raen & Bows, their headquarters at least, were open to the public as if it were any other day. Located in the Adalith district, Thea and Namara strode through the streets with their destination in mind. The sun had come out to warm the frozen ground under their feet, but the wind whipped that little warmth away.

The bridge over the river, Silver Thread, marked the threshold of the district. Up until then, the cobblestone roads had been uneven with stones missing to create jarring potholes for carts and buggies. They were dull gray in color with moss and weeds growing between the cracks. It wasn't so much that the roads were unkempt, but in comparison to the smooth, squared sandstone starting at the bridge and making its way through Adalith, the roads everywhere else looked as if they hadn't been worked on since the turn of the century.

Beautiful flowers, spelled to stay alive even through the worst temperatures, decorated the bridge and the sills of windows of every business and home in town. Some of the townhomes were the color of the clouds in the sky, decorated with wood ornamentations and black shutters. Others were made from dark red brick with green, metal trimming around the windows and doors. The people who lived in these buildings were just rich enough to settle down in the fancy district, but true wealth lay beyond the high-class, compact little borough of Cascades. People like her parents and some of the blue cloaks lived farther out in towering mansions with sprawling yards and ornately decorated bushes. But even the less expensive townhomes and high-rising apartments with peekaboo views of the waterfall were more than Thea could ever afford.

Maybe not on Rafe's new salary.

Thea nearly tripped over her own feet, and she couldn't even blame the cobblestone road because, well, there wasn't one.

"You okay?" Namara asked, and she didn't conceal her concern as well as she might have thought she did.

"Yeah, I'm fine." She wasn't going to linger on the thought that had tripped her up any more than the other thoughts waiting to be let loose in her head. Add it to the growing pile behind the curtain in her mind, right beside the memories of her telling Rafe she loved him just before they were supposed to die. She didn't want to think about what that would mean for their relationship now that they had very much *not* died.

She sighed, ignoring Namara's pointed look, and brought her chin up as she waded through the white-collared populace. These beings, though neighboring Borlimane, were braver than those in center Tolvade. Bolstered by ignorance and arrogance alike, Adalith's people continued on as if the day were a normal one. She met their gazes head-on, ones that flitted down to her silver insignia and filled with either mocking amusement or flat-out disdain. They could tell by the pin on her cloak that she couldn't afford even a meal here, but if her insignia hadn't given her away, her rugged boots and plain corset would have. Even her demon companion was not of high enough class to be impressive (but should anyone attempt to say so, it wouldn't be the kelpie they'd need to worry about). The disgusted looks Namara got as water trailed behind her were not new, and the demoness appeared as unfazed as ever.

Up ahead, Raen & Bows was the face of a row of high-reaching buildings that split the wide street into two one-way paths. It was several stories high with its metal, clover-green roof. At the very top, a small, gold flag whipped wildly in the wind. The red-bricked bank stood out among the sleeker, more modern shops, and the dark stain of the wooden double doors gleamed in the sun as Isabel — having waited for them to catch up — pulled them open. Thea was hit with the scent of cleanser cleaning magic and old coins. The emerald and gold-flecked tile clacked under her feet and echoed around the high-ceilinged room.

You mean there aren't any more floors above us? Just a bunch of empty air? How much does it take to heat this place?

Thea dropped her gaze down from the ceiling and looked around. A dark wooden countertop ran half the length of the building on either side, divided evenly for the six leprechauns on both the right and left. Customers were checking on their accounts with several of the beings while the tellers not working with clients scribbled down on scrolls with feathered quill pens. At the back of the room, a separate desk stood alone with a single, older leprechaun speaking to a very miffed customer.

Thea had never seen so many leprechauns in one room before. The smaller branch in the center of town employed anyone. What Thea was most surprised to see was just how many leprechauns didn't have ginger hair. Another stereotype for the books.

Isabel made a beeline for the center desk, and Thea and Namara begrudgingly followed after her. The older leprechaun came up to Thea's knees, but he was sitting atop a red, high-backed, plushy chair that elevated him a few feet in the air. As soon as he spotted Isabel striding toward them, he immediately hopped down off his perch and dismissed the woman still talking to him with a "Yes, yes, Mrs. Sundill, we'll take care of the issue right away. We'll contact you first thing tomorrow morning." He then walked right past the woman and beamed a bright, white smile at the redhead.

Isabel was quick to return the grin with one of her own. "Yo, Isaac, how ya been?"

"Ms. Thomas, always a pleasure! Anything we can do for you today? Perhaps you've come to make another deposit?" Isaac looked oh-so-hopeful, clamping his small hands together in front of him while his bright, golden eyes positively shone. Thea wondered if he was restraining the urge to rub his palms together like a greedy villain. His accent was fluid, pitched high on the vowels, and he spoke like he was pressed for time, yet there was nothing but patience on his round face.

Thea watched in bemusement as the woman Isaac had previously been speaking to left with a huff, sending the party a withering glare. Neither the leprechaun nor Isabel spared her a look.

"Mmm, not today. Actually, I came by to make a large withdrawal."

Instead of disappointment flashing across the leprechaun's face like Thea imagined might happen, Isaac merely appeared curious. "Of course, of course! Mission must be a quare one if you're comin' by the bank. Come along, then." He spun on his pointed, leather shoes polished to a shine and guided them to a door behind the desk.

Isabel waved off the creature's concern as they were led through a hallway. Massive, shuttered doors ran the length of the dull gray path on either side, and glowing runes were printed on each one, sealing them magically shut. "Just remember to donate my assets to the research department should I ever keel over," Isabel reminded, continuing the conversation.

This time, disappointment *was* clear to read on Isaac's face, and he sighed quietly. "I'm well aware, Ms. Thomas, but we shan't speak of such things. Now then." He halted before one particular door and stared expectantly at the redhead.

Isabel made a face, and it was the first time anything other than absentmindedness or amusement was scrolled over her features. Thea watched as annoyance transformed Isabel into a cold, hardened soul. She fished out a tiny vial from her pouch with wooden, jerky movements. In her hand, a tiny, glass jar of gold dust glittered in the hallway's artificial light. She sprinkled some onto her fingertips, just enough to give the digits a light sheen, before pressing them to the door. The glow was soft, minute, barely even visible from under Isabel's palm, but it was enough of a magic signature for the rune to activate. It lifted the spell, and the metal door rolled up in a ruckus.

Inside, a mountain of gold awaited them.

Isabel shook the dust off her hand with a look of disgust and waltzed into the room with purpose, leaving a gaping Thea and Namara in her wake. The kelpie rushed in and twirled about in amazement. She bounded over to one pile, then another, and then another, inspecting the mass of treasure as closely as possible without actually touching any of the jewels, coins, or antiques littered throughout the vault. Thea hesitantly stepped in, and she too pivoted on her toes, trying to take in the massive amount of wealth around her.

"What in the name of magic?" Thea wondered aloud.

The woman had to be as rich as her parents.

Isabel peered down at Thea from atop the mountain of coins she was standing on and proclaimed boldly, "Magic's got nothin' to do with it."

Thea thought the statement was a bit odd, but not as odd as what the researcher was doing on top of all that gold. Isabel was surveying the treasure at her feet with detached curiosity. She pursed then unpursed her lips, tilted her head this way and that, and hummed to herself as if she were thinking about what the best course of action to take was. She squatted down, and a few coins shifted under her feet much like the brilliant-gold sand in the desert would have. Another pang of guilt hit Thea square in the chest when she was reminded of Blythe, so she turned her attention away from the researcher.

Isaac cleared his throat and waved at the trio. "If that's all, I'll leave you to it. Save travels, Isah—!" The squeal of high-pitched shoes slipping and tumble of limbs had all three of them turning in the direction of the noise.

"Are you all right?" Isabel hollered from atop the mountain of gold.

A groan followed by a strained reply, "Aye, all's well here. Just slipped a little on something wet … Going to need to get this cleaned up …" The last part was muttered quietly, but Thea and Namara still cringed.

The kelpie whispered, *"I'm so sorry,"* up at Isabel, who would hopefully convey her sincerity to the poor leprechaun, but Isabel was already distracted once again.

They stood around for a while after that, waiting for the redhead to be done doing … whatever it was she was doing. Eventually, though, Namara got bored and began scouring the generous piles of trinkets and gold all around them. Thea continued to watch the researcher scoop through the coins she was sitting upon, much like a squirrel trying to find where they buried an acorn.

A soft gasp from Namara had her turning around to see the kelpie dangling something shiny from her fingertips. It looked like a necklace, but it was the gaudiest piece of jewelry she had ever laid her eyes on. The chain was enormous, each link the size of Thea's thumb, and the pendant was in the shape of a cat. The cat was a substantial collection of tiny black gems. It was hideous.

Ma would have killed someone for it.

"Ooh, whatcha got there?" Isabel jumped up to her feet, slid down the large pile of gold, and hopped over to where Namara was twirling the necklace in the air still by the tips of her fingers. "I remember finding that at the bottom of Lorvo Lake. Scrubbed it with a toothbrush for, like, three days trying to get the grime off it. Real ugly, but I knew it'd come in handy one day." She plucked the accessory out of Namara's grasp and stuffed it into the satchel at her hip.

"It's going to come in handy how, exactly?" Thea queried, brow arched and arms crossed.

Isabel snickered, her earlier gloom having dissipated completely. "Bartering, Miss Spellweaver. We're gonna need some ammunition if we want intel."

That certainly had Thea's attention. She despised going into a mission blind, and she was honestly surprised Isabel wasn't the type to go in wands blazing. However, something told Thea Isabel had some sort of aversion to magic. Yet, she clearly wasn't magicless.

Rather than letting her thoughts wander further, she straightened up and peered around the treasure trove of a vault. "What exactly are we looking for that can be used as a bargaining chip?"

Isabel was already digging through another pile a few steps away, but she paused and hummed briefly. "Anything that screams gaudy, antique-ish, or downright weird."

Namara looked like a little kid in a potion shop the way she immediately jumped on the task and began scavenging through all the gold.

Thea let loose a sigh through her nose and began her own investigating. She'd look up at the occasional *"Ooh"* and *"Ahh"* from both researcher and kelpie, and eventually they managed to collect an assortment of odd treasures. A rolled-up parchment with a crumbling leather tie holding it together, one jewel-encrusted goblet, a sparkling garment that was more revealing than Thea had the pleasure of imagining, a magnifying glass with a bone handle, several raw crystals and gems of varying shapes and sizes, and a handful of gold coins thrown in at the last moment for good measure.

Thea glanced at Isabel. "And how are we going to carry all of this out of here? Unless your informant is in Adalith, we'll be mugged as soon as we cross the border." There was also no way on Raen Thea would be caught lugging around that one article of clothing—if one could even call it that—lest someone think it was hers.

Isabel jumped to her feet and whipped out a small bag tucked into her belt pouch, a gleam of pride in her features as she waved it around like it was going to solve all their issues. It looked like it would hold a couple of gold coins. Maybe.

"What's that?" Namara asked in wonder.

If possible, the redhead puffed up even more. "A researcher has to bring back specimens of whatever they're studying to the lab. I run into all kinds of things I have to carry with me, and rather than drag around a big ole backpack, I got this nifty Morgan le Fay bag."

Thea sputtered. "A what?"

A boastful grin spread Isabel's lips wide. "How do ya think I got all this back here?" she asked, gesturing to all the treasure around her.

Thea did a quick glance about the vault and considered how large some of the treasure in there was—a massive chest, an ivory statue as tall as herself, and a full-length mirror that glimmered from within a silver frame would surely have been difficult to carry without the help of several people—or one Morgan le Fay bag.

She nodded curtly. "All right then, let's get this all gathered up and head over to your informant. I'm curious to know how anyone outside the Coven has relevant information to our mission."

She only received a playful smirk in response.

Chapter Five

The Flustered Patron

Thea looked up at the building in front of her and, honestly, wasn't surprised she was there. At this point, Isabel could have led her to Leslie's house and told her Ma was a double agent.

Ha. As if.

At least at this shady establishment, the food wouldn't make her want to vomit. Thea squinted her eyes up at the Flustered Dragon. Maybe.

The tavern sat alone smackdab in the center of both the seedy, crime-infested Borlimane and the uppity, better-than-you Adalith. It acted as the border's heart for the morally gray customers found on either side of the fence, pumping patrons in and out of its chambers on a regular basis. It was decorated in grime and gold and somehow managed to blend the aesthetics of both districts flanking it.

Thea turned to make some comment, probably not to take too long, but stopped when she got a good look at her pet. Namara had the appearance of someone who'd just seen a ghost—which was pretty hard to accomplish considering she was a literal demon. She was fiddling with her dripping wet locks and smoothing her drenched dress of all its wrinkles—a fruitless effort.

"What are you so twitchy for? Have you never been to one of these joints?" Isabel asked with a snicker.

Dark green flushed Namara's face. "Well … it just so happens a certain being moonlights here as a musician … and, well …" If possible, the kelpie's face became even darker.

Thea stared at her pet in awe. "You're seeing someone?"

Isabel's brow quirked, and she looked up at the sky. "Well, the moon ain't out, so I don't know what you're worried for."

Thea sent her a stiff expression.

"We're not … like *that*. I don't even know if he knows who I am. I've seen him a couple times around HQ, and Mokana actually told me about him." Namara scratched the back of her head.

Thea hummed. "Mokana probably knows every demon just as her owner knows every Coven member. If you see him, point him out to me. I want to know what he looks like."

"No way!" the kelpie snapped, though it was more in embarrassment than anger.

Thea grinned, and it was not a nice smile. "Fine. I'll just ask Mokana."

Namara gasped. "You—She won't tell you anything!"

"Ladies, ladies." Isabel cleared her throat and held up her hands between the two. "Forget the moonlighter, you first gotta worry about if she'll make it out of this establishment without swooning for the bartender."

Thea and Namara both paused and looked at the researcher in confusion. "What?" they said in unison.

Isabel, looking proud of herself for having interrupted their spat, aimed her determined gaze at the Flustered Dragon. "The guy we're wanting to talk to is a real schmoozer and the biggest flirt this side of Tolvade. Actually. Probably all of Tolvade. If it moves, he's gonna wanna make out with it."

Thea wrinkled her nose. "That's disgusting."

"Ain't nothin' wrong in loving multiple people."

"It is if they're not willing."

Isabel snorted and waved off her companion's concerns with a flick of her wrist. "He's nothin' like *that*. Guy's harmless. Well." She pursed her lips and propped her chin up in her hand as she thought about her next words. The stretch of silence that followed was doing absolutely nothing to prove her case. Then she snapped her fingers as if a golden thought bubble had burst inside her head. "Let's put it this way: he's gonna press, but if you're totally uninterested, he's got a line of beings—female, male, both, and neither—just waitin' to replace you."

Thea stared at the redhead. "How comforting."

Isabel groaned. "Oh, come on! Let's go already, we're burnin' daylight. We stand around here too much longer, Namara's wanna-be lover will show up."

Namara looked wholly uncomfortable with this being said out loud and, flushing a dark green again, marched off in the direction of the building.

Isabel and Thea shared a brief look before quickly following after her. They didn't have to go very far as the kelpie had been stopped by the bouncer guarding the entrance. Or *bouncers*, one would say, once she got a closer look. The creature was a giant—though he (they?) was much,

much smaller than the giant Thea had encountered in the rainforest. This giant was specifically called a jötunn. They were stunted versions of the giants in the Jeweled Canopy who had descended from Titans (or so the legend went). However, jötunns were no less intimidating with their double limbs and double … well, everything.

Hence, one being a bouncer.

"… only beings who know the owner get through this early," one of the jötunn's heads was saying. He had an irritated scowl adorning his features, though it appeared to be less directed at Namara and more directed at having to stand guard so early in the morning. The three females were the only ones there, it seemed.

"Yeah, go *away*," the other head mumbled with a sleepy yawn, rubbing a large hand over his exhausted-looking face.

"Oi, wake up, Cleatus!" Isabel barked as she made her way over to the giant. Said giant jerked at her loud, abrasive tone and peered down at the tiny, gutsy woman before him.

Isabel spared him not a second glance as she moved her attention to the being's other half. "Shoo, Eurytus, quit scarin' my friend with that mean mug of yours."

Instead of getting angry, Eurytus's expression softened just a tad, but he still sighed in exasperation. "You know you're the only reason he lets certain beings in this early, right?"

"Yeah … Yeah," Cleatus interjected, still trying to rub the sleep out of his eyes as he yawned. "Why you gotta come so early in the morning, Izzy?"

Isabel crossed her arms over her chest and cocked her head to the side. "Aww, well, don't that just make me feel all warm and fuzzy inside. Quit complainin' like you don't like the extra coin on your checks."

The jötunn grinned, and the being stepped aside and waved the three of them on through. "All right, go on in," Eurytus said.

"See ya boys later," Isabel called over her shoulder as she pried open the Flustered Dragon's doors.

"Bye-bye, Izzy," was Cleatus's sleepy reply.

The inside of the establishment reminded Thea of the mouth of a dragon swallowing her whole with its wine-red color scheme. What windows there were to afford light were still closed off by heavy, plum curtains.

Isabel led them straight down to the bar area, where the room opened up. A few of the windows had been freed of their curtains, letting just enough of the morning light filter in so one could see without bumping into the many booths and chairs clustered around. The stage on the far side of the room would light up the place later that evening, but for now it was empty of performers and silent of the music that would attract countless patrons. The enchanted tree beside it glittered in the limited lighting, but the fruit it would bear wouldn't bloom until customers started shuffling in.

Thea took it all in as she was led to the obsidian bar shoved into the room's corner. The granite counter ran the length of the wall, giving plenty enough space and seating for those needing to wet their whistle. When she was motioned to take a seat by a grinning redhead, she did so cautiously. It still didn't prepare her for the stool to plunge a couple of inches out of nowhere.

"What the—?" she yelped, scrambling to hold onto the counter while Isabel cackled from beside her. The researcher plopped onto one of the seats herself, but hers raised her until both women were the same height. Namara was more prepared for her chair to rise, and she giggled when she met Thea's annoyed gaze.

"Ha ha, yes, it was very funny."

Namara's dark eyes twinkled. "I thought so."

The Spellweaver huffed and turned to Isabel, who was currently digging the dirt out from under her nails. "Where's this guy we're supposed to talk to?"

Isabel looked up and peered around the bar. "Ummm … hold on." She hoisted her body over the counter and dragged a silver bell closer to her. Then she proceeded to bang on it obnoxiously. The ringing echoed throughout the large room, persistently calling for the owner.

A crash sounded somewhere off behind the stage. "That's it!" a voice snapped in the same vicinity. "I'm gonna fire that no good Molionids!"

Isabel snickered but thankfully stopped her incessant ringing. "You better not!"

Silence descended, followed by shuffling and scrambling of feet. A head popped out from behind the stage curtains, and viridescent eyes rounded when they spotted Isabel casually waving from her seat at the bar. The being's head, surrounded by a wild, red mane, quickly disappeared back behind the curtains, and more muted shuffling could be heard. Then the curtains were thrown back by tanned arms, and the being before them practically oozed charm as he waltzed out.

"Well, well, well, if it isn't my *favorite* redhead."

The being's hair was a little more tamed, and he strutted down the length of the stage as if he were about to put on his own show. With tight leather pants and suspenders—that had to be there just for styling purposes because those pants weren't going *anywhere*—over a naked, muscled chest, he could certainly play the part of entertainer. Twin horns adorned his head as scarlet hair bled down into a burnt-orange color, then, finally, a bright, startling yellow. His tail was thick with onyx scales, and clinging to the tip of that tail was a tiny, chubby, smoky creature with nubs rather than hands that held on for dear life.

Isabel snorted. "Vice, I've literally heard you say that to two other redheads. In one night. And one of them was you talking to yourself in the mirror."

"Ah, but for *you* it's the truth. I keep this place open to those I know just so you can march your cute butt in here and make my day." Vice smirked and sauntered on over to the bar, thick tail swishing behind him. The wisp went flying up into the air, where it hung suspended for a moment as if in confusion before it floated down to burrow itself inside Vice's hair.

"Yeah, so I've heard. What have you got there?" Isabel propped her chin in her hand as she watched the graceful Dragonkin sweep by her. His tail flicked out to tug on one of her locks. She swatted at the limb, but it was already out of reach.

One of his clawed fingers came up to scratch the little being behind its tiny head and cooed at the creature. "This is Wispy. Isn't he cute? I had him resurrected by a witch down in Herbon. They have to be guarding something, otherwise, they combust into a glittery pile of ashes. So, I thought, what better thing to guard than an immortal? Now he's my little bodyguard."

Isabel hummed. "He's got a very original, unique name."

Vice sighed, expression drying up along with the charm in his voice. "Why are you here? Not that I don't *love* seeing your beautiful face," he quickly amended with a salacious grin. "And what's more," he continued, "you brought me two other beauties to fawn over." His comment was punctuated by a leer that Thea frowned at, but the one he sent Namara kept the kelpie at a near-permanent dark green color. He chuckled at her reaction before moving over and sliding open a handleless door that blended into the wall. The sound of ice being shoveled was heard before Vice appeared once again.

"They're not interested in the likes of you. One's gotta man who's high up in the Coven now, and the other is swoonin' over someone who works here."

Thea's cheeks flared with heat, and Namara made a scandalized noise. "I'm not swooning over anyone!"

Vice dumped his shoveled ice into the bin beside the bar's sink and blinked up at the kelpie. "Is it Freddie? Please, for the love of the goddess an' all her holy children, don't go stealing Freddie from me! I've never met someone so skilled at the saxophone!"

Dear goddess above, Namara was turning into a furnace from all the blood rushing to her face. "It's not—it isn't, uh, whoever that is."

Vice sagged in relief, but he quickly straightened up and pointed a clawed finger at Namara. "Is it Mavrinn?"

"Oi," Isabel yelled, slapping the bartop with her palms. "We're here on business, Vice, quit pesterin.'" She sighed dramatically. "I can't believe you haven't complimented me for a whole two seconds."

Quick as an air nymph, Vice was draped over the countertop in front of the researcher with a smile as vile as his intentions. The adorable little wisp still clinging onto his tresses swayed with the motion. "Oh, baby, this business better be all pleasure because the things I'd do if only you'd let me …" He ended the thought with a shiver.

Thea wanted to comment, but the less Vice paid attention to her, the better.

For what it was worth, Isabel didn't even so much as blush at the being's crude talk. She only leaned over the bar, moved close into his personal space, and whispered, "Tell me how to get through the Red Tipped Mountains."

Vice straightened with a *tsk*, and all the tension the two had created dissipated completely. "No way, doll." He backed away and pointed at the three of them, tail lashing behind him. Isabel opened her mouth, but Vice was having none of it. "Uh-uh, *nope*. The last time a group of wanna-be heroes made their way to my bar, I had to call in the Cleansers to clean up a black magic fiasco. No way. Take your cute behinds elsewhere. I've got to set up the bar, and when I get back from the storeroom, you had better be gone." He began to walk off, paused, then threw a smoldering look over his shoulder. "Unless you're wanting to spend some quality time with me, then—by all means— *stay.*"

Once his back was turned again, Isabel pulled out her Morgan le Fay bag and made a show of dumping the contents of it onto the bar. Loudly. The clang of gems and coins hitting the counter resonated throughout the room—

effectively halting Vice in his tracks. His tail flicked once, twice.

"Do I even want to know what—"

"Don't you think I'd look hot in this, Vice?"

Thea had never seen a creature spin around so quickly in her life. Her own head was dizzy from the way Vice whirled around and rushed back over to them, snatching the immodest clothing from Isabel's hands and holding it out in the air to get a better look. Then he peered down at the jewels, coins, goblet, and other items they'd brought along with them. His gaze narrowed at the smug researcher.

"Oh no," she said in a most sarcastic voice. "I dropped all my things. How clumsy of me. Will you be a dear and help me pick them up?"

Utterly trounced, Vice sagged against the bar, forehead nearly touching the countertop, and his flaming hair fell over his face to hide his defeated expression. Wispy peeked out from behind the strands and made a face like it was giggling, but no noise escaped the tiny creature. Then Vice was springing upright and glaring at the woman before him. "Fine, you win this time, but you stay right here," he said with a pointed jab at the black granite. "I'm not letting anyone into the dragon's belly ever again."

Isabel looked affronted. "You let someone see your treasure hoard! You never let *me* see it!"

"Lesson learned, babe!" Vice shouted over his shoulder as he disappeared around a wall.

Isabel slumped against the bar with a pout. Silence descended on the group once again, and Thea awkwardly coughed into her fist.

"Um," she said intelligently, trying to break the quiet. "So … you and Vice … are you like, a thing?"

Isabel glanced over at the Spellweaver with her brow pinched. "Huh?"

"You know, are you guys together?"

Isabel stared at her for a good, solid minute before bursting into laughter. Her cackles filled the room, and Thea honestly missed the silence when the researcher started gasping for air like she was dying.

"Oh, good goddess above, *no*," she wheezed. Finally, her laughter subsided into more bearable chuckles. "Vice and I could *never* be a thing."

Namara piped up from behind Thea. "Why? Is it because he's a …?"

Isabel seemed to sober up at the question that was left to hang between them. "No, him being part dragon has nothing to do with it. We're just … opposites."

"Opposites can attract," Thea said.

Isabel snickered softly. "Not like this. 'Sides, I got my eye on someone else anyway."

Thea wasn't one to press, though she certainly was curious about who could have managed to snag and hold onto Isabel's short attention span, but she hardly knew the woman. Rafe might know. Scratch that, Rafe might know everyone in town, but she doubted he knew everyone well enough to know who each person had their eye on. Still, the two had seemed quite chummy this morning—

"Sorry to keep you ladies waiting," Vice called from somewhere past the wall he'd disappeared behind earlier. He popped around the corner with something rolled up in his hands, though it was not a typical scroll by any means.

He slipped behind the bar once again and met each of their gazes head-on. "This is very precious to me, so don't go dying up there on the mountain. Otherwise, I'll never see it again."

Isabel huffed a laugh but nodded along, nonetheless. Vice then rolled out what Thea could only describe as a wooden scroll. It rattled against the granite until it was fully spread out. It had to be as long as Vice was tall, and the Dragonkin was taller than Rafe. Each wooden piece was about a foot in length, as wide as a ruler, slightly curved at the edges, and affixed together with very thin twine along the sides of the scroll near the top and bottom. The color of the wood did not appear to be stained, but it was a unique, golden-yellow color that Thea had never seen before. An illustration of the mountains was spread out before her in deep-stained ink with minute details etched out cleanly despite the age this thing must have been. Characters that did not look like runes were written sporadically, but Thea couldn't make heads or tails of them.

"You'll need to start the journey here," Vice started to explain, pointing at the base of the nearest mountain. Rather than going up, his finger smoothed over the wood and trailed around the side of the mountain. "There will be a path that will save you time and possibly your lives. It's not noticeable at first, but once you find it, you'll be able to stay on it. I don't know where you're trying to go, but you'll want to meet the Huǒshān Clan—"

"People live up in this mountain range?" Thea queried, furrowing her brow at the map in front of her.

Vice flicked his long, multi-colored hair over his shoulder. Then his eyes widened when he realized he just sent the wisp careening through the air and caught the little guy before it could splat against the wall. "I know, I know, I'm sorry!" he shushed and cooed at the small creature before shoving it into the strands of his hair once again for safe (hopefully) keeping. He then cleared his throat. "Where were we?"

Thea, having watched the whole thing in bemusement, said, "Clan. In the mountains."

The Dragonkin gave her a full body glance, though it lacked any passion. "You're a fun one in the morning."

"Is it even still morning at this point?"

"All right, all right," he griped. "Yes, there's a clan in the mountains. The people are hardy—they have to be. This place is no fairy garden. You—" he nodded at Thea in indication, "how good are you with your combat skills?"

She heard Namara give a horse-like snort in amusement. Well, she did have her downfalls, though, so she settled with, "Good enough to be recently promoted to Summoner." She hadn't taken the job yet, but it was the offer that counted.

Vice didn't look that impressed, but he wasn't unimpressed either. He did give her another once over, though, and Thea could not mistake the heat she found in his gaze this time. It made her want to pull her facemask back up over the bridge of her nose.

Vice turned his gaze onto Namara, opened his mouth to say something, but then—as if realizing for the first time that he was facing a *demon*—reverted his attention to the researcher who was enthralled with the wooden map before them. As if memorizing it, her dark brown eyes flickered from one corner of it to the other. "Izzy, you still got that mouse on you?"

Isabel didn't even acknowledge him. Vice didn't repeat himself either. His lips quirked up in a half smile, revealing the tip of a fang just long enough to dent his bottom lip. He leaned over the counter on his elbows, tail swishing high behind him, and his long hair draped onto the granite. The little wisp swung into view as it held on dearly to a lock of hair. There was amusement in his ancient eyes, and Thea could appreciate their beauty when they weren't directed at her.

The silence was what broke the redhead from her trance. She blinked and looked up, darting her gaze between the three of them. "What? What I miss?"

Vice glanced over at Thea and Namara with a smirk. "And that's how you get her attention."

Isabel frowned. "What did you want?"

"Do you still have that mouse thing?"

"He has a name, ya know."

Vice stood upright as gracefully as a predator and waved his hand in the air. "Oh, whatever, as long as he's still around, I shouldn't have anything to worry about. However …" He tapped the wood with the pad of his finger against a certain spot on the map. "Do not go up to the peaks of the mountains. There's nothing up there worth risking your life over, and that's where *they* live."

He didn't need to specify who *they* were. If a Dragonkin was warning them away, then the rumors about dragons living in the mountains were rumors no more.

"You'll probably need a mountain guide," Vice said next. He was rubbing at his chin in thought.

Thea was snapped out of her thoughts. "Mountain guide? There're beings who know their way up the mountain?"

Even Isabel looked confused. Thea had a hunch if someone in Tolvade knew how to get up the mountain successfully, Isabel would have already sought them out. Rafe hadn't volunteered anyone while they held court with the blue cloaks, so he didn't know anyone with that kind of knowledge either.

Vice smiled, and it was all teeth. "Oh yes. My son being one of them."

A woman sauntered up to the bar, set down a large duffel bag, and leaned over the edge. Her blonde curls were pulled up into a sloppy bun, and she wore sweatpants and a large, baggy shirt. Her face was clear of any makeup. No one would be able to tell who she really was until she got up on that stage. She was chewing a wad of bubblegum as she watched the Dragonkin shelving glassware above the counter. On the bartop, curled up in an empty wine glass, was Wispy sleeping the day away.

She blew a bubble and let it pop loudly. The Dragonkin paused in what he was doing and bent down to see who was lounging at his bar. A salacious grin broke out over the being's face. "Mad Mary. How have you been, my dear?"

She popped another bubble. "I'm not Mad Mary right now."

Vice shrugged and went back to putting up the glasses. "You are always mad, though."

"You're always flirting. Do you want me to call you Vice the Dogkin?"

Vice dropped a glass, and only the swift action of his tail kept it from shattering against the floor. "Maryanne! That's offensive!" He hopped down off his stool and crossed his arms over his chest. He was positively pouting.

The blonde shrugged and chewed her bubble gum obnoxiously. "Offensive or not, it's the truth. Speaking of flirting, was that Isabel I just saw leaving?"

Vice's pout evaporated, and he sighed as he slouched against the black granite. "Yes. That flighty little fairy is off on some grand adventure." He sighed again.

"You know," Maryanne began before popping another bubble, "you keep sighing like that, and we're all really going to think you're in love with her. She's never going to sleep with you, Vice."

The Dragonkin blinked and met the woman's gaze. "Oh. Oh, no. I'm not in love with her. It's just—"

"You want what you can't have?"

"No," Vice sighed once more, and a fond look entered his ancient eyes. "She just reminds me of someone, and I'll never sleep with her because of that. I just like teasing her."

Maryanne pulled the duffel bag off the bar and hoisted it over her shoulder. "If you say so," she muttered and began walking toward the back of the stage to get started on an early rehearsal. It was a big show tonight.

The soft look Vice wore melted into a lecherous grin, and he turned to chase after the blonde. "*You*, on the other hand—umph!" The words he was about to say were cut off from a towel smacking him right in the face.

Chapter Six

Crystal Roots of the Mother Tree

Thea and the others stood on the hill bordering the waterfall (the side belonging to Vemeese) in the middle of a small neighborhood of single houses. Mature trees grew between them, and uniform stone fencing squared off the lawns. Though part of the Vemeese district, the homes were more expensive than what Thea alone could afford, as they were built right outside the city and had many conveniences the rural homes further out did not.

One address among the few belonged to Vice's son. Isabel, Thea, and Namara stepped up to the covered porch and eyed over the face of the large, stone structure. The roof was terracotta red and had two conical peaks, and a tall, rock chimney jutted into the sky. Smoke was puffing up into the air and being carried off by the breeze coming from the cliff.

Namara gazed longingly at the waterfall. "I want to live here," she muttered to herself.

"Remind me when my parents keel over, and I get all their money."

The kelpie choked. "Thea!"

"Yeah, okay, that was a bit much." The nasty thought hadn't made her feel better like she believed it would. It made her feel worse. Like she had stooped to their level of hurling hurtful words. She sighed. She was better than that.

Her thoughts were interrupted by Isabel striding up to the door and banging on it with a closed fist. "Hello?" she called loudly.

Thea flinched and hissed out, "He's going to kick us off the property before we have a chance to talk to him!"

Isabel looked over her shoulder. "Why would he do that?"

Thea scrubbed at her face and let go of a sigh. The sheer audacity this woman had. "Let me do the knocking from now on."

Isabel shrugged. "Pretty sure he heard me. I was knocking kinda loudly."

The whole neighborhood probably heard you knocking.

After a short moment, the door swung open, and another redhead answered the door. A familiar one.

Thea balked. "Tasgall?"

The tavern owner was blinking sleep from her eyes and rubbing at her face. She was wearing a tank top, and around the straps were Me'Glach and O'Glach with their tiny hands clutching the material as they continued to snooze. Tassie staggered a little bit—either from sleep or from having sampled the goods last night—and met all three gazes in alarm. "Wha—?" she slurred, voice still thick with sleep. "Thea? What are you doing here? What time is it?"

It was Isabel who spoke. "We thought someone else lived here. Vice's son—what was his name again?" she directed at Thea.

"Uh, Fatik."

Realization dawned in Tasgall's stormy-blue eyes with sharp clarity. Her gaze narrowed, and her voice had lost all its weariness. "Why? Did my dad send you?" The sudden seriousness in her voice startled the pixies awake. Eyes that reflected autumn and another pair that held all of winter blinked sleepily at the trio on the doorstep.

Thea's brow pinched together. "What? No—"

But Tasgall wasn't listening. "He needs to mind his business before I make him mind it! Just because I'm his daughter doesn't mean he can dictate who I let into my own home. I am a *grown woman*, and if he's concerned about him and his *ethnicity*, well, let me tell you, he's gonna be more concerned with me when I show up at Coven headq—"

As Tasgall raged on, Isabel whistled, brown eyes shining in amusement. Thea was waving her hands desperately in front of her, trying to cut off the ranting barkeeper before she could keep going.

"Tassie, we weren't sent by your dad! We were sent by—" Thea jerked back when Me'Glach flew right up into her face with the most severe expression the Spellweaver had ever seen on a pixie. Her leaf-like wings were flapping more like a hummingbird's in her anger.

"What's with all the noise?" a deep voice from inside asked.

All four heads (plus the two pixies') turned to watch a tall, lean being come to the door. He was as bright as a crystal with pale eyes surrounded by pearly lashes, feathery-white hair that reflected like an opal, and a thick, scaly tail as stark as a sheet of paper before the ink drops. He had wings on his back, but they did not resemble those of a dragon's. There were scales, but they were iridescent, see-through, and shaped like long feathers. The wings reached high over his head and draped over his back.

He crossed his pale arms over his exposed, snowy-white chest. "Mom, you can't get in a being's face like that."

Thea balked for a second time. "What? Mom?" Her gaze homed in on the pixie in front of her.

Surely not … there was no way! Was there …?

As if her thoughts had been heard, Me'Glach spun around to glare at Thea again with her tiny fists placed on her hips. A minuscule brow rose, and those upturned eyes of hers narrowed.

Isabel threw back her head and laughed. "Oh, this is the most fun I've had in a long time. I gotta keep you around, Thea."

Thea sent her a withering glare.

"*Mom*," the Dragonkin in the doorway admonished.

"Why don't we all settle this in the dining room?" O'Glach requested calmly. "I will serve tea."

Thea looked at Tasgall. Tasgall looked at Isabel. Isabel was staring at Fatik in curiosity. Namara wasn't even paying attention.

"Okay, fine," Tassie sighed and waved them all in. "As long as Dad isn't the one who sent you, then I'll hear you guys out. Bit early, though," she grumbled the last part.

Thea stepped into the warm abode and glanced over her shoulder at Namara to see if she was coming. The kelpie was still gazing off in the direction of the water. The Spellweaver opened her mouth to say something, but she thought better of it and instead unpinned her silver insignia. "Here," she called out to the creature.

Namara jerked around. Her dark eyes zeroed in on the pin, and she aimed a silent question at her owner. She took it, nonetheless.

"This has got my magic imprint on it, but anyone worth their magic dust can tell you're not feral. Still, Coven members are flinging spells and asking questions later right now. So, keep this on you."

Namara's face broke out into a grin before tossing her gratitude over her shoulder and racing off toward the cliff. She tipped her head back, and a shrill whinny left her just before she threw herself over the edge and transformed mid-air. Thea winced at her antics but smiled even as she shook her head in exasperation.

The maple-brown wood of the dining table was smooth to the touch as Thea sat herself next to Isabel. The room was cozy and secluded from the kitchen with its own fireplace on one side. The rustic theme of burnt-orange walls and wooden cabinets holding emerald-green dishes within lent the room a warm quality that had little to do with the fire crackling next to them.

O'Glach and Me'Glach came fluttering in with empty, ceramic mugs and set them around the table before whisking themselves away back into the kitchen. Metal diffusers with the loose-leaf tea inside were already hooked onto the cups' edges. Isabel immediately started fiddling with hers as they waited.

Fatik and Tasgall had disappeared into the kitchen to do who-knew-what, but Thea had a suspicion they were going over a game plan of sorts. What to tell, what not to tell if certain questions came about. Thea was, of course, curious about Fatik, but they were really only here to hopefully get the being to agree to take them up the mountains. She doubted Isabel could bribe the Dragonkin as easily as she did his father, so they would have to play their divination cards just right.

The piercing whistle of the kettle alerted the home that the water was done boiling. Soon, Fatik and the pixies filtered into the room and sat themselves at the picnic-style dining table. Tasgall carried the heavy, cast-iron kettle effortlessly, and she made quick work of filling up all the mugs.

"Thank you," Thea said and cupped her hands around the mug. The heat through her gloves was enough to make her sigh contentedly as it warmed her chilled fingers.

Tasgall set the kettle down on the center of the table, where a matching cast-iron kettle holder prevented it from damaging the wood underneath. "No problem. It's my special blend. Great for headaches, body aches, and keeping your energy up."

Thea snickered. "I can see why you'd make something like this."

"Hey now," she griped in return, but a grin belied her tone. She plopped herself down on the bench beside Fatik and propped her elbows on the table with her chin in her palms. "*Sooo*," she dragged out the word. "Why are you here if my dad ain't the one who sent you?"

Straight to the point. Tasgall was many things, both good and bad, but she was always direct. Her curiosity simply wouldn't allow her to beat around the berry bush.

"Oh, we're here to take Fatik up the mountain."

Isabel was also direct. Too direct.

Thea quickly picked up her drink as Tasgall lunged across the table and grabbed Me'Glach around her tiny waist before the pixie could barrel into Isabel. The table was lifted off the ground for a second before slamming back down on its legs. Everyone had managed to secure their drinks as well—everyone except the unsuspecting Isabel, whose cup wobbled but, thankfully, didn't spill.

The pixie's wings flapped uselessly against the woman's hand as she kicked her little legs trying to free herself. Fatik, who had grabbed both his and Tasgall's cup, had recovered from his mother's sudden fit of rage and was currently gaping and pointing to his (now clothed) chest as if he wasn't the only Fatik in the room.

Thea cast the redhead beside her a look. "Let me do the talking, please."

Isabel's nervous, wide eyes darted from the enraged pixie to Thea several times before she quietly nodded.

"What she meant to say," Thea began, and all eyes were on her. Me'Glach had settled, but she still wore a dark look on her face. "… is that we've been entrusted with a high-class mission that requires us to travel up to the mountains. Isabel had us visit Vice because she believed he might know how to get up there."

At the mention of the Dragonkin, Me'Glach calmed down completely. A pensive look crossed her face, and her ever-changing eyes shifted to Fatik, but the being wasn't looking at her. His features were stiff, but Thea couldn't quite read what he was thinking.

Tasgall brought Me'Glach up to her chest like the pixie was a little doll. She also eyed the Dragonkin next to her, but concern was easy to see in the upturned pinch of her brow. "That's your dad, right? Vice?"

Fatik's expression gentled when he met her gaze. "Yes. I haven't seen him in a long time, but I remember when he used to take me up the mountain to go camping."

Thea couldn't believe her ears. Vice had really thought taking a child up the mountain—which he himself warned them was extremely dangerous—was a good idea?

"He told you I could take you up there, didn't he?"

Thea realized Fatik had directed the question at her. "He did. He said we'd need a guide and gave us your address. If you don't want to accept, that's fine. We don't really have anything to give you, but I can contact the Coven and request compensation. Also, I can't disclose the details of the mission because of its high-class status, but we've been assigned this for the sake of Aeristria."

It was O'Glach who spoke up next. "What does that mean?"

The Spellweaver glanced at Isabel, but the researcher had locked her lips and was waiting for Thea to explain. Thea turned back to the group before her and chose her next words carefully. She wanted their help, more so Fatik's, but in order to gain that, she'd have to reveal some details. What details she chose to reveal were what truly mattered. If Fatik said no, they would be forced to leave, and Tasgall could blab their secrets to the whole tavern. Panic could incite just when things were starting to calm down, and it would all be traced back to Thea. That was not something that she needed to happen, especially after recent events with the sanctuary.

"Essentially, Aeristria's well-being is in question. A yearly spell needs to be done to keep everything in check, and we've recently learned that part of that spell is in the mountains."

"Why the mountains?" Tasgall piped up.

Thea only stared at her. Tassie knew the drill. Her father was a blue cloak, and she had grown up knowing she'd never know all his secrets, no matter how many times she asked.

The redhead slumped in her seat. "I see. Worth a shot, at least." She glanced down at Me'Glach still in her grasp when the pixie tapped her hand. There were no traces of anger there in her features, so Tasgall slowly let her go. Thea braced for the creature to come flying over, but Me'Glach ignored them and instead flitted over to her son.

Fatik watched her as his mother's tiny hands went to cup his jaw. The silence stretched between them before he finally nodded. "I'll be careful, Mom."

Thea, having gone to sip her tea, perked up in her seat. "Are you accepting?"

Tasgall was quick to reply, "Not without compensation."

She should have seen that coming. "Right. I'll make a call to the Coven then." She took a quick sip of her tea before getting up and grimaced as the beverage was still blistering to the tongue. Though it didn't really taste like anything other than hot water, the aftertaste was bitter. Definitely a hangover recipe.

She made her way through the home and stepped outside only to be assaulted by an icy gust of wind. Taking out her crystal ball, she made a call to the only one she knew who could authorize compensation.

Winona's silver gaze was as sharp as ever. "Second Chosen Cavett speaking … ah," she hummed as recognition dawned. "Spellweaver Bauer. I heard you made it back in mostly one piece. Glad to see it's true."

She felt her face harden. "No thanks to you," she bit out. "You mean to tell me you didn't know the blood mages were going to launch a massive spell on the night of the *blood moon*?"

Winona had the decency to glance away, and what might have been contrite surfaced, but it was snuffed out quickly. "We evacuated the citizens beforehand, and we had the Celestial on standby should any of the blood mages have tried to escape Herbon. Trying to combat against them in their own territory on a night they are strongest would have been a blood bath—literally. We would have walked right into their hands. I do apologize you were caught up in the chaos. However, *you* know of the Blood Moon Festival as well, so I cannot fathom why you decided to tread through the district on its most dangerous night."

Trust Winona to turn things back on her. "It wasn't my intention. I'm sure Rafe's made a detailed report on what happened."

"Yes, well, as much fun as it has been scrutinizing your reports, I have other things to do. So, I would appreciate it if you could inform me on the nature of this call, unless it was simply to critique the Coven's battle strategies?"

Thea resisted rolling her eyes at her superior. She did not need to take out her irritability on a Second Chosen and get that promotion offer swiftly rescinded. "I was calling to see if I could request compensation for a tour guide. We've found someone who can lead us up the mountain."

Winona looked impressed. "You've managed to find yourself another out-of-town mission that could possibly get you killed. Two for two, Thea, I admire your tenacity."

This time, Thea did roll her eyes. "Second Chosen C—"

"Yes, yes, I know," she interrupted. "Unfortunately, I do not oversee this mission of yours this time around. I frankly do not know more than the gist of the assignment. Due to the severity of the mission, I will have to patch you straight through to the High Priests in charge."

Thea closed her eyes and prayed silently to the Goddess that it was Mia. Or at least not Torro. Goddess above, if Tasgall heard her talking to her father, she'd kick her and Isabel out of the house and slam the door before they could explain themselves. She opened her eyes and looked down to find the dark gaze of Leto Remes watching her.

She flushed at having been caught with her walls down. "Sorry, I was …" She couldn't even find the words to excuse herself.

"Don't be," he said casually. "I imagine Isabel has dragged you all over the city by now. I apologize for her excitable behavior."

It was hard to believe she was speaking to a blue cloak. Leto spoke to her as if they were the same rank. He hadn't changed at all since he'd scrunched his polished toes in Rafe's carpet no more than a few weeks ago. And why did he feel the need to apologize for Isabel?

"It's all right, you don't have to apologize," Thea quickly assured. "I didn't know you and High Priest Remes … uh, High Priest Lilith Remes were overseeing this mission."

Leto's lips quirked up into a smile. "Just call us by our first names when we're talking privately, Thea. I know it might be confusing. And as for the mission, the Celestial believes this is a good way to initiate my sister and me as blue cloaks."

Thea was at a loss for words at the sheer casualness of the conversation. She had had a certain etiquette pushed onto her since she could talk, and now she was allowed to speak to her boss, nay, her bosses' boss, like a friend. She was uncomfortable, but it wasn't a … *terrible* experience.

"Oh, okay, um … Well, I was wondering if I could request compensation for a guide. Isabel found someone to lead us up the mountains."

Interest flickered in Leto's gaze. "Of course, she did. Lily!" he called over his shoulder. His eyes tracked something out of Thea's vision, and she could only assume it was his sister. "Izzy found a guide, but they want compensation." Then she was being passed over until equally dark eyes—broken up only by that patch of startling, cornflower blue—met hers.

"Thea," she greeted just as casually as her brother had.

Thea remembered to reciprocate. "Um, hello, Lilith."

The noirette flicked her dark hair over her shoulder, and her eyes crinkled in amusement. "Isabel's got you running around the city on your day off, doesn't she? I'll make this quick: offer two thousand gold. They'll probably refuse but accept nothing over ten. You good with that, Lee?"

"Yeah," she heard Leto say in the background.

Thea felt so awkward. Was this what other blue cloaks acted like when they weren't sitting on their thrones? She supposed they were never truly off the sundial, but the ease in which they spoke to those under them was so … relaxed. Were they like this with everyone?

"You're overthinking things," Lilith said suddenly.

Thea glanced down and found a fond smile on the twin's face. "What?"

Lilith huffed and slumped down in a chair or couch, Thea couldn't be sure, but it jostled the woman's image for just a moment. "We've been Summoners a long time, Thea. We're used to speaking to other Summoners and Spellweavers like equals, and that's probably not going to change anytime soon. Unless we're in a Council meeting, of course."

Well, it's not what Thea would do, but she understood at least where they were coming from. "Oh, well, okay."

"And don't think you're off the hook either. You still owe us."

Thea's brows pinched. "Wait, I owe you? How do I owe you?"

She was passed back to Leto. The man's amused smile was back, but it had sharpened into a devious little smirk. "Did you forget how I found you in the jungle? How we kept whatever secret you and Rafe had going? Surely you didn't think we were going to let that slide?"

"But I thought Rafe becoming your Second Chosen was paying you back?"

"That was *Rafe* paying us back. Not you."

Banish a banshee, how many more hoops was she going to have to jump through to clear up her past mistakes? She tipped her back and sighed up to the heavens. She'd never act this way in front of the Celestial, or any of the other blue cloaks for the matter, but if the twins wanted her to let loose around them, she was truthfully too exhausted to pretend she wasn't happy about the situation.

She peered down at the little orb and gave her new boss a hard look. "What do I need to do?"

Leto was hardly paying attention to her. It appeared he was writing something down or signing paperwork. At the end of the day, he *was* a High Priest. He looked up briefly at her before returning his attention back to whatever he'd been doing. "Oh, that's easy. Just don't screw up this job. I told you this mission was our initiation as blue cloaks, so if you look bad, *we* look bad. Got it?"

That was it? "I wasn't exactly planning on fumbling this assignment anyway, though I guess you two will look bad if I die. Can't really help that though," she grumbled.

The orb was yanked out of Leto's hand, and Lilith's stern glare filled the glass. "You are not allowed to die."

Thea froze. At that moment, Lilith sounded exactly like a High Priest on the Council commanding respect and order. She nodded mutely.

Lilith's expression softened, but her voice did not waver. "Don't forget you have someone waiting on you to come back. Now, get home and rest, Thea, and see to it you secure that guide." Then the connection winked out.

Thea stared at the darkened orb before pocketing it. She wanted to slump down into the grass and sleep. She wanted to yell her frustrations out to the sky. She wanted to cry and let go of everything overwhelming her. She wanted to be home in her bed and close herself off from the world.

Home.

Don't forget you have someone waiting on you to come back.

As if she could forget. She took a deep breath, turned around, and walked back into the house. For now, the thoughts behind the curtain had quieted.

Chapter Seven

A Home to Come Back To

Thea opened the door to Rafe's duplex and shut it softly behind her. She felt the exhaustion finally steal what little strength remained in her, and she slumped against the wood with a heavy sigh. The house was blissfully quiet. Namara had stayed at the waterfall after Thea had finally detangled herself from Isabel with the promise to meet at the city's center fountain at sunrise.

A door opened and shut somewhere in the house, and Thea opened her eyes. Heavy footsteps let her know it was Rafe coming down the hall, and when he entered the living room, he stopped at the sight of her weary form.

Their fight from this morning was the first thing that went through both of their minds. The way he lingered as if unsure of what to do and the way his mouth bobbed open but no words came out told her he was feeling every bit as awkward as she was. She was still upset with him for what he'd done last night, but she understood why he did it. It didn't make it okay—taking the decision to fight away from her hadn't been his choice to make. But if the roles had been reversed … She wasn't perfect. She never had been and never would be. She wouldn't have put it past herself to do the same thing.

Another sigh escaped her. She had never been good at smoothing over ruffled feathers. She pushed off the wall and marched straight over to him. Rafe tensed, but he kept direct eye contact with her until she stood toe-to-toe with him. They stared at one another for a long, quiet moment. Their gazes flickered back and forth between one eye and the other, reading the emotions playing out from behind the windows to their souls.

Then she let her head fall forward onto his chest, and the fatigue returned. She felt his arms slip around her, one curling through her tresses and scratching at the back of her neck. She returned the embrace loosely and closed her eyes.

"Did you know Me'Glach has a son?"

The scratching paused before it resumed. "I did not."

Thea brought her chin up to rest on Rafe's sternum, tired eyes full of mirth. "Guess who the father is?"

Rafe's eyes were that calm, blue-green color she loved so much. A slight smile upturned the corner of his lips. "Who?"

"Vice."

Rafe's eyes widened comically. "What?"

A giggle bubbled out of her throat. "Apparently, pixies can change their size for short periods of time for certain … things." At least that was what Vice had told them when Isabel had badgered him about how he had a son she'd never heard of before now.

She watched as the man visibly tried to piece together the logic in his mind. It made her huff another laugh.

"I'll never be able to look at her the same way," he muttered. "Now all that strength packed into that tiny body makes sense."

Thea hummed in agreement and closed her eyes again. She was about to doze off right there in the entryway when he spoke up again.

"Can we talk about what happened?"

She didn't want to—well, she did, but confronting her feelings was difficult. She was used to bottling them all up. It was easier that way. She could hide her hurt. She could pretend she wasn't mad. She could shut down so that she didn't have to *feel*. And then, when it became too much, she could explode at the person who had wronged her. And they would leave. Or she would. Either way, the problem would go away.

But she didn't *want* Rafe to leave.

So, she nodded, eyes still closed. "Yeah. We can talk. Hot chocolate first?" She didn't care if she sounded like a little kid. Rafe's hot chocolate was the best. Hellfire, everything the man made in the kitchen was good.

His fingers massaged the back of her neck. "Is that all you want?"

No.

She opened her eyes and peered up at him. He seemed to know exactly what she wanted, for he leaned down and captured her lips with his. It wasn't fireworks or stars bursting or weightless wonder.

But it felt like home.

"I'm sorry about what I said this morning," Rafe murmured to her. They had commandeered one corner of the couch after the Summoner conjured a steady fire in the hearth. His arm was around her, idly fiddling with the ends of her curls, and she was nestled next to him, holding her mug of hot chocolate. On the coffee table were their now-empty bowls of stew. Thea hadn't realized how hungry she was until she'd walked into the kitchen and the smell hit her with the force of a rebound.

She stared at the marshmallows swirling around the contents of her cup, leaving a white film in their wake as they melted. "I'm sorry for how I reacted. I shouldn't have snapped at you like I did … I was just so mad. I was so scared when you went off by yourself. I was furious you forced me to stay behind."

Rafe nodded at her response. The fire crackled and popped, and a spark of purple magic danced in the flames as the starter log kept it going. "I was scared when I saw you cough all that blood up. It—It was everywhere, Thea. You were so pale, and you were shaking. I didn't think either of us were going to make it, but I didn't want you going out under their control." His hand left her curls to wrap around her shoulder, and he squeezed. "I thought if I could distract them, maybe Blythe could get you out of there. Give you a drop of the wyvern blood so you could recover."

"I should have taken a drop right then and there. I …" She sighed and dropped her head on his shoulder. Why hadn't she just done that? What if a drop could have not only cured her, but boosted what magic she did have?

"Panic makes it hard to think. Even for us. We rely on instincts on the battlefield. That's what keeps us alive. We don't have the time to go through every option in our heads. We think about the options we had later when we're not dodging death." Rafe dragged his hand down his face, looking nearly as weary as she felt.

"It was that giant lizard that got me," Thea said after a moment. "That had to be what made me … ill."

The crackling of the fire and the wind outside had filled the silence, and Thea noted how the sun was going to set in the next few hours. The days were still unfairly short this time of year. Namara would be getting home soon. Mokana was apparently out at the tavern, so no one knew how long she'd be.

Rafe nodded. "I thought about that too, later, after everything settled down."

Thea took a sip of her drink and lay her head back down on his shoulder. "I know I yelled at you about not doing that again—risking your life. I don't want you to, but I understand why you did. I knew why you did it *when* you did it … I just … I think I would have done the same thing if the roles were reversed, and you'd rightfully be mad at me for it. But that's why I want you to hold yourself to the same standards you hold me to. Our job is dangerous, it's always going to be that way, but if you wouldn't let me throw myself into a situation because you know I'd end up dead, I don't want you to do the same thing. And I … I'll promise not to be so rash, too."

Usually, she wasn't. She tried to think things through, but she had been reckless lately. Now, she was going on another mission where she could potentially lose her life at the smallest mishap. A big part of her thought it unfair. She'd already risked her life on a much grander scale than normal, and now the Coven was asking her to do it again.

This mission was bigger than her, though, just as the last one had been. The threat of blackmail was no longer hanging over her head, but the fate of her country and magic itself was.

"Call me whenever you stop."

Thea lifted her head and met Rafe's gaze. "What?"

The Summoner went back to curling the ends of her hair around his fingers. "It's not going to stop me from worrying, but call me when you can. I don't care how late it is, or if you think I'm busy. Call me often, please."

She felt herself smiling. "All right."

"Pinky promise?"

She tipped her head back and laughed before offering up her pinky finger. A simple spell, really. A tiny vow that bound the other person to keep their word. If they didn't, their pinky would feel like it had been dunked in ice-cold water. He hooked his much larger one around hers.

"I promise."

Chapter Eight

New Horizons

Thea stood away from the spray of the fountain. The last thing she wanted to do was get her clothes wet when she was about to head up an icy mountain. It was also why Namara's constantly dripping body stood away from her, banished to a three-foot distance. The order hadn't been taken seriously, but Namara wasn't about to miss an opportunity to frolic in a fountain that was not supposed to be frolicked in. Thea moved back another step.

She was clad in her thickest drawstring shirt and a heavy wool cloak that only came down to her hips so as not to get in the way of climbing. She had skin-tight stockings under her cargo pants, her boots had been switched to lighter, fur-lined ones with better tread, and her gloves were the thickest pair she could find that didn't diminish her fingers' dexterity. Her facemask was pulled over the bridge of her nose to keep the wind from freezing her cheeks.

Her Coven insignia was pinned securely to her person, and she kept running her fingers over it every few moments just to soothe the anxiety sitting in her chest. She was not going to climb down the mountain with a two-hundred-year-old tablet chock-full of magic powerful enough to take out a horde of blood mages on their strongest night. She was going to teleport straight back to HQ as soon as it was in her possession.

She carried a traveling pack with her saddle blanket poking out of the top, and her sickle was secured on her back with her arrow launcher strapped to her leg. The Coven had put in a rush order to get the rune fixed. Which really just meant Rafe had pulled the new strings he'd been given. He'd also gone out and gotten her spell pouches refilled with every dust and spell ingredient she could need while she slept like a hibernating nandi bear after their fireside talk.

He'd made her a smoothie when she woke that morning. She hadn't choked to death drinking it this time, either. He'd kissed her forehead. She'd said goodbye. Then she'd walked out the door with Namara, and it had taken everything in her to not turn right back around.

Thea sighed and adjusted the strap on her shoulder. The sun would be rising in twenty minutes' time. She wanted to be out of Tolvade and starting up the mountain before then.

"Do you sense Isabel coming?" she called over to Namara, her voice just loud enough to be heard over the endless splashing of water. They would convene with Fatik at Tasgall's before heading out. Why they didn't all just meet up at Tassie's was beyond Thea, but she had been too tired to question the researcher yesterday.

Haggling with Tassie about the compensation had been like pulling teeth from an imp. The price had flown from two thousand to fifteen thousand gold, but eventually the Spellweaver managed to get the greedy redhead to agree to a hefty six thousand five hundred and seventy-five. The extra seventy-five had mattered, apparently.

Namara paused in her antics and twirled around in a circle, green-tinted lips pursing in thought. "A little," she said. "Isabel's rakshasa is hard to miss even when he's not in his true form. They should be here soon."

Thea hummed. "I've always wondered why you can sense things that others can't. Mokana is a little similar to you, but she can't sense things the way you can."

Namara shrugged and stepped out of the fountain. She was positively drenched. "Moka also doesn't need to constantly stay wet."

Thea snorted. She figured Namara wouldn't know either. She watched the water fall off the kelpie's gown and saturate the ground under her, but Namara paid no mind to the droplets already leaving her body as she stretched her limbs. Thea hadn't said anything about the spell she'd memorized back at the Skrittish Library yet. She wanted to test it out first before she got Namara's hopes up.

"Ah! You're already here!"

Thea flinched at Isabel's obnoxious bellow and turned to find the redhead jogging up to them. She was wearing similar gear as Thea, though not a trace of spell-casting ingredients could be found on her person. Isabel seemed to be appraising her too.

"Nice!" She gave her a glove-clad thumbs up. "Thought you'd come all decked out in magic stuff, but it looks like you don't rely on potions too much. You ready to head out?"

Thea let the comment slide in favor of getting a move on. She nodded and gestured for the researcher to take the lead. She had the map after all. Unless she'd managed to lose it already.

"Not much of a talker first thing in the morning? That's all right, I know I talk enough for two." Isabel pulled up the hood of her fur-lined cloak and waved for them to follow.

Namara hopped away from the fountain and shook herself like she was a wet dog. "Rafe made her drink a protein smoothie rather than coffee this morning."

Isabel cackled as Thea repressed the urge to sigh.

Their walk through town was brisk and blissfully quiet. By the time they made it to the neighborhood on top of the hill, Fatik was waiting for them. He was dressed in simple winter gear—the kind Thea would wear around town on a chilly day. His coat wasn't even particularly thick, but at least the tread on the bottom of his shoes was. Thea marveled at the outfit, but she knew anything extra would be overkill as he was, for the most part, adapted to harsher elements like most other magic-based creatures and demons. The dragon genes inside of him no doubt attributed to his ability to stave off the cold. Frostbite was going to be a concern for her and Isabel, but Namara, Agni, and Fatik would be fine.

"Good morning," he greeted with a small smile. His chin-length hair was pulled back out of his face, still reflecting a myriad of colors in each strand, and Thea noticed for the first time that his skin had a hint of blue to it without the sun shining down on him.

"Morning!" Isabel cheerily returned. "Let's go! I've been waiting forever to get up these mountains!"

Fatik nodded quietly and started leading the way without a word. Thea glanced over at the bubbly researcher and raised a brow. "We just got this mission yesterday. Are you that impatient?"

Isabel scoffed, though she beamed a huge smile the Spellweaver's way. "You think this is the first time I've thought about going up to the mountains? Heck no! I've gone up to the Council exactly thirty-seven times trying to get funding to go explore. After, like, the twenty-fifth time of being rejected, I told the Council I was just gonna save up and go by myself. Freakin' Mama Mia threatened to tie me to a chair because it was 'too dangerous.'"

Namara's eyes blew wide. "Thirty-seven—? Are you crazy?"

"Duh."

Thea choked on a laugh. "Okay, but why were you trying to get up to the mountains so bad?"

Isabel's eyes went wide this time. "Are *you* crazy? No one's ever gotten to research up there! Who knows what's up there! And besides all of that, dragons, man, dragons! I packed so many notebooks, baggies, vials, artbooks—"

"Artbooks?" Namara questioned.

They were approaching the top of the hill. At the peak was a bridge that crossed the small—but terrifyingly deep— gap of the gorge. On the other side, only those who maintained the watermill wheel for the waterfall ventured this far.

"Yeah," Isabel was babbling on, "I've gotta document what I see properly, so I make tons of sketches. I've gotten pretty good, if I do say so myself. And I do it really fast, too, 'cause you never know when something could change or if you're in a hurry."

Fatik paused near the bridge and peered over his shoulder. He cleared his throat, and Isabel was distracted long enough by the sudden sound to stop speaking. "One at a time. I don't know how stable the bridge is. It's likely not accustomed to the weight of multiple beings."

"I'll go first," Namara volunteered. "Doesn't look like anyone's used it for a while. If it snaps, I'm quick enough to grab onto the cliff face."

Thankfully, as Namara slowly crossed over the bridge, it did not snap. Fatik went next, then Isabel. Thea brought up the rear, and when her weight pressed onto the wooden planks, the protesting squeak sounded louder to her ears than it had for everyone else. Of course, that wasn't true, but the swaying motion made her hands tremble as they gripped the rope railings. Sweat trickled down her temple, and chills traveled through her limbs. She held her breath the entire way, exhaling only when her foot touched solid ground once again.

She'd been so preoccupied staring at the end of the bridge that she didn't realize the view she was coming up on. The hill after the bridge plateaued out into flat land for miles. The waterfall came from an enormous river that followed a winding path, cutting through the frosted grassland until it rounded one of the mountains in the distance. Where the plateau ended, large boulders jutted up from the ground. From them, massive foothills grew, and monumentous mountains were borne. The peaks were blurred by thunderous winds picking up and hurling snow and ice around. The summits were as breathtaking as they were perilous.

The sun had started peeking over the horizon, throwing the range into sharp relief by highlighting the snow that refused to melt. Thousands of crystalized evergreens dotted the massif, only parting for enormous bluffs. The sky opened up to pink and gold-stained clouds, and the stars began to disappear completely.

"We're going around," Fatik announced after the sun had left the horizon and broken the spell over them all. "We'll find the path that will lead us up. It's a long walk."

Thea shook herself. She could enjoy the view from on top of the mountain. "Right. Namara?"

Namara was already stretching her arms above her head, crossing one over her chest as she loosened up, then the other. She bent her knees and quickly stretched the muscles in her thighs. After cracking her knuckles, her body began to transform. Her hands fisted before they were quickly sheathed in hardened hooves. Her skin darkened, her hair whipped about as if alive, and her mouth opened to expel a terrifying whinny. The cries of her victims, having met their ends in another lifetime, wailed their anguish to the skies. The rest of her body quickly followed the transformation until she was a towering, dark green, sopping-wet horse.

She reared up, hooves razor sharp and slashing at the air, before slamming them down into the dirt. Unlike her other form, which was better equipped for swimming, her tail was that of a normal horse's, which slapped against her flank. Thea approached with her saddle blanket out and tossed it over the creature. Her fingers clenched through the slimy, black strands of Namara's mane, and she hauled herself up.

She met Fatik's wary gaze, but he nodded. It was instinct to be on edge around a demon. She peered over at Isabel, who was staring in awe. "That was so cool!" she gushed. She flung her bag around to her front and opened up the flap. "Agni, oi! Wake up." She stuffed her arm into the bag and brought out the tiny mouse Thea had seen yesterday. The rakshasa. "Your turn, buddy! It's time to saddle up!"

The mouse blinked sleepily before hopping out of her open palm. His transformation was much faster than Namara's. Black smoke wafted off the rodent until its body grew and grew. The rest was a blur of smog and quick motions. Thea squinted as she tried to follow the change, but it was over before she could tell what happened. Agni's form was now also that of a horse, and he was as large and tall as Namara. His coat was a speckled black and gray color, and his mane was tangled and as dark as an inkwell. It reached his knees while his tail's length dragged across the ground. His eyes were all red. No iris or pupil within. The most disturbing thing about him, though, was just how eerily quiet he was. No nicker, no whinny, huff, or snort. Silent and deadly. He was truly a walking nightmare.

And sitting atop him was a beaming Isabel. "Ready?" she chirped.

Thea glanced over at Fatik. The being already looked as if he regretted his decision to guide them. She could only sympathize.

Chapter Nine

The Mountain's Eyes & Ears

It was as if Thea had rewound time and found herself back in the aftermath of the annual blizzard as Namara had to hike her long horse legs high in the air to get through the thick snow that accumulated near the piedmont. Their guide hadn't spoken much, and Isabel was surprisingly quiet. The redhead was balanced perfectly on her demon steed as she scribbled incessantly in her thick, yellowed journal. The quiet allowed Thea to take in the sounds of the natural world waking up as the sun was now in full view. Before they knew it, they had reached the beginning of the frozen forest. Birds chirped and sang, squirrels chittered and rushed from branch to branch, and an owl called out to the woodland creatures as it retired for the day.

Fatik paused before they could breach the treeline and turned so he could meet their gazes. "Keep your eyes peeled from here on out. There are things in these woods you will have never seen before, and most of them will want to kill you."

If anything, Isabel looked like she was three seconds away from combusting from pure giddiness. Thea's lips thinned at her excitement, but she didn't say anything. Instead, she unstrapped her crossbow from her leg and quickly secured it to her right arm. If she had to defend herself quickly, she didn't want to be fumbling with her equipment when every second counted. "How well do you know these woods again?"

"Well enough," he replied. He was staring into the treeline, his otherworldly eyes seeing what she couldn't. "My father took me out here when I was younger, if you recall."

Isabel was craning her neck up at the sky. Her gaze swooped down to land on the mountain's peak, and the gleam in her eyes hadn't withered in the slightest. "Camping, right? Lil' dangerous for some father-son bonding, don't ya think?"

Fatik shouldered off his backpack and rooted around inside. "Yes, well, it wasn't so much bonding that we were doing. It was survival training. The dragons up in the mountains aren't as volatile and … prejudiced as the dragons that were driven out are. They tolerated our presence only as much as someone would tolerate a fly." He found what he was looking for and pulled out a retractable walking staff. Flicking it in the air, the pole shot out to its full length.

Thea was left reeling from the shock of what he'd said so casually. "Wait, the dragons up in the mountains aren't volatile?"

Fatik paused briefly before peering over his shoulder. "Not as much to their own kind. But anything other than a dragon …" he trailed off, looking toward the forest once more. Staff in hand, he began making his way into the woods. "Let's just say you don't want to be caught by one."

Thea and Isabel's demonic steeds followed after the Dragonkin. The redhead didn't seem bothered by the warning, but she hadn't seemed bothered by the prospect of dragons to begin with. "So, basically, your dad wanted you to visit your relatives? For like, what though? The holidays?"

Thea heard Fatik snort a laugh, which he quickly covered by clearing his throat. He'd found them a winding path through the evergreens, covered completely by snow but easy enough to follow. "Um, no, that's not why he did that. He wanted to make sure that if the Dragonkin were ever driven out of the city, I would know where to escape to."

Oh.

Dragonkin had never been exactly wanted in Tolvade. She'd nearly forgotten that in the face of Vice's successful charm and schmoozery that they had always been ostracized from society. Beings probably flocked to Vice for his attentions as a sort of achievement, a dark secret that morphed into guilty pleasure, or perhaps a passing curiosity. And Fatik, for however much his draconic genes had dwindled, still appeared with all the same Dragonkin features. It was as if the dragon within him refused to be snuffed out, especially by a pixie's genetics.

It would make sense as to why Me'Glach and Tasgall had been so overly protective. Fatik didn't have the same self-assured aura as his father. He was easy pickings.

Thea glanced at Isabel and noticed the researcher's face had darkened. "It's stupid he felt he even had to do that."

Fatik ducked under a low-hanging branch and flicked off the snow that had dusted his shoulder. "That's just how the world is."

Isabel was quiet for a moment, and neither Thea nor Fatik were inclined to break the silence. Thea's gaze swept over the nearly untouched landscape. The lack of tracks and wildlife made the hairs on the back of her neck rise. It wasn't as deathly quiet as when she'd been encroaching upon the Vemeese village. Birds still chirped and flapped their wings in liftoff, squirrels chittered and argued with one another, and a wolf's howl had sounded far off in the distance a few moments ago. Yet, still, a lingering feeling of dread overshadowed what could have been a peaceful hike.

Isabel must have felt it too, but she couldn't remain quiet for very long. "What type of creatures are we likely to see out here?"

"Well, for one," Fatik paused and stepped closer to a large pine tree, inspecting a small, broken branch. "You have your usual woodland animals: deer, wolves, foxes, bears. Then there's the sprites, wisps, nymphs, and others." He moved onward but kept surveying the land around them. Thea also kept her eyes peeled and her arrow launcher at the ready. "While the first few are inconvenient at worst, the last few are tricky and could cause us harm if they wanted to. But, they're not what we should be worried about."

Thea both wanted to know and did not want to know what they should be worried about, but she dared ask the question, "And that would be?"

Fatik stopped again, and his iridescent eyes narrowed on another branch that had been snapped intentionally. Thea summoned a magic arrow, and she felt Namara's shoulder shiver in response. "Aoyin, for one. They resemble an ox, only they're twice as big and will attack with the sole purpose of mauling travelers to death before eating them."

Isabel was scribbling all the information down with lightning quickness. She didn't seem unnerved by the sudden tension in the air, and Agni did not appear fazed either. Namara, however, was flicking her tail irately behind her and stomping her hooves. She sensed something.

As much as Thea wanted to stop and scout out the area, she also needed to know what dangers could be lurking nearby. It was helpful that Fatik had also noted that something was amiss and wasn't just listing off potential threats while waltzing through the woods carelessly. "What else?"

Fatik pulled a curved dagger out of the holster around his hip and continued forward. "Mafu. Has the body of a large cat with black stripes. Its face is more humanoid, and it likes to hide up in the trees."

Thea felt the hair on the back of her neck rise again, and she quickly scanned the branches above her. Even Isabel stopped what she was doing and looked up. She must have felt confident in Agni protecting her, for the redhead went back to scribbling away in her notebook.

"If you hear a baby crying in the woods, take caution if you feel the need to go check. It could be the mafu luring you in for a trap," Fatik continued. "In addition to any feral demons that could have escaped into the mountains, there's only one other thing that I would warn you to be wary of."

Namara halted and flung her head from side to side, jostling Thea. Agni had also stopped and peered up into the trees. Thea reacted swiftly and aimed her crossbow at the evergreens, magic arrow blazing a fiery amethyst.

"*Azbanonites.*"

The forest exploded around them.

Namara roared and reared back, and Agni let loose a terrifying scream that forced every hair on Thea's body to stand at attention. She cursed viciously as she was bodily slammed off the kelpie by a blur of white. She struck out her arm, and the weight of her crossbow collided into her assailant.

She crashed to the ground and only had a second to kick her legs out and connect with the blur of movement that launched itself at her. Isabel was hollering in the background, and Fatik was dancing on his slender feet, dodging left and right before parrying with his own blade against their small, cloaked foes.

Thea scrambled to her feet but was rammed into again in her side, and a wicked punch just under her ribs had her bellowing in pain. The blur was gone, replaced by Namara's razor-sharp hooves and enraged scream. Isabel was by her side in an instant. She yanked her up to her feet and shoved her against the tree. Then she whirled around to use her body as a barrier.

The cloaked figure darted out from under Agni's massive form and narrowly missed the kick the demon sent back with his hind legs. Isabel hoisted her left leg in the air, body canting to level the weight onto one foot, and just as their hooded attacker launched itself at her, she swung her leg as hard as she could. The distinct sound of metal slamming into flesh was *loud*, and the creature went flying back, but not before having ripped the researcher's pants in attempt to maul her leg. However, instead of bloody flesh, the gleam of brass peeked through the shredded material.

The creature crashed into the tree adjacent to them, and the forest descended into silence. The rest of their attackers retreated and surrounded their fallen comrade, baring sharp teeth as they stood protectively around them.

Thea felt wetness trickling down her stomach, and when she peered down, her breath caught in her throat. Blood soaked the front of her shirt, and a dull throbbing pain started to pulse through her body. She yanked her shirt up and found the source of the blood from a shallow knife wound just under her ribcage.

Movement in her peripheral had her flinching back on instinct, but it was only Namara who had transformed and was pulling Thea's hands away before the Spellweaver could blink. She registered hot and cold sweeping through her, and she let loose a grunt when the kelpie slapped an ice-cold hand across the wound.

"What are you …" but she trailed off when she noticed how Namara's palm seemed to melt and then congeal around the wound.

"I haven't used this little technique in a long time," Namara murmured. She kept her dark eyes on the wound. "I used to use it so that whenever my victims tried hopping on my back, they'd stick to me, trapped, and wouldn't be able to escape as I dragged them into the water to drown them." She pulled her hand away after a couple of moments, and only a trickle of blood seeped out. "You don't have any internal bleeding. My little trick just now couldn't have stopped the blood if you did. Heal yourself, Thea."

The order seemed to snap the Spellweaver back to reality. Her fingers were a bit clumsy, but she dipped them in the dusts needed for a healing spell and whispered her touch over the torn flesh. Healing spells could only do so much, and a scar would remain since they had no access to a doctor right now. She was adequate at healing wounds, nothing like a nurse would be, but she would still need to be careful for the next few days as she stacked healing spells, or she'd undo the magic and open up the wound again.

She looked up to find Isabel staring at her. The expression she wore wasn't easy to decipher, and the redhead looked away before Thea's slowed mind could analyze it. Her attention was brought back to their assailants still crowded around the base of the tree. The tension in the air was thick, palpable as Fatik and a much larger creature stood towering over the azbanonites. Thea realized belatedly that it was Agni.

Agni was freakishly tall—double Isabel's height—with blotchy, gray skin. His wild mane of hair was a dark, blood-red color, and the massive limbs he sported were as thick as some of the smaller tree trunks around them. Bull-like horns grew out from his head, and as Thea and Namara neared the gathering of creatures, she eyed the large fangs curving up and out of his mouth like tusks. Flickering fire coiled in his palms, caged by ivory claws, and it was most likely the only thing that had kept the azbanonites from attacking again.

"*You* attacked *us*," Fatik was growling.

"And as we have said, it was a *mistake*," one of the creatures hissed back. The hood of its white cloak had been removed, revealing that they belonged to the Yama Clan. The Yama Clan azbanonites were all tanukis and resembled a cross between a fluffy dog and a raccoon. They were all white except for the charcoal markings around their eyes and pawed hands, and they stood as tall as an imp.

"A *mistake* doesn't heal stab wounds," Fatik continued with a hard edge to his voice.

The tanuki that had spoken turned its dark eyes on Thea for a split second before it glanced at the rest of its clan.

The one Isabel had sent flying was being supported by two others, but it was evident in the small movements of its chest that it was still alive, just unconscious.

"Why did you attack us in the first place?" Namara demanded as she came to stand in front of Thea.

The anger in her pitch-black eyes had the tanukis' already fluffed tails bristling further. They huddled together in the face of her animosity, bodies easily sliding into defensive positions. Agni's hands twitched, and the fire in his palms crackled. Thea placed a hand on Namara's shoulder and nudged her back behind her. The kelpie glared at her but allowed herself to be moved. Isabel also slipped in front of Agni with her hands on her hips. The beast flared his large nostrils but didn't move otherwise.

"We saw demons. Thought you were like the others," one of the tanukis holding up its unconscious friend managed to say, though fear made its voice choppy.

Understandable.

Fatik's wings shifted restlessly on his back, catching the light filtering through the trees. "Are there a lot of ferals running around here?"

The tanuki that had originally spoken nodded quickly. "In groups. They camp in clearings and move at night, rotating where they stay. They never move up the mountain or down to the city. They just stay in the forest but are always moving."

Thea shared a look with Isabel. She was chewing her cheek and tapping her foot, fidgety as always. Thea couldn't rely on her to come to the same conclusion as she could if Rafe were here, but she'd inform him of the situation later.

He was the Second Chosen (to be) for Lilith and Leto, so she killed two roks with one stone by reporting to him.

Her thoughts began to race as she mulled over the tanuki's words. Demons were grouping together and camping out in the woods. For what reason? That didn't sound like feral behavior, but the only other demons that lived on the surface were those tied to Coven members. Unless …

Thea's gaze shifted to Agni. Agni wasn't tied to Isabel the same way Namara was tied to Thea. He'd once belonged to a Coven member, but no more. For whatever reason, he chose to follow the researcher willingly, but at any point, he could leave and go somewhere else. So that led Thea to wonder … *Were once Coven-issued pets congregating in the woods?*

She had no proof, but it was the only thing that made logical sense. Regardless, their intentions wouldn't be hostile … would they? Maybe in the eyes of small creatures like the Yama Clan, they would be. They were demons after all.

"What did they look like?" Isabel suddenly asked. "Did you see where they went off to? Was anyone else with them? Did they try to eat you?"

"I think that's enough, Isabel," Fatik intervened before the woman could keep going. She only took out her notebook in response, quill poised over the page and at the ready.

The azbanonites had flinched at her barrage of questions, and their answers were vague. "We see them, we flee. Their groups are small in number, but each time we see different faces. Your group was the smallest so far, so we attacked to keep you from finding the trail up the mountain."

Fatik peered over his shoulder as he searched for something only he could see before looking back. "The trail is still a couple miles north. It will take us another few hours to get there."

Another tanuki piped up. "That trail is old. Useless. Landslide took it out two years ago when the blizzard hit. New trail is closer."

"Show us the way there," Thea ordered without delay. The tanuki shirked back from her stern voice, but she lifted the hand still holding her wound. The pressure helped some of the lingering pain. "Or did you forget that you now owe us?"

The azbanonites looked at one another for a brief moment before the one who had done most of the talking, their leader it seemed, stepped forward and nodded. "Okay, I will show you the way. But no further than that."

Thea nodded and met Fatik's dazzling light eyes. "Once we're on the path, we'll be fine, right?"

Fatik sheathed his dagger and went to pick up his fallen walking staff. "More or less. There might be some twists and turns I'm not expecting to come across, but I'm confident I can still navigate us up the mountain correctly."

Thea huffed and went to collect her backpack that had gotten tossed in the skirmish. She winced as she bent over. "Twists and turns, huh? I think we've handled our fair share already."

"Welcome to the mountains," he replied. "This is but a taste."

Thea refrained from huffing again and put the pressure of her palm back on her wound. The healing spell and whatever trick Namara had done had helped tremendously enough. They'd been quick enough to stop her body from going into severe shock, but the pain wouldn't disappear completely.

As Namara and Agni transformed back into their hellish horse forms, Isabel helped hoist Thea up onto her kelpie. Namara's skin did the same thing it had earlier. It started melting around Thea's thighs, and she felt herself slipping into the demon's body. Stuck like this, she couldn't move.

I won't have to put so much strain on myself to stay upright like this, she thought to herself. She gave Namara's shoulder a pat as thanks.

The demonic sounds released from both steeds left the huddled azbanonites frozen in fear, and even their leader stood stock-still with a bristled tail until Fatik made an impatient noise.

Thea winced as they began to move. She tried leaning back, leaning forward, even leaning to the side. Finally, she resigned herself to just being uncomfortable for the foreseeable future.

Chapter Ten

A Cry for Help

As nightfall encroached later that evening, Thea had been banished to the edge of the campsite and out of everyone's way so she could rest up. With nothing to occupy herself, she'd decided to call Rafe.

"The journey is going smoothly then, I presume?" he asked after she told him they'd found shelter in a cave for the night.

Thea looked away from the crystal ball in her hand. Everyone in the group had chosen a task to attend to. Her gaze found Agni carrying wood over to the firepit Isabel had set up. Fatik was carving up the deer Thea had shot down earlier when the group had crossed paths with a small herd. Namara was keeping watch at the edge of the cave. Guard duty would most likely be the only task the kelpie would be able to do on their trip. Her hands would only dampen the wood, put out the fire, or ruin the meat.

She turned back to the glass sphere in her palm. "We had a rough start in the beginning. Not even ten minutes into the woods, and we were attacked by azbanonites."

Worry flashed in those blue-green eyes of his before confusion took over. "Wait, azbanonites attacked you? Why?"

Thea thanked the goddess above that he hadn't asked her if she'd been hurt. She already felt terrible for withholding the truth, especially after she kept her last injury hidden from him, but what could he do in this situation if she told him she'd been stabbed? Worry endlessly? She *was* going to be okay, she didn't need to tell hi—

"I was stabbed," she blurted out. Immediately, her face exploded in color as she realized what she'd just said.

Rafe's jaw had dropped slightly, and he blinked once, twice, before she saw him jump up from his chair and bellow, "*What?*"

"Shh!" Thea snapped, hunching over the crystal ball as if that would stifle the volume, but his voice boomed and echoed off the cave walls regardless. All eyes had turned to Thea at the loud noise, and she felt herself becoming dizzy as all the blood in her body seemed to shoot straight to her face. She glared down at Rafe, who only looked mildly chastised. "Can you please *keep it down?* I'm trying not to alert the entire mountain of my location!" she seethed in a harsh whisper.

"I'm sorry," he snipped back. "You can't just tell me you were stabbed and not have me react like that!"

"Yeah, well …" She looked away and huffed. "I didn't want to tell you in the first place because there's nothing you can do besides worry, and I didn't want you to worry when you have so much packed on your altar right now. But, I figured, well—" she sighed in frustration, "I figured that after our talk I should, um, I should be honest with you over things like this. So … yeah," she finished awkwardly.

"You're okay, though, right?" Rafe asked after a moment.

Thea still couldn't seem to meet his gaze. "Yeah. I'm okay. There's no internal bleeding. I've already healed it well enough. It's just uncomfortable right now."

Rafe let go a deep sigh. "All right, well, if you've healed it then I won't worry as much. Now, tell me about the azbanonites."

With the topic shifting back to business, Thea found it easier to meet the Summoner's gaze as she recounted what had transpired between them and the Yama Clan and their reasons for attacking.

"That doesn't sound like feral behavior."

"I know." She could see the wheels starting to turn in his mind.

"The only other demons would be Coven-issued pets."

"Exactly."

"But they're tied to Coven members."

"Which means we have only one possible scenario here."

"Coven members are involved?"

Thea blinked. She hadn't thought of that. "Not really what I had in mind."

Rafe's eyes narrowed, and she could see how they flicked over her and scrutinized every detail of her face. "You're being intentionally vague."

Thea glanced at Agni and Isabel. The giant rakshasa was placing logs carefully onto the firepit, but not carefully enough, as the entire thing crumbled into a pile. Isabel groaned and ran her hands through her hair messily like a child throwing a temper tantrum.

"What about demons that were once Coven-issued pets but are no longer tied to Coven members?" she whispered.

She knew there was a good chance that Agni could hear her, but she hoped Isabel's childish antics had him distracted. She didn't want him thinking he was a suspect, and she definitely didn't want to offend the demon.

Rafe's eyes widened. He looked away, and she could tell he was trying to piece it all together in his head. "What would be their motive, though?" He asked quietly.

"That's what I don't get. Nothing else makes sense, though. Especially if they're ferals because they're not attacking anyone."

"They could be lying in wait? Setting up ambushes."

"That still doesn't sound like feral behavior. And they're rotating their camps."

Rafe's brows pinched. "They could be tracking something."

"What could they be tracking that requires multiple groups of demons?"

The Summoner hummed. "Right. Okay. I'll report this to the twins, and I'll have Mokana start asking around. She knows every demon in town seems like."

Hmm, wonder where she gets it from?

Thea shifted in her seat as a gust of icy wind not blocked by the trees surrounding the cave blew through her clothing. She was going to start griping if Isabel didn't get that fire blazing soon. "I'll keep a lookout for anything else suspicious. I'll report back tomorrow if I can."

Just as Thea was about to cut the connection, Rafe stopped her. "Wait," he said suddenly. She peered down at the glass with a silent question in her eye. "Thanks. For telling me about what happened."

Confused, she said, "Well, yeah, you are the Second Chosen for the twins. I mean, not officially —"

"I meant about being honest with me earlier."

"*Oh*." Now Thea's face was burning up all over again. "Yeah, um. You're welcome."

She was left staring at the crystal ball after they said their goodbyes, face flushed and no longer cold.

The piercing cry of a baby woke Thea in the dead of night. She bolted upright in bed only to wince and hiss at the skin stretching over her wound. She bit through the sting and grabbed her arrow launcher. Her breath puffed out in front of her, and her cold fingers ached even through her gloves as she gripped her weapon tighter.

From the corner of her eye, and with the small fire her only source of light, she saw Namara skulk near the cave's entrance. Her movements were fluid like the water that dripped from her every pore. With two demons and a Dragonkin in their party, there had been no need for keeping watch during the night. Not with their excellent hearing.

Fatik had settled down behind Thea, and she could hear the slightest rustle in his sleeping bag as he sat up. Thea peered around and caught Isabel's alert gaze. The redhead had come to sleep beside her to keep warm, and next to Isabel was Agni, crouched low to the ground. His blazing-red eyes were trained on the forest surrounding the cave.

A baby crying far off in the distance again made the hair on Thea's arms stand on end. The sound was agony. Frantic, in pain, the baby wailed with all its heart in desperate hope someone would come to its rescue. Thea had never been overly motherly, but a baby in need in the coldest climate this side of Aeristria had her struggling to get out of her sleeping bag. Only a large hand clapping on her shoulder stopped her movements.

She whirled around to find Fatik having placed a hand on Isabel's shoulder as well. The Dragonkin wasn't looking at either of them, though. He, too, was staring into the shadowy abyss of trees.

"What is it? Why are you stopping me?" Thea whispered, though she didn't try to dislodge herself from him. As much as her heart tugged at the sound of the helpless child, something didn't seem right.

"Mafu," was all he whispered back.

Thea and Isabel shared a look.

"What?" Isabel asked as quietly as she could. Her eyes kept darting back and forth between him and the treeline, and her fingers kept fumbling with the zipper of her sleeping bag anxiously.

Fatik elaborated in a slow, quiet voice, "That's the sound of a mafu."

Thea froze. That was right. Fatik had warned them just before the azbanonites attacked what the cries of a mafu resembled. She turned her head slowly, but even her trained eyes couldn't see past the first few trees. She swallowed, and the crying started up again. Try as she might, it still sounded like a baby. To the point she wanted to question Fatik and get up just to check. Logically, though, she knew a baby would not be in the middle of the woods in the mountains. It wouldn't survive more than a few minutes.

"At least we know it's a few miles away," she offered in comfort. She gauged it was anywhere between two to three miles out.

"No," Fatik whispered, catching her attention again. "Mafu can throw their voices."

Thea's eyes widened. Fatik's gaze darted through the trees before anchoring onto something. Namara hissed loudly, startling Thea and Isabel. Agni rose to his impressive height, and a deep, rumbling growl shook the ground on which they sat and had Thea's stomach swooping in fear. A cold sweat had started to break out all over her body, and she couldn't stop the shivers of adrenaline and dread.

Both Spellweaver and researcher whipped around when a twig snapped, and Thea pointed her weapon at the woods. She watched in horror as something stepped through the dense underbrush. As large as a manticore, the mafu prowled closer than comfortable. The fire had died off, but the remaining glow had the cat's round, human eyes lit up like liquid gold with pitch-black slits for pupils. The fur around its face was patchy and as brown as fresh soil with even darker stripes on its forehead and legs. It had lips like a human's, spread thin like it was smiling at them.

Namara crept closer toward the others, and Agni stepped forward in slow but sure movements. Fatik unfurled his wings and spread them high above his head to make himself look as big as possible. Thea's eyes never left the mafu's, and she could see the way it took in the entire campsite. Its slitted pupils shifted from Namara, to Agni, to Fatik, before resting on Thea and Isabel.

It lowered itself to the ground, pupils widening slightly, and the campsite itself seemed to lunge forward in defense.

Agni roared, deafening Thea momentarily as he sprang forward. Namara jumped in between the large cat and her owner, and Fatik's wings shuddered and flapped before spreading even higher. The mafu flinched back, but the fact that it hadn't took off running unnerved Thea. After another moment of sizing up the group, the cat eventually turned and prowled off.

No one dared to relax until several moments later. The sound of the mafu crying, deceiving its prey and luring it closer, pierced the night once more. Only this time, it sounded as if a baby was crying right beside Thea.

It had moved on for now. She felt like she could breathe again as she lowered down her quivering arm. She liked to think she had nerves of steel, and maybe she did when it counted, but she wasn't going to pretend that wasn't terrifying. She watched as Namara stepped over to Agni, and a silent conversation played out between the two demons as they gazed into each other's eyes. Then Namara glanced at Thea.

"We're going to patrol the perimeter again. I won't feel better until I make sure it's clear."

Thea nodded silently. She didn't feel like she could get the right words out at the moment.

Isabel didn't seem too talkative either, but she saw the two off with a quick, "Watch each other's backs!"

The two nodded and left, and Isabel settled back in her sleeping bag. Fatik had also relaxed and turned over to get some shut-eye. Thea tried to do the same, but it was difficult. The mafu's crying baby imitation kept on starting up just when she thought the beast would give it a rest. Weariness returned to the Spellweaver, and she could feel it pulling on her bones, but with the sound of a distressed child in her ear, she was kept awake for most of the night.

Chapter Eleven

The Night is Not Endless; Dawn Will Come Again

That same night …

Blythe stared up at the midnight sky, but the stars were dimmer here than they were in the desert. Fewer were visible now that the moon had reached its peak. It was time.

She turned her gaze to the creatures surrounding her. A hundred or more had shown up in the past day, loitering around the edges of woods when the sun was out before closing in on the sanctuary at night. They had remained quiet, waiting, giving her time to mourn. But they were mourning, too. Most had all known Cressida for longer than she had. They wanted to see her put to rest.

She nodded, and a large leshy stepped forward. Old burn marks scarred his ashy green skin. His mossy beard nearly touched the ground, and locks of ivy crowned his head rather than hair. His eyes, a hazel clash of sage and chestnut, swam with sadness that threatened to overflow. He bent down and scooped up a body of bundled cloth and held it close to himself as he stood.

A plump, female brownie wept quietly as he passed, and around her, seven more tried to comfort her. Two fauns, brother and sister from their identical humanoid features, stood on tawny, furry goat legs with hands intertwined. The sister looked away, hiding her pain behind long, mahogany tresses. Beside them, a small group of moss folk huddled close to one another. Their olive faces were bleached of color, and their lichen hair hung to the ground like heavy cloaks that seemed to drag their already sagging postures down even further.

Some of the other creatures Blythe caught glimpses of were mermaids in bubbles of water floating above the ground, nymphs of several different elements drifting to and fro, a unicorn with a fractured horn and a lame leg still posing elegantly under the moonlight, and a gorgon sitting on the outskirts with deep scars marring her skin. She kept her gaze downcast so as not to turn anyone to stone. Dozens of other creatures had gathered around Srbeveara to mourn the loss of their once powerful caretaker, yet none of them had been any the wiser as Cressida had spiraled in endless agony.

When she died, and the amplifiers could no longer work properly, fear and confusion spread like black magic. Creatures had lingered outside their useless rooms, watching in alarm as Blythe swept by them with Ma leading the way. Their distress had only been partially quelled once the amplifiers reinstated their abodes, but they knew what had caused the magic to cease. They knew. And before the sun could rise to mark the new day, every creature that Cressida had ever cared for would know too.

Ma had done her best to help, but Cressida had dabbled in the dark arts for so long it was no wonder the amplifiers had not only been tied to Cressida's magic but also her life force. Which were one in the same and yet … not. Amplifiers were not selfless tools—they were give and take, fickle to work with, and could be deadly if used incorrectly.

Ma had found Cressida's notes in her desk on their inner workings. Cressida had always been powerful—that was without question, though whether that was nature or nurture remained to be seen—but the amplifiers had been a major reason as to why. Not only had they made the sanctuary more powerful, but her as well. When simply tying her magic to them hadn't yielded good enough results, she had resorted to tying her life force to them as well. The notes hadn't mentioned how, just that black magic had been involved. The amplifiers had syphoned off any excess magic she allowed and slowly whittled away at her life force to produce the pocket dimensions and fill them full of magic. Whatever creature came through would benefit from this, but whatever magic they didn't contain in their weakened states would also be syphoned off and cycled back to Cressida. And because no one else had tied their life force to the amplifiers, her own would be cycled back to her as well.

The sanctuary had become a living, breathing entity.

It was the only reason Cressida had remained alive for so long. She had never intended to die at all. She had backup plans for her backup plans, but she had overestimated the amplifiers' abilities.

And her own.

Though her magic was still alive, when it jumped to Blythe, it had altered itself so that it could not be transferred again. The amplifiers no longer recognized the magic as Cressida's. So, with only her life force remaining tied, and with the crippling urges of black magic crawling through her veins, she was reduced to nothing more than a living corpse.

More and more of her life force had been taken from her, and only a little had been given back. Just enough to keep her alive.

The dark magic withdrawals had caused her horrible, aching pain. The amplifiers had forced breath into her lungs so she could endure it for longer.

Unknowingly, she had created her own personal Hell.

Blythe blinked, and a hot tear fell down her cheek. She recalled Ma teaching her how to tie her magic to the amplifiers. Srbeveara wouldn't run as smoothly as it had before. She could only cut corners so much, and eventually, she would have to do more than place a temporary fix on the situation.

Right now, however, was the time to mourn.

The leshy placed Cressida down on a flat, wooden board. Tulips in pinks, yellows, and oranges surrounded her. They were her favorite flowers. Under the board was a massive pile of wood.

A pyre for the woman who'd always had a fire in her soul.

A beautiful lorelei stepped forward in a layered gown of white silk. She was the same lorelei that had sung for Blythe and Cressida's oath-binding ceremony. Her lilting voice had been captured with a wave of Cressida's hand and would forever bounce off Srbeveara's walls. Her lustrous skin was as dark as shadows, her sharp cheeks holding hints of silvery blue. Her hair was a mass of loose, black braids, some thicker than others, that pooled at her bare feet. Her pupilless eyes were the color of platinum, and her plush lips parted to lull the night with her song.

Blythe approached the unlit pyre. In her hands, she held a white candle, and the flame flickered with each step. She knelt down beside the pile of wood, closed her eyes, willed her magic forward, and blew at the candle's flame. Rather than snuffing the fire out, the flame sprang forward and started consuming the wood.

The lorelei's voice crescendoed as the fire swallowed Cressida up. The creatures surrounding the clearing tilted their heads back and wailed alongside the hauntingly beautiful song. Blythe felt her lip tremble and her eyes water, and a wild beast thrashed against the cage of her heart. It hurt. It hurt so much. She felt her fingers clench the material at her chest, but the beast inside wouldn't be calmed.

Not until she let it out.

Thea woke with the dawn. She'd gotten a measly two hours of sleep after the mafu's crying had been eerily cut short during the night. Either it had found something, or something fiercer had found it.

She slowly sat up with a wince. Her wound still ached, but it was now comparable to the soreness she felt from sleeping on the ground. She blinked the sleep out of her eyes, but when she opened them back up, she was met with a slab of thin jerky shoved in her face. She looked up to find Isabel squatting in front of her with her own piece of jerky hanging half out of her mouth.

"Breakfast of champs," she said with a grin, words muffled from the jerky.

"Mm, thanks," Thea mumbled back. As soon as she took the jerky, Isabel was springing up to her full height and stretching with an obnoxious sigh.

"Ah, *man*, I didn't get any sleep last night. Not gonna lie, that mafuku cat or whatever scared the crap outta—oh! I should write that down in my notes. Didn't even think about it last night. I was way too scared."

Thea rose to her feet and stretched as Isabel continued chatting to herself. Jerky wasn't the best breakfast, but it was nice to even get breakfast on overnight missions. She'd seen Fatik still carving away at the deer when she'd gone to sleep, so he must have filleted the leaner portions into strips and set them by the fire to dry out.

The smell of that deer carcass had to have been what attracted the mafu in the first place, but it had been disposed of before any of them had gone to bed. They'd just have to be on their guard at all times.

She looked down at the jerky in her grasp and took a bite. She made a face but kept chewing. The texture wasn't perfect, and the taste was more of the same gamy flavor, but at least it was chock-full of protein …

She already couldn't wait to brush her teeth.

Chapter Twelve

Falling For You

Isabel gave a long, low whistle as Agni stopped in his tracks.

"What is it?" Thea asked from behind. The path they were on was narrow. On one side, it dropped off sharply by hundreds of feet, but there was some comfort in the thousands of trees that rose up from the ground to act as a buffer should one fall. Thea had chosen to follow behind everyone else to ensure nothing could sneak up on them. She didn't trust Isabel not to constantly get distracted, but that meant the redhead was currently blocking the view of whatever lay ahead.

Shuffling over as far as the mountain would allow, Isabel leaned to the side with an amused expression so that Thea could see their newest obstacle.

And what an obstacle it was.

"Are you kidding me?" she griped, eyes widening at the sight of the massive avalanche that had decimated the path before them. Fatik had his hands on his hips, and it was clear from the tension in his wings and shoulders that he was exasperated as well.

"What do we do now?" Isabel called out to the Dragonkin.

Thea patted Namara's shoulder. "Heads up, I'm sliding off." As she did, she felt Namara's sticky skin shift to follow her as she threw one leg over and hopped down. There wasn't much room to stand on the narrow path, so Namara's skin stuck to whatever touched Thea like glue to keep her from tumbling over the edge.

Thankfully, the tacky substance didn't leave a residue.

The Spellweaver shimmied past both the kelpie and Agni until she stood beside Fatik. Unsheathing her dagger from its holster at her thigh, she tapped at the ice with the tip. Her lips thinned as she tapped harder, but her blade couldn't pierce through the packed ice unless she really put effort in. That could result in a landslide if she broke off some in just the right way, and they couldn't afford to be caught up in that. "It's frozen solid. There's no way we'll be able to clear it without endangering ourselves."

Their guide didn't look pleased one bit at that news. If it had been loose, Agni might have been able to melt a way through, but it would take a lot longer to melt such compacted ice.

Fatik's bright eyes flicked over the massive blockage critically before he turned to the edge of the cliff. "I suppose we could scale down and around it. That or turn back. There might be another trail we can follow since this isn't new."

"Why don't we just go through it?" Isabel piped up from the back.

Thea peered over her shoulder. "We don't have the right equipment to scale over ice."

Isabel's face scrunched in confusion, and she gestured to both Agni and Namara. "Dude. We have demons. And

Agni can turn into—I don't know, a mountain goat or something if he wants to."

Thea turned to fully face the researcher. "And what about you? Are you going to ride the goat as it hops and skips over the ice? We don't even know how far the avalanche stretches, and Namara isn't equipped to tread ice or haul me on her back in any of her forms."

Isabel's lips twisted to the side as she considered those thoughts, but they appeared to be quickly tossed out the proverbial spellbook as she brightened up. "What if Agni scales the ice first just to see how far it goes? If it's not that long a stretch, surely we'll be able to get over it. He can even haul us back and forth until we're across. Is that okay with you, big guy?"

Agni rocked his head up and down silently.

"Why can't he transform into a giant bird and fly across the ice instead?" Thea countered.

Isabel crossed her arms over her chest. "Why can't you ask him yourself? He can speak in this form too, ya know."

Thea balked and met the red eyes of the rakshasa. She supposed she had been talking about the being as if he wasn't even there. "Um, Agni …" she glanced up at Isabel, and the girl nodded in encouragement, "are you able to change into a, uh, like a big bird and fly us across the ice?"

Agni only swung his head back and forth, and Thea took that as a horse's version of *no*. She didn't know exactly why, though.

It must have been obvious to Isabel because she rolled her eyes. "Ugh, jeez. It's 'cause Agni's powers are limited to creatures that already exist, and he has to have been in their presence before." Well, there went him turning into a rok.

"So, like, he can't turn into a bird and then supersize it, and he can't turn into other demons. Plus, transforming constantly takes a massive amount of energy. Man, you shoulda just asked me to begin with."

Thea squinted at the redhead.

"What?"

She went to open her mouth but thought better of it and simply turned away. Her lips thinned at the predicament they were in. She peered over at the barricade once more. "And if this blockade is larger than we thought?"

Isabel merely shrugged. "Then we turn back." She flicked her hands at Fatik and continued, "Or whatever you guys decide."

Thea looked to their guide, who shrugged as well. His iridescent wings shuddered as he readjusted them against his back, and he squinted at the sun above them, but it was still hidden from the mountain this early in the morning. "It would save us a lot of time. Going down and around or turning back could set us back by a whole day."

Thea wasn't happy about the idea, but the sooner they got the tablet and got back to Tolvade, the better. None of the options were particularly safe to begin with. She sighed. "Okay, Agni can scout ahead."

Isabel clapped like an excited child and slid off the large creature on the safer of the path's sides. Agni was soundless as he transformed back into the towering rakshasa form. He shook his dark red mane and stretched his wide, meaty arms above his head. His bare torso wasn't riddled with muscle definition, but rather he was barrel-chested and as sturdy as a building. Long nails the color of porcelain flexed, and then the demon was stalking off toward their blocked path.

He crouched low to the ground for a second before pouncing into the air with the power befitting his rank. His talons sank into the ice, but his feet slid without traction against the slippery surface. Thea winced but kept her eyes on him as he used his arms to propel himself forward until the bend in the mountain placed him out of sight.

Isabel hummed without worry, but Thea counted to sixty before starting over to keep track of how long it took Agni to come back. She'd cut the time in half to account for a one-way trip. Minutes passed in silence with the exception of Isabel's soft humming. Fatik also searched the ice like a hawk, waiting for the demon's return. After five minutes had passed, Agni came back into view. He was careful as he judged when to lunge, where to step, and what to do next. Thea was at least thankful he showed good judgment.

When he had made it back to the path, Isabel was bounding up to him with a big smile on her face. "All good?" she asked with a proud glint in her brown eyes.

Agni nodded. "One part is tricky, but I can manage," he said, and his voice sent shivers of alarm through Thea. She'd never heard him speak before, but his voice was deep, guttural, rough like swords scraping over stone. Thea had nearly forgotten just how terrifying higher-ranked demons could be. She glanced over her shoulder at Fatik and noticed the slight widening of his pale eyes.

Isabel, however, was completely unaffected. Her smile seemed even bigger as she roughly patted the rakshasa on his stomach (as that was as far as she could reach) with the back of her hand and said, "Ya did good, bud." Then she clapped her hands together and aimed that broad grin over to Thea and Fatik. "Eh? Eh? What'd I tell you? We got this in the bottomless bag. Let's do this! I'm up first."

Fatik stepped forward. "I should probably go first," he countered. "With the additional weight he'll be carrying, if Agni slips and I fall, at least I'll be able to glide back to the mountain."

Isabel pouted. "Ah, come on, there's no way Agni will even feel you on him. He's as strong as they come."

Agni turned to face the Dragonkin and gave a wordless nod.

Fatik looked hesitant for a moment, but he persisted. "I insist. For safety. Then you can go."

Isabel sighed again, loudly. "*Fine*, but I go afterward."

"Of course," He agreed with a patient smile. He began tightening the straps on his pack around his shoulders to prevent any slipping as Agni walked over to him, turned, and knelt so Fatik could climb onto his back.

The sight of an incredibly tall Dragonkin on the back of an equally tall rakshasa was a ridiculous sight to behold, and Thea may have found herself laughing if the situation wasn't so serious. That, of course, didn't stop Isabel from chortling as Fatik secured his ankles around the demon's waist.

Thea heard the sound of bones crunching, skin shifting, and a low whine and spun around to find Namara transforming into her more humanoid form. She slinked up to Thea just as Agni launched himself and Fatik onto the packed ice. The Dragonkin's wings flared frantically, and Fatik himself looked two seconds away from panicking. His thighs flexed to hold on tight, and his arms were barred over Agni's thick neck. Hopefully, he wasn't choking the demon.

"I'll go last," Namara said quietly once the two were out of sight.

Thea turned to look at her. It would be a few minutes before Agni came back. "What? Why?" It wasn't like she minded, but she was curious about the kelpie's reasoning.

Namara moved her thick, black, soggy hair off her shoulder and brought her hand up for Thea to see. It was glistening in the light from the water that dripped from every pore. "I'd rather not have you slip and fall because I climbed on first."

She didn't look upset, but Thea's heart clenched all the same at the grim reminder. She'd been partners with Namara for so long, and they'd always had to make sacrifices on some of their missions because of the kelpie's *affliction*. There had been nothing either of them could do about it at the time, so they'd move on. They wouldn't talk about it. It was what it was. But now there was hope. Thea nibbled on her lip, and she cast her eyes away as the words of the spell came drifting back to her mind. She'd already memorized the incantation. She had wanted to wait until after the last mission, but now she realized there would always be *one more mission* on the horizon.

She'd start working on it tonight when they made camp.

"Okay," she managed to say in response.

Namara gave her a puzzled look, but the low grunts of Agni making his way back distracted her. Thea looked up and followed Isabel's bouncing bob of blood-red hair as she bounded over to the demon.

"My turn!" she yelled as if anyone would dare to refute her a second time. Agni turned and knelt to the ground, and Isabel scrambled up onto his broad back like a child would their parent. They were gone and out of sight within the minute. The path must have become familiar enough by now for Agni to know where to grip and hold, and Isabel was probably much lighter than Fatik. Although that metal leg Thea caught a glimpse of the other day may be weighing her down.

Thea turned as the wind blew through the tops of the trees below them. The view from where they were standing was beautiful, but they weren't that high up (as high as mountains were considered anyway), and it was the reason Thea could stomach looking down at the sea of trees before them. The path Fatik had been following had led them around the mountains on the eastern side that faced The Black Forest. Thea couldn't tell where the regular forest and The Black Forest collided, if it was even in view from here. The large hill in the distance could be cutting off the sight of it.

"Do you think Agni is attractive?"

Thea blinked, and all the thoughts in her head came screeching to a halt. She turned her head to catch Namara's gaze and noted the flushed features on the kelpie.

"What?"

Namara flushed harder, but she held her ground. "Objectively, of course. I know you're in love with Rafe and all that," she said casually.

Thea sputtered. "Wha—I mean, ah—I … You think Agni is attractive?"

Namara shrugged. "Isn't he? He's really strong, too." She pushed back a strand of wet hair behind her ear and looked away in embarrassment. "He didn't let me out of his sight when we patrolled last night. He's very attentive. To be honest, I'm kind of nervous about getting on his back. Do you think he's going to be disgusted with …" She trailed off and gestured to herself.

Thea still couldn't wrap her head around how they'd gotten here. "Aren't you seeing someone?"

Namara huffed. "No, like I said before, I don't think the other guy knows I exist. I've only ever seen him from a distance. I don't even know if we would … click. I'm just tired of being alone, Thea. I want what you have with Rafe. Actually, I could probably skip all the side-stepping and get right to the point."

The Spellweaver could feel her cheeks heating up once more. Again, she bypassed the topic of Rafe and her and said, "I don't think Agni will be disgusted, Namara. He doesn't come off as the judgmental type."

Namara groaned quietly. "There's a difference between not being judgmental and not wanting to carry a waterlogged weight on your back."

"Oh, stop it," Thea snipped, but she paused as she noticed Namara's low-spirited posture: the hunched shoulders, the fiddling of her fingers, and how she picked at the skin around her talons that would surely heal before anyone noticed, the way her gaze stared off into nothing. It was like looking into a mirror of the past. Namara wasn't *just* thinking of Agni.

"Look," Thea began, and she was already regretting this, especially when Namara turned to her. "I may have a spell that will work for you."

Confused, Namara's brow pinched. "What?"

Thea scratched the back of her head. "In the Skrittish Library, there was a book with a spell made for humans to keep hydrated in the desert by replenishing the water in their body that they sweated out. I thought maybe I could convert it into working for you."

Namara's dark eyes lit up, but she remained conservative. "Really? Do you think it'll work?"

Thea hesitated, but the truth was the best answer. "I don't know. I didn't tell you about it because I didn't want to get your hopes up. I wanted to test it out first. I just haven't had the time to."

Namara nodded and looked away. "Well, I won't put too much faith in it until we test it out." But Thea could tell the news had lifted the self-loathing, if only by the way Namara had eased her hunched shoulders back. The tension had left her, and there was a light in her abysmal eyes that wasn't there a moment ago.

Thea would have to do everything in her power to make that spell work. She wasn't going to be the one who let that light die.

Agni was back before long, and it was Thea's time to climb up on his back. She was reminded of the Cyan Spider Monkeys in the rainforest the way she clung to his back, and she might have made a similar screeching sound when he leaped into the air and dug his nails into the ice. The pain in her torso flared up, but she thankfully did not feel the skin pull or the warm flow of blood.

"Sorry," she muttered loud enough for him to hear, but she only heard him grunt in reply. Her thighs ached from how hard she clung to him, and she feared she was going to choke him to death every time a large gust of wind threatened to tear her away from him. She kept her eyes shut most of the way, but as the moments ticked by without any harsh, jarring leaps, she felt confident enough to open her eyes.

Big mistake.

Stiffly peering over her shoulder, she felt her stomach drop, and the air in her lungs escape her. The ground was hundreds of feet, maybe even thousands, below her now. They had been scaling diagonally with the mountain rather than horizontally, like Thea had thought they would. The sky was wide and free and clear of anything disrupting its view. The trees that once towered over her were now twigs in comparison, melding together in a sea of rolling green. In the far distance, she could see the spires of HQ no longer blocked from view of the hill, but they were so tiny Thea might have confused them for another civilization had there been one. Her sense of direction had never been good.

Another strong gust of wind rushed by, forcing its way between Thea and Angi, and the Spellweaver gritted her teeth and flexed every muscle in her body in hopes it would be enough to keep her attached to the demon as she screwed her eyes shut. With one final, powerful leap that rattled Thea's teeth together, Agni was patting her arm and signaling her to get down. She could feel the soreness of her muscles, and her limbs and fingers shook as the adrenaline still held her by the throat.

She exhaled a slow, deep breath when her feet hit the ground, and Fatik was by her side to ease her away from the cliff face. He steered her toward Isabel, who was perched on a large boulder and digging through her sack. Half a granola bar with the wrapper still clinging to the end of it hung from her mouth. She glanced up as Thea approached and proceeded to shove the whole bar into her mouth, stuff the wrapper back into her bag, and when her hand came back out, it was holding another protein bar.

"Want one?" she asked, mouth still very much full.

Thea snorted at her poor manners and dropped down beside the redhead. "Sure. Thanks." She peered up at Fatik still hovering nearby with his gaze firmly on the blockade of ice and snow. "How's the path up ahead?"

The Dragonkin looked at her over his shoulder for only a moment before he returned to staring at the bend in the mountain. "All clear. I couldn't see very far, but from what I could tell at this distance, there will be no more avalanches to cross."

Thea nodded. "Good. I don't think my stomach could handle something like that again."

Isabel coughed as she roughly swallowed the dry snack before she turned on the Spellweaver to quickly ask, "How's your wound? Did it open?"

That wasn't quite what Thea had meant, but she looked down to check on her wound anyway. Thankfully, there wasn't a fresh red stain to deal with. "Oh, no. It's fine." She reflected back on her earlier thought and smiled. "Wasn't the greatest feeling leaping about like a Cyan Spider Monkey, but no harm done."

She heard a gasp beside her, and suddenly Isabel was hacking and coughing all over again. Banging on her chest, she finally cleared her throat enough to ask in a hoarse yell, "You've seen the Jeweled Canopy?"

Caught off guard, Thea couldn't mask her grimace at the memories that came flooding back to her. "Not by choice."

"Ah, man, I wanna go there *so bad*. I can't ever get funding, though," she whined. "Though I've thought about just packing a bag and heading out there by myself. Well, I'd have Agni, of course. Same with the desert, too, but I just can't handle the heat. Mama Mia knows this, so it's probably why she won't let me go to the jungle either."

That's not the only reason.

Fingers no longer shaking from the adrenaline, Thea peeled open the protein bar and took a bite. She chewed as Isabel continued on. Only after she had swallowed did she utter, "I wouldn't recommend going out that way. I can't say much about it, but the magic is … messed up there. It's finicky. Coven may never see you again."

Isabel was staring at her with that curious look of hers, not intimidated in the least. Then she snorted a laugh and looked away. "That's all magic, though. It's all … finicky."

There it was again. Isabel's distaste in magic had reared its head once more. And yet, she was able to use it. Did she only have so much? Did she resent the fact that others had more than her?

Thea felt it wasn't her place to ask. She wasn't friends with Isabel, and after this mission, she may never see the redheaded researcher again.

The scrape of claws over ice had Thea looking up. She couldn't see the two demons yet, but it sounded as if they were fast approaching. She hopped up from her spot on the ground, and she, Isabel, and Fatik neared the ledge. If Thea stayed a little further back than the other two, no one mentioned it.

A fiery-red mane came into view, but just as Agni became visible, Thea's blood ran cold. Namara was barely hanging on to the rakshasa. Her face was twisted in frustrated concentration, her arms nearly shaking as her slippery skin made it difficult to keep a hold of Agni's neck. Her legs would come up to wrap themselves around the demon's thick torso, only to fall away with each movement Agni made. The rakshasa's motions were fast, hurried, even more jarring as he tried to rush toward the edge, no doubt the exhaustion from going back and forth taking its toll.

Fear of heights forgotten, Thea raced toward the edge and fell to her knees as the two demons approached. Fatik crouched beside her, holding out his hand since he was closer and much stronger than either of the humans beside him. Agni paused to catch his breath, large chest huffing and puffing from the exertion, before readjusting Namara's arms around his neck. Namara had given up on her legs and was letting them now dangle freely in the air. The large demon's shoulders suddenly hunched, his body poised to launch himself. The three of them scrambled out of the way lest they be flattened.

Agni leaped into the air, and his nails sank into the packed dirt below. Fatik grabbed ahold of Namara by the arm and yanked her over to him, but before she could find purchase on the ledge, she slipped out of Fatik's hold.

Thea launched herself over the ledge, trying to snatch the kelpie out of the air, only held back by Isabel's arms snaking around her waist. "NAMARA!"

Namara's claws sank into the face of the cliff, and a rough, pained growl escaped her. Thea could barely see anything other than the top of her head, but she could tell the kelpie's shoulders were shaking from holding herself up. Agni was trying to climb his way down, but his feet kept slipping. A vicious growl left him as he continued to try to reach her but couldn't.

"I can't fly down there," Fatik announced in a panicked voice as his wings fluttered frantically behind him. "The best I'm able to do is glide!"

"I have some rope! We can pull her up!" Isabel yelled over the howling wind.

Thea blindly shoved Isabel away and ripped open her dust pouches, barking roughly, "She'll slip right off it!" She yanked off the arrow launcher from her arm and threw it on the ground. Once the spell powders were in her grasp, she married her hands together and shut her eyes.

"Forge the bonds, imbue the bow, weaken the blade upon the soul." Once the rushed spell was uttered, she parted her hands and let the dust fall over the weapon. The rune fixed on the arrow launcher glowed a deep red. She looked over the edge and yelled down below. "Namara! Look at me!"

Namara's pale green face peered up at her owner, and Thea would immortalize the look of terror she saw in the kelpie's features. "I can't hold on," she croaked out, and her shoulders were shivering.

Agni snarled as part of the mountain fell away from his grip, leaving him dangling from one arm. Terrified they were going to lose a second demon, Fatik rushed over and held out his hand. The beast below swung his arm up and grabbed hold, and they managed to haul him over the side.

Thea returned her attention to the kelpie. "I got you," she said softly. "Close your eyes."

Namara did, even turned her face away as if she knew what was coming.

Thea aimed the arrow launcher at the creature, but a moment of hesitation passed through her. Was she really going to shoot Namara? The Spellweaver squared her shoulders and took a deep breath. She couldn't throw the dust down on Namara. Even now, the wind was relentless as if trying to pry the kelpie off the mountain by sheer force alone. Any moment, the creature's strength was going to give out, and she would fall. Demon or not, Thea didn't think Namara would survive a fall like that. And she wasn't going to watch Namara die right in front of her.

Keeping her eyes on her pet, Thea shot the arrow and yelled out, "Feather Fall!"

The arrow snapped upon impact rather than penetrating the skin, just as Namara's strength abandoned her. She plummeted for only a moment before weightlessness engulfed her, but it was a moment too long for Thea's heart.

"Aim for the mountain! Try to climb back up!"

The weightless feeling would conserve her strength and help her climb as long as she had something to hoist herself up with. They couldn't afford to stop moving now to operate a rescue mission.

But no matter what Namara tried, her kicking and wildly flailing arms did not move her closer to the mountain, only softly downward.

Chapter Thirteen

Fall to Flight to Fright

Thea cursed and fell back on her haunches in defeat, scrubbing at her face as a massive sigh left her. Namara was safe at least. That was what really mattered. She would have to find a way to get down to her and then bring her back up the mountain, though.

"I can glide you down there," Fatik offered softly after a moment.

Thea nodded and let go another sigh. "Thank you. I have plenty of dust for more Feather Fall spells. It'll enable us to climb the mountain without actually using any strength."

Isabel cleared her throat and stood to her full height. Her demon companion couldn't seem to tear his gaze away from the mountain's ledge. "Agni and I will uh … scout up ahead. It's still too early to find another place to camp, but maybe we'll find something useful nearby."

Thea nodded again, but she also couldn't tear her gaze away from the ledge. "Right. Good idea."

Fatik's wings fluttered before stretching out to their full length. How he couldn't fly was beyond her, but she wasn't going to question Dragonkin anatomy, and with the way he panicked earlier, she knew he wasn't lying about it. He crouched low to allow Thea to climb onto his back, and she had the unwanted flashback of climbing onto Agni hit her. Only this time, instead of climbing up, they would be soaring straight down.

"Let's hurry," she grumbled, wincing at a twinge of pain from her wound. She'd completely forgotten it in her panic, but her rough actions hadn't done it any favors.

Fatik nodded wordlessly and vaulted himself over the edge. Thea screwed her eyes shut and hoped to the goddess above he wouldn't get them killed. The wind was harsh, but the force was great enough to catch in the scaly, iridescent feathers. Thea felt the air in her lungs vanish when that force was suddenly gone, and they dropped like dead weight out of the sky.

Her eyes snapped open, and the trees that were so tiny below came rushing up to meet her. "Fatik!" she screamed in fear.

She nearly let go with one arm to prepare another Feather Fall spell, but she paused when the Dragonkin ordered, "Wait!"

The trees were so close now Thea could tell what kind they were, and she yelled over the useless air around them, "We're going to die!"

"Wait!" he yelled again.

Just as Thea was about to go digging in her pouches despite what he said, the wind picked up in a huge gust once more. Their dramatic plunge was slowed to near hovering, and Fatik was able to glide them to a clearing.

When Thea's feet hit the ground, her knees completely gave out on her. She gasped for air on the cold ground as her nerves zipped through her body, adrenaline forcing her heart into overdrive. "We …" she gasped, "are never …

doing that … again." She lifted her hand up to eye level and observed her fingers trembling in bemusement. "Banish a banshee, I should have just spelled us from the get-go."

Fatik had remained standing, but he rested a hand over his chest and huffed out a small laugh. He hadn't been completely unaffected by the fall either, it seemed. "I have to say, I was worried there for a moment." He offered her that same hand to help her up, but he had to use a little more force than he thought. "Goddess above you're—" he abruptly stopped.

Thea's eyes snapped to the side and widened. The clearing they had landed in had already been occupied. The remains of an abandoned camp took up most of the open space. Pitched tents made from patched-together fabric were ripped apart and lay trampled along the frozen ground. Blotches of dark, dried blood were spread sporadically all over the place. The firepit was knocked about as if something had run through it, causing the ashes to smother out the pure white snow surrounding it.

The absence of her left behind arrow launcher was more apparent to her now than ever. She strained her ears, but only the whistle of the wind through the thick evergreens greeted her. The hair on her arms raised, and soon the feeling shivered its way up her spine. It was quiet. Too quiet.

A twig snapped to their right.

Thea's arm whipped behind her, gloved hand already seizing the sickle in her back holster before the intruder made themselves present. It was just Namara slipping between two spruces. Her green skin was paler than normal, but Thea figured that was more from the recent fright than any lack of water. Her bare feet were covered in snow as she trudged her way closer.

"Thank the goddess," Thea breathed out. She let go of her sickle's bone handle and rushed to meet the kelpie halfway. Namara held out her hands, palms up to accept Thea's own gloved ones, but that was as far as they could safely come into contact.

"I'm not having you risk hypothermia," Namara chuckled and squeezed Thea's hands before nodding at her injury. "You're pitiful enough as it is."

The Spellweaver could only grin back. "I'm just glad I didn't lose my ride."

Namara gasped in mock offense, slapping lightly at her owner's shoulder. Her bottomless-black eyes slid over to the ruined campsite, and seriousness returned to her features. "What is this?"

Thea peered over her shoulder. "My only guess is one of the camps set up by those demons the azbanonites were talking about."

Fatik walked up to them, holding a large, broken-off horn. "Whatever happened here, it wasn't good."

Thea hummed as she took the heavy horn in her grasp. It was thicker than her palm at the base and curved into a wicked point that could easily gore them straight through. As evidence of the red-stained tip. "Was there a fight within the group of demons?" she wondered aloud.

"It would make sense if they were feral after all," Namara replied.

Suddenly remembering something, Thea chucked the horn over her shoulder and dug into the pouch at her side. She brought out her crystal ball and stared at the orb until she found the floating icon she remembered using in her bedroom back at Rafe's. With some finagling, the image of the bloody campground was captured on the sphere and pocketed. "I'm going to see if I can send those images to Rafe later. If not, they'll at least remind me to tell him about it when I call him next."

Namara looked around again, eyes trailing over the blood splatters and torn tents. "You think you'll forget something like this?"

Fatik looked up at the sky. "The day is still pretty young. Who knows what we'll run into next that could be worse?"

Thea hitched her thumb at the Dragonkin. "What he said."

"Well, just jinx us, why don't you?" Namara grumbled under her breath as she looked toward the cliff she'd fallen from. "Can we get going now? The mountain isn't too far from here. I landed pretty close by, but I heard you guys when you were falling and tracked you down."

"Yeah, we don't need to waste any more time down here," Thea agreed.

They looked over the campsite one last time, but there was nothing of any value strung about the mess. As they walked toward the base of the mountain, the thick spruce trees concealed the remains of the devastation from view. The area was perfectly located. It was sheltered from the sky, the surroundings, and near noticeable landmarks. If only Thea knew what had transpired there.

She shook her head. It didn't matter. She pulled out her pouches and stuck her hand into her powders. After tossing the dust on each of them, she whispered, "Feather Fall."

Immediately, weightlessness engulfed them, and they each grabbed hold of the base of the mountain.

"Such a long way to go," Namara grunted as she hoisted herself up. Her back legs floated up behind her as she used the rockface to climb.

"Be quick, but don't be reckless," Thea warned, using the jagged surface to heave herself up. "This spell isn't designed to last more than a couple minutes, so look for stopping points where you can land safely while you climb."

After several minutes of scaling the slope, Thea felt herself becoming heavier and heavier. She already had her eyes on an overhang, so she pushed herself to climb faster until she reached it. Just as her full weight came back to her, she grabbed onto the jutting rock and heaved her body over the edge.

The ledge turned out to be the front porch of a cave burrowed into the stone. It was small, but all three of them could easily fit inside. The kelpie's senses hadn't gone off, so there was most likely nothing within that would bother them. Maybe some bats, but they wouldn't come shooting out unless the trio was up for some exploring.

Thank the goddess Isabel wasn't here with them.

Thea crouched low to catch her breath, and she huffed a laugh as Namara flopped onto her back beside her. Ascending for the last couple of seconds had nearly winded them. Thea was fit, but climbing mountainsides was a whole new breed of exercise. Her fingers were throbbing and, if not for her gloves, would have looked like she'd shoved them through a shredder.

"How many more times can you make that spell?" Fatik asked after a moment.

Thea didn't even have to glance at her belt. "Enough. It doesn't take much to get it going, and we're already a third of the way up."

He hummed and gazed out at the view in front of them. Miles and miles of trees were spread out before them, but the cave wasn't high enough to see over most of them. "It is going by a lot faster than I thought it would."

Thea rose to her full height and stretched her hands high above her head. She faintly heard a crack somewhere and sighed in the relief it brought her. "Ready to start climbing again?"

Namara groaned but rolled to her feet as well. "Yeah, let's do this."

Thea shoved her hand into her dust pouches, but something stopped her from pulling it out. Something from within the cave. A low, beastly growl reverberated through the ground. Thea felt the vibrations travel up through her feet until they were knocking her heart off its rhythm and throwing it into a frantic sprint.

"What the heck is that?" Namara hissed quietly, hunched down low and backing up toward the ledge.

"I don't know, I thought you could sense things," Thea whispered back fiercely. She yanked out her hand and pelted the kelpie with dust before turning and doing the same to Fatik and herself. "Feather Fall!" The feeling of weightlessness returned, and Thea waved at the two to follow her as she began climbing again.

Shadows moved in the cave, and the Spellweaver began frantically pulling herself up. Namara was scaling rapidly beside her, and Fatik was keeping up as best he could. Below, another angry growl ruptured from the cave. Thea glanced down just in time to see something burst out of the opening with an ear-splitting bellow of rage.

She gasped as the massive beast turned toward them. Fiery-red eyes homed in on her, surrounded by the features of an enormous bull. Two giant horns on its forehead shot straight up in the air while even larger ones curled down from its head and scooped around its back. One was missing the top half, and fresh wounds on its face bled freely. Thea couldn't tell if there were any more on its body as the beast was covered from the neck down in dark, woolly locks of hair so long it covered its limbs.

"Climb!" Fatik yelled from above her. "It's an aoyin!"

Her gaze darted up to find both Namara and Fatik had left her behind. She started climbing with all her might, scraping her gloved hands over the rocks as she dragged herself up. The aoyin below roared, and Thea dared another glance down to see that the monster had started to climb. Cloven hooves found purchase on the rocks, and it hoisted itself up as if it weighed nothing. The mountain buckled under its force, and more and more of the stone crumbled away as the beast chased up after them.

Thea cursed and started hoisting herself up as fast as she could. Handful after handful of jutting rock and vines embedded into the stone, she pulled and pulled until she realized she was slowing down. She cried out as the rock she grabbed onto fell away from her, and below her, the aoyin howled. It was closer, but she dared not look again. She felt her weight coming back to her, but she couldn't stop now. There was no place for her to stand. There was no time for her to stop.

"Thea!" Namara screamed.

She threw her gaze down at the creature and shrieked as it was nearly upon her. She scrambled to pull herself up, now relying on the muscles in her forearms and thighs to propel her as the spell wore off. She grabbed onto the mountain with one hand and growled in pain as she let go to grab a handful of dust. If she didn't work fast, the wind would rip it away.

She showered the beast below her with the powder and yelled out, "Emblaze!"

Fire consumed the dust as it landed on the bull, and it screamed in fury as the embers caught on its woolly coat. The creature swiped at her with its razor-sharp hooves and snapped its massive jaws full of spiked, gore-stained teeth.

Thea swung her free arm up and grabbed onto the mountain, hoisting herself up while the monster was distracted. She just needed a little more room between them. She needed a ledge, a large protruding stone, anything that she could stand on where she could respell herself. The pain in her arms was weakening her, slowing her down. She could barely feel her fingers anymore.

She chanced another look down, but the beast was still preoccupied with shaking off the flames. Glancing up, she spotted the perfect spot to haul herself up and over. It wasn't a cave, but it dipped in and provided enough room to kneel. Her legs nearly gave out on her when she ducked under it.

The aoyin below her roared so loud, Thea felt her ears ring. It reverberated through the mountain with such a force it nearly knocked her off her perch. But then it kept going, and growing, until Thea's head peered down over the edge, but the beast's maw was no longer open. The sound, however, continued, rumbling so loud that the loose rubble by Thea's palms bounced and skittered around.

She peeked up and felt her blood run cold. Massive boulders came hurtling down toward her, and behind it was a tidal wave of snow and ice. Forgetting the Feather Fall spell, Thea ripped out her sickle and, with all her might, jammed it into the mountain.

"And now it is what it has pierced, left alone, rigid, fierce," she gritted out.

The spell took hold just as the landslide came shooting past her. She ducked her head and held onto the sickle with all her strength. Dust bloomed in the small space, and the light from the sun was blocked out as thousands and thousands of pounds of dirt and debris came sliding off the mountain, the roar of it all so loud Thea couldn't hear anything else.

The ground below her gave way, and she screamed as her feet came out from under her. Her hold on the sickle remained, and the spell kept the weapon from detaching. Her vision was swallowed up with brown and gray as more and more of the mountain crumbled away. Her lungs filled with dust, and the pain in her arms flared as she hung onto the weapon with everything in her. Her gloves were slipping, and with an agonized howl, one hand let go of it and ripped open her pouches. She grabbed a handful of powder and flung it on herself, screaming, "Feather Fall!"

The ache in her arms vanished, but the mountain kept raining down around her. The sound was deafening, and she was continuously pelted with debris, only somewhat sheltered by the part of the mountain that hadn't given way yet. The part of her sickle was spelled to remain attached to.

Time was skewed. It felt like hours passed rather than mere moments. She didn't know what had happened to Namara and Fatik. She didn't know if they were alive or dead. Had they made it up to the others? Or were they buried along with the aoyin?

Eventually, the sound of the falling rubble lessened and lessened until there was nothing but the ringing in her ears. While Feather Fall was still activated, she began climbing again. She jerked the weapon out of the stone once she was above it with a quick, "*Release*," and rushed to grab onto anything that would propel her forward. Almost everything she was grasping onto was loose soil, though, and if she wasn't careful, she'd cause another landslide.

One that would bury her by far more than six feet.

Chapter Fourteen

Sprucing up the Place

Her fingers sank into the loose dirt, grasping onto nothing substantial and hindering her progress. She growled in frustration and pushed off with her toes, but that only managed to get her up a short distance and caused her legs to float up behind her. She narrowly accomplished another few feet by grabbing onto thick, splintered roots before she was back in the same boat as before.

"Thea!" someone shouted from above, though the ringing in her ears made it difficult to discern who was calling out to her.

Thea squinted up before a coughing fit racked her body. The air was thick and foggy with dust, making it nearly impossible to breathe and see ahead of her.

"Thea!" someone shouted again.

"I'm down here!" she croaked, but the sound refused to carry. She looked around her for the next handhold to climb up to, but everything around her had transitioned from loose dirt and unstable boulders to ice. Even with Feather Fall aiding her, her options didn't look good.

With dread, she realized her weight was slowly returning to her. Her legs gradually came back under her until they rested on the mountain. She would only have a few moments to secure herself before the spell wore off. She cursed viciously when the thick tread of her boots still couldn't get traction, and she nearly slipped on a slick patch of frozen soil.

Something heavy *thunk*-ed beside her head, and her heart leaped into her throat as the thought of the aoyin tearing up the mountain crossed her mind for the briefest of seconds. Instead of the monstrous beast, it was a thick piece of rope dangling beside her.

A lifeline.

One she grabbed just as the rest of her weight returned to her. Her footing hadn't been stable enough, and she grunted as she dropped a few feet and landed hard into the mountain's side.

"Banish a banshee," she snarled. Her breathing became labored, her muscles working overtime to keep herself holding on. Planting her feet and using her thighs to push her legs into straightening out, she wrapped the rope several times around one arm until it was taut and used her free arm to gather the dusts in her pouch. The burn in her lower abdomen was excruciating, and it radiated throughout her back as she remained perpendicular to the mountain. "Feather Fall," she gasped out, and heaved a massive sigh of relief when all the weight went away.

She got to work scaling the mountain, walking upright at a sharp angle and using the rope to pull her along. There was no heaviness to her body, but her shoulders began to burn from the back-and-forth motions.

The ledge eventually came into view, and with it were four worried faces. "Thea!" Namara called out. The Spellweaver's progression had slowed as the burn in her upper back became too much, but thankfully, Agni and Namara grabbed onto the rope and began hoisting her up.

Agni, Namara, and Fatik all pulled her up once she was at the edge, and she flopped onto the solid ground beneath her. Dust coated her mouth, but she was too tired to ask for her canteen.

Namara's stricken expression filled her vision as the kelpie leaned over her. "I was so worried you'd gotten buried under the avalanche." The anguish in her voice was undeniable.

Thea slowly sat up and felt a damp palm at her back, assisting her. She peered over her shoulder at her bag and waved a nearly numb arm at it, but words failed her. Isabel, who had been pulling up the rope and bundling it back up, raced over to the backpack and brought it over.

"Thanks," Thea managed to rasp out. She clumsily pawed at her canteen before frustration had her ripping her gloves off so her sore fingers could grab it easier. She downed half the reserves in a mere few gulps, but even when she forced herself to stop, she wanted to keep going. She cleared her throat, but the dry feeling remained. "I managed to find a shallow hole in the mountain just before the avalanche," she clarified. "I heard it coming and was able to spell my sickle into part of the mountain. The ground under me gave out, so I'm sure we won't need to worry about the aoyin again. It was definitely buried under all that."

"Its bellows had to have been what caused the avalanche in the first place," Fatik said with a sigh. "Thankfully, Namara and I had climbed high enough for

Isabel and Agni to see us. We were able to grab onto the rope just as the avalanche came down."

Namara looked agonized. "I didn't want to leave you, but I couldn't get to you either."

Thea huffed a small laugh, but the action caused her to start coughing. She cleared her throat, but it didn't help. "I'm glad you did. When the spell wore off, I was so worried about you guys."

Fatik rotated his arm and gripped at his shoulder with a groan. "Thank the goddess for Isabel's insanely long rope, but climbing it was no walk in the meadow." He gazed up at the sun's placement in the sky and frowned. "We need to get moving soon. Think you can stand?"

No, Thea thought immediately, but she pulled herself to her feet anyway. Her knees instantly buckled, but Namara was there to catch her.

"Agni, carry her on your back," Isabel ordered. There was no playful lilt to her voice as she said the words. "You guys also need to conserve what little strength you have, so stay in the form you're in now. Transforming a whole bunch will just make you guys weak."

"I'm fine," Thea grumbled. "I'm too heavy anyway."

The redhead snorted and waved her hand at Thea. "Puh-*lease*. You're not heavy to Agni. Right?" She looked up at Agni to confirm, and the demon nodded firmly.

It was Thea's turn to snort. "Fatik doesn't think so."

Since meeting the Dragonkin, this was the first time any sort of color graced his pale skin as he flushed a deep red. "I—What are you saying? I don't think that!"

Agni silently turned and crouched in front of Thea despite her protests, and rather than arguing any further, the

Spellweaver slipped onto his broad back with ease. She was too exhausted for modesty and nervousness, and she chuckled at Fatik's flustered expression. "Don't think I didn't hear your comment right after we landed."

Namara put her fists on her hips and stared the Dragonkin down. "Is that any way to talk to a lady?"

"'A lady' is pushing it, Namara," Thea mumbled sleepily. She could hardly keep her eyes open now that the adrenaline had worn off.

She heard Namara reply, but the words didn't register. She felt Agni move under her as the demon began walking. The group had gathered everything and was moving on. To where Thea didn't know, and, as she began to lose consciousness, she really didn't care either.

Thea woke when the sun was setting. Her face was buried in Agni's thick mane, and the smell of brimstone and musk filled her nose. It wasn't bad, but it was as pungent as any creature hailing from below.

She tapped him on the shoulder, and Agni paused to let her down. Her muscles protested when she sat up, and she groaned as she slid off the giant demon. Namara was instantly by her side to settle her after she stumbled the landing.

"Whoa there," the kelpie chuckled. "How do you feel?"

"Like the mountain tried to eat me," Thea grumbled. She pushed her hands to the sky and stretched with another groan. She was going to be sore for the next day or two, but she'd live with the stiffness. She had already used more dust than anticipated for the second day of their journey.

Then it hit her.

Goddess above, it was only the *second* day. Was every day going to be like this? Fatik had told her right after the azbanonites had attacked that that was just a taste of what the mountain could throw at them.

"We're circling back to another abandoned campground we saw about fifteen minutes ago. Don't worry, this one's in a lot better condition. No tents, though," Namara continued on, filling in Thea on what happened while the Spellweaver was asleep. "Fatik caught a rabbit. It's not much, but we can pair it with some of the deer jerky."

Thea nodded and rubbed the grit from her eyes. "I'll take the first watch tonight. I could probably even take the second watch, too. I slept like a rock."

She heard Isabel giggle. "Yeah, ya did. We came across some wolves earlier. Agni let loose this ferocious growl, and you didn't even flinch."

Fatik scoffed from beside the redhead. "It was hardly ferocious, and wolves are actually timid by nature."

"Timid by nature when confronted with *demons*," Isabel quipped.

Namara nudged Thea with her shoulder. "They've been like this the whole time. I think Isabel reminds him of Tasgall."

Thea laughed quietly. "They are both short, passionate redheads."

They marched on for several more moments, Fatik leading the way and Isabel antagonizing him. Agni brought up the rear, and every once in a while, Thea had to look over her shoulder to make sure he was still there. How something so large could be so quiet was beyond her.

They diverted off the main trail and hiked through thick forest and large piles of snow for a good while before the campsite Namara mentioned came into view. If Thea hadn't been looking for it, she would have missed it. The underbrush had been flattened and saplings ripped out of the ground to make a clearing, and all around them, the giant spruce trees hid them from anything passing by.

"We need to make a fire," Fatik announced as he set his bags down by the edge of the clearing, and Isabel and Thea tossed their bags into the pile as well.

Thea eyed the blackened firepit in the center, now cold from the long absence of use. "We can't make it too big, or the smoke will give away our location."

Isabel was already grabbing supplies out of her many pockets. "If you guys find any maple trees nearby, their wood produces low smoke. Also, I wanna try my hand at building a certain kind of firepit."

Thea shrugged her shoulders. She didn't know how one firepit differed from another, but it would keep the researcher busy. Eyeing the trees around her, she set off a little past the clearing and unsheathed her sickle. Namara followed closely behind.

"What are you doing?"

"Making shelter," Thea responded after eyeing a particularly thick spruce branch. Nodding to herself, she reared back her arm and hacked at the branch. The sharpened gargoyle bone sliced effortlessly through the softwood. "The trees around here are good for camouflaging us, but they won't protect us from the falling snow."

The branch she tossed down was as tall as she was, and she got to work on the neighboring trees. She left the ones closest to the campsite alone, and she didn't take too much from one tree at a time. The fuller they remained, the less wind that could get through. Namara followed her lead and began breaking off similarly shaped limbs with her superior strength, but each time she would pause and grimace at the gooey pitch that coated her palms.

Thea's shoulders protested, but the impossibly sharp edge of her weapon made the job quick and easy. After a few moments, they grabbed the wood and hauled them back to the camp, where they were dumped by the clearing's edge.

Fatik was preparing the rabbit, and Isabel had cleared a spot from snow and debris. Agni was crouched by her, using his massive claws to dig a hole in the frozen ground at her insistence.

Fatik looked up from his task. "What's that?"

"Shelter," Thea replied with a smirk. "I don't know about the rest of you, but I don't feel like getting snowed on." She peered up, and already the clouds were rolling in over the graying sky. She turned toward Namara and handed her the sickle, handle first. "Here, use this. I'm going to get to work tying these up. *Don't* cut yourself," she warned as Namara took the weapon from her.

"Oh, *drat*, and here I was thinking I'd look lovelier without an arm."

"I'd have to put you down, though. What use is a horse with only three legs?" Namara swatted at her partner, and Thea jumped back and nearly fell over the bundle of branches. "Easy there, or *I'll* be the one without an arm!"

The kelpie only snickered. "Call me a horse again and you will be."

Chapter Fifteen

After Life

Thea nibbled on her piece of deer jerky from under the shelter she'd built. She'd tied the thickest part of the branches together so that the limbs fell in the shape of a cone with only a small opening in the front. It hadn't snowed yet, but the wind that managed to sneak through the trees around them was further buffered by the makeshift tent. She made one for herself, Isabel, and Fatik, but the two demons had declined the offer.

They all sat around the buried fire pit Isabel created. Thea had to admit that, despite the look of it, it was just as warm—if not warmer—than a normal firepit. Two holes in the ground connected, one at an angle to allow air to the fire, and another where the fire was kept insulated by the ground. Little to no light escaped the hole, so their location wouldn't be given away so obviously, and the maple tree kindling Namara had found produced very little smoke at all.

The kelpie slipped around Thea's tent from behind, having traveled a long way off to bury the rabbit carcass, and sat a few feet away from the silent Agni. Right in the snow. Thea resisted the urge to laugh. The sun on a normal spring day could dry the kelpie out but bury the creature in snow and she was completely fine.

Fatik had fallen asleep right after eating. His stamina wasn't as high as a demon's (even though it was fairly impressive), and he'd continued walking the rest of the day while Thea had been conked out cold. Isabel should have gone to sleep as well, but even with the two spruce shelters cushioning the sound, Thea could still hear the redhead scratching away at a notebook with her pen.

All the hair on her arms rose to attention when the wails of a baby crying started up. She sat stiffly in her shelter and felt the blood in her veins run cold. The entire campsite stopped as if someone had put a pause on time itself.

"It sounds close by," Namara murmured after a moment.

Thea nodded. "Which means it's actually far away."

Little by little, the campsite relaxed. Eventually, after a few moments, the crying abruptly cut off. Thea waited with bated breath, but sooner or later she had to breathe. She exhaled slowly and felt her heartbeat relax. Something had fallen victim to the mafu's cries, and that meant they were safe from another encounter.

She kept her eyes on the fire, feeding it when the already weak light dimmed further. Soft crackles and pops greeted her each time she stoked it. She let her mind wander in the now quiet night. She briefly wondered how Rafe was faring. She'd have to call him tomorrow. He was going to absolutely love being told of her more recent near-death experiences.

Then she remembered the spell she wanted to try out on Namara. Grabbing her canteen and twisting off a twig from her shelter, she set the items on the ground as she recalled the words of the spell. Her hand rummaged around in her pouch until she found her gold powder, and she sprinkled just enough to dust her fingers. She remembered going over the incantation so many times back in the library, and the words came flowing back to her. She opened her eyes and picked up her canteen. It had been restocked sometime during the day. Fatik had told her right before he fell asleep that he'd brought along a small, handheld filter. With all the snow around, they didn't need to search for a cold creek or underground spring. Carefully, she hovered the open container over the spruce needles and repeated the spell.

"Fluid of infinite shape and form, doth by which we all are born, reverse the untaught flow forevermore, henceforth no longer shall thou endure."

The water droplets clung to the twig, but each one fell away as they normally would. Thea leaned over and held it over the fire, and within moments the wood and needles were dry again. Her brow bent, and her lips thinned in annoyance. Did the spell need to be applied to something living? Was the plant already considered dead? Or, would the spell really need to be applied to something that created its own water?

She was so absorbed in her thoughts that she didn't hear the quiet rustle beside her.

"So … I'm sorry … about earlier," Isabel said suddenly.

Thea's brow pinched. "What are you talking about?"

She heard the redhead sigh. "I just feel like it's my fault, ya know? What happened today."

Isabel didn't sound like her typical chipper self, and that disturbed Thea more than anything. Still, she was confused on why the researcher thought any of what happened was her fault. "Because you suggested we go around using Agni?"

"… Yeah."

Thea grabbed the edges of her shelter and shuffled it so the opening was more pointed in Isabel's direction. She couldn't see the redhead from how thick the branches were, but she knew Isabel was listening and not daydreaming in the silence.

"There's no way you could have predicted something like that. And, anyway, I agreed to the plan, remember?"

"Yeah," Isabel agreed quietly. She scuffled around in her own shelter. Then, after a moment, she giggled. "Those two are getting real chummy."

Thea's eyes flicked up to see Agni and Namara having already dozed off and sleeping face to face, merely a foot away from each other. Namara would usually distance herself so the ground wouldn't become soaked next to the person she was sleeping beside, but Agni didn't seem to mind—especially since he, too, was curled up in the snow. "Seems like it," she hummed in agreement before she went back to focusing on the spell.

"Angi feels bad, too. He doesn't say anything, but I know."

Thea repressed a sigh and dusted her hands off. She wasn't going to be able to concentrate with Isabel there, but she wasn't exactly annoyed at the distraction necessarily. She looked up again and watched the two demons in front of her, and her lips ticked up in a smile. "Namara has a small crush on him."

Isabel gasped, and Thea snickered. "No way. Dude, that's so cute. Agni's always been so self-conscious because beings judge him so harshly. I was afraid he'd never find someone to look at him as more than just … ya know."

Thea quirked a brow at the researcher, though Isabel couldn't see her. "Agni is self-conscious?" She picked up a stick and stoked the fire, and the embers floated high into the sky before burning out. Fatik rolled over off to the side of them with a soft snore, and she heard his wings shuffle slightly on his back in his new position. She'd had to make his shelter a lot bigger, but, even then, she knew it was cramped for the tall being.

"Oh yeah, man. Beings are straight terrified of him. They'll cross over to the other side of the street if they see him coming. It's why he's always in a small form so I can carry him around, and he never talks much because others get scared of his voice. Even demons will stay away from him. Makes me so mad!" Fatik's abrupt snore had Isabel shutting up. She lowered her voice as she repeated, "It makes me so mad. Like, he was once a Coven-issued pet. He ain't feral, so why does everyone gotta be afraid of him?"

Thea winced as she recalled she had done the same thing earlier that day. A part of her wanted to argue it was instinctual to be afraid of demons, but he had never once done anything to her to confirm her need to be wary. Another part hated herself for even judging him to begin with. As if she were one to talk.

You'll never find a man who'll love you.

Women were meant to be soft, Thea.

You're an embarrassment to our family.

At least I don't look like a man.

The fire crackled, and somewhere off in the distance an owl hooted as if to announce the hour. It brought Thea out of her daze, and she cleared her throat. "Others will judge you for every little thing. It's your choice if you let that affect you."

"You make it sound like it's so easy."

Thea stoked the fire again. "I never said it was."

Isabel was silent after that. She hummed a sigh, and the shelter beside Thea's creaked and shifted. "What are you doing? You were pretty quiet before I interrupted."

Thea chewed on her lip. "I was working on a spell."

"Oh." An awkward pause hung in the air. "For what?"

"For Namara."

Isabel was quiet again for a moment. Then, "Is it something only magic can fix?"

"I'm not sure even magic can fix it."

"Magic can't fix everything like everyone likes to believe."

Ah, there it was again.

"Is that why you seem to dislike it so much?" Thea queried, looking up at the stars. They were at home cradled between the peaks of mountains and treetops, surrounded on all sides by the clouds that had parted and allowed them to shine. She was reminded, just for a second, of the desert. Were these the same stars? She remembered Blythe speaking so highly of the sights, and a sharp pang flared in her chest.

She heard Isabel sigh and tilted her head toward the researcher. The memories faded away, but the ache in her chest remained.

"I don't … like, *hate* it, okay?"

Thea scoffed. "Could have fooled me."

The light of the fire dimmed, and Thea reached over to grab a medium-sized stick to feed to the hole. Isabel must have used that time to pick her words carefully, for they sounded well-thought-out when she spoke them.

"I just hate how reliant people are with it. No one can seem to go two minutes without pulling out some powder or flinging around a wand."

That sounded a bit like an exaggeration, but Thea wasn't one for nitpicking. "We *do* live in Aeristria, which is the heart of magic."

"That doesn't mean we should use it for every little whim and fancy just so our lives are a little easier. Everyone has gotten so lazy. And the jobs beings could do, they get replaced with some magic device that does the job better, supposedly."

Now Thea had seen that firsthand, and she agreed with Isabel on that front. She didn't see how using magic to make one's life easier was such a problem, but with the Wild Hunt spell being done incorrectly for the last two centuries … she supposed they *were* taking more than they were giving back.

"And you not using magic does what for who?"

Wait, that was way too blunt.

But before she could rectify what was said, she heard Isabel giggle beside her. "Dude, ouch."

She winced. "Sorry."

"Ah, it's okay. But I don't really do it for others. I don't think of me not doing magic as some silent protest. I just … I don't want to use it. Mom never did, and she got by just fine."

It clicked. "Your mom was magicless." It wasn't a question.

"Yeah. When we were little, she used to teach us all the games she played as a kid. Magicless ones. Hattie and I didn't even notice until the kids at school wanted to play. They got bored real quick 'cause there wasn't any fun in something if magic wasn't involved. Hattie and I realized later we had some wicked magic—got it from dad, of course—but I just remember being so upset because I wanted to be just like mom."

Thea listened with a small smile. She imagined Isabel's mother, a natural redhead like Helena, beaming with pride at her two daughters, even though one of them was throwing a temper tantrum. She wished her own mother had celebrated her first day discovering her powers. All she'd gotten was a disinterested wave.

"I tried too hard to be like mom that I flunked my magic class 'cause I refused to learn anything about it. I got yelled at, but Hattie secretly agreed to do my magic homework if I did her math homework. Don't tell my dad."

Thea chuckled. She didn't think she'd ever get to meet the man, but she agreed anyway. "I won't."

It was then she realized Isabel had said, *"Don't tell my dad,"* and not, *"Don't tell my parents."*

Isabel snorted a laugh, but Thea could tell it was fake. "Even mom's death was magicless. She died in a carriage accident. Someone ran out into the road and spooked the horses. Driver was new and freaked out right along with 'em." She huffed another fake laugh. "I never used magic when mom was around, but I swore it off entirely after she died. I don't even like using it at the bank."

That would account for all the scars on her body that could have been mended with healing spells. "Helena didn't feel the same way?"

"Nah. Mom saw magic as a gift, so Hattie continued to use it and became a Summoner. I know mom wished the same for me, but I wanted to be just like her. I don't need magic to live. If I can do something without magic, then why use it in the first place?"

"Save time, money, strength," Thea listed. She was reminded of Isabel's metal leg when a metallic *clink* was heard as the redhead shifted again. "You take on really dangerous explorations for someone who doesn't use magic."

"Dangerous smangerous, I got Agni, and half the time he's all I need."

Did Agni save your leg? She wanted to ask, but that wasn't her place. For all Thea knew, Isabel could have been born without the limb. Instead, she countered with, "Isn't using Agni for protection the same as using magic for convenience?"

Isabel didn't skip a beat. "Some may think so. I used to. But Angi's not a thing. He's his own being, and he wants to be by my side all the time. He wants a purpose. He told me once that he was so lost after his Coven partner died. There's no contingency plan for demons, ya know? Never has been. They just assimilate them into society and expect 'em to be, what? Quill pushers? Clerks? Beings like Agni live close to forever, and they don't even spend a fraction of that time playing bodyguard before they're left to their own devices in a world taught to fear them."

Thea felt the words resonate in her as another pang shot through her chest. She stared at Namara on the ground, breathing slow and easy next to the hulking rakshasa. To think, one day Thea would die—whether on a mission or of old age—and Namara would be left behind. Looking exactly as she did now. And then what would she do afterward? Who would be there for her? For Mokana when Rafe ultimately passed away?

"Ugh, sorry," Isabel said after a moment. "Sometimes I get carried away. Dad says I'm just a passionate person, but I know I can kinda get annoying."

Thea shook her head and chuckled. There was definitely a point where she found Isabel annoying. Now—well, she was still annoying. But it was endearing in a way. "It's okay, Isabel. It's something worth getting passionate about. I wish more people thought like you—"

"Beings," Isabel cut in.

Thea's brow quirked. "What?"

"You said 'people,' which kinda implies just humans. I hear it a lot from others, so don't take it as a personal attack, but without realizing it, you exclude a lot of others when you say that instead of beings."

Thea felt her mind reeling. Had she really … been doing that? She knew she said the word beings here and there … She hadn't intentionally meant to exclude anyone, but who was she to decide who felt excluded and who didn't? She nodded to herself and made a mental note to change that.

"… Beings," she corrected herself. "I wish more beings thought like you."

She could practically hear the self-satisfied nod the redhead gave her. It stuck with her, though, what Isabel had said. She peered over at Namara and wondered, *Has Namara ever felt excluded by me? By something I've said? She would have said something, right?*

When the quietness settled around them, Thea thumbed awkwardly at the twig at her feet. "So," she began and then regretted speaking. It wasn't like she had anything to say. Her gaze flicked over to the two sleeping demons for something to latch onto. "Are you going to be third-wheeling the two new lovebirds, or are there going to be double dates in the future?"

Isabel snorted. "If anyone's third-wheeling, it's Namara. Agni and I are the bestest buds out of anyone. And double dates are lame. 'Sides, I can't get with anyone anyway."

That … That's a weird way of wording things. "What do you mean?"

Silence. Almost like Isabel hadn't meant to let that slip. Thea looked over at Isabel's shelter, but the redhead was still fairly well-hidden. She tried again.

"What do you mean you 'can't get with anyone,' Isabel? I thought you said you liked someone back at the Flustered Dragon?"

"Uh, well, it's complicated." Thea waited for her to elaborate, but after a few moments, she knew that wasn't going to happen. The silence must have gone on long enough for Isabel to shift in her shelter and sigh. "Goodnight, Thea."

"Night," she responded quietly. Thea didn't know if Isabel went to sleep after that, but she didn't speak again.

She was left alone with her thoughts for the rest of her watch.

Chapter Sixteen

Mothers of Nature

Blythe clutched the piece of paper in her hand and looked down at it once again, rereading the words for what had to have been the hundredth time. This had been her choice to make, but that didn't stop the nerves from festering within her. Cressida had always handled these affairs without so much as a hint of what exactly she was doing. Blythe hadn't minded so much at the time. She never needed to know what Cressida did to keep the sanctuary running. She never needed to know the connections Cressida kept. She never needed to know anything. She was never supposed to take over the sanctuary in the first place. Cressida was going to make sure everything was taken care of.

But Cressida wasn't there anymore. She hadn't been for a week now.

She had made the choice to come here, to meet the owners of the other sanctuaries in Aeristria. Now that she was the head of Srbeveara, she had Cressida's very large shoes to fill. She'd already managed to comb through the paperwork that kept the sanctuary running financially, but now it was time to forge her own connections with the other three in Lorvo, Borlimane, and Adalith.

Blythe took a steadying breath as she peered over a swaying field of grass, seemingly untouched by the receding winter's chilly temperatures. The ground was warm, dewy. A sure sign of magic thrumming through the air and seeping into the soil below. In the center of the lush field, an old schoolhouse that was longer than it was tall stood against the test of time. The red, faded brick was riddled with cracks and tattooed in flowering vines. A large, brass bell at the school's peaked roof refused to budge in the wind that carried across Lorvo Lake just a few miles away, indicating its heavy, burdensome weight.

She folded the piece of paper that had short, simple details on the once-school-now-sanctuary's owner and slipped it into her long, burgundy cloak pocket. She stepped into the field of grass and felt a pulse of mild heat shoot through her. It was pleasant yet intimidating, and Blythe wondered if this was what others felt when crossing her own barrier. What had it felt like crossing Cressida's?

The thought sent a twinge through her chest and brought sharp prickles of tears to her eyes, but she swallowed her emotions and pressed onward. She marched up to the double doors, ready to knock and introduce herself, but she hesitated. Quickly, she patted down her bright yellow dress and brushed her fingers over her bee-hived hairdo to make sure no strand was out of place before she hesitantly rapped her knuckles against one of the doors.

Only a few moments of silence were afforded to her — long enough for her stomach to start brewing anxiety — when the door was opened by a young woman who couldn't have been more than a few years older than Blythe.

It was as if she had been teleported back home.

Dulce Maina, the owner of Matron Manor, hailed from the Golden Sea. Of that she was certain. The woman was tall, much taller than even Thea. Her doe eyes were kind, welcoming, and surrounded by the thickest of lashes. Her coily hair was pulled up into a large puff-ponytail that sprawled over the crown of her head and the red, patterned headscarf she wore. The motherly aura she seemed to exude brought warmth as soothing as the magic whispering over the grassy field. Her skin was ocher in color and just as warm as the rest of her, and she radiated light from every pore when she flashed Blythe a gentle smile.

"Goodness me," she exhaled, "been a long while since I've had a visitor of the human variety. Come in, darling, you must be cold!" She opened the door wider, and Blythe gracefully slipped in. The woman's voice was unique to this land, but not to her. To her, she heard *home*.

"Thank you, you are very kind. My name is Blythe … Do you … Do you mind me asking something?"

She had to know. She hadn't seen many people hailing from the desert since she left it all those years ago, and after recently traveling back through the Golden Sea … She already missed it.

The woman's beaming smile softened. "You may call me Dulce. Or *Delmec*, if you prefer. And I have a feeling I already know what you're going to ask."

That didn't dissuade Blythe. If anything, it bolstered her confidence. "Do you … speak Ernimoen? *Irnomuin?*"

"Ah," Dulce winced and began messing with the fine, curled hairs around her ear. "I am rusty in that language. My parents were Hondonese, but even then, I do not speak much of that either. They wanted me to learn the common tongue here while I was growing up."

Blythe could feel herself deflating. "Oh …"

As if sensing her inner turmoil, Dulce began helping the sorceress out of her coat and placed it on the elaborate hall tree by the door. The tree's branches swooped out, perfect for hanging coats and scarves, and the massive trunk of the tree formed into a large bench at the base.

Blythe flicked her eyes around the lobby and noticed that the rustic theme continued throughout the institute. The floor tiles were made of clay, and the open ceiling boasted dark, wooden beams that hung chandeliers of glowing orbs. Double doors of the same rich wood led to other rooms, and Blythe counted five of them. In the middle of the lobby and backed against cream-colored walls was a tall desk. Blythe assumed that was where creatures made their reservations.

She brought her attention back to the woman in front of her and smiled. "You have a lovely place."

"It's not much, but it is home." Dulce sighed and eyed the room around her. "My *bibi* and *emmi* fell in love with the rustic design when they immigrated out here. My old family home was made of big, round logs and wood floors, but I still remember the canvas walls of my childhood when we traveled through *Eltom Dimoz*."

That must be the Golden Sea. It was similar to what the Ernimoens called the desert in their mother tongue.

As she peered around again, she was surprised the building had no Hondonese flare whatsoever. The people of the Hondonis tribe were more eccentric than Blythe in their patterns and colors. Most of the clothing she wore came from the stalls in town where merchants sold the tribe's wares.

The Ernimoens traded occasionally with them along select trade routes, but they didn't venture too far away from *Gaygha*. The Hondonese people, however, were true nomads. They crossed the entirety of the Golden Sea over and over again and never settled in one place.

"Would you like a tour?"

Blythe blinked at the sanctuary owner. "You offer tours?" Cressida would never.

Dulce chuckled, and the sound suited the tall, curvaceous woman. Her figure was that of an hourglass, one with a bit of extra sand. She seemed so soft, so comforting. Blythe felt the urge to run toward the woman and be enveloped in her arms and cry away her troubles. The prickles behind her eyes returned, and she sharply looked away, feigning interest in her surroundings.

From her bright blue and gold, floor-length skirt, Dulce pulled out a tiny, silver bell. "Not to the general public, but another Keeper is a different story," she said before giving the bell a jingle.

"Keeper?"

"Oh, it's what I call those who look after the other sanctuaries," the woman explained, but before Blythe could question how she knew Blythe was Srbeveara's "Keeper," a short creature with skin that seemed a touch too baggy for its body with large, pointed ears jutting out from its head came jogging around a corner where the desk was. It wore nothing more than rags.

"You rang, milady?" Its guttural, deep voice was a shock coming from such a small creature. Blythe had never actually heard any of the brownies at Srbeveara speak.

Dulce went a little red at the title and glanced at Blythe bashfully before addressing the brownie. "I keep telling you that you don't have to call me that, Noll. Anyway, will you be a dear and please watch the entrances for me? I'll be giving our guest a tour of the place."

Noll looked Blythe up and down with his large, twilight-blue eyes and then nodded firmly at the sanctuary Keeper before plodding back to somewhere behind the desk. Dulce sighed in fond exasperation before bringing her twinkling gaze down to Blythe. "Would you believe me if I told you I've tried giving him nicer clothing to wear? He finally threatened to leave me to my lonesome if I presented him with so much as a scarf. Apparently, it's offensive."

Blythe, having known this bit of information already, smiled in understanding. "Cressida had warned me never to offer them anything, no matter how much my, um, what did she say—'*bleeding heart*' wanted to."

Dulce tipped back her head and laughed. "Cressida is a gem. Not many seem to think so, but she's always had a quick wit and certain charm about her."

Blythe swallowed. "Yes, that is very true."

Dulce waved and led her over to a set of doors on the right side of the desk. When she pushed them open and stepped through, Blythe gasped softly. The old gymnasium was massive, dilapidated beyond repair, and overgrown with wildlife. A gargantuan sycamore tree with a ginormous trunk curved upward against the ceiling and had, at one point in time, broken through the roof and left a gaping hole in the structure. Dim light from outside streamed onto the ground, and the gentle breeze now trapped in the space whispered over the grass that grew in between the cracks in the old, wooden floors. Saplings crowded around the base, flowering bushes sprouted in clustered patches, and a dip in the rotting foundation had become somewhat of a shallow watering hole. Nature had taken over the space and reclaimed it as its own.

"This is the common room," Dulce was saying with a fond smile. "Guests can mingle here without feeling trapped inside their rooms as they recover. They're a little shy right now, but some of our residents are here."

Blythe peered back into the old gym and spied some wood nymphs, not completely camouflaged anymore, pry themselves away from the great tree. They gracefully descended from the branches to get a better look at their newest visitor. Water spirits reformed from within the shallow contents of the pond and peered at Blythe with equal curiosity. Pixies fluttered from behind the flowering bushes, now realizing there was no danger, and went back to zipping around the common room in what looked like a game of tag.

"So creative," Blythe commented. "They feel more at home here with some of the outside on the inside."

Dulce hummed in agreement. "I can't take credit for this, unfortunately. When I found this place in such disrepair, I couldn't bear the thought of my old school falling to ruin. My magic has never been that great …" She found Blythe's curious gaze and went on to explain. "My *bibi's* parents were from Tolvade originally, but he was born and raised in the desert. He had lots of magic in him, but he only passed on a little bit to me," she chuckled. Waving her hand, she had Blythe follow her as she moved toward another set of double doors on the far side of the room. "None of the contractors I spoke to wanted to fix the place. They all just wanted to tear it down, and it was going to be demolished if the city condemned it. So, I petitioned to turn it into a sanctuary of sorts for the magic folk in the area. Don't think I'd have had a leg to stand on if the other two sanctuaries in Adalith and Borlimane weren't already well established."

Blythe listened with rapt attention. So, she had magic in her, too. Not only that, but all the other sanctuaries were older than Cressida's … "You went to school here?"

"Oh, honey, I may not look it, but I'm a proud forty-six-year-old." Her smile fell a little as she looked up at the crumbling ceiling around the huge tree. "I was in the last graduating class. Afterward, the remaining students were zoned for the new school that had opened up earlier that same year. I felt like, as the only one in my family to receive my diploma and one of the last students to walk the stage, it was my responsibility to keep the place alive somehow. Maybe I'm just a softie for nostalgia," she giggled.

Blythe looked back at the giant tree. "What about that tree, then? Surely it couldn't have grown that fast?"

Dulce hummed and glanced over at the towering sycamore. "You can thank the magic fauna for that. She's been pumped with magic ever since she was a sapling. I had to stop them after she broke through the roof," she sighed, but it was accompanied by an indulgent smile. "Took only about a decade for it to get that big."

They both reached the doors and pushed them open. A long, wide hallway stretched out before them. Cracks ran along the wall, and weeds peeked through the tiled floor, but at least the ceiling was still in good shape. This hallway was where the classrooms were once located. Staggered on either side, fifteen in total branched off from the corridor.

"Each classroom is a room for a creature in need. As you can imagine, nothing bigger than a nymph can live comfortably here. It's a shame, but I have to keep reminding myself that I'm relieving the other sanctuaries by taking in the smaller folk so they can have rooms for the bigger ones."

Some of the doors were left ajar, some propped open completely, and some were firmly shut. Dulce politely informed Blythe that she could peer into the ones left open, but that was it. This was a sanctuary after all. No one wanted to have their privacy invaded in a place that promoted a safe space.

One room was completely overgrown in trees with only a small clearing in the center. Various fruits grew from the branches, and vines roped around the trunks and hung limply. The windows were overtaken in them, leaving little view of the outside.

"I keep the trees trimmed from breaking through the ceiling like the one in the common room. The next resident might not like rain coming in while they're trying to sleep," Dulce said in passing as she sauntered down the hall, and Blythe followed after her.

Another had the window left wide open, letting the balmy breeze from outside blow in. Giant boulders took up one corner of the room, a small but deep pit of water in the other. Grass and fresh soil had been carried in and took over the entire floor. The large nest of moss must have been the creature's bed.

The other rooms were similar. Some had more trees and bushes to hide within, some had more grass to rest on. The other hallway on the opposite side, she learned, was much the same except for the cafeteria and kitchen. The kitchen remained for its original purpose, but the cafeteria was another common room. It was practically a mirrored image of the gymnasium, except the tree the guests had chosen to nurture was a willow tree, and it was nowhere near tall enough to reach the ceiling yet.

It was only when Blythe was led outside behind the school that she felt that same sense of wonder she felt in the first common room. The school was backed up to a towering forest, overflowing with dense shrubbery and smaller plants at the trees' trunks. An incredibly large pond was cradled between the woods and the building. It was nearly as big as the gym. The water was dark and littered with aquatic plants that flowered in beautiful colors. It flowed from a small, manmade waterfall that kept the pond from becoming stagnant. Moss grew over the rocks bordering it, and Blythe was cautioned to be careful from the slippery hazard it could be.

Creatures took to it just as they would any other pond in the wild. A mossmaid was floating on her back without a care in the world. Her long hair of rushes and reeds drifted around her in a mass of green, corkscrew curls while her scaleless, slimy, dark brown tail navigated her lazily across the water's surface. A swarm of brightly colored butterflies and dragonflies danced around her, landing on her outstretched fingers and dipping into the water by her hair. A jewel-toned hummingbird was also buzzing about, drawn to the aquatic plants of the pond.

A cecaelia was resting his heather-colored human half against the rocks, and Blythe only caught a glimpse of the tentacles that flickered under the water. The creature eyed Blythe with cat-like silver eyes rimmed in fire-red, but he dismissed the sorceress when he realized she was no threat. The last creature Blythe saw meandering about the pool was a peryton with sage-green fur. It drank slowly from the water, only lifting its stag head to curiously gaze at the sorceress. Its pure white wings shifted on its back before it resumed drinking. The shadow it cast on the rocks was one of a human. That was a good sign. It hadn't killed anyone. Should that change, its shadow would form into that of its own shape.

"Should we go back inside?" Dulce called out to her from the doorway.

Blythe acquiesced quietly and slipped back into the Matron Manor with a contented sigh. Though it was warmer just outside the sanctuary than it was the rest of Tolvade, it held not a candle to the toastiness of the manor.

Blythe was ushered into what had been the principal's spacious office. It now doubled as a lounge area and Dulce's bedroom, though that had been blocked off with room dividers.

"I hope you enjoyed the tour," Dulce said as she set down a tray holding a glass pitcher and mismatched porcelain cups onto the wooden coffee table. The room was probably in the best shape in the entire building. As much as Dulce seemed to love nature, she didn't want it extending to her sleeping quarters. It also had much more Hondonese flair. Everything from the patterned, gold curtains to the woven rugs at her feet held a touch of the desert and the people who made them.

"I did very much," Blythe responded, taking the offered cup. The scent that wafted from the tea had her eyes and mouth watering. The spice infused with the floral scents was enough to set her tongue ablaze. Her eyes widened, and she let loose a giggle as she watched the herbs and dried petals float around in the pitcher. "I haven't had something that hot since I went home." It was nothing like the sharp, tart tang of a good Ernimoen brew, but it was good.

Dulce settled herself into the high-backed loveseat and sipped at her own drink. "I got my *emmi*'s recipe from her old journal. It was all written in Hondonese, so that was fun. Feel free to come by whenever. We can exchange recipes if you have any. I don't get much company, none that I can chat with anyway," she giggled. "I know she's not one for social interactions, but bring Cressida next time too."

Blythe froze before her cup could reach her lips again. She slowly put it down on its saucer on the table and found her gaze wandering to the intricate designs of the room dividers. "I …" she whispered after a quiet moment, and then let loose a shuddering sigh. "That won't be possible."

Dulce noticed the shift in the air and put down her own cup. With nothing to fill her hands, she fiddled with the thread on her skirt. "Is she really so busy these days?"

Blythe smiled, but it fell quickly. She swallowed, and when she opened her mouth to speak, her lips quivered and distorted whatever words she was about to say.

"Oh." It seemed to hit Dulce all at once. "Oh, dear." She scurried up from her seat and fluttered over to the sorceress and plopped down beside her. Her hand had barely grazed Blythe's shoulder before the sorceress turned and flung herself into Dulce's motherly embrace. She couldn't stop her fingers from gripping harshly on the woman's blouse, nor could she stop the way her body shook despite trying so desperately to hold in her sobs. When Dulce's arms wrapped around her tight, Blythe wailed.

She thought she was done crying. She thought she had cried all there was to cry. Her eyes had hurt for days. Her head had pounded with relentless headaches even as she pushed herself to keep the sanctuary running. She fell into bed each night mentally exhausted but unable to sleep. She wondered what was worse: sleeping beside your loved one as they struggled to live or coming back to an empty bed with only the memories of what was, of what could have been, to keep you company at night.

Would she ever be complete again? For all the lies she told herself that kept her going, that kept Srbeveara going, she knew she would never be the same. She would not be okay. She would not be okay for a very long time. She would never walk through the halls of her home and not hear Cressida's laughter. She would never walk into Cressida's office and not picture the woman sitting at her desk, feather quill in hand, staff leaning against the wood. How she'd look up from whatever she was working on and smile. She would never bustle about the kitchen and not think about the path that would lead down to the cellar — the cellar she would never go down to again. Because if she did, whatever progress she would make in moving on would crumble at her feet. Just as Cressida had done that fateful day.

When Blythe pulled away, it could have been an hour or merely a few moments later. She couldn't tell how long she sat there and cried, but her eyes hurt from the strain, and a headache was already pounding away. She sniffed and apologized profusely, but she couldn't look at Dulce as she did so. She felt so ashamed. She barely knew this woman and had gone ahead and flung herself at her.

Dulce offered her a small smile, full of warmth and quiet understanding, and pulled out a thin notebook from the table's front drawer. "Here, darling. I know a couple spells that will remedy that headache. Some to sleep, too, and one that will clear up those red eyes of yours."

The headache was already making it hard to focus, but Blythe forced a nod. "Thank you. Really."

"Anytime, darling. Anytime."

Chapter Seventeen

Every Sanctuary has its Secrets

A few hours later …

Blythe looked left. She looked right. She then peered over her shoulder, brows quirked in confusion. She turned back and stared at the small stone hut in front of her. *This* was the Borlimane sanctuary? It was no bigger than her closet. She had a nice-sized closet, albeit, but still.

She glanced down at the intricately detailed map she'd procured from Cressida's office. Marked right where she was standing was labeled: *Passage (Borlimane Sanctuary)*.

Blythe looked up and around at her surroundings. The area just outside of Herbon had come out mostly unscathed in last week's battle. Some of the taller buildings sheltering the small shack sported charred markings in places, but the stone each building was comprised of had withstood the war with the blood mages.

There was no point in standing around any longer. Hopefully, Nathaniel—the Keeper for this sanctuary—was just as nice as Dulce had been. She hadn't been able to learn much about him from Cressida's records, but the ex-sorceress had praised the man's ability to keep Passage well-guarded despite the location of the safe house. Any praise from Cressida was high praise indeed.

Blythe squared her shoulders and made sure her hair was still secure. It had been a few hours since she'd met up with Dulce, but the remedy spells the Keeper had given her had already worked their magic on her headache, and she knew they would come in handy every time the feelings rattling around the cage of her heart were too much to bear.

She brought up her fist and knocked firmly on the door. She stood there a few moments, ears strained as she tried to hear if anyone was coming, but no one answered. She fidgeted with her gloves, peered up at the gray sky still blanketed in clouds, and checked her surroundings once more. She didn't know if the outskirts of Herbon would be better or worse than the center of the borough, so she made sure to keep watch.

Out of the corner of her eye, a shadow darted down an alley. Blythe felt goosebumps rise over her arms, and she quickly knocked on the door once more. The shadow had since disappeared, but she kept glancing over in that direction just in case. She liked to believe that most beings were good, just unfortunate, and that everyone should be given the benefit of the doubt. But she had every right to be paranoid. The last two times she'd walked through Borlimane had been enough to scare her from ever coming back.

Yet here she was trying to make connections with Passage's owner. Key word: *trying*.

After several more minutes, she knocked again, contemplating if it was worth opening the door and walking right in.

What if this isn't the place? her mind whispered. *What could possibly be safeguarded in such a small building? What if no one even lives here anymore? It could have been moved to another location.*

After another long stretch of silence, she sighed. She'd have to do a little more research before forging out into Herbon again. She didn't think her nerves could take strolling through the streets searching for something when she didn't even know what it looked like.

She adjusted her bag over her shoulder and turned—only to stop abruptly. A cold dread bled from her heart out to the corners of her soul, and she found herself frozen stiff in fear. The building directly facing the small shack now had three men hovering around the doorway. They were all wiry in build, scruffy, and their eyes gleamed with ill intentions. Their naked chests were on display, skin sallow from malnutrition, and backs hunched over from years of slumping.

"Look what we have here," one rasped in a voice like serrated knives.

Blythe's eyes darted in the direction she came from. She could run for it, hit them with some magic if they grabbed her—*if* her magic worked for her like she wanted it to. She didn't have a weapon. She wouldn't know what to do with it even if she did. Escape was her best option. She'd have to beg Thea to come with her next time, should she ever gather the courage to come back here.

One of the men advanced, and the other two followed like his shadow. Blythe felt her heart beat hard and fast against her chest, and despite the fear gripping her and keeping her rooted in place, she was going to run for it. Any second now. She was going to get moving.

They took another step. They were toying with her, their smiles all teeth and laughter sharp and grating. She was going to run. Right now. *Right* now.

Blythe felt her breath catch in her throat. She was going to run—she was going to run now. Run. *Run*. RUN.

The door handle behind her jiggled, and the slow creak of the door opening halted the men in front of her. Silence descended over the area. Blythe was too afraid to turn around, too afraid to take her eyes off the men before her. She watched their smiles fade, wariness replacing the vigor in their eyes, and they backed away as slowly as they had advanced.

A large hand dropped down on her shoulder, and she couldn't help the muffled shriek that escaped her. Her head whipped to the side, and her eyes widened as her gaze was ensnared by the fierce expression the man beside her bore. Scars of three decorated his pale face from his hairline to his chin, whiting out one of his once-blue eyes to the color of stone. His hair was a washed-out shade of gray and tied back in a low ponytail, and his height belied his strength. Though shorter than Blythe by a good half a foot, he was built stronger than the hut behind him. His aura was the most intimidating one Blythe had witnessed from a human, and she had a fleeting thought of Cressida and all those she used to so easily scare.

When the three men slunk back into the building they'd come from, Blythe felt her breath leave her in a giant *whoosh* of air. She placed a hand on her frantic heart and flinched when the heavy weight on her shoulder disappeared. She met the man's gaze once more and opened her mouth to thank him, but he was already turning around and walking back into the shack.

"Wa-Wait!" Her tongue felt like it was made of lead, but she hurriedly continued. "Are you the—the Keeper for Passage?"

The man paused in the doorway. His shoulders were so wide he'd have to side-step his way through it. They shook with what was maybe laughter, and he turned around to stare at the sorceress. His lips, surrounded by a heavy shadow of stubble, were pulled up at the corners in a faint smile.

"See you've met Dulce already." His voice was deeper than the sand dunes. He said naught else before continuing into the shack, but before he could disappear into the shadows, he lifted his large arm dusted in fair hair and waved for her to follow him.

Blythe glanced around once again, swallowing nervously before she squared her shoulders and strode into the unknown.

The stone shack was *not* the sanctuary known as Passage. It was its entrance. Passage, the real Passage, was a sanctuary completely underground. She'd heard of the tunnels that connected the safe house to the other sanctuaries, including her own, but she hadn't expected the entire thing to be buried below the surface. When she'd entered the small building, she'd been met with a dirt staircase that went deep into Tolvade's underbelly. Her long dress had not been the best choice for this trip.

Nathaniel—who merely grunted when she asked if that was his name—had offered her his arm without a word, and she'd taken it just as quietly. Now, he was leading her through the tunnels of solid dirt and rock. He didn't say much, but that was just the type of man he was.

The flickering flames inside the orbs that were strung up through the main tunnel illuminated his many scars. They littered his arms, and one went up his neck in a vicious curve. They reflected the same silver color as the man's hair, and Blythe had dozens of questions bombard her on their origins. But she wasn't one to pry.

The underground corridors were humid and warm despite the chill that still remained in the air above ground. The scent of the rich soil surrounding them had been overwhelming at first, but slowly she'd gotten used to it. It vaguely reminded her of the homes in the desert.

Tunnels branched off this way and that from the main corridor into complete darkness. The dim lighting they walked under made no attempt to penetrate the seemingly endless black halls. Blythe had wondered about a tour before her arrival at Passage, but now she would politely decline if offered. She was still shaken up by what had happened earlier to be in the shadows for too long.

It was so quiet underground. No noise from the surface could pierce this far down. This led to a slightly awkward silence between the two. Only the sounds of their shoes scuffling over the packed soil could be heard. It may have been the fear she had felt earlier lingering, but she was a bit unnerved with the silence.

Movement out of her peripheral had her nearly jumping out of her skin. Her head whipped around to see a blur of an old man, tiny as a toddler, vanishing into one of the adjacent tunnels. Nathaniel stopped and found her gaze when she looked back at him in confusion. His half-smile was back. "Just the knockers," he said. "Curious folk."

Blythe forced her heart to calm itself. "Knockers. Right." Similar to brownies, knockers looked like someone's grandfather who had been shrunk down to the size of an imp. It was hard getting details on such shy creatures, but they were usually depicted with long beards and carrying around pickaxes. They loved being underground, and Blythe wouldn't have been surprised if Nathaniel told her it was them who had carved out these tunnels and made Passage what it was.

A loud knock echoed through the dark, and Blythe swiveled in the direction the sound had come from.

"You're good people."

Blythe offered him a pinched expression. "What?"

Nathaniel wasn't looking at her anymore. He carried on, leading her further underground. "They like you. The knockers."

"They do?"

The man grunted. "Keen senses they got."

Blythe swept a few strands of hair behind her ear. "Oh. Well, I am glad they approve of me."

The awkward silence returned.

"Um," she murmured after a few minutes of shuffling footsteps had taken them deeper underground. "Where are we going?"

"Almost there."

That wasn't the answer she was really looking for, but she didn't press. She did notice, though, that the lights strung up above the conjoining tunnels were getting brighter, and up ahead, a large, metal door with a circular lever for a handle announced the end of the road. It was illuminated by round, glass orbs that floated in the air all around it.

Nathaniel took back his arm and used both hands to grab the lever and heave it upward. The squeal of metal on metal made Blythe flinch, and the noise resounded throughout the tunnels until the sorceress wasn't sure if the echoes were getting fainter or if her ears were ringing.

Shadows lapped at the threshold, giving away not one secret of what could be held within. Nathaniel plucked a floating orb right out of the air and pushed against the void that soon swallowed him up. Blythe hesitated for only a moment before following him in.

She gasped upon entry. On the other side of the door, the room was bright and … utterly magical. It hadn't been shrouded in darkness. It had only been a barrier spell, quite like the one Blythe had tried to form in the bathroom of her home for Thea.

The floor was made of polished labradorite that shifted from amber to turquoise, covered by a plush, red runner rug that slithered up to a large desk of cherry-stained wood. An enormous map took up nearly the entire back wall, and Blythe couldn't keep up with the twists and turns of the different colored tunnels that it presented. The entire city of Tolvade sat above a network of pathways.

Bookcases with scrolls and tomes rose up to the dirt ceiling. Roots and vines dangled from above, hanging low and curling like slender fingers as they picked up tools and strips of leather haphazardly tossed around and placed them back where they were supposed to go. Handcrafted accessories such as purses, tote bags, scarves, and belts hung on every available hook and corner. Baskets of material scraps lined the floor along the wall. The smell of leather oil and latex permeated the air. Lanterns of different styles and candles of various colored wax floated around the room, much like the orbs that hung about outside. To the side of the entrance, a centaur-sized portal took up the corner of the room. The portal was a swirling vortex of varying shades of purple that could transport anything to and from anywhere. To keep it continuously open must take an enormous amount of magic.

Muffled humming stole Blythe's attention, and she turned her gaze back to the desk where someone's head was pressed into a book. Their hand, the color of rust, waved about lazily in the air, spurring a needle to thread through some fabric in front of them.

Nathaniel purposely cleared his throat. He had let go of the orb he'd been holding, and it had floated back through the barrier to its spot outside the room.

The humming stopped, and slowly the book was placed down on the desk. The creature's face was the same color as her hand, as if she had smoothed rich, wet, red clay all over her body. Her eyes were twice as large as a human's. The sclera (normally white on a person) was gold in this case, and her irises were the exact replica of the swirling portal behind them. Her hair was the color of lilac blossoms, knotted and tangled like the roots that came down from the ceiling. Trinkets hung from some of the strands, while others had grown around and were now embedded in the locs.

"Has one never laid claim to seeing a Fae in one's such modest lifetime?"

Fae … Fae?

Blythe blinked owlishly. She was staring at one of the *Fae.*

"I—" she tried, but her voice got caught in her throat. The creature's gaze shifted to Nathaniel, and it was like a spell had been lifted, and she could breathe again. Fae were as old as the dragons in the desert and perhaps even more mysterious. There was almost no lore on them—none that was factual, at least. Most passages of the Fae were based in speculation and myth. Only once, many years ago, had she found a book with a single sentence on the history of the Fae.

A great war had broken out amongst them and their foes, and they were driven underground where they remained forevermore.

Now, she was in the same room with a creature whose entire history and magic capabilities were more mystifying than the Celestial's.

Blythe's gaze flicked between Nathaniel and the Fae. They seemed to be having a wordless exchange. Suddenly, the Fae's otherworldly eyes found hers.

"Ah," was all she said and stood with the grace of swans drifting over Lorvo Lake. A section of clumped roots plucked a scroll off one of the bookshelves and dropped it into the Fae's waiting hand. The being walked around the desk on the balls of her feet, wearing dark brown tights with large, hand-sewn stitches up the sides. A layered skirt of many folds hung off her hips, and loose fabric of the same dingy white color was wrapped around her torso and up over the back of her neck. Separate sleeves were tied around her elbows, and the material belled out and fell near the ground where her bare toes sank into the soil.

"It best not be to give one a tour," the being said and offered Blythe the scroll in her hand. "Yet should ever arise the need, one may take this and find one's way back 'ere—or anywhere under the Mother's eye."

Blythe rolled out the piece of paper and found a miniature version of the map on the wall in her hands. The Fae's words had been a little confusing, and it took Blythe a moment to understand she had meant anywhere in Tolvade.

She had so many questions, but she rolled the map back up and looked the Fae in her strange eyes. "Thank you. Any creatures not suited for the underground can always be sent to Srbeveara."

The Fae nodded, but her attention was ripped away and found Nathanial's gaze. Her swirling, purple irises hardened before they flickered over Blythe once more. "One wishes to go straight home?"

The sorceress had to look away from the intensity of the being's gaze. She felt as if any moment she was going to be sucked up into those twin portals. She focused on the map in her hands. "Yes, I must be going. I really should not be away for too long."

The Fae made no noise, but she waved her hand in the air. A leafy vine dropped the large strip of silk it had been holding and swooped over to the desk, where it rummaged around, shuffling papers out of the way and knocking over a few upright notebooks. The Fae glared at the creeping plant, but it eventually found what it was looking for.

It placed a small stone attached to a cord in the Fae's waiting palm before it went back to putting the silk away. The creature held the trinket out by the cord, and Blythe took the offered item.

"The surface be fraught with more perils than what lurks 'neath the ground. A guide is given to you. Query one's thoughts aloud, and it will answer in kind."

Upon closer inspection, Blythe recognized the object as a pendulum. The light-green stone was smooth and tapered down to a rounded point. The cord affixed to it was made of thin, braided leather. She'd read up on pendulums months ago as a passing fancy. Only yes or no questions would reveal answers. Usually, they would swing back and forth for a *no*, and around and around for a *yes*. One didn't even need to possess magic to use them, and that was what had gained her interest in the first place.

Nathaniel moved toward the map at the back of the room, and under it was a small door. Blythe hadn't even seen it when she first entered. "Ever need anything, come through the tunnels," he said in way of parting words. "Couldn't hear you earlier. It was Morgan who knew you were in trouble."

Blythe had stepped over to the door, about to be on her way, but she paused and looked back at the mysterious being. "You knew I was in trouble?"

Morgan had gone back to her book, brooding over its contents with a sharp, pointed nail guiding her eyes. She didn't bother looking away from its pages as she said, "Though under the surface, the senses are roots that burrow through the soil. When a fellow kin cries for help, a choice is given to them. Should one enter the window to the soul, or should fear consume?"

Blythe's brow quirked in confusion. She ran the Fae's words through her head several times, but nothing connected.

Nathaniel had leaned against the wall by the door, and a fond sigh left him. "She senses whenever something's in danger in the area. Keeps out of human business, though. Well, most of the time. Whenever somebeing needs help, she opens up a portal and lets whatever's in danger decide if they want to go through or not."

Blythe glanced back at the … Keeper. Was that the title she should be using with him? "It is up to the being to decide?"

"Choice magic," was all he said in reply.

The sorceress hummed, and her brow furrowed. Choice magic could only present itself when a choice was to be made. The caster did not get to make the choice themselves … But that wasn't what confused her. The only beings in Aeristria said to be able to perform the specialized magic were Dragonkin. Legends claimed dragons created the magic as a way to trap greedy humans, and their descendants still claimed the skill. No one knew anything about the Fae, though. Had they come up with the magic first? Had they seen the dragons using it and decided to steal their technique?

She needed to write this down. She needed to talk to someone about this—someone she could trust.

Blythe glanced down at the rolled-up map in her hands, then to the giant map behind her. Up close, she could see just how many tunnels there were under Tolvade. They were all marked by different colors, but what did the colors mean? She was getting overwhelmed just staring at the starting point. The thought of being stuck in an underground maze, possibly lost forever, had her wanting to turn around and try her luck on the surface, creepy locals loitering about or not.

"Um," she muttered, looking back between the map and the door. "Will I run into anything while I am finding my way home?"

"Kin," the Fae said. She flipped a page in her book but went silent after that.

"Kin … as in more Fae?" She wasn't opposed to meeting more of Morgan's kind—if they were friendly. She wasn't sure exactly how they viewed humans. She wasn't sure about anything when it came to them.

The being looked up from her book, but her gaze was far away. "To know of certainty is to know when the wind will blow next. The moon has not been gazed upon for so long that even time does not recall. When war shaped the land, it was the land that ripped us from the sky the father had gifted us and buried us underfoot. Scattered like mice, we have not converged since the last viewed dawn."

… they were driven underground, where they remained.

Blythe inched closer. She thought she understood what the Fae was saying—somewhat. "You went to war? With who? When was this?"

Morgan blinked, and her otherworldly eyes flicked back down to the book lying on the table. "When the body of one could swallow a town, and the clouds could not reach the farthest heavens as well as we could. We were borne of the Father who ruled the sky, they the Mother who blessed the land."

The sorceress knew there was weight to the Fae's words, but they went over her head. She looked back at Nathaniel, but he only shrugged his large shoulders. The words tumbled through her mind over and over as she memorized them. She'd be sure to ask Thea or Rafe what they could mean later.

Satisfied with her time spent here, she thanked them both for the map and the pendulum and set off through the door.

It was only later when she found herself amidst the endless maze of branching corridors, pendulum glowing brightly in the dark, that she paused and looked up from the illuminated map.

Morgan the Fae … Why does that sound so familiar?

Nathaniel watched Morgan flip another page of the book she had already memorized.

"You almost told her too much."

She began humming once again. It was an ancient tune that had not touched an instrument in a millennium. "One thinks so?"

"Just because she runs a sanctuary doesn't mean we should trust her fully."

"One senses malice? The roots must have shriveled in these trying times." Another page flip, then another.

Nathaniel sighed and rubbed at his eyes. The brightness of the room was starting to give him a headache. *"Knockers approved of her, too. Don't think she's bad. You telling her the Fae used to be dragons is what could be bad."*

"Never such words crossed the lips," Morgan hummed. She straightened and, without any cue, the closest cluster of roots pulled some scraps of fabric out of the baskets and deposited them into her waiting hands.

"She'll figure it out," Nathaniel persisted.

The Fae sighed and finally turned to meet the man's gaze. "One is ageing, friend of the fallen. Let the knowledge of the past trickle into the minds of the blossoming. The secrets of the mother and father's world will have the light shining upon them before the moon can next hide under the life star."

"They do not even know about Saellah, what makes it a good idea to tell them about Unsoul?"

Morgan's wine-red lips turned up into a secret little smile. "The one who came and went as frantically as a passing butterfly follows neither of those who birthed the flow of magic. The desire to witness the events that should unfold once the knowledge sinks into the depths of the soul is …" a giggle escaped her, "*most* plentiful."

Chapter Eighteen

Fractured Rainbows

The words on the paper blurred together, and Rafe heaved a sigh and pushed the document away. It was the seventh witness report on Isolde's escape, but there wasn't anything new that hadn't already been addressed in the previous reports. They were all starting to bleed together, and it didn't help that his mind kept drifting.

Thea hadn't called him in a few days, and he had stayed up well into the night worrying. He knew she was strong, capable, smart. But there was a reason researchers could never get funding to go into the mountains, and why missions were never placed that far out. The fact a team hadn't been sent with her because the High Priests wanted to keep the tablets a secret even from the rest of the Coven was ludicrous. They had basically announced that any of the Summoners and Spellweavers up to the task weren't trustworthy. He was trustworthy. He could have gone. The twins could have waited on their Second Chosen.

And yet … here he was, sitting at a desk signing documents. "I should have gone," he uttered to himself. It was probably the hundredth time he'd said those words, but he couldn't stop them from coming every time a *what if* spelled its way into his mind.

"Coven needs you here," Mokana interjected in a drab voice. She had repeated that response back at him just as many times.

Rafe tossed her an unimpressed look, but she wasn't even paying attention. Sprawled inelegantly on the massive couch in front of the desk, Mokana lay on her back with her white hair falling over the edge to brush against the floor. She held her purse up in the air and twisted it this way and that so the light coming in from the windows refracted rainbow colors all over his walls.

"My duties here could have waited," he argued, not for the first time. It's not like he could have stopped the ex-Council member from escaping or prevented Dmitri's death.

Mokana dropped her arms and pushed up onto her elbows, throwing him her own unimpressed stare. "Are you going against the Council's decree?"

Rafe frowned. "Of course not, I just think—"

"Surely the straight A, always upholds the law, stickler-for-the-rules Rafe MacBain isn't *questioning* the *Council*." Mokana flopped down into the cushions again. "What would Thea say in this scenario?"

A frustrated growl left him. "Mokana—"

"Ah," she interrupted, "inconceivable! That's a big one."

Rafe brought his hands to his face and tried to drag the stress away that the world and his pet were dumping on him. "Why do I put up with you?"

"Dunno, I never had a choice in being here," she replied flippantly. She sat up again and tossed the purse onto the other side of the couch. "Look, I'm right there with you. I don't want to be stuck in here listening to you mope about

Thea going on that expedition every single day. You think I like feeling left out of the action? I didn't get to go with you on the last Dark Market mission, I didn't get to go with you guys when you went to the desert, and now I'm missing out on going to the mountains. The fact that you came home battered all to Hell and that Thea was—not just knocking but *pounding*—on Death's door hasn't escaped me."

Rafe felt the heat creep into his neck, and he scratched the back of his head and glanced off to the side. "I'm sorry, Mokana. I wish things had been different. I wish I could have taken you with us. I know this also probably isn't what you wanted either, now that I won't be doing as much field work."

Mokana looked away. "A life of boredom or a life living as a monster … if I had to choose one, I'd happily file papers with your horrible handwriting on them every time. Besides, I know it's not going to be all bad. Especially if I get to room with Namara from now on."

The heat was in his cheeks now, but he wasn't going to comment on it. "My handwriting isn't horrible …" is what he uttered instead.

Mokana chuckled. "Sure, it's not."

"*And* I wasn't *questioning* the Council."

"Oh, sweet goddess who shuns me," Mokana groaned and fell back against the couch. "We all know whenever it comes to Thea, you're willing to bend the rules—or, ya know, obliterate them into tiny pieces and then burn them until they're ashes—so don't act like you don't."

Rafe sputtered. "I—when have—t-that's—who is *we* anyway?"

Mokana went back to fiddling with her purse. "Oh, you know," and waved her hand about in the air as if the answer was obvious.

Confused and exasperated, he groaned in annoyance, "What are you talk—" but the gentle whirring from his crystal ball cradled in its clawed pedestal stole his attention. He cleared his throat and brought the glass sphere up to his face. "This is Rafe MacBain."

Ell appeared on the other side with a nervous smile. "Hello, Ra—uh, Summoner MacBain, I have a guest here who is very adamant about seeing you."

"Guest?"

"Yes, she claims she needs to speak to you about something."

"*Oooh*, I'm telling Thea you're seeing other women behind her back," Mokana teased from the side.

Rafe glared at the rusalka before turning his attention back to a flustered Ell, who likely heard the comment. "What's her name, Ell?"

"Blythe Castel. She says she's the head of the Vemeese district's sanctuary."

Mokana sat up from her sprawled position on the couch. Her expression had shifted to match her owner's. She mouthed, *"Why is she here to see you?"* at him, to which he shrugged.

"Send her up, Ell, she's a good friend. You can give her clearance from now on."

Ell's eyes widened, and she started nodding hastily. "Sure! I'll get right on that. She'll be up in a jiffy! *Erk*—Why did I say that?" Ell's cringe was the last thing he saw before the glass darkened.

Rafe set the crystal ball aside. His fingers drummed against the wood of his desk for several seconds before he looked up at his pet. "Was it just me, or was Ell acting weird?"

"She's kind of normally weird, isn't she?"

"Mokana," he admonished. "Ell isn't weird. She's … quirky."

The rusalka huffed. "I don't know, she probably heard about your promotion. I've been wandering all over HQ today, and it's one of the many things beings are gossiping about. She could be intimidated?"

Rafe hummed and rubbed at his chin. "Should I … I don't know, send her a card or something? For all her hard work? That way, she might not see me as some bigwig."

"I think that would intimidate her more."

Rafe threw his hands up in the air. "Then what do I do? I don't want everyone to change how they act around me. I spent a long time making connections with everyone in the Coven. It'll all be for nothing if everyone starts acting like I'm their boss." He groaned for the umpteenth time. The day was definitely going to end at Tasgall's.

"Relax, Rafe," Mokana soothed and hopped up from her seat. She came around behind him and started twisting the ends of his hair. She couldn't braid it anymore, but she could ruffle the locks into odd styles. It had already grown more than a knuckle's length since he had it cut. "Just act like you normally do, and everyone will go back to normal. Eventually." Her nails grazed his scalp, and she could see the tension start to leave his large shoulders.

A soft knock on the door alerted them of Blythe's arrival. Rafe batted away Mokana's hands and flattened his hair back down. The rusalka acquiesced with a sharp yank on one of the locks before dodging his counterattack and skipping back over to the couch.

"Come in," Rafe called out and stood from his chair.

The door squeaked open, and Blythe stepped into the room with a bright, lime-green frock. It was sheer in the front so that the dark blue underskirt could be seen. Her coiffed hair was parted into small buns that ran down the center of her scalp, each dressed with a ruby hairpin, and her gold and orange eye makeup was as bright as a sunset. "Hello. I am sorry for bothering you. You must be busy."

Rafe greeted her with a smile. "Not at all. I was just thinking of taking a break, actually. Would you like something to drink?" He gestured for her to get comfortable on the couch as he took his own seat.

"Oh no, thank you." She aimed a smile of her own at Mokana and sat beside the rusalka. "Hello, Mo—oh!" she gasped, gaze focusing on the purse. "Where did you get that? I must have one."

Mokana grinned and pulled the purse up to her chest. It caught the light from the windows, and more rainbow hues bounced around the room. "I got it from the street vendor down the way. It's a new design they came up with to stay in competition with Morgan le Fay's brand."

Something flickered in Blythe's brown eyes, and she snapped her head around to find Rafe's curious frown.

"Is something the matter?" he asked.

"No, no," she assured and fidgeted with her skirts. "I just remembered why I am here."

Rafe's brows rose in question, and Blythe took it as her cue to elaborate.

She moved a stray strand of hair back behind her ear. Her demeanor had changed, and the bubbly person they both knew disappeared. "Where do I begin?" she murmured to herself. She suddenly looked fatigued, older. "I guess I should start with the night we last saw each other. How is Thea, by the way?"

"She's … good," Rafe said after a moment's hesitation. "She was angry with me for the stunt I pulled, and now she's on another mission to recover one of the last tablets. How is Cressida faring?"

The sorceress was staring at the hourglass collecting dust on Rafe's desk, but the look in her eyes was glazed. "Cressida …" she trailed off, and Mokana and Rafe shared a look, but they could do no more than that before Blythe continued. "Cressida is no longer with us."

Mokana dropped her purse, and her hands flew to her mouth. Rafe's jaw had unhinged. His brow pinched together in confusion, and he stumbled over his words. "Wha—how is that—what do you mean she's no longer with us? The cure—?" He abruptly stood up from his desk, and the chair behind him screeched in protest.

Blythe had not flinched at the startling noise. She merely watched the Summoner pace behind his desk as the thoughts in his mind raced, clear as day for all to see on his face. "I do not understand it myself. I can only recall what Asmo said to me that night in the desert. That she was 'too far gone' and that it would kill her. I did not believe him. He is … *evil*, yet he told me the truth." She sighed and slumped against the couch. "I know he did it for his own gain, but there were no other options for her recovery, so I chose to not believe him."

Rafe paused. "I need to contact Dr. Snow. She's been experimenting with the wyvern blood. If patients have been 'too far gone' like Cressida, maybe she'll have more information."

"I would appreciate that." Her smile was genuine, but it was a shadow of its former self. "This is not the reason I stopped by, however."

Rafe had reclaimed his seat once again, and he was currently jotting down notes. He looked up in surprise. "Oh?"

She took a few moments to compose herself again and brushed that same strand of hair back behind her ear once more. "Since her death, I have taken over Srbeveara. I do not know what I am doing most days, but I have managed. I set out yesterday to make connections with the other sanctions in the Lorvo, Borlimane, and Adalith. I have not had the chance to see the last one … I wanted to talk to you about what—*who* I found at the Borlimane sanctuary."

Mokana had brought her knees up to her chest as she listened intently. Rafe, too, was all ears, and he leaned back in his chair.

"I was introduced to a Fae."

Silence fell upon the room. Mokana's jaw had dropped, and Rafe's eyes had blown comically wide. He slouched over his desk and ran his hands through his hair, letting go a massive exhale as the news settled.

"That is certainly something."

"No kidding," Mokana remarked. "I've lived a long time, and I've never seen one."

Blythe's gaze drifted as she recalled the book's words, how all the Fae had been driven underground. If the rest were as versatile as Morgan, they had adapted fairly well. She was brought back to the twin vortexes of the Fae's eyes, the rich color of her skin, the riddlesome way she spoke, and the hidden meaning behind her maze of words. Blythe straightened her posture and took a deep breath. If she was right about what she was about to say … well, she didn't know what would happen. "That is not all. I did not fully understand her at the time. She speaks in riddles, but I have since written down everything I can remember her saying and …"

Rafe leaned forward in his chair. Mokana had pulled her knees impossibly closer to herself as she hung on the sorceress's every word.

"I believe the Fae were once dragons."

Chapter Nineteen

The Magic Touch

Thea woke from gentle prodding to her shoulder. She groaned as she sat up from her position on the hard, frozen ground. For the past week and a half, Thea had repeated the same sleeping arrangements when they couldn't find a safe cave for the night. For every evening they were stuck out in the open, she'd haul thick branches back to the camp and tie them together. Fatik would fillet whatever animal they managed to catch for dinner, Isabel would recreate her hidden firepit, and while Thea was awake during one of the watch shifts, she'd work on the spell for Namara—with little to no luck.

Each morning, they all woke up stiff. There was no room to lay out their bedrolls completely, but by the amount of fresh snow covering the spruce shelters, they all would rather curl up under the branches than wake up under a pile of white powder. Well, all of them except Namara and Agni.

"Rise and shine," her partner called to her quietly.

"The sun is hardly shining, Namara," she grumbled in reply before standing to her feet and stretching out the soreness. While the sun had indeed risen over the horizon, it was hidden by the gray clouds dominating the sky.

"Today we should reach the Huǒshān Clan's caves," Fatik announced to the group.

Thea groaned again as she twisted her back, and the sound morphed into a sigh as the telltale pops and cracks met her ears. She went to pick up her bag and paused, thinking of something suddenly. She dove a hand inside and felt around until she sighed in relief.

"What?" Isabel, having noticed her antics, asked as she brushed out her hair. Already the blood-red color had faded to a watermelon hue, and the roots were much more prominent than before.

"I was checking to see if I still had the barrier breaker oil. That way we'll be able to understand them, and they'll be able to understand us."

Namara giggled from the sidelines. "No imps this time around."

Thea pulled her hair out of its tight bun and grabbed her comb. "Thank the goddess herself," she said with a roll of her eyes. The last thing she needed was Leslie tagging along. It had been bad enough in the desert. He had been vital for their survival, but that didn't mean he hadn't been annoying.

They quickly and quietly gathered their things after that. The day was going to be a long one if they were supposed to find the caves. Thea hoisted herself up onto Namara's transformed back and sighed in relief as the action didn't cause pain to flare up from her stab wound. Thankfully, the nightly healing spells had remedied it down to a discolored blemish.

Thea let go of Namara's mane and removed her gloves. She curled her fingers slowly and inspected the digits. They were near frozen stiff, but frostbite hadn't set in. There was no numbness or prickling feelings of pain, no discoloration.

Her gloves were thick, but they wouldn't totally protect against her fingers falling off if she didn't keep an eye out. She checked her other hand before scrunching her toes in her boots.

The only thing out of the ordinary was the pinky finger she'd used to swear with Rafe. It had been growing colder and colder with each passing day she didn't call him. She was going to need to soon or the feeling would persist. Every time she did call him, he was running errands and couldn't talk for more than a few moments. When he called her, she was about to go to sleep and was too tired to think straight. It sufficed enough to know the other was okay — or as okay as they could be. However, the constant wall they kept hitting had Thea waiting longer and longer between each call.

There hadn't been much to report — thankfully — but she knew it was selfish to keep him worrying. She also wanted to dedicate as much time as possible to the spell for Namara while she had the brain power during her watch, but that would have to take the back burner tonight, or she'd start losing feeling in that pinky.

What was practically numb already was her arm from hauling around the arrow launcher all day, every day. She wanted it ready at all times to fire if they were ambushed from anything stalking them (not like it was super effective the last time that happened, but she wasn't taking chances). It hadn't felt as heavy strapped to her leg, but the aches brought back memories of her training days with her sickle. She smiled to herself as they came flooding in. With them came memories of sparring with Namara, Mokana, and Rafe.

She *really* needed to call him today. She shook herself out of her daze and glanced around her as the world refocused. What she *needed* to do was stay alert. She promised herself and the memories that tugged at the edge of her consciousness that she'd reach out to Rafe whenever they stopped for their midday rest.

She wondered how his Second Chosen activities were treating him. How was Mokana doing? Surely, she was having to make some major adjustments, too.

Thea huffed and straightened her spine. She was doing it again, letting her mind wander when she should be paying attention.

From underneath her, Namara nickered and swung her head gently up and down. A question. That or a comment on her partner's restlessness. She couldn't be sure.

"I'm just thinking about back home," Thea said in response.

Namara made a very loud snort, but the Spellweaver took it as understanding rather than mocking. She was sure Namara missed being home, too.

She reached behind her to take a sip of her canteen when an alarm began blaring from her crystal ball. She jolted in her seat, and even Namara flinched at the loud noise. It wasn't just coming from Thea's crystal ball, either, but Fatik's was blaring in alarm as well. Isabel's head whipped between the two in confusion, but Thea couldn't tell her what was going on over the commotion. As quickly as she could, she connected her magic to the glass sphere. Fatik picked up his and together the transmission went through.

"*This is the High Priest Council urging all beings to remain within city limits. Due to dangerous conditions outside Tolvade's borders, we advise any and all beings to remain inside the city until the Wild Hunt ritual is completed at the end of the month. If you need assistance with something outside the borders that cannot be put off until the given time, seek an audience with a Hunter status member to file a request report. Thank you, and have a good day.*"

Within seconds, a message popped up and wrapped itself around the curved glass. It read:

All Coven members are on light duty and information retrieval scrolls until further notice. Three hours of minimum magical training are to be conducted daily, and spell usage is to be reported to headquarters until the day of the Wild Hunt ritual. The city and the inhabitants are our top priorities. We are to prepare for the event as usual with added precautions. Report any sketchy behavior and events that seem out of the ordinary as soon as they transpire to the Coven.

Blessed be,
The High Priest Council

Thea chewed her lip and silently sheathed her crystal ball. She *really* needed to call Rafe.

Blythe peered up at the sky and frowned. The sky was gray and dreary, but, thankfully, it wasn't very cold out. In fact, it was a little muggy with the recent rain they've had. Blythe couldn't think of a worse combination—cool and muggy.

She glanced down at her pure white dress and brushed away wrinkles that weren't there. It was a little late, but she'd finally managed to dig through her entire closet and find her mourning garments buried in the very back. She'd only ever worn white once, a long time ago. When her parents hadn't made it back from the trade route, she'd worn the color for the customary time of one week before she'd packed a bag and left the only home she'd ever known.

She hadn't had the strength to find the clothes sooner. She hadn't wanted to admit Cressida was gone even as she'd watched the woman's body go up in flames. But she couldn't keep running from the truth. So, today she stood before the last sanctuary on her list dressed in a layered frock of alabaster and ivory. The thin, satin scarf around her neck whipped in the breeze. Her hair was a simple updo that held no personality whatsoever, and her makeup … she hadn't worn any today. But that was okay. This wasn't about her.

White represented the purity of the soul and its departure from this world to the next. She had been taught that to wear white and dress down was to rebuff the soul from coming back and losing its way. Instead of wanting to come back to what was familiar, the soul would be attracted to the bright colors of a new life and new opportunities while being dissuaded from the lifeless colors of those mourning.

But Blythe had not wanted to rebuff Cressida from coming back. Even if it meant coming back as her familiar and nothing more.

This—wearing white—was for her more than it was for Cressida. She had made progress everywhere else to move on. Now, with this, she was finally letting go completely.

Blythe let go a soft sigh and walked up the curved, stone steps lined on either side with potted plants. A pointed, wrought-iron fence squarely sectioned off the tiny corner lot. The sanctuary was also pretty small and shoved nearly up to the fence, and Blythe wondered if, like the last sanctuary, this one held secrets underground. More lush plants overtook what little yard there was and twirled up the metal spires of the fence. The building was the same color as the pewter clouds above and made up of varying stones. Three chimneys on top of the oddly curved roof puffed away.

She knocked lightly on the door and held her breath. She hoped the woman inside, Branwen, did not look at her with the same scorn as the rest of Adalith had. The district was beautiful. The people, however, were terrifying.

The door slowly opened, and Blythe's teeth plucked at her bottom lip in anticipation. A hunched-over figure came into view. Her hair fell down to her ankles in a silver stream over her knobby shoulder. Her face held deep wrinkles around her cheeks and hazel eyes, which were bright with wisdom and sharp with wit.

"What do you want?" the old crone asked bluntly in a rough, croaking voice.

Blythe floundered. "Uh—well—um, my name is Blythe, and I'm in charge of the sanctuary, Srbeveara."

Branwen closed her eyes and nodded her head as if gathering patience. "Yes, yes, I know *who* you are. I asked what you *wanted*."

"Oh." Blythe blinked and felt a flush take over her cheeks. Her colorless nails scratched at the back of her neck. The words she had planned to say, the ones she went over in her head countless times on the way over to Adalith, were lost to a nervous laugh. "I wanted to introduce myself and—"

"Well, you've met me. Goodbye."

"Wait!" Blythe shot her hands out to keep the old woman from closing the door, but they fell just short of the handle. Branwen paused, though, and peeked around the frame in mild annoyance. Then her hazel eyes, so much like a field of sun-dried grass under a hazy day, shifted to something behind her. Her gaze hardened.

Blythe glanced over her shoulder to see the neighbor across the street's window curtain quickly falling back into place.

"Ugh," the crone sighed. "If you must bother me, at least come inside." Then she hobbled back into her home without so much as a backward glance, leaving the door wide open and grumbling along the way. "… gossip mongers … whole neighborhood … them nosey little …" Blythe was glad she couldn't hear that last bit, but she had a pretty good idea of what was said.

She hesitated for only a moment before lifting her gown's hem over the threshold and stepping inside. As soon as she closed the door, warmth enveloped her, but it was unfortunately just as muggy indoors.

Wide-planked, wooden floors that were in desperate need of a sweep stretched out before her, adding contrast to the pale rock walls. A large hearth interrupted the flow of the stone, lit within and burning under a bubbling cauldron. Cast iron pots and pans hung from the ceiling along with twine bundles of herbs, garlic cloves, peppers, and mushrooms. Bottles of potions and jars of powders were lined up and crowded in the bookshelves shoved up against the walls. A cluttered table sat in the center of the room with cards, candles, crystals, and thick, leather-bound tomes spread out and piled haphazardly on top of one another.

The short curtain over the window allowed little natural light to filter in, but there were plenty of candles already lit. A floor-length candelabra stood by the table with each of its milky-white candles alive and flickering as fire danced atop the wicks. Potted plants overtook what little space remained of the floor. The humidity in the sanctuary amplified the multiple different smells layering over one another, creating a musty, sour scent that had the sorceress's nose twitching occasionally.

Next to several large ferns, Branwen was clunking away at the butcherblock countertop of her small kitchenette. A heavy-looking ketal was in one hand, two jars in the other. "Care for some tea?"

That seemed to be all Blythe was drinking recently. The caffeine helped keep her going. "Sure," she answered. The wood floor creaked under her white flats as she sidestepped a striped snake plant in a shiny, red pot.

"Quit standing around," the crone snapped with a wave over her shoulder, and with that wave of her hand, a chair from the table was yanked out. "Make yourself comfy. That nervous energy is going to upset Gypso."

Blythe gaped. She hadn't seen any powders or magic enhancers come from the woman's robe pockets. She didn't even bother to ask who Gypso was as she slid into the seat. The ambience of the home was cozy, if a little overwhelming, but it felt a lot more welcoming than the woman lumbering over to the table with two mugs of steaming tea.

"So, Cressida's dead, eh?"

Blythe stilled. Her heart clenched painfully in her chest, and she closed her eyes as she tried to right her breathing. "Yes," she admitted softly after taking a moment to gather herself.

Branwen set the tea in front of her and plopped down in the opposite chair. There wasn't much room with all her eclectic crafts taking up so much space, so she just held the hot mug in her gnarled hands. "Ah," she made a sound of understanding, but she didn't apologize for her crass words. It hadn't meant to be a jab or insult. Branwen was as blunt as a dull blade, but a blade was still a blade, and the words *had* hurt.

Blythe busied herself with taking a sip of her tea, hoping to gather herself more before she spoke next. She blinked in astonishment as the flavor hit her tongue. She jerked back and stared at the dark, honey-colored liquid in the crude, handmade mug.

"This is so good!" she exclaimed, aiming her surprised gaze at the old woman before her. The tea had a certain bitterness to it, but it left behind the taste of smoke and a flare of heat from a spice she couldn't place. It smelled of pine and honey, and Blythe quickly took another sip. It was nearly comparable to what she could find back home.

Branwen wore a similar expression of surprise before she huffed a soft, throaty chuckle, and her expression morphed into a smirk. "It ain't mine. I got it from Dulce."

She should have known. "Oh, really? I really will have to trade recipes with her."

Branwen stared at her for a few moments. "… You don't look like much, but you've got a sense of taste at least. Can't stand that flowery crap myself."

A soft pitter-patter of feet came from behind her, and Blythe only had time to look down and flinch in shock as a huge skunk came tottering past her calves. It was bigger than a small dog and wandered over to Branwen's ankles before stopping and looking up. The old woman chuckled again and reached down to scratch under the creature's chin.

"Um," Blythe cleared her throat as she eyed the animal with apprehension. "Is that … Gypso?"

"You needn't worry about him. He only sprays those hoity-toity neighbors of mine when they stop mindin' their own business."

The skunk sat back on his haunches. "Elizabeth and Jeanette have been particularly nosy as of late."

Blythe choked on her tea, and she felt some dribble down her chin, which she hastily wiped away after her coughing fit. "Oh," she said hoarsely. "It's a familiar." A soft pang of longing passed through her, but she shoved that feeling out of her mind.

Branwen took another sip of her tea and hummed into the mug. "Aye. Taught me everythin' I know. We been together now … what say you?"

"Sixty-seven years," the skunk said.

Blythe wore her surprise easily. That was a long time together. Familiars were not as rare as beings liked to think, but they blended in so well with other pets that most people couldn't tell the difference. And, unfortunately, not everyone took to their familiars as easily as they took to animals who didn't constantly nag them about their magic. So, most of a familiar's knowledge never got passed on to the recipient.

But Blythe knew that was not the case with Branwen. She couldn't get a sense of aura pouring off the woman, but that sharp wit in her eyes gave her away. She was the skeleton key that would unlock the door to Blythe's capabilities. She just had to find a tactful way of acquiring that key …

She glanced between the two of them and blurted out the first thing she could think of. "Could you please teach me how to use my magic!"

Both Branwen and Gypso stared at her. Then they looked at each other.

"I don't teach," was all the crone said after a moment.

Blythe visibly deflated. Well, there went that idea.

The old woman sniffed and took a sip of her tea. "How do you run a sanctuary without knowing anything about magic? You just too lazy to learn? Cressida — ah, well, she didn't teach you anything?"

Blythe leaned back in her chair and sighed. She found the lines in the wooden table from the tree it'd been carved from and traced the patterns with her eyes. It was easier than looking at Branwen while admitting the truth.

"This magic was not always mine. It was a gift from Cressida before she died. One I never asked for."

Several seconds of silence passed by before Blythe dared look up. She had just admitted to her lover's crimes, but what could Branwen do? Have the ashes thrown in jail? Blythe gave a wry smile at the thought, but even she felt how fragile it was from the soft tremble of her lips.

Branwen shook her head in disappointment. "Enzou would have been so disappointed."

Blythe's brow quirked. "Who?"

The old crone looked up. "She never told you? I've known that little spitfire ever since Enzou brought her home."

"Wait," Blythe set down her tea, "I'm confused. Who is Enzou?"

Branwen set down her own tea and crossed her arms over her chest as a faraway look entered her eyes. Gypso went and curled up on a large cat bed by the fire. Whatever was in the cauldron continued to bubble and boil a frothy-green color.

"Enzou was a kind man. A weirdo, but a gentle soul. He came down from the mountains … let's see … four decades ago now? Hailed from some clan long forgotten now, way up at the summit of those mountains. I thought for sure he was lying. There's all kinds of trouble up in those mountains besides dragons. But his accent was thick even with a translation spell. Back in my day, we didn't have oils to do the work for us. We had to use the dust the goddess gave us. You all just throw around fancy little bottles thinkin' you're all that and a bag of runes. Anyway, where was I? Oh yeah—his accent was thick, and he just plain looked different."

"Different how?" she queried softly.

"Just like how you look different than the folks around here," the old crone stated bluntly. "He was tan, but I bet the sun had nothing to do with it. Was in his blood. His hair had texture to it, some real weight. But it shone so brilliantly. His features were different, too. Didn't look like anyone I'd seen in Tolvade. A breath of fresh air, honestly."

Branwen looked softer as she described Enzou. A small smile had made its way onto her face, but it died when she came back to the present. She cleared her throat and sipped some more of her tea. "Anyway, he came down the mountain and thought this place was some hotel. Heh. The nerve. Still, I took him in. He taught me a few things, I taught him a few things. He stayed here all of a month and then left, saying I'd inspired him to create a sanctuary of his own. It's why ours are so similar. The other two do the job right, but they don't have the space like we do. Nor the magic."

Blythe hung onto her every word, but her gaze darted about at the last part. Confusion flitted across her face. The home was tiny, and she hadn't seen one creature—other than Gypso—meander through.

"Don't believe me?"

The sorceress looked back with wide eyes. "Huh? Oh—no, I just … um," she trailed off as the words she wanted to say left her. Branwen was more terrifying than any of the people walking Adalith's streets, yet she liked her presence all the same. The woman was fiercely intimidating and brash, but she wasn't wholly unkind.

Branwen groaned as she pushed herself up from the table and set down the mug on the counter behind her. She hobbled over and rummaged through the tomes, candles, and bottles. A crystal ball almost rolled off the table before it was snatched up and put back on its pedestal. A curved wand was excavated from the messy pile with, "Aha, blasted stick."

The wand glowed dully.

"Don't catch an attitude with me."

The wand stopped glowing.

Branwen looked over at Blythe and flicked her wand in an upward motion. "Follow me."

Blythe popped out of her chair and rushed to catch up with the old woman as they made their way over to what looked like a skinny broom closet. Upon opening it, that's exactly what it was.

"Um," Blythe paused when Branwen held up her gnarled hand, wand pointed at the closet. She swung the door shut and then proceeded to touch the wood lightly at several points. Each time, the wand glowed a different hue of blue. The wood expanded, widened, and Blythe stepped back with a small gasp.

When the old crone opened it again, a long, *long* hallway was in the broom closet's place. The same wide, wooden planks stretched out before them, and the cozy feeling from the kitchen bled into the impossibly long corridor. Hundreds of doors on each side greeted them, every one adorned with a green wreath of succulents.

Branwen closed the door and double-tapped the wood. The entrance to the hall shrank back to the size of the broom closet once more, and the older woman hobbled back to her chair, leaving Blythe near speechless.

"You use amplifiers?" She asked after a moment, scurrying back to her own chair in her excitement. If she could convince Branwen to teach her how to use her magic, if she could help her with the amplifiers, she would be able to finally run the sanctuary just as Cressida had.

Branwen took a sip of her tea and made a face. It must have cooled. She waved a hand over her mug and then waved at Blythe's. Steam curled up from the cup, and the strong smell wafted into the air once more. Taking another sip, this one being satisfactory, she responded with, "Yes, it was one of the many things I taught Enzou on how to use properly. He had the gift of being magically talented, and we traded information quite regularly. He was a very smart man." She sighed. "Died too soon. Left that little spitfire to run the place all on her own. Seems it's a cycle."

Blythe scooted closer. "Will you please teach me how to use the amplifiers at least?"

Branwen stared at her hard for a few moments. Blythe kept eye contact with her, though it was admittedly hard to do so. She held her breath and waited.

The old crone shifted in her seat. "Fine. On one condition," she added quickly when Blythe went to jump from her chair in excitement. "Tell me how much magic knowledge you possess."

Blythe did. She sat back down in her chair and looked up at the ceiling as she recited all that she had learned over the years in the desert from books the traders would bring through, from the journals she would devour in Tolvade's libraries when she first came to the city, and from everything she picked up from Cressida when she moved into the sanctuary.

Branwen listened with what looked like endless patience. Her features gave nothing away. She could be interested, or she could be waiting for Blythe to finally shut up. The young sorceress didn't know, but she kept going over everything in her head that she could remember.

Once she quieted, Branwen didn't skip a beat. "Now, from all your knowledge, tell me something I don't know."

Blythe balked, her mouth opening and closing like a fish's. "What—but I—"

"The condition can be met by telling me something I already know," Branwen interjected, "but I want to *see* just how much you know. And I want to test that by asking you to tell me something that you feel only you know."

Blythe sat back and ran through everything she'd learned. All of it was common knowledge to those of the craft, and while she retained a lot of it more than most people who specialized in one branch, she had absorbed so much with the thought that she'd never be able to specialize because she would never get to practice. Everything she learned by picking it up from Cressida she could tell now was child's play, as Cressida never did more than show off little tricks for Blythe's amusement.

The conversation she had with Rafe yesterday flashed through her mind. Her head jerked up to find the crone's gaze. "I believe the Fae used to be dragons."

When she'd divulged that information to the Summoner, they'd spent the better part of the afternoon going over the Fae's riddlesome speech and everything she had said to Blythe. They hadn't known what to do with the information, and when everything was said and done, they'd all been silent as they contemplated the news. What it meant to them now was irrelevant, yet it felt as though the secret was something vital and worth holding onto. For what, they didn't know.

But Branwen, the crone who seemed to have been alive for the birth of the sun, merely scoffed. "So, you've met Morgan. That's hardly something newsworthy. What, pray tell, do you plan on doing with that information? How is that going to help you with anything?"

Blythe sagged in her seat with a frown. She had run into the same roadblock the other day with the others.

The look of defeat must have been obvious on her face. "Care to try again?" the older woman sighed.

Blythe's eyes danced back and forth across the wood floor below her as she went over everything she had ever learned once more. She kept going back to that conversation with Rafe … but then her eyes widened. Rafe. Rafe and Thea. Rafe and Thea in the desert.

The tablet. The tablet that mercilessly laid waste to all the blood mages in Herbon. The tablet that was a necessary piece to the Wild Hunt spell. The spell that the country's leaders have been doing wrong for over two hundred years.

She looked up and found Branwen's gaze once more. "Magic is dying in the world."

Branwen scoffed again and went to say something snarky, but Blythe cut her off before she had the chance.

"Because the Wild Hunt spell has been performed wrong for the past two hundred years, and the tools used to complete the spell have been split up into four temples."

Whatever the old woman was going to say died on her tongue, and her hazel eyes sharpened as they landed on Blythe. It was an intensely curious look. "How do you know that?" was all she asked.

Blythe squared her shoulders. "Because I was there in the desert temple when I was told as much. It was guarded by sylphs who said they had been trapped there for two centuries. I was also the one who used a fraction of that power to dispel the blood mages in Borlimane when they attacked us recently."

Branwen stared at her again for a few more seconds before bowing her head and letting loose a hearty chuckle. "Aye, I like you. Now," she said and held Blythe's gaze, "tell me everything you know about it, and I'll help you with those amplifiers. I might even throw in how to properly use that magic of yours if you have anything else interesting up your sleeve."

"Really?" Blythe's eyes lit up at the prospect. "But, wait, you really didn't know?"

Those hazel eyes were equally bright. "I may have been around a long time, but even I was not alive during the division of the humans and elves. I assume that is why the Wild Hunt is done wrong. Am I correct?"

Blythe was in awe of how witty Branwen could be. And she was ever so happy to reveal to the old woman something even she didn't know.

"Partially."

Chapter Twenty

Valley of Beasts

"You can't seriously think that," Thea scoffed at Isabel and crossed her arms.

"Of course, I do!"

"I can't believe you like eating stiff bread."

"Look, I'm sorry you like charcoal over lightly toasted goodness, but some people actually prefer to taste what they're eating and not its burnt remains," Isabel snipped over her shoulder. "Lightly toasted toast is the best toast, and I stand by that!"

"It's not burnt," Thea sneered. "It's just *actually* toasted."

"This coming from the same one who doesn't like spicy food."

The Spellweaver reeled back at the change in subject, but, honestly, she shouldn't have been too surprised. It had been like this—the constant back-and-forth nitpicking and arguing over the most trivial things—for the past three hours.

"I'm sorry I don't like being in pain when I eat something?"

Isabel threw back her head and wiped her hands down her face as if washing away the frustration she was feeling. "I like how you're this super warrior who's constantly fighting for her life, but the thought of a tiny kick that adds flavor to your food is somehow a deal breaker. It's not even painful, it's just a little hot!"

"A little hot? My nose ran for an hour after I tried that street vendor's food, and my mouth felt like it was on *fire*."

She waved at Thea dismissively. "Oh, sure, ya big baby."

Thea squawked. "What—you—"

"*Ladies*," Fatik interjected in a tone that bordered somewhere between pained and exasperated. "As entertaining as this has been, I simply can't do this anymore."

Isabel, the ever-persistent, aimed her attention at him. "Okay, but surely you agree, right? Tell me you can at least *handle* spicy food."

Thea sputtered from the back of the group. "I can *handle* spicy food, I just don't like eating it!"

Fatik sighed. "My soul is too weak for this."

"Your soul is too weak for spicy food?" the redhead piped up.

"No," he groaned and spun around, halting Agni and Namara and thus Isabel and Thea. "We should go ahead and take a break for lunch. I need to recenter myself because this constant arguing has disconnected me from the world."

Both Thea and Isabel peered down at the Dragonkin in confusion.

"You're connecting with the world?" Isabel asked.

Thea shifted atop Namara with her brow pinched. "I'm not following."

"It's a long story," Fatik said with another sigh, which must have meant he was too mentally drained for further explanation. He swung his retractable walking stick up and, with the use of his own magic, the rod shrank back to its portable size. "It's just hard to tell what's around me when I can't even hear my own thoughts."

Thea and Isabel mirrored a wince and muttered, "Sorry," simultaneously.

Fatik nodded and peered over his shoulder. He took a deep breath and closed his eyes for a moment. "There should be a massive valley just up ahead. We'll take a break there."

Thea couldn't see anything from her vantage point atop Namara, but she saw Isabel pull out the wooden scroll that clattered against itself as it unraveled. With a gentle nudge of Thea's foot, Namara hurried on over to walk flank-to-flank with Agni. The trail they were on now was thankfully wide enough to accommodate them both, and they were surrounded on each side by thick forest. They hadn't come across a sheer drop off all day, and Thea was thankful for it all the same.

Isabel unfolded the center of the map, leaving the edges rolled up so that the long chart wasn't difficult to hold up. The moment the woman set her eyes on the detailed mountain drawings, it was like another person had taken the reins over Isabel. The researcher in the girl came out, and she studied the contents with keen eyes and an organized mind.

Isabel pointed at something on the map. "Look here," she instructed, and Thea leaned over as far as she dared and spotted what Isabel was pointing at. "This is the valley he's talking about."

Thea couldn't tell if it was really that large when comparing it to the sizes of the mountains, or if the illustrator had purposefully made it bigger for the viewer to see it.

Turns out, it was really that large.

As Namara and Agni halted upon entering the clearing, both women atop them gasped softly. Rolling hills were carpeted in lush grass so green Thea had only ever seen the color reflected in gemstones. Wildflowers of all kinds dotted the landscape in cobalt, lavender, scarlet, and gold. Hundreds of mountain peaks rose up over the horizon with evergreen forests creeping up their sides. In the far distance, a massive waterfall sprayed over the side of one of the mountains and misted the air. The runoff from that waterfall seemed to end in the valley in the form of a giant, crystal-blue lake mirroring the clear sky above. Large deer with massive antlers drank from the other side of the lake, and woolly mountain goats grazed nearby in a clustered herd.

It was warmer in the valley. So much so that Thea hadn't noticed on the trail, but her breath was no longer visible. The wind was still biting, but it wasn't as harsh nestled between the mountains. The sun had come out in full force over the last couple of hours, and only the peaks of the highest mountains remained clouded and snow-capped.

"It's so beautiful," Thea muttered in awe.

"I wanna go running through that field of flowers, but like, super slowly. Agni, you gotta do it with me and catch me in your arms like those cheesy romance plays mom used to take us to. Remember?"

Agni snorted, and Thea hid her smirk by looking away. Fatik had wandered off to a massive, fallen log. The Dragonkin sat himself on the aged, gnarled perch and closed his eyes. His wings behind his back stirred only a moment before stilling.

Thea slid off Namara and pulled the leather saddle blanket off with her. "Go take a dip in the lake, but stay in this form just in case we need to escape at any moment. I don't want it taking a lot out of you, especially if we encounter any danger."

Namara bumped her with her nose and nibbled at her shirt, jumping back when Thea went to swat at her. She let loose a high, piercing whinny as she galloped off in the direction of the lake, spooking the deer that were near the edge. The goats also scattered when the kelpie dove into the water with loud, crashing splashes. Water elementals jumped out of the lake in shock and raced up the attached creek before slipping into the stream and disappearing once more.

Thea turned back to see Isabel—having apparently given up on convincing Agni to join her—frolicking in the field of flowers without a care in the world. She looked like she was about to burst out in song any moment.

She smiled. She didn't know when she started looking at the redhead as anything more than a noisy nuisance, but that was just Isabel's effect on those around her. It was hard not to like her. She wasn't fake or rude or believed she was better than anyone else. She may have looked down on magic and those using it, but Thea knew it was mostly aimed at beings who overused magic. Regardless, despite her hang-ups, she wasn't a bad person by any means.

Then there was Fatik. She hadn't gotten the best read on the Dragonkin over the last week. One moment, he was helpful and relaxed, the next, he was stiff and quiet. There was still the question about his wings and their capabilities, and the comment about his soul being weak earlier had piqued her curiosity in him.

She glanced over and found him watching Isabel. A look of amusement was scrolled onto his features as he observed the redhead dance (quite badly) around and around. No longer feeling like she was going to disturb him, she made her way over and sat down quietly next to the pale creature. In the sun, his entire being seemed to glow this ethereal, iridescent color.

"She's something else, huh?" she asked with a chuckle.

Fatik glanced at her out of the corner of his eye and huffed a quiet laugh. "She's definitely more of a handful than Tasgall. Never thought I'd find someone to say that about."

Thea giggled before leaning back with a sigh. It was such a beautiful day now that the sun had come out and it wasn't blocked by endless trees. "Do you feel recentered now?" she asked after a moment.

She wasn't looking at him, but she could sense the flush that covered his face. "Yes. Sorry about snapping earlier."

"No need to apologize. We were arguing about stupid stuff anyway, but … what did you mean? About your soul being too weak?"

Fatik didn't answer her for a long moment.

She shifted to look over at the Dragonkin. "You don't have to tell me. I was just curious, but I think it's best to know the weaknesses of those I'm traveling with so I can cover them with my strengths. And vice versa."

The Dragonkin nodded, but he still wouldn't meet her gaze. His wings shifted, and they glinted like glass in the sun. "It's nothing serious. It comes with being only a quarter dragon."

"Only a quarter?"

Fatik sighed, but it wasn't one of annoyance. "Dad's Dragonkin. That's half. Mom's a pixie, which dilutes the blood of the dragon even more."

She was still confused. "That's a bad thing?"

"No, not at all. I wouldn't trade my mother for the world. She gave up her voice to give me a name. She—"

"Wait, what?" she interrupted. She brought her hand to her mouth at Fatik's wide-eyed expression. "Sorry, I just never knew. I assumed she was always mute."

He gave her a wry smile and looked away. "Giving birth to a dragon soul, however diluted it is, is still essentially giving birth to the purest magic of all. And magic is all about give and take. Mom gave up her voice so she could have me. The last thing she ever said was my name when I was born."

Thea felt her eyes water, and she blinked the would-be tears away quickly. She didn't understand why that hit her so hard, but she looked at Me'Glach in a whole new light now.

"Being only part dragon makes it harder to do a lot of things. It's harder to hide the parts of me that are obviously dragon. Even dad keeps his wings hidden because it takes too much out of him to pop them in and out. In a bar, they'd just knock things over, so he keeps them in. For me, it's harder to keep them contained, so I just keep them out."

She eyed the large, glassy wings and hummed. "How do you … uh, never mind."

"What is it?"

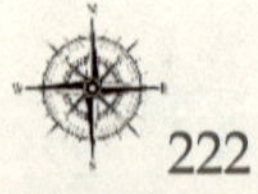

She could feel her cheeks heating up. "I was just wondering how you put clothes on … with your wings out like that."

Fatik smiled softly and peered down at his coat. "It's a bit expensive, but Tasgall spoils me. I have to have my clothes custom-made, and the thread they're woven from is enchanted. They morph around my wings."

"Oh," she mumbled and eyed over the material he was wearing once more. "That's …"

"Annoying? Irritating? Yeah, I know. Don't worry about it," he sighed. "Being only part dragon also makes it a lot harder to get a feel of the land's layout than it would be for Dragonkins like my dad. But dragons weren't borne of land magic anyway. They were borne from his breath. If I could fly, I'd be better than any bird in the sky." He sighed again. "I can't even do that."

Thea was confused once more. "Wait … whose breath?"

To that, Fatik only chuckled again. "You think the goddess rules alone?"

Her jaw dropped, and her mind blanked, but before she could gather her thoughts, Isabel came bounding over boisterously. She was out of breath and straddled the huge log before slumping over and lying out on the rough surface. Her face was red and splotchy as if she had been lying out suntanning all day rather than frolicking through some flowers. "I've danced all there is to dance. I can't dance anymore," she admitted breathlessly.

"I'm so glad to know the limitations to your dancing last—" Thea glanced up at her sun as if actually calculating the time, "all of five minutes."

Isabel flopped over onto her back with a groan. "I give it all I got in those five minutes, and that's all that matters. I'm gonna nap now. Wake me when we leave."

Thea snorted at the sight and peered over to see Agni lounging in the flowers, legs tucked up under him. He was watching the other demonic horse swimming circles in the lake like a tipsy duck, and she smiled softly at the two. Soft snoring had her looking down to find Isabel passed out already. The dance session must have really tired her out.

"We should get going before long. I'm going to make a call out to Rafe and grab a snack." She needed to catch up with the Second Chosen—her finger still feeling as if it was dunked in that freezing lake along with Namara—but she wasn't sure if she was going to mention the bomb Fatik had just dropped on her. She needed to get more information first.

She slid off the log and felt around her belts for her crystal ball. Her fingers met cool glass, and she let herself smile as anticipation coursed through her. But just as she brought up Rafe in her mind, the ground beneath her feet rumbled. She stiffened, and when Rafe's surprised yet relieved face popped up on the sphere, she only had a moment to meet his gaze before the connection winked out. She whipped around to find Fatik and the now awake Isabel frozen on the log.

The very log that began to move from underneath them.

Agni let loose a hellish squeal as he bounded over to them just as bright, fire-orange splotches began to glow all over it. Fatik jumped off, snatching Isabel by the wrist and yanking her away. All three scrambled back just as the thing they believed to be a fallen tree ripped itself away from the soil to reveal the head of a massive salamander.

The creature swung around to show off its molten lava-colored eyes with narrow, pitch-black, slitted pupils. Bright red and charcoal pulsed across its slippery skin, and from its mouth, a large tongue darted out to lick its eyes.

"Run," Fatik whispered, horrified. "Run!"

Thea took off in a sprint across the valley, Fatik and Isabel close behind her. Agni was screaming in the distance, and when the Spellweaver chanced a glance over her shoulder, the stallion was kicking out at the sluggish salamander and distracting it.

Namara was bellowing her own cries, galloping across the clearing and reaching her owner before the valley's halfway point. Thea didn't stop running, but her hands shot out and became glued to the kelpie's skin. Pushing off the ground, she leaped onto the creature's back. Fatik was somehow keeping up with Namara, his wings tipped to give his body the perfect streamline.

She threw her head back over her shoulder to find where Isabel was. Angi had angered the monstrous amphibian long enough and was now bolting over the clearing faster than any normal horse. He slowed only to gather the researcher up on his back before he was racing over the fields once more.

Thea whipped around and held out her hand to Fatik. "Grab on!" she yelled over the wind whipping around her. He latched onto her, his wings flaring to catch the wind and lift him off the ground. He landed behind her, and his arms secured themselves around her waist. She leaned over, thighs straining to keep her elevated as the slippery being galloped underneath her, and wrapped her fingers tightly in the seaweed-green mane. "Go as fast as you can!" she directed at Namara, and the kelpie immediately picked up speed.

Thundering footfalls chased them over the valley, and Thea could only peer over her shoulder in horror as flames spewed across the ground behind them and burned the grass and wildflowers into ash as the salamander chased after them. Grumbling noises left the colossus, booming over the valley and threatening her eardrums as it rushed after them. Lava dripped from its mouth, and its sticky, flaming tongue darted out to catch. It lashed out just behind Agni, who had almost caught up with Namara.

Thea screwed her eyes shut and trembled from the strain in her thighs. The entire mission had been torture on her body, but she knew if she sat down completely on Namara's back, even with the glue-like substance keeping her from being bucked off, it would jostle her hard enough to kill her. Namara wasn't the average horse.

She opened her eyes to see the forest at the edge of the clearing just up ahead, and it would hopefully provide them with enough coverage to escape the salamander. She whipped around to find the amphibian nearly upon them, and her blood ran cold as it clamored after them with its sticky tongue darting out, blasting the ground and ripping large chunks of the terrain out. Its scrambling footfalls were so loud her ears felt like they were bleeding.

Everything suddenly darkened, and a large gust of wind blasted them. The sound of air walloping them was enough to finally blow Thea's eardrums. Sharp pain flared in her ears and raced down to her jaw, and she felt herself scream.

The trees swallowed them, and Namara and Agni skidded to a halt and spun around. Thea felt for sure that blood was now trickling down her ears. Her vision blurred for only a second before her gaze homed in on a massive, red being of *death* holding down the squirming salamander.

A dragon.

A living, breathing dragon. It was twice the size of the wyverns in the desert, and it snapped its enormous jaws down on their assailant's head before rearing back and swallowing the salamander whole. Its body took up nearly half the valley. Scales the size of an oxcart glittered a deep, blood red under the sun. Massive horns of obsidian protruded from its head, flanked by scarlet spikes that flared out like fins. Muscles bulged, and its gigantic wings blocked out the sun and cast the world in its shadow. Its jaw opened, revealing hundreds of razor-sharp teeth of incredible length, and goopy, red-tinged drool connected them in viscous strands. Smoke billowed out of its wide nostrils, fogging up the surrounding area in plumes of giant clouds.

Thea couldn't hear what Fatik was saying, but she felt the vibrations from his chest on her back. She glanced over to Isabel and saw blood smeared around the redhead's ears. She had a dazed expression, but even she was frozen as she stared at the monstrous legend before them.

The dragon didn't even bother looking at them, so tiny they were compared to it, and it flapped its wings once, twice, before lifting off. The towering trees around them thrashed and swayed from the force of the blast, and Thea shielded her face with her arms. Namara reared back and toppled over, and once again Thea felt a scream of agony rip out of her throat as she was nearly crushed under the kelpie's weight. Namara rolled as quickly as she could, and the glue-like substance of her skin brought the Dragonkin and Spellweaver up with her, but sharp, throbbing pain flared up Thea's leg. A high-pitched ringing sounded in her ears, and the world slowly faded to black.

Chapter Twenty-One

Caveward Bound

Thea felt the heavy rhythm of being rocked before she was fully awake. Her eyelids peeled back, and a forest—most specifically the tree trunks—lazily passed her by. She sat up slowly and winced at the throbbing in her left thigh from where Namara had nearly crushed her under her weight.

"Are you okay?"

She swiveled slowly to meet Fatik's gaze over her shoulder. Her hearing had returned, most likely from being healed, and besides the minor ache in her leg, she felt fine. She slowly nodded.

"I healed your ears as best I could. Your leg too. I know it had to have taken the brunt force when we fell—mine did anyway. It's been a while since I've used powders, so it probably wasn't the best job, but thankfully being part dragon has its benefits."

Thea stared mutely. Fatik's wings shone brilliantly under the sun. His thick tail swished behind him contentedly. His eyes were clear and full of concern.

He was nothing like the monster Thea had witnessed earlier. Her mind helpfully shuffled the memories of that massive beast to the forefront of her brain, and she felt herself shudder. The wyverns in the desert had been intimidating. Scary, even, when faced with one. However, in comparison, where the wyverns were lean and smooth like river rocks, the red dragons were as jagged and rough as the mountains they resided on. She finally realized why the mountain range was called the Red Tipped Mountains. The dragons here were absolutely huge—big enough that they could be seen perched at the tip of a mountain from far below.

She blinked, and her vision cleared. Fatik was still staring at her, either still waiting for her response or simply observing her. "Thank you," she mumbled after a moment, referring to his earlier comment.

He smiled softly at her, but his smile faltered when he glanced over at Isabel. The redhead was passed back out, and Agni was somehow keeping her from slipping as he strode up the steep path. "I wanted to heal Isabel as well, but she refused. I … I healed her when she finally went to sleep." The Dragonkin was flushed with guilt and didn't want to meet Thea's eyes. "I didn't want to, but without medical attention …"

"No," she interjected, placing a hand on Fatik's forearm. "You did the right thing. Isabel's choices don't just affect her anymore. We have to do whatever it takes to survive on this mission, and if that means sacrificing morals … I've had to do it before in order to live with the guilt the next day. If she were alone, that would be her call. But we depend on her at her best, and she can't be at her best if her hearing is shot."

Fatik nodded, but he didn't look too convinced.

Thea nibbled on her lip as silence returned. She eyed the redhead once again and met Agni's bored stare. Then the thought hit her—why couldn't Agni just transform into a dragon and fly them up the mountain? Why hadn't they thought of that from the beginning? They could have avoided—*everything*. But that was just it ... Maybe some of them already did think about it.

"Agni," she called.

The rakshasa must have heard the question in her voice, for he paused his walking. Namara halted and looked back over her shoulder in curiosity.

Thea hesitated for some reason she couldn't explain. It was as if she already knew the answer would be no, but she had to at least ask. "Can you transform into a dragon? It's not a demon—and you have seen one now."

Agni seemed to ponder that fact, but it was Fatik who spoke up. "He wouldn't be able to do that."

Thea turned in her seat to find the Dragonkin's pale eyes watching her. Her brow furrowed. How would Fatik know that? Just because he was part dragon—did he have some sort of secret sense? "How do you know?"

Fatik gave her a small, patient smile. "Do you remember what I said earlier?"

Thea thought back, but she was drawing blanks. So much had happened between this morning and now.

"Something that might have been unknown until recently?"

Her eyes widened. The only thing that came to mind was what he had said about the goddess not ruling alone. And he had said "his" breath, implying it was a male god. She peered up at the Dragonkin with an inquisitive stare. "There's a god working with the goddess?"

"Well, I wouldn't say he's 'working' with her, but there is a god. He created the dragons to take to the skies, so no creature on land—or those who hail from below—can copy his creations."

"He can do that?"

"He is a *god*, Thea."

Her mind reeled, and she felt the subtle shift of Namara begin walking under her as they resumed their journey. She wanted to know more. She wanted to ask Fatik everything there was to know about this mysterious god and why no one else seemed to know about him. Isabel's curiosity held not a candle to her own in that moment, and she wished above all else Rafe was here right now to—

"Oh!" she exclaimed, suddenly remembering that she had called Rafe right before everything had gone down. She felt around for her crystal ball and heaved a sigh of relief when she felt cool, uncracked glass under her fingertips. She dug it out of her pouches and frowned at the way it pulsed and glowed. Rafe had no doubt made countless attempts to call her since the connection blinked out.

She thought of the Summoner in her mind, and within seconds, Rafe's frantic face filled the glass. "Thea? Thea, thank the goddess! What happened?"

She couldn't help the tired grin that spread across her face, and her shoulders sagged as the stress from the trip seemed to have lifted from her being. "I'm okay. You wouldn't believe what I've been through the last—well. Since the mission started, if I'm being honest."

Rafe grimaced, and she could tell he was inspecting every inch of her from her bloodstained ears to the bags under her eyes. "Well, I want a full report, Spellweaver Bauer," he said in his best business tone, but it was a mask.

She snickered at his attempt at keeping his cool. She was not concerned in the slightest with appearances at the moment.

"Of course, Second Chosen McBain," she giggled in a mock professional tone.

"Is that Thea?" she heard someone say on the other end, and Rafe was shoved aside as Mokana's aqua eyes filled the screen. "Oh, double-dip a candle stick, Thea! You had us worried sick! I swear I saw Rafe turn green with worry. I thought for sure the man was going to puke!"

"Mokana!" he chastised, batting away the long limbs of the rusalka. "I may have been worried, but I wasn't going to throw up."

Thea could still hear Mokana in the background, though she could no longer see her as the demoness replied with a snippy, "Could have fooled me."

The Spellweaver laughed, her giggles remaining even as Rafe aimed her an unimpressed frown. "Okay, okay, I'll bring you up to speed."

Rafe sobered and nodded. "Then it's my turn. I need to fill you in on something."

"How close are we to the caves?" Thea asked over her shoulder. She still held Rafe in the palm of her hand as the Summoner had refused to let her go after her relay of what happened. He had been horrified, impressed, and then horrified all over again at the stories she spoke of since their last actual update. Fatik had even leaned over her shoulder to give his perspective of things once or twice.

But Rafe had equally horrified and impressed her with his own updates. Isolde's escape, Dmitri's death, the third tablet's miraculously fast retrieval, and the way the Coven members were already being thrown for a loop at the last broadcast message. It had been a lot to take in.

Now they were idly chitchatting while they had the time. Thea looked over her shoulder to see Fatik contemplating her question, his eyes closed as he concentrated. Isabel was still passed out, and the trip was all the quieter because of it.

"I say we should reach them just before sundown."

Thea nodded, and Rafe was scribbling notes on a piece of paper. She still hadn't told him about what Fatik had said to her earlier. It wasn't because she didn't want to or that she was afraid to with Fatik sitting right behind her. She wanted to do her own research on the topic of a possible god, and she knew just the hidden library to do her research in once she got back. Rafe was busy enough with his duties to go galivanting off chasing hearsay.

Isabel groaned loudly beside them. Thea turned in time to see the redhead groggily push up from her steed. She rubbed messily at her face with the heels of her palms, clearing away the haze of sleep from her caramel-brown eyes. She peered over at Thea and Fatik and squinted, but she didn't say anything yet. When first waking up, Isabel could go one of two ways: she was either boundless in her energy like a squirrel who'd found a piece of candy, or she was a mindless husk who communicated with grunts and groans rather than actual words. Looked like they were getting the latter of the two this time.

However, just as Thea was going to tell her they were almost to the caves—hoping that would spur the researcher's excitement and wake her up a little more—Isabel's eyes went wide, and she inhaled sharply. Her hands flew over her person until she found what she was looking for, ripping out a notebook from her pouches before shoving her hand back in to rummage around for something to write with. As soon as she procured a pencil, she began furiously scribbling down notes.

Thea glanced over at Fatik, and the Dragonkin made eye contact with her and whispered, "Hopefully she's so distracted she won't notice I healed her."

The Spellweaver nodded. She didn't blame him for his guilt, but it was as she said earlier. Sacrificing for the sake of the group was the name of the game on dangerous missions. She would never force someone to do something they didn't like if it only affected themselves, but having one's ears shot on a perilous expedition could be the thing that ends one or all of them. Healing her had been the best option.

She was just glad they bypassed a confrontation.

"Is that Isabel?" Rafe piped up from her hand.

She glanced down and met his gaze. Another surge of relief washed through her, and she caught herself before a smile could spell its way onto her face again. It was nice having him there, even if he wasn't really there. "Yeah," she replied. "She just woke up and is already scribbling away. Probably recording the description of the dragon. Or salamander."

Isabel gasped, and Thea turned to see her flipping to a new page before she was jotting down even more notes. Thea snickered.

"Probably both," Fatik huffed a laugh.

Thea hummed in agreement. "She'll be writing even more when we actually get to the caves. I hope her hand doesn't fall off."

"Trust me, that girl's got more strength in her wrists and fingers than either of us. She could write the Coven's whole library down word-for-word and still not be tired. Especially when she's zoned in on something. Nothing else matters," Rafe said with an exasperated expression, but his eyes were fond.

Thea looked back, finding Isabel's gaze so focused on her notebook that she failed to notice the small branch heading her way. Thea leaned over and grabbed the redhead by the shoulder, pulling her toward herself and out of the way of the tree limb that surely would have smacked her square in the face. To her credit, Isabel didn't even look up as Thea pushed her back upright with a chuckle.

How she seemed to collect the most eclectic company, she'd never know.

Chapter Twenty-Two

The Gorge's Guards

Fatik tugged on her shirt sleeve, and Thea hummed quietly in acknowledgement. She squeezed softly around Namara's girth to wordlessly halt the demon. Agni also paused in his steps beside them.

Rafe had long since ended the call with her once he'd received a summons—most likely for training of some sort. The weeklong deliberation period had ended a few days ago, and now his true training had begun. The walk on the trail afterward had been quiet for the most part, but, in the distance, Thea could hear the roaring of a waterfall or a large, fast-moving river.

"We're here," the Dragonkin whispered softly. He peered over at Isabel, who was done with her notes for now, but her notebook-slash-sketchbook was resting in her lap. "Keep your voices down so as not to alarm anyone."

"That reminds me," Thea muttered before digging around in her bag. She sighed in relief when she easily found the barrier breaker oil in one of her pockets. She uncorked the vile and dabbed the smallest amount around her lips before dabbing another drop to both the insides of her ears. She peered over her shoulder at Fatik and asked, "Can you speak and understand them?"

He shook his head. "I've never made contact with them. Dad did a long time ago, and he says they're friendly, but I won't be any help as a translator."

She eyed him for a moment. "I know this won't work on demons, but you're not a demon, so it's worth a try."

Fatik's iridescent gaze dropped down to the vial in her hands. "What is it?"

"Barrier breaker oil. It's not really produced a whole lot since everyone—for the most part—speaks common tongue. It doesn't work on demons, but even still, there's always some stored in HQ just in case. Anyway, it allows the user to speak the native language of another person when dabbed on the lips, and if dabbed on the ears, it allows them to understand any language spoken to them."

"Except demonic languages?"

"And Draconian, apparently."

Fatik blinked at her.

She handed him the oil. "We didn't bring it when we were in the desert trying to search for the myth about wyvern blood. We just used an imp."

"I see," was all he said as he dabbed some of the oil on his lips and then in his ears. "How long does it last?"

"A day, so use it sparingly."

He handed the bottle off to Isabel, but the redhead only sneered at it. "No thanks."

Thea narrowed her eyes. "Isabel, just use it. It's not even your own magic."

"I said no. You said use it sparingly, and we don't know how long we'll be here, so it's better if I just don't use it."

"That's all well and good, but like you said, we don't know how long we'll be here, and I am not going through the hassle of translating everything to you."

Isabel's brow furrowed, and she looked ready to say something, but Thea cut her off with a wistful sigh. "I'm sure they'll have some really interesting information on how they've lived up here all these years. Maybe they'll even have clues as to how to sustain future populations up in the mountains. Or maybe they'll have certain plants that aid in medicine that we have no current knowledge of. Goddess above, I do hope I remember everything, but, alas, I only have one notebook. A shame, really."

Isabel growled and snatched the oil from Fatik. "Ugh, fine!" Though her actions were anger-fueled, she took Thea's advice and applied only a dab of the oil to her lips and ears. "Happy now?" She snipped and tossed the bottle back at Thea.

She caught it one-handedly and smirked. "I'm so happy you were able to see my side of things, Isabel."

"Let's just go already," the redhead huffed and spurred Agni into motion first.

"That was a bit devious," Fatik said behind her after Thea nudged Namara.

She sighed. "It's clear Isabel's not used to working with a team or a partner outside Agni, or—if she is—not on a mission of this caliber. Like I said before, each of us must make decisions that benefit the group. If we split up inside the caves and gather information, it won't just benefit us but all of Tolvade. I'm not having this mission hindered by dead weight, and anyone who refuses to communicate in a situation like this is dead weight. I'm a Spellweaver, not a babysitter."

He chuckled behind her. "Still a bit manipulative, don't you think?"

"I learned from the best," she grumbled under her breath. How her mother and sister used to use any method under the goddess to get their way with her father. Arabella especially used to weave her way into the hearts of the servants, their father, the men at the galas, and just about anyone else with her purple prose poems and adorable looks. Anyone but Thea, and after the third or fourth failed attempt, Arabella started showing her true colors. She'd been a bully to her older sister ever since. After a while, she'd batted her tear-filled doe eyes at their mother, and Colleen's narcissism had split all motherly ties with Thea. Arabella was the golden child. Thea was a mistake.

I wish I could have skipped giving birth to you. If I had had Arabella first, I wouldn't have needed a second child. But I always knew something was wrong with you.

"Thea?"

She blinked, feeling a distinct hotness in her eyes. She blinked some more and discreetly sniffed. "Hmm?"

"We're here."

She let go a laugh. "I feel like you just said—*that.*" Namara halted abruptly, forcing the rest of the words out of her in a rush of air. Her eyes widened as she looked down, down, and *down* some more. The ground just in front of them gave way to a deep, vertical gorge speared through by a narrow waterfall. At eye level, the waterfall was partially hidden by juts in the rock that bridged over to the other side of the gorge, but they were too skinny to hide any sort of passageways.

"This is the entrance?" Thea asked quietly to no one in particular. Isabel had already slid off Agni and was hastily drawing up a rough sketch a few feet away. Agni's demonic horse form melted away like a sinister shadow, unveiling his true (and much more intimidating) form.

A pale, claw-tipped finger pointed over her shoulder. "Do you see that narrow bridge in the center of the gully?"

Oh, she saw it. She did not like the implications that came with it. "No."

She felt Fatik shift behind her, pointer hand insistent as it motioned to what was clearly *not* a bridge. "It's right there. In the middle where—"

"I see it," she hurriedly cut him off, "I meant *no*, I'm not crossing that."

The Dragonkin chuckled behind her. "Thea, the Huðshāns have been crossing this bridge for generations."

Her lips thinned. "Great, so it's worn down is what I'm hearing."

"Where's your sense of adventure?" Isabel called out with a laugh as she put away her sketchpad. Their earlier conversation was no longer weighing the researcher down. Her eyes were practically sparkling once again.

"The same place you keep your sense of rationality," Thea grumbled lowly, eyes never leaving the "bridge."

Namara, having had enough of her nonsense, tossed her head, snorted, and turned, ambling over to the natural structure.

"Namara, wait—"

Namara did not wait, and when the kelpie stood in front of the stone pathway, Thea's dread doubled. It was much too narrow for Namara to walk over it in her horse form. Meaning … Thea was going to have to walk this by herself.

Her gaze plummeted to the deep, dark pool of water at the bottom of the gorge.

Isabel squatted down by the very edge, which was enough to nearly send Thea into an anxiety attack. She whistled lowly, and the sound bounced around the rocky walls. "Hey, at least it's not like it's a bunch of stones that'll break your fall."

"Will you please step away from the edge?" Thea hissed. She only let go a sigh of relief when Isabel rolled her eyes and scooted back some.

"I bet the water feels nice down there," the redhead said with a thoughtful hum.

Thea peered back over the edge and immediately shook her head and started digging in her pouches. "Nope. Nope, I'm not doing this without a balance modification spell."

"Of course, you got a spell to help you walk a straight line," Isabel griped, and Thea could practically hear her rolling her eyes for a second time.

She fished out a tiny, black potion bottle no bigger than the barrier breaker oil and dabbed a drop on her forehead. "Body in mind, feet be kind, steady the soul, keep control."

Only once she could see a faint, peachy-colored mist swirl around her did she feel comfortable sliding off Namara. The kelpie's transformation was not as quick as Agni's was, but going back and forth between forms so often—while still stressful—had gotten her body more used to it.

Namara stretched her seafoam-green arms toward the sky and groaned. Her eyes found Thea's and gave a reassuring nod. "Just like the bridge on the edge of town. I'll go first."

That didn't make her feel any better, though, because if Namara fell off the edge, Thea might just have a heart attack.

Agni stepped forward before Namara had the chance to and wordlessly stuck out his hand for the kelpie to take. Namara's face flushed a dark green, but she only hesitated a moment before she placed her hand—dwarfed in comparison—in his.

While the two carefully made their way across, Isabel shifted over to Thea and crossed her arms over her chest. "I see how it is. I'm being replaced."

Thea snorted. "You're not being replaced."

Isabel glanced over at the Spellweaver beside her, and an impish grin transformed her heart-shaped face into something akin to that of a goblin. Maybe that was all in Thea's head, though. "Want me to hold *your* hand?"

Nope, Isabel was a goblin through and through.

Thea pursed her lips and started walking right over the so-called bridge. She faltered only a little when some rubble fell off the side, but she forced herself to look forward and keep walking. She also wouldn't admit to anyone that Isabel cheering her on was helping. Only a little bit.

The spell Thea had placed on herself did generally improve one's equilibrium, but it acted more as a placebo than anything else. Regardless, it gave her the confidence to put one foot in front of the other. The waterfall was near deafening as she reached the middle of the gorge, and a tad wetter from the water's spray.

She avoided the larger of the damp spots along the rock structure, which was sure to be thick with algae slime. She had her eyes glued to the area just in front of her feet and, before long, she was on the other side. She let go of a large breath of air and felt her nerves calm as solid ground was beneath her feet once again.

Her hands trembled only slightly as they grabbed at the wall of the gorge. Agni and Namara had dipped around the bend out of sight, and already Isabel and Fatik were halfway across the bridge—seemingly much more confident that the thin, stone walkway would hold their weight—and Thea wasn't going to take up any more room than the limited space provided on the other side.

She went to move out of their way and catch up with the demons, but a shrill, haunting sound stuttered and echoed throughout the gorge. Thea halted as her blood ran cold and her heart jumped in her chest. Fear forgotten, she took off around the bend and kept running along the edge of the circular gorge. She could feel the ground beneath her feet chip away, but her only focus became the sounds of a skirmish under the roar of the waterfall that blocked her view.

Just a little further!

The flattened area just behind the cascading water was now a battleground between three humans and Agni and Namara. The men fending off the demons had to have come from the pitch-black cave entrance in the wall.

"Wait!" she cried out, and she could briefly feel the faintest tingle against her lips as the barrier breaker oil activated.

Agni and Namara jumped back at the same time, and the three people whirled around and stared in disbelief at the stranger who just yelled at them in their native tongue. Thea skidded to a halt, shielding the two demons with her body as she raised her palms up in surrender.

"They're with us," Thea spoke quickly, gesturing to Isabel and Fatik, who were now barreling around the waterfall and forming a defense barrier around the two demons.

The three men wore identical robes of light green and had their thick, black hair tied up on top of their heads in neat buns the likes of which Rafe could never have managed to achieve. Their features were unique and different, and the way they kept eyeing Thea and Isabel explicitly, the Spellweaver wondered if they were making the same observations about them.

Then their dark brown eyes shifted and widened as they landed on Fatik. They took in his large wings, softly swishing tail, and iridescent features and jumped back in alarm. Their weapons were raised defensively, and they all hissed, "Dragonkin!"

Fatik was quick to back away with his hands up. His wings shifted closer together, trying to make himself look smaller even as they loomed over his back, and his tail came to hide behind him. "I am not *their* kin. I wish you no harm. I am merely a guide up these mountains. If the red dragons were to see me, I would be no better off than the moss mammoths."

Thea and Isabel shared a quick glance. *"Moss mammoths?"* The Spellweaver mouthed at Isabel. The redhead only shrugged her shoulders.

One man straightened up and pulled the large halberd he had been wielding to his side. His jaw was strong and square, and his beard was short and neatly trimmed. The wrinkles around his eyes were the only sign that spoke of his age. "How do you know our language?"

Thea stepped forward and let her arms fall to her sides slowly. "It's a magic spell we used before coming here. It does not work on demons—but they're not vicious. They're our friends."

The man's eyes narrowed even further. Suspicion swirled in the dark depths, and he shared a look with his companions. The one beside him with a leaner build nodded, but the one in the back without any facial hair looked particularly angry at the situation.

"What do you want?" the first man asked in his deep, baritone voice.

Thea pinched at her Coven insignia, and it gleamed in the shafts of light coming in through the gorge's open ceiling. When she noticed their gazes had dropped to the pin on her coat, she said, "I'm here on official Coven business. I—We're from the south, below the mountains. Somewhere up here is a temple up that contains a tablet that completes a spell we need to perform in a few weeks."

The angry man in the back barked out, "If it is something you need for your sloppy magic spell, why is it in our mountains?"

"Control yourself, Tiōng!" the first man snapped in an equally aggressive tone.

Thea steeled herself from reacting to the harsh words hurled at her. She didn't quite understand the "sloppy" comment, but she elected to ignore it as she went on to explain. "It's a long story, but it was placed here over two hundred years ago." She took a deep breath and let it out silently to settle her nerves. Her strengths had never been in diplomatic affairs. With a quilled pen and a piece of paper, she could accurately relay exactly what needed reporting. But her words had always fought her tongue on the way out. Especially if the stakes were high. "Essentially, if we do not perform the spell with that tablet, the magic in the land will eventually disappear."

A heaviness seemed to settle over the group. Thea's fingers twitched, ready to use her weapon if she needed to. Her eyes flashed between the three of them, lingering on Tiōng, and praying to the goddess above that they would believe her.

"It is as we feared," the second man with the leaner build stated. He looked directly at Thea and, with a voice that brooked no argument, said, "You will meet with our clan leader before you are permitted to leave. We cannot blindly trust what you say, so we will leave it up to his discretion."

Thea hoped the clan leader was as hospitable as the village matriarch had been in the desert. A soft pang filled her chest as she briefly wondered how Madam Odine was doing.

Tiōng was the first to turn and leave, apparently done with them. The last to follow was the first man they'd spoken with, whose name Thea had not yet learned. He nodded for them to follow. "This way."

Thea glanced back at Namara, but the demoness had managed to dodge every blow the quick-moving guards had dealt. Agni only sported a minor cut along his forearm, but it had thankfully stopped bleeding already.

"Are you okay?" she directed at both of them just to be sure.

The rakshasa grunted—which Thea was slowly learning to differentiate the meanings of—and her partner nodded.

"What did they say?" Namara whispered as the group followed after the guards. The cave they were entering was more of a tunnel, and quickly the light faded until pitch darkness surrounded them.

Isabel tripped. Several times.

"They told us we needed to meet their clan leader first before we could go any further," Thea informed. She heard Isabel trip and curse once more, a small grunt from Agni, and then some shuffling.

"I'm fine," the researcher hissed quietly, though her voice still came out a bit loud in the cramped space. "You don't have to corral me like a cow, Agni."

Agni only grunted again.

Thea sighed. Hopefully, this would all go well, and the initial resistance they faced was their only bump in the road.

Hopefully.

Chapter Twenty-Three

Life Whispers Quietly in the Darkest of Places

Thea hated tight, dark places. The worst one she had ever had the misfortune of enduring was the curved staircase at the bottom of Srbeveara. She felt her throat close up just thinking about it, and the conditions now weren't all that dissimilar. The sounds of the shuffling footsteps echoed off the stone walls around them, accompanied by the occasional *drip-drop* of water falling from the ceiling. She was having a hard time seeing, but her steps were careful and her reflexes fast enough to catch herself with every dip and groove in the floor. They also helped her avoid crashing into the guards in front of her after she heard their footsteps halt.

She couldn't see what they were doing, but she wished she did. Rough scraping sounds skittered and bounced off the walls, biting at her ears and sending dreadful shivers up her spine as she hunched away from the noise. She felt hands gripping her shoulders and then a sudden, heavy weight hoisted itself onto her back. Her immediate reaction was to grip the slippery legs anchored around her middle so Namara wouldn't fall off.

"What do you think you're doing?" she hissed even as she continued to support the kelpie on her back. She grimaced at the feeling of cold arms slipping around her neck and a slimy, wet strand of hair grazing against her cheek. A part of her—a small one—was thankful for the distraction from the claustrophobic space around her.

"I can see in the dark but not over your shoulders, and I want to know what's going on. Besides, I thought it was fitting that I get to ride around on you for a change."

Thea snorted and shifted to get a better hold of the demon. She could only imagine what she looked like with Namara—a veritable cave goblin—crawling all over her back. "Well, can you tell me what that sound was just now?" she whispered.

"Looks like they opened up a door."

Isabel must not have heard the whole ordeal, for the redhead proclaimed (a little too loudly), "What's going on?"

By the sound of swishing fabric, Thea assumed the guard in front of her had turned just enough to explain. "Chhêu is going on ahead to alert Clan Leader Renkilo. You will refer to him as such or as Clan Leader. You are not permitted to call him by his name only."

A claw-tipped finger ticked gently at her shoulder, and Thea remembered Namara couldn't understand what was being said. "They're getting the Clan Leader. Telling us what to call him and not call him and such."

This must be how Leslie felt, Thea thought to herself.

"Oh," she remembered, "Fatik, I'm glad the oil is working."

She could hear his wings shift in the darkness. "Me too. Thankfully, I won't be kept in the dark—"

"Hah," Isabel snorted at the irony.

"—which makes it easier on you, I suppose. Only having to translate for two rather than the three of us."

"Agni won't care about what's going on unless he thinks it's life-threatening," the redhead helpfully supplied.

Thea could feel Namara's huff on the back of her neck. "Great, I love being the odd one out."

"Don't worry, I felt the same way in the desert. I'll let you know what's going on."

"I'll try my best to assist as well," Fatik assured.

For a little while longer, they waited in silence—something that was clearly too long for the antsy researcher, as Thea could hear the sighs and shuffling around coming from behind her.

"Behave yourselves," the nameless guard warned suddenly, and more scraping noises clawed at Thea's eardrums as rock scraped over rock. The soft swishing of fabric continued, and Namara took this as her cue to hop down and allow Thea to hurry after the guards.

Light began filtering into the tunnels, and before long, the narrow walls surrounding them became visible, and the guards were no longer creeping shadows slipping through the abyss with ease. Thea could already see around the guards' heads just how massive the clan's dwelling truly was. They filed out of the tunnel, and Thea squinted up at the light that shot down from the cave's ceiling. She heard Isabel gasp out, "*Whoa*," and blinked rapidly in the hopes her eyes would adjust.

The caves turned out to just be one cave, one that was *massive*. Soaring ceilings towered far above them, allowing mist from the clouds to come rolling in from what small openings there were in the roof. It was warmer in the caves, but a cold breeze kept wafting in from above. Far off in the distance, away from the elevated livestock pens and fenced-off beds of crops, was a small waterfall pouring in where it had weathered away a hole big enough for the stream to fall through. The narrow, bubbling river wound its way through the entire cave, looping through unchecked, flourishing forests. A wild underbrush made the thick woodland even more dense, barricading the fruit-bearing trees within.

In the center of the cave—and by far the most eye-catching thing Thea had come to witness in a long time—was a colossal chunk of the mountain floating in midair. Bits of rubble levitated by the enormous rock, and a few trees had even grown out of the stone. Long roots dangled in the air or curled and clung to the rock like a spider as wide, sweeping branches reached for the summit. An ornate building decorated the immense boulder like a cherry on top of an ice cream cone. It was a gem amidst the brown and gray, and it was painted a brilliant shade of red. Several gold and black roofs stacked on top of one another in a way Thea had never borne witness to.

Thea's attention was snared next by the small homes clinging to the rock walls of the cave. The houses were not built into the rock like the Ernimoens' homes in the desert, but rather made from stone and anchored to the walls. They were clustered tightly and compactly together, with a convoluted system of pulleys rigging the lifts, ladders, and bridges that connected one collection of homes to another.

The people who milled about were also mindboggling in the way they tended to their homes. Though they appeared to be working hard as any other villager outside the mountains would be, upon closer inspection, most of them weren't lifting a finger. They stood by fields of crops and waved their bodies in a fluid dance of limbs and—

without any magic reagents to work with like potions or wands—the crops were lifted out of the ground and into the baskets at their feet. A middle-aged man fanned himself with one hand as his other moved through the air. Before him, on a flattened rock, chunks of wood splintered in two with every wave of his arm. Another person stood by the pulley system, and with just a few jabs at the air, the platform was moving up with people on it faster than any lift operator back in Tolvade. To say Thea was stunned was an understatement.

Like the villagers in the desert, the clansmen here were uniform in their dark hair and eye coloring, and—even though their skin had not been subjected to the sun as harshly—their complexion was that of soft bronze. One's person hair was so black it reflected midnight blue, while another's was a brown so dark one could only tell when the light hit it. Unlike the Ernimoens, though, their long hair was not done up in elaborate works of art but rather left either free flowing or in thick buns, and not one man sported a beard longer than their chin. Their clothing was similar to those in the desert and yet not at all. Swishing, loose robes billowed around their feet and arms as they moved swiftly from place to place, but the colors were muted blues, greens, and eggshell whites. The women bore simple designs such as flowers, clouds, and bird silhouettes. Thin ribbons decorated their clothing around their waist and in the simple hairdos that some wore.

"I can feel them staring at me," Fatik whispered tensely.

Thea looked back at the clan's people and noticed that they were, in fact, staring at Fatik with a mixture of surprise and unease. Some even stared so hard that they dropped whatever they were manipulating with their magic.

Agni crowded close to the Dragonkin as if in protection, and Thea wondered if they were also staring at Agni with the same looks or if it truly was all directed at the creature who was part dragon.

"It's okay," she tried to assure. "We won't let anything happen to you."

Fatik forced a chuckle. "You'd think I'd be used to the stares by now, considering I always got them back home."

"You never really get used to them," Namara whispered. "The best you can do is pretend they're not there."

Thea felt her heart squeeze in her chest. Coven-issued demons were common in Tolvade, but if one looked particularly wicked enough, they could get stared at. But Namara, for all intents and purposes, should have been an ordinary demon in the Coven's ranks. But she came with things that weren't so ordinary. The water constantly dripping off of her, landing everywhere, soaking through everything … it turned people off. Thea remembered the gross stares hurled the kelpie's way on nearly every occasion the creature was in the public eye.

She wanted to reach out and promise Namara she'd complete that spell if it was the last thing she'd do, but the kelpie's black eyes met hers with a small nod and understanding smile.

Don't worry about it right now, her gaze seemed to say.

"Clan Leader Renkilo approaches," their nameless guide announced, peering up at the floating chunk of rock. Thea glanced up again just in time to catch a winged animal leap off the edge and flap its dragon-like wings in the air. It soared through the mist curling around the top of the cave, a single person on its back as it slowly descended.

When it landed, Thea was struck by how bizarre the rare creature was. It was called a longma and had been a prevalent mode of transportation in the Elvan Era, but they slowly disappeared with each passing century. The creature looked as if someone had slapped scaly armor on a horse and given it wings. Steam blew out of its wide nostrils as it landed with a snort, and its yellow eyes seemed to glow in the dim lighting of the cave. Its wings flapped once before resting back against its silvery, scaled hide.

The brave figure riding such a tall beast dropped down onto the dirt with ease, even though his snow-white hair and high-brow wrinkles declared a golden age. He was dressed the nicest out of all those present, but there wasn't anything too ornate and gaudy attached to him outside of a simple headpiece embellished in small jewels. His robes were a dark, wine-red that brushed against the ground in a whisper.

"Clan Leader," their guide said and dropped to one knee. He bowed his head quickly before moving to his feet again in one fluid motion. "Those before you seek out the Divine Temple with claims that they can cease the waning of mana in the land. They are here to request permission to investigate further up the mountain. They are able to understand and speak our language."

The words were bellowed out and rang loud in the cave with no sense of secrecy. Thea could feel everything from her cheeks up to her ears grow hot with embarrassment as every single person wandering about stopped what they were doing to stare.

This has to be what Fatik was talking about earlier. There was no pretending the stares weren't aimed at them either.

Renkilo did not look surprised. In fact, his serene face broke out into amusement as a soft laugh escaped him. His eyes found Thea's, and then they seemed to drift about her person curiously. "My, we certainly do not receive guests very often, though I'm afraid you've come at a bad time."

Thea felt dread form in the pit of her stomach. "What do you mean we've come at a bad time? We can't afford to come back later—"

"You dare question Clan L—"

A raised hand was enough to quiet their guide. "Enough, Fông." Renkilo turned back to address Thea and said, "Fear not. We won't turn you away, but I will warn you that your endeavors will be dangerous if you should continue to pursue them past this point."

Isabel snorted, earning a glare from Fông that she easily ignored. "The entire trip up here has been one big danger after another. We've almost got eaten twice—wait, no, three times!"

Renkilo's fluffy, white eyebrows rose high on his head, emphasizing the deep-set wrinkles even more. "Ah, how perilous a journey you've had," he stated in a way an amused father would after listening to his children's exaggerated adventures. His gaze swept over them all, but his eyes did not linger on either of the demons or Fatik. "A true test of your convictions, and Fông has said all in the name of stopping mana from dying out?"

Thea paused, unsure as to why they referred to magic as such. At the end of the day, it didn't matter. She pressed on and stated simply, "Yes."

Dark eyes full of secrets and wisdom flicked to her, and she held her breath as she awaited his reply. Once again, she felt as if she was being assessed by the way his eyes danced about her person. It wasn't lewd or haughty by any means, but it was still strange. She wondered what he was thinking in that moment. He'd already said he wouldn't turn them away, and he didn't seem to have any notion of stopping them. However, beings who lived this long always had something up their sleeve. Thea was just waiting for it to drop.

"I would like to discuss this further in a more … private setting," he said after a moment, and his gaze drifted toward the onlookers. Quickly, people dropped their stares and got back to work without a word. He brought his attention to Fông. "Escort them to the Bamboo Pavilion and have …" he trailed off as he looked around, "Ah, Siàu!"

Nearby, a tall, lanky woman jerked up from grappling with a duck, a basket of eggs on her arm, and quickly ran over to them. The duck honked after her as if the feathered foe was boasting a win. She bowed to the Clan Leader—catching the basket on her arm before the eggs could slip out—before casting a wary gaze at the travel party. Her onyx eyes narrowed slightly at Fatik before dropping to her feet as she awaited her orders.

"Siàu, our guests are to be escorted to the Bamboo Pavilion. I would like it if you would act as their guide."

Siàu bowed again with a quiet, "Yes, Clan Leader," and turned toward them fully. It was then that Thea realized that the woman was taller than her by a good half a foot. She possessed a thin, willowy body with espresso-colored hair that for the first half hung free around her shoulders before the second half was captured in a thick, loose braid that swayed around her hips. Her lips were full and formed a natural pucker, and the dimples on both of her cheeks were prominent enough to show up without her smiling. Her long sleeves were tied back and wrapped around her arms to keep them out of her way, and her yellow, wicker-woven sandals were thick enough to keep her feet out of the muddier areas.

Renkilo mounted the longma with a swift kick off the ground, which had his body looking as light as a feather in the air. He peered just over his shoulder, acknowledged them with a small nod, and the beast started a slow gait down a weathered path that led to the dense clumping of thin, pole-like plants.

"What are those things?" Isabel piped up from the group, pointing to where the Clan Leader was heading. Siàu turned to the researcher and studied her silently for a moment.

"Bamboo," the tall women said plainly.

"That would explain the name of the pavilion," Namara commented after Thea quickly translated. The demoness was idly combing her fingers through her wet locks as she took in their surroundings. If she was bothered by the stare Siàu sent her, she didn't make it known. Thea caught the woman opening her mouth as if to say something, but she closed it all too quickly and turned around.

She pointed to the area she had come from. It was a cleared-out section surrounded by more towering, dense forest. Light from the small openings in the cave ceiling highlighted the tops of the trees that swayed in the chilly mountain air. In the clearing, an elevated platform the size of

Tolvade's city center held a moderately sized barn with a thatched roof. A small, manmade pond sat in the center where the ducks were collected, and the pigs lounged nearby. Domesticated mountain goats and—*Camels?*— grazed on the grass. A few people were stationed inside brushing the fluffy, two-humped camels, feeding the ducks, or sweeping the area next to the barn. All with the help of their intriguing magic, of course.

I didn't know they also had camels in the mountains, Thea thought to herself. Out of everyone here, she was the only one who'd gotten to see the one-humped, desert variation.

"This is where we keep our livestock." She didn't elaborate, and Thea couldn't tell if she was being cold with them or if she was just an awkward individual. Isabel hadn't seemed to pick up on this—that, or she didn't care.

"What's that thing?" she pointed to one of the camels.

Siàu blinked at the redhead and swept a loose strand of hair behind her ear. She had a bit of sweat on her brow, and her hands were smudged with dirt from working in the livestock pen.

How curious. If they need not lift a finger, why is she doing manual work?

"It's a camel," the taller woman stated.

Isabel hummed and wrote something down in her notebook. "Fascinating. What are those things on its back?"

This went on for a while. With everything that Siàu introduced them to, Isabel had questions, Siàu had simple, straightforward answers, and Thea was trying her best to keep up with translating as Namara's curiosity was just as insatiable. Some of the things Isabel asked were more for personal interest, and others were asked for the research she would divulge to the Coven upon their return. Thea zoned in and out throughout the conversation despite Namara's constant tugging on her shirt. "How much precipitation do you average year-round?" or "What are these plants called? What do you use them for?" or "What's the material you use to make clothes?"

Other questions, though, had Thea zoning back in as her own curiosity perked up.

"What makes that giant rock float?"

Siàu stopped walking and glanced up at the enormous hunk of stone levitating in the center of the cave. Thea leaned forward in anticipation. She, too, wanted to know how such magic maintained a floating structure of that magnitude … and why. What was the point?

Fông, who had not grown impatient throughout their tour despite the frequent stops and barrage of questions, answered instead. "Clan Leader Renkilo keeps it floating. He is a powerful master of mana. It is not like your magic. Mana is pure, and therefore we are able to do things that those outside the mountain could only dream of."

Thea stiffened in indignation at the words. What did they mean "pure?" Because they somehow didn't have to use powders or wands or staves? She turned on the guard, her mouth open to defend her craft, but Isabel cut her off before she could.

"Yeah, yeah, yeah, that's great. No one asked about your magic there, bucko. I shoulda guessed that's what was makin' that thing float. Don't get me wrong," she hurried to say as Fông balked at her bluntness, "it looks cool. For sure. But I don't care if magic's involved. Anyway, moving on—*ooh*, what's that over there?"

Now it was Fông's turn to pinken with indignation, and Thea felt a smidgen of satisfaction at the color his cheeks were turning. She was quick to jump in before he could cut their journey short and escort them back out the way they came. "Don't worry, she's like that with all magic. Even our 'impure' kind."

Okay, she couldn't help but make a small jab of her own.

Fông's mouth clicked shut, and he nodded stiffly. The Spellweaver looked over at Isabel, who was pointing at the houses attached to the cave walls along with their many pulley systems and noticed the curious look Siàu was giving the redhead. Like she couldn't quite understand the tiny person by her side.

Same, Siàu, same.

Now that they had moved past the previous subject, Thea was still curious about what Fông had said. Renkilo was keeping that monstrous rock floating, but for what purpose? And how could he keep it floating so effortlessly? She also had questions about the Huŏshān's so-called "pure" magic—or mana—and how it differentiated from Thea's outside of the lack of reagents.

She wasn't going to ask Fông for his pompous opinion, and, judging by how Siàu's answers were forthright enough to be almost unhelpful, she wasn't going to get anything substantial out of the woman.

It looked like her best bet was interrogating Renkilo, but that was assuming he hadn't lined the proverbial chessboard with traps first.

Chapter Twenty-Four

The Bamboo Pavilion Parley

The Bamboo Pavilion was a sectioned-off seating area surrounded on two sides by a thick bamboo forest. The pavilion's cusped roof was reminiscent of the one on top of the floating rock. The peak didn't come to a pointed tip, but rather it was flat at the top, and the corners of the roof were sharp and ornately carved like flames. There was a short table made of stone that sat in front of them, the top polished to a smooth finish. One had to sit on the round, padded cushions on the ground to access the table that was no more than a foot or two tall, and Thea and the others had been instructed to sit with their legs up under them.

That did not stop Isabel from lounging about and picking at her toes—shoes had been forbidden on the grass-woven mat under the pavilion.

Silk curtains of sheer gold draped around the supporting beams and, if desired, could be loosened to give more privacy. However, Renkilo left them open so that Thea and the others could take in the view of the waterfall on one side or look through a large opening in the sidewall of the cave that acted as a window to the outside world. Thea could see for hundreds of miles out the hut-sized hole, and she could feel the breeze that wafted in and blanketed the area in the mountain's chill.

Renkilo had already been situated at the small table when they arrived, but he had only picked up his handle-less cup once they sat down. Tea was a welcome surprise and served in a flatter-styled teapot similar to the one Blythe had in her room back at the sanctuary. The pale chartreuse drink offered a roasted, nutty aroma and faint taste that actually became more pronounced after swallowing.

After the tea had warmed them up, Renkilo directed his attention Thea's way. "I see you have an emblem pinned to your person where the others do not. Would this make you the leader of this expedition of yours?"

Thea shifted in her seat and, out of the corner of her eye, saw Fatik lean over to quietly translate to Namara. "Not necessarily. This insignia represents my position in the Coven."

The elder man raised a brow as he sipped his drink. "A coven?"

"It's the governing force in the city below the mountain. I'm the only one enlisted into its ranks. Namara," she gestured to the demoness beside her, "is my partner that I summoned. She's tethered to me and was imbued with an intelligence spell. She's not a threat by any means."

Renkilo studied them as Thea explained, and he made no move to interrupt.

"Isabel is a researcher conducting a wide variety of studies, as this is one of the few times beings from Tolvade have crossed the border of the mountains. Agni here is also her companion. Fatik—"

"I notice you did not include the same introduction to Agni as you did Namara," Renkilo interjected with an amused expression. His hawk eyes flicked over the rakshasa in scrutiny.

"His original partner died. He's my best friend now," Isabel said without looking up from her sketchpad. She had pulled it out as soon as they'd sat down and had begun scribbling away with small sketches, interrupted here and there with hastily jotted down notes. It had kept the researcher quiet until now.

The Clan Leader gave a sagely nod before leveling his dark gaze Thea's way once more. "Continue."

Thea cleared her throat. "Fatik offered to be our guide. His father once made contact with your people. He goes by the name of Vice."

It was the first time genuine surprise crossed Renkilo's face. A hand came up to rub at his smooth chin in contemplation before recognition lit up the dark depths of his eyes. "Ah, yes. I was just a boy when we received a visit from a Dragonkin. My mother and father stayed up all night talking to him, even though he ended up lodging here for nearly a week."

Fatik's scaly tail swayed as he perked up beside Namara. "He left on good terms then? I wondered why he never went back."

Renkilo's brow furrowed as he thought back. "He snuck off with family heirlooms that were centuries old and had been in my family since before the Great Migration. My mother was particularly upset. So, no, I don't believe he did."

Fatik's expression crumbled and, if possible, he grew even paler. He cleared his throat, and his iridescent eyes shifted around nervously. "I'm … I'm actually adopted."

Thea buried her face in her hands and cursed under her breath. No wonder Vice refused to come up the mountains with them. Actually, she was thankful he'd refused. They would have been chased clean off the nearest cliff.

Isabel's head popped up from its bowed position over her sketchbook. "Would one of them happen to be a map?"

Renkilo's eyes widened. "Yes. Topography was my fourth great-grandfather's strongest suit. He painted the land we now reside within in vivid detail when he was just a young man himself. Why do you ask?"

Isabel had only been half listening after the initial "yes" and was already digging in her satchel. With a louder than necessary "Aha!" she pulled out the wooden map Vice had so clearly ordered them not to lose.

Well, it wasn't like they were losing it. Just returning it to its rightful owner.

The map clattered on top of the table despite the careful (Isabel's version of careful) way in which she set it down. Immediately, the Clan Leader was hunching over the wooden scroll. His long, elegant finger hovered over the foot-length, golden-yellow pieces of wood that Thea now recognized as halved bamboo. The pitch-black stains that brought to life the very mountains they'd climbed had not suffered despite the perilous journey. It was still in near-perfect condition, given its now estimated age of about three hundred and fifty years. Give or take a few decades, depending on how old Renkilo's great-great-great-great-grandfather was at the time.

He swiftly leaned back and discreetly wiped at his eyes, but Thea could see the shine that had been brought to them and the bob of his throat clogged with emotion. She took that moment to bring Namara up to speed. The kelpie had been looking back and forth between the man and the map in confusion for the last few minutes.

When Renkilo collected himself, he aimed a genuine smile at them. "You have my gratitude. I will ensure you the best hospitality while you stay here."

Thea held her palms out and gently waved off the grand gesture. "That won't be necessary. We don't plan to be here long. We'd hoped to gain permission to locate the temple, secure the tablet, and head back home. The spell that requires that tablet is vital to Raen's survival."

A thoughtful expression smoothed out over the older man's features, but a soft sigh coupled with a downcast look made the feeling of dread within her stomach bloom once more. "Ah, that brings us back to what I had said earlier. Unfortunately, you have come at a bad time."

His gaze drifted to the side, and Thea turned and watched as a few men were effortlessly carting a giant slab of wooden planks bound together with the use of their mana. They disappeared behind the dense wall of live bamboo, and they reappeared and stopped just under the massive hole in the wall. Using a series of fluid movements, the slab of wood was lifted into the air and deposited onto large, metal brackets embedded into the mountain. Another dance of limbs and the metal brackets began to warp and bend over the wood at the base, middle, and top to secure it in place.

"They do that every night?" Isabel questioned curiously, twirling her pen around her fingers with amazing dexterity.

Renkilo sighed again. "No, only when a bad storm is forecasted."

The feeling of dread came back with a vengeance. "But it's been sunny all day. Are you saying we're going to be trapped in here for who knows how long?" It was hard to keep the panic out of her voice, but Thea managed to squash it just enough not to sound hysterical.

"We have lived on this mountain for a very long time, my dear. We are more than capable of predicting when the next snowstorm is about to come blowing down. You can feel it in the air, taste it on the back of your tongue. Even our bones and joints recognize the change. There are subtle warnings, but we have tuned into those warnings for centuries."

Thea sagged in her seat and peered hopelessly over at their now covered window. The sun had begun to set while they'd spoken over their tea, and even now the departing rays dared to peek through the cracks between the planks.

She couldn't help the poutiness that came over her voice, though she'd deny it at every opportunity. "Do the warnings by chance tell you how long the snowstorm will last?"

Renkilo laughed but shook his head. "No, my dear. Unfortunately, not even I am privy to the mountain's schedule. However," he continued when she seemed to only slump further in her seat, "I would say that if it's anything like the past few snowstorms, it should clear up in the next few days. A week at most. Though I cannot stop you, I urge you to stay in the safety of the cavern and wait out the storm. We do not venture too far away from the caves for obvious reasons, so it has been a long time since I've last saw the temple. I do not know how the land around the temple has fared. We go as far as the Pools of Time, yet even that can be dangerous."

Thea mulled over the words in her head and nodded in resignation. As eager as she was to return home, she wasn't going to risk death to get to the temple. The yearly blizzard was dangerous enough in Tolvade. She couldn't imagine the type of damage a blizzard in the harsh mountain terrain could cause. She'd be frozen solid in minutes and buried alive under hundreds of layers of snow.

"Come now," the Clan Leader said suddenly, tapping the table to bring them out of their daze. "We cannot prepare a feast so suddenly to welcome you, but you will not go without. Siàu!"

At his command, the willowy woman came around the thicket where she'd left them and bowed. "Yes, Clan Leader."

"Have Khien prepare a special meal for our guests and deliver it to their sleeping quarters at the Heavenly Temple."

Siàu bowed again. "Yes, Clan Leader," before she was off, nearly tripping over her feet in her haste.

Renkilo was not done, and with a shout of their guard's name, Fông came around the corner next. "Send word to have beds prepared at the temple." He leaned over the table as if to whisper a secret to the group. "We don't receive guests very often, so regrettably, we do not have a building designed specifically for visitors. However, our temple has rooms that can be converted for sleeping arrangements."

"We appreciate this, and we're sorry to impose," Fatik said gratefully, no doubt trying to give a much better impression than what his father left behind.

Thea leaned back after having translated everything to Namara and nodded in agreement. "Yes, thank you. You've been more than kind."

Renkilo waved away their gratitude. "Returning my fourth great-grandfather's map has more than covered a few days' lodging. Think nothing of it." He turned back to Fông, still patiently awaiting any other orders. "Afterward, deliver a message to Phú to recall all troops. The storm is well on its way."

"Yes, Clan Leader." Fông bowed and turned away quickly to carry out his tasks.

Renkilo collected the wooden scroll and stood gracefully from his seat, and Thea and the others were quick to scramble after him as he began walking down the pavilion's steps without a word.

It was as the tinkling of her crystal ball began to chime that Thea remembered that she had not gotten to interrogate Renkilo about mana *or* the floating rock. She groaned at the realization and stepped away from the group to fish around in her belt pouches until her fingers brushed against hard glass. She held up the sphere to show Namara and the others that she had to take a call before jogging back up the stairs of the pavilion, where she'd be afforded more privacy.

When her gaze met the person calling her, she did a double-take. "Rafe? We just talked earlier."

The Summoner smiled in greeting, but it was a tired one. "I know, but I forgot to mention something important earlier with all the chaos going on. We just received intel from a source the other day that blood mages are gathering with feral demons in the Black Forest and around its borders.

It lines up with your findings, so we know it's legit. I wanted to make you aware."

Thea felt as if the breath had just been punched out of her lungs. "Blood mages? But we—we just—" Blythe had just annihilated a huge number of them only—what was it, a little over a week ago now? How had they reformed so quickly?

"Think of them as the cockroaches of the casting world," Rafe tried to joke, but it fell flat as he rubbed at his eyes rimmed with exhaustion.

Thea let her gaze drift to the covered window and noted that the fast-fading rays of the sun had died away. Night was upon them. "Suffice to say, we won't be trekking back down the way we climbed up. Not that I had *any* intention of doing that, regardless."

She'd hogtie Isabel—and Agni too if he tried intervening—before she'd journey down the mountain rather than use her insignia to teleport them straight back to Coven HQ.

Relief washed over his features, and a genuine smile brightened his blue-green eyes. "Good to know your insignia is on you. How is your wound healing?"

Thea felt around the area through her clothes, and while it was a tad tender still, she was out of the enchanted woods with that injury. "All good. Was that all you had to report?" She only asked so she didn't cut him off in the middle of whatever he needed to tell her before she informed him of her latest findings.

"Eager to get rid of me?" he teased regardless.

It did the trick, and she could feel heat creep into her cheeks. "No!" she yelped out a little too loudly. She snapped her gaze around to check if anyone had heard her before turning her flustered expression back at the chuckling Second Chosen.

Rafe had leaned back in his high-backed chair and, maybe it was the way he crossed his arms over his broad chest, or maybe it was just how his crystal ball was situated to make it look like he was taller than he really was—or maybe she just missed his insufferable presence—but the heat in her cheeks didn't fade. If anything, it worsened as her heart started tripping over itself. "No, it's not actually," he pressed on, oblivious to her inner turmoil, "I told you already that Spellweaver Peterson had secured one of the last remaining tablets. I was handed a copy of the report just a little while ago, and the twins told me the Celestial has already decoded the spells listed on them all. I didn't think it was important enough to tell you so soon, but then I forgot to tell you about that blood mage report that landed on my desk yesterday." His gaze drifted to a stack of papers on his right, and the glare he aimed at them had Thea assuming they were the affronting reports. He pointed his full attention back to Thea once more, and her stupid heart gave a traitorous squeeze at the eye contact. "So, all that's left is your tablet. With your Coven insignia pinned to your cloak, we should expect you back soon, right? What's your progress?"

That expectant look of his had her feeling something else entirely, and she looked away to sigh as guilt started to surface. It was silly, she knew, to feel guilty over something she couldn't control. It wouldn't stop the sense of failure, though, nor would it halt the thoughts of letting Rafe down with her progress report.

One failure after another, a quiet, familiar voice hissed.

She sighed again. "Unfortunately, we just received news of an impending snowstorm. At best, we're looking at a few days' delay."

"Are you safe?" came Rafe's concerned voice through the glass.

She finally met the Summoner's eyes once again. "What?"

His expression matched his tone. "Are you safe, Thea? Are you able to take proper shelter? What's your current location?"

She felt her mouth bob open as his barrage of questions continued. "Yes, yes, yes," she hurried out, effectively shushing him. "We made it to the caves—cave, I should say. This thing is massive, Rafe. But, yeah, we made it with no time to spare, it seems. They've prepared everything for us. We'll be safe while we ride out the storm."

Rafe slumped back in his chair. "Thank the goddess." He gave her a small smile, and though it was as genuine as the last, she could see it was taking everything in him to press on. "Don't worry about the delay then."

She blinked. "What do you mean? I mean—I mean I know it's not ideal, but I'll get the tablet back—"

"I believe you. You're very capable, and I'm not just saying that because you kiss me all the time."

Thea sputtered. "Rafe!" she hissed, color exploding on her cheeks. She glared at the small sphere as Rafe tipped back his head and laughed.

"I'm kidding, I'm kidding," he conceded after his laughter died down. "Well, maybe not *completely*—"

"Goddess help me."

"—but anyway, as I was saying, I know you're capable, Thea. Don't worry about this little delay so much. You've got a couple of weeks before the Wild Hunt spell needs to be conducted. The storm shouldn't last that long, and you're *right there.*"

She sighed once again, but it wasn't as heavy this time. She let a small smile grace her lips, and she felt light enough to tease back. "That's if you didn't just jinx us."

Mock offense played out on the Summoner's face. "I would never. How dare you say something like that. I thought you loved me?"

A giggle escaped her. "Get some sleep soon, moron."

Rafe wiped at his face and gave a sigh of his own. "Yeah. I have a few more reports that need a signature on them by tomorrow morning, but after that, I'll head home."

"Use the telepads."

He rolled his eyes. "Yes, *mom.*"

Her nose wrinkled. "I don't think I can ever kiss you again if that's how you really see me."

Now his eyes widened. "Wait, no—"

It was Thea's turn to laugh, and it felt good to let go of the stress she'd been holding onto, the fear, the anxiety. She just hoped that when she cut the connection with him, it didn't all come crashing back down on her.

Chapter Twenty-Five

Father of the Realm Above and Mother to Those Who Dwell Below

The temple hadn't been hard to find, and as Thea had followed the river and asked a few kind strangers where to point her, she realized she shouldn't have bothered. The temple was tall, skinny, and looked like three small houses stacked on top of each other. Much like the building on top of the floating rock.

When she first walked into the temple, she was graced with a large, lavish room with a shrine in the very back. A smooth, white, stone statue of a woman with six arms, all holding various tools, was fluidly posed around a striking male statue of pure onyx, who was also holding objects in each of his six hands. Around the shrine, the supporting beams were ornately carved and decorated with draping curtains, banners with things written on them in a language she couldn't read, and thin ribbons of all different colors.

She had stepped forward to gather a closer look at the statue, but before she could discern what the figures were holding, one of the doors on the side of the room slid open sideways. She was greeted by a familiar face, Siàu, holding an empty tray in her hands. The woman blinked slowly at coming to find Thea in the temple's entryway before she stepped aside and allowed Thea to bypass her.

Once Thea had passed through the door and aimed a soft, "Thank you," the woman's way, she'd been assaulted with the strong odor of grilled meats and alcohol. She blinked at the sheer amount of food spread out on the long, thin table in the middle of the room. Boisterous laughter harmonized with the soft twang of music. A woman in the corner of the room sat on her knees with a long, wooden, rectangular instrument hovering over her lap. Her fingers plucked delicately at its many strings, and the faint notes were peculiar but pleasant.

"I thought you said you didn't have time to prepare for a feast," she said as she took a seat beside Renkilo. The old man already sported a flush to his cheeks, and a tiny, minuscule cup in his hands that couldn't have been practical for drinking out of. "And where's Namara and Agni?"

Isabel was laughing at Fatik's failed attempts to eat with what looked like two delicately carved sticks. The redhead snorted another laugh as the brown noodles Fatik had grabbed with his utensils slipped back into his bowl before she addressed Thea. "Renkilo ordered some of the clansmen to bring in a tub of water for her to sit in, so she doesn't get anything 'drenched in water'—her words, not mine. Agni went with her, probably to carry the thing."

Thea turned toward the Clan Leader, who was expertly wielding the wooden implements with one hand and knocking back his drink with the other.

"Thank you, that was very kind of you," she commented before reaching for her own sticks. She studied them a moment, eyed Renkilo's way of grasping them, adjusted her fingers accordingly, and attempted to pick up some of the noodles in her bowl.

Renkilo caught his breath after swallowing his drink, and she could smell the potency of the liquor on his tongue. "Of course, I couldn't let her dry out and become our next course!" He chortled good naturedly, jabbing his elbow into Thea. She'd managed to shakily grasp a few noodles—a feat for her first attempt if Fatik was any reference to go by—but, at the jab, the noodles all fell back into her bowl, throwing Renkilo into another laughing fit.

Thea couldn't find it within herself to chastise the Clan Leader, but she did send him a playful glare he paid no mind to. Isabel started telling the older man of their adventure from the beginning, of course, exaggerating a few things here and there, and Renkilo was too enraptured in the tale to sabotage Thea's attempts at eating. She picked up a heavy-looking ball of dough with a twirled design as if someone had pinched the top and twisted. She took a bite, and flavor exploded on her tongue. The meat inside melted in her mouth, and the smoky tang stayed with her even after a drink of water. She grabbed a skewer with what smelled like duck and a myriad of seasonings she couldn't quite place and nibbled on the meat.

Big mistake.

Her eyes rounded, and she dropped the duck on the plate and hastily seized her cup of water. The redhead across from her noticed the action and burst out into hysterics, so bad that she nearly toppled over.

"Oh—yeah," she gasped out in between bouts of laughter. "That's the spicy dish!"

Thea wiped her mouth with the back of her sleeve to no avail. "And you didn't warn me?" she snapped.

Isabel only laughed harder, her cheeks flushed nearly the same color as her hair. Renkilo had joined her, too sloshed to find anything not funny, and Fatik looked like he was gaining a headache. He'd pushed the noodles away from him and started chewing on the spiced duck.

The door opened, and Agni strode in with a giant tub in his arms, filled to the brim with sloshing water and—to the astonishment of several people crowding behind him— Namara. The kelpie was giggling at the show of strength, but her eyes widened at the scene playing out in front of her. She leaned over the rim and looked around the room.

"Uh, what'd we miss?"

"Just give me your hand already," Thea sighed as she held out her own hand in waiting.

The room was now bare except for the tub Namara would be sleeping in and Thea and Isabel's futon beds. She had tried to tell the women preparing their room that they had their sleeping bags, but the chipper ladies were having none of it. She had decided not to press any further when she sat down on the cloud-like bedding. Isabel was passed out already, snoring away in the dimly lit room.

The candle beside Thea was acting as the only source of light as well as a channel to shift her magic energy for the spell she was trying to perform. The men had been escorted out to the room on the opposite side of the shrine, and now Namara was pouting because her new sleeping buddy wasn't around.

The kelpie's lips twisted in uncertainty, but she finally held out her hand at her partner's insistence. Thea had dug around in her pouch pockets for her blue dust to enhance her magic and her gold dust to perform the spell. Together, they worked nearly the same as the rune on her crossbow.

She grasped onto Namara's hand and closed her eyes, letting the world fall away as she concentrated. Isabel's snores faded into a gentle thrum, the heat of the candle spread to her entire body, the tingling sensation of the dust on her fingers fizzed out, and the wetness she felt from Namara dissipated.

She took a deep, steadying breath and began to whisper in her mind. *Fluid of infinite shape and form, doth by which we all are born, reverse the untaught flow forevermore, henceforth, no longer shall thou endure.*

Her eyes snapped open, and they homed in on a single droplet of water forming on the tip of Namara's finger. It pearled bigger, growing and growing, and Thea's breath caught at the thought that she had *finally* perfected the spell.

The droplet fell.

Thea let go of Namara's hand and fell back onto the futon behind her, groaning in frustration. She scrubbed at her face and sighed, staring at the coffered ceiling in contemplation. What was she missing? A specific reagent? Was her mind not clear enough to perform the spell? What conditions was she not meeting?

"It's okay, Thea," she heard Namara say from the tub. Her feet sloshed over the side as she lounged back and relaxed. "You'll get it right. You won't stop until you figure it out, so it's not like I'm worried."

Thea sat back up and blew out the candle, shrouding them in darkness. She pushed the taper away and crawled back onto her bed. She didn't want to have Namara see the crestfallen expression she was trying to hide. The kelpie's eyes were exceptional in the dark, but Thea didn't want to think about that. Darkness equaled privacy. If she couldn't see her failure, neither could anyone else. She swallowed the emotion that dared rise up in her. "Every day I don't get it right is another day you're burdened by this."

"You act like I haven't lived with this since my creation. It's only really started bothering me after being summoned, but it's nothing new. Agni doesn't seem to mind."

Thea huffed out a chuckle. The demoness was smitten through and through. Her smile quickly disappeared, and she turned over on her side facing the kelpie. "I'll get it right soon."

A soft splash. "I know."

She closed her eyes and tried to let sleep take hold of her. The thoughts in her head swirled about as if to taunt her, though. She wanted to know more about mana. She wanted to know what was up with that giant, floating rock. The snowstorm closing in, trapping them here. The temple being *so close*, yet so far away. The failure of once again not successfully performing the spell. How much she missed Rafe. Blythe and … everything that needed to be said between them.

She swallowed down a choked sob, refusing to let the sound escape her. Refusing to allow that weakness to penetrate the stillness of the night. She couldn't stop the lone tear that slid down her cheek, but she closed her eyes and ignored it. Ignored the pangs in her chest and focused on the softness of the bedding under her, the quiet splashes of Namara in the tub, and the smell of agarwood incense in the air.

Waking up knowing it was morning but still being surrounded by darkness was disorienting. It was early, sure, but not early enough to escape the morning rays from filtering in from a window, nor late enough to not hear the birds chirping their sunrise songs for the world to hear.

Her eyes were tired. Her body was sore, but she knew it was because she'd been sleeping on the hard, frozen ground the past few days and not the comfortable bed under her. Her mind was foggy, and thoughts came to her slowly, but she pushed herself out from under the covers regardless. She sat there for a moment, staring off into space, before her brain caught up with her.

Rolling over and dipping her finger in the dust pouch propped next to all her other belongings, she then pinched at the wick on the candle beside her bed. A flame sprang from her fingertips, and dim light engulfed the room. She grabbed the bottle of barrier breaker oil and dabbed a drop onto her lips and in her ears. It likely hadn't worn off just yet, but she didn't want to take any chances.

She got dressed quickly and ran her comb through her curls, grimacing at the knots she found. She wanted to ask about taking a shower and maybe a change of clean clothes—or at least find somewhere to wash the garments she had—but first she needed breakfast. She hadn't partaken in the drinks last night as she was still technically on the sun dial, but Isabel had drunk herself into a stupor. She would *not* be waking the redhead anytime soon.

Namara was also still asleep, and as Thea peered over the tub, she was reminded again how different demons and humans were. The demoness was still below the tepid water. Like a weighted corpse, not even air bubbles escaped her olive-green lips.

She stepped around the tub, over Isabel's prone form, and tried to grasp at a doorknob that wasn't there. She looked down in confusion before realizing she had to slide it open. When she finally managed to escape the room, she found Fatik stumbling out of his own.

"Good morning," she offered with as amicable a smile as she could first thing in the morning and handed over the barrier breaker oil. The room was not that much brighter than it was last night, but candles adorning nearly every surface lit the room aglow.

The Dragonkin scratched the back of his head and stretched his wings out fully. Spread out, they were truly magnificent and larger than one would think. "Mornin'," he yawned out before reapplying the oil. Something caught his eye right after, though, and he peered over at the shrine.

She glanced over as well, struck once again by the statues in the back of the room. "What is that?" she couldn't help but ask, even knowing Fatik was probably as clueless as she was.

"*That*," he said with significance, weighing his tone and stepping closer. Thea followed him, looking between him and the statues. "That is the god and the goddess."

Chapter Twenty-Six

Under the False Moons

Thea stopped in her tracks and whipped her head in Fatik's direction. He wasn't looking at her, but he seemed amused nonetheless at her astonishment. She dashed over to the figures and leaned down to get a better look.

"You're telling me that I *just* learned about a god and *that's him*?" She pointed at the black statue for emphasis.

Fatik had closed in on the shrine and was standing tall with his arms crossed over his chest. His pale eyes glanced over the stone sculptures in scrutiny, but he nodded. "Yeah, that's what these two represent. Unsoul and Saellah. Sometimes, Unsoul is depicted with a different mask in each of his hands, but this one is pretty accurate too."

The Spellweaver felt her jaw unhinge, and her eyes slowly traveled back to the shrine. "Unsoul and Saellah," she whispered, and a tiny tingle of … of *something* shot through her and stole her breath away. She clutched at her heart as it throbbed in her chest, but the feeling wasn't a horrible one. Her eyes were suddenly hot, and she hurriedly blinked back the tears before they could spill. She didn't know what had just come over her, but, "That felt … that felt like I—like I just came home," she said in awe. The words were more spoken to herself, but she didn't miss Fatik's hum of understanding.

She wanted to know more. She *needed* to know more. As if a cord had tied itself to her soul, she found herself being pulled closer to the sculptures. The yellow light of the candles flickered and played across their features as if the two were truly alive.

The white nephrite statue of the goddess held soft-brown tints around the finer details, and no such detail had been spared. She was dressed in a flowing gown that draped over a full, pregnant belly. She was poised on one tiptoe, and her six limbs and long hair swayed as if in dance with the figure before her. Her eyes held no iris or pupil, just left blank, yet tears streamed down her tranquil face. In each hand, she held some object, but it was only upon closer inspection that Thea could make out each item. Saellah held a wand, a book, a crystal ball, a talisman paper, magic dust that was slipping between her fingers, and a small bundle of flames.

Unsoul was just as imposing as his counterpart. Carved from raw nuummite, the god was sweeping forward as if to embrace the goddess before him. His eyes were closed, and his face placid. His six arms were outstretched like he was going to hold her, but his hands were also occupied. The two in front of him that were separating him from Saellah held a large book open. One hand held a mask of his identical face, but the mask was smiling. Another held what looked like a few souls, formless, yet their expressions cried out in anguish. One hand held nothing, but his two fingers were crossed as if he were lying about something. The last held fire like Saellah, but in his palm, the flames were wild and licked up his arm.

Thea had so many questions. Unsoul didn't look nearly as welcoming, and Saellah was crying. Yet, she didn't appear sad. The Spellweaver turned to Fatik, a question on the tip of her tongue, but the door to the temple snapped open and revealed a fresh-looking Clan Leader on the other side. He was dressed in a bright white robe with wide sleeves that hid his hands within. Two women, one of them being Siàu, scurried in behind him and went to the two opposite rooms of the temple.

"Ah, I am glad to see you are awake," Renkilo said with a smile. A loud groan rumbled out of the room Thea'd slept in, and the Clan Leader tucked his lips in to hold back a laugh. "Well, most of you anyway."

"Good morning," Thea greeted in return, Fatik nodding beside her. "I was wondering if I could perhaps bathe today. Also, I …" she trailed off and peered back at the shrine. "I have some questions."

Renkilo nodded. "A marvelous idea, and I see you've become acquainted with the Mother and Father of Magic and Curses. Not to worry, we'll have plenty of time to discuss them while you meet with Merrjewl and Cel'dion."

Thea felt like she had just received whiplash. "Who?"

Renkilo was already leaving out the door, but he tossed over his shoulder a smirk only a wise, old man could manage and said, "Two of the few remaining children of the Goddess Saellah. Siàu will show you where to wash up."

Then he was gone.

A loud bang startled her, and she whipped around to see Isabel shoving the door to the side and rubbing her forehead with the groggiest expression she had ever seen on the redhead. Fatik laughed and got a mean look for it.

Namara came walking out, stretching like a cat and making a beeline for the door.

"Where are you going?" Thea called after her.

"The river!" she hollered over her shoulder.

Thea snorted. As if the tub full of water wasn't enough to get a good soak. She turned as Agni also walked out, looked around, and then also turned for the door. The Spellweaver rolled her eyes.

Those two are so obvious.

Isabel was groaning about something as she refused to take the oil from Fatik, eyes still closed and swaying on her feet. Thea sighed and swiped the bottle from the Dragonkin and applied the oil quickly—and a bit harshly—to Isabel's lips and ears. The redhead only batted her hands away in annoyance.

Siàu emerged from the room after presumedly cleaning up a bit, and Thea felt relieved as the prospect of washing herself seemed nearer. At the request for a bath or a shower, the taller woman nodded and shut the door behind her, but she nearly tripped as the hem of her robes was caught inside it. She huffed, reopened the door, snapped the material away, and reclosed it. She smoothed the hair around her face as if embarrassed by the action, but Thea couldn't tell from her expression.

Stepping outside the temple, she was once again disoriented by the fact that it was morning, yet everything was so dimly lit. The homes affixed to the cave walls gave off a soft, yellow glow from the windows. Tall torches with fluttering flames lit up various spots of the cave, but they offered little warmth against the early chill. With the snowstorm howling outside, catching glimpses of her breath didn't surprise Thea. She eyed the giant slabs on the cave ceiling when she heard them rattling, but she stopped walking altogether at the sight above her.

Isabel bumped into her and grumbled a complaint, but Thea was hardly paying attention. Fatik came up beside her, and she could hear the wonder in his voice. "It's neat, isn't it? I saw them last night when I went for a walk."

She nodded. All along the cave walls, darkened by the lack of sunlight, thousands of shining, sapphire lights glinted from the stone. They glowed and pulsed as if alive, and as Thea pivoted, she observed that they covered nearly the entire cave. She shook Isabel beside her, but the redhead only grumbled some more.

"Isabel," she hissed, "look at this! You're going to want to see this."

Isabel huffed and began rubbing her eyes. "What?" she griped, but as soon as she squinted up at the cave ceiling, her eyes nearly popped out of her skull. "Wh—What is that? I gotta get a sample! Where's my notebook …" she began mumbling incoherently as she frantically slapped at her body as if she could procure her notebook out of thin air. Unlikely for someone who didn't perform magic.

Siàu approached them with a confused look on her face, which only grew as Isabel ran back to the temple. Thea merely pointed up. "What are those lights?"

A look of understanding smoothed out her features. "Ah, those are the moonglows." When Thea thought that would be all, as typical of Siàu and her short answers, the woman surprised her by continuing. "They are insects that burrow deep in the cave walls, only coming out when it is dark. They eat the minerals from the cave walls. When we dig up their nests, we find a wax hive containing their food and pupae. The wax we use in dying patterns on our clothing. The pupae are wrapped in silk cocoons, which we use to make our silks. There's not that much, however, so we are limited—"

Redness blossomed over Siàu's cheeks as she caught herself rambling on too much, and she abruptly closed her mouth. She nodded her head for Thea and Fatik to follow her to the baths, and the two hurried after her. They turned and paused when Isabel burst out of the temple and, spinning around like a tossed coin, she found Agni in the river a ways off, lounging beside Namara in her horse form. Without even a look toward Thea and Fatik, she jogged off toward her demon companion.

"Guess she won't be joining us," Fatik snickered as they began walking once more.

Thea shook her head in fond exasperation. They stepped onto a well-worn trail enclosed on either side by tall, broad-leafed trees. The branches swooped over them in an arch and blocked out the cave ceiling, casting the path in deep shadows. White paper lanterns dotted the walkway and hung from the branches to ward off the darkness with their soft, candle-lit glow. "Did you see the jar she was holding? She'll probably try and catch a dozen or two."

Fatik hummed as he peered up at the trees. "Let's hope they don't die before she gets them back to her lab."

"If they do, I won't be around to hear her cry about it." Somehow, though, she didn't trust those words. She and Isabel weren't the closest by any means, but not having the redhead in her life ever again felt … odd. She had a feeling she'd be seeing the researcher long after this mission, and a large part of her wasn't even upset about that. Isabel had definitely kept her on her toes throughout their adventure.

"We're here," Siàu said as they stepped out from under the canopy. They were a ways off from the river now, but the humidity had only swelled as they neared the baths.

Thea looked around, but all she could see was a large tunnel carved into the cave's wall. Already, goosebumps were dancing over the skin of her arms despite the mugginess wafting from the tunnel. It was dark, tight, and she didn't know where it would lead.

Is it too late to change my mind about a bath?

She huffed and steeled herself. She was gross, grimy, and probably smelled. The last thing she wanted to do was meet the literal children of Saellah (and probably Unsoul, she didn't know how that worked), looking like she just rolled around with the barn animals.

Siàu entered the tunnel without looking back, and the duo hurriedly strode after her. Thankfully, though, after only a few feet in, candles were lit on the floor along the rough walls. The passage was small and forced Siàu and Fatik to hunch over as they walked, and it was tight enough to only allow one person at a time to comfortably travel through. Be that as it may, it was a blissfully short walk.

The tunnel opened up to another, smaller cave that was sweltering and had Thea feeling like her clothes were sticking to her. Steam clung to the surface of the water before wisping up into the air, trapped against the low ceiling. Candles were placed everywhere, bestowing their warm light all over the enclosed space and offering those bathing a sense of comfort and coziness. Crystalized stalactites jutted down from the top of the cave, and massive stalagmites breached the water and reached for their parallels. One was so massive it split the hot spring nearly in half.

Fatik and Thea shared a look before glancing around the cave once more. After seeing no indication of privacy, Thea pointed to the right. "I'll take that side. I know I'm as dirty as my clothes, so I'll just change when I'm in the water."

She had barely trudged to the edge of the hot spring before Siàu was grabbing onto her jacket and exclaiming, "Wait!"

Thea looked over her shoulder in alarm. The usually quiet woman had never seemed this frantic, and she hadn't made an effort to physically touch any of them either. "What is it?"

Siàu let go of her and stepped back a few steps. "You must not enter the hot springs in your clothing. It is not allowed."

Thea's brows pinched, and she threw a look at Fatik, who threw up his hands in surrender. He wanted no part of this. "I'm not going to change in front of him! I'd rather go without a bath at all." She peered back at the Dragonkin. "No offense."

Fatik quickly shook his head. "None taken. Tasgall would kill you *and* me."

Siàu waved a hand in the air as if telling them to wait before she raced over to the wall and pried off a slab of stone that was nearly hidden by the entrance. It looked heavy, but she handled its weight with ease and set it down onto the ground on its metal, claw-foot legs. It stood on its own when she stepped away from it, and then she pulled at its top corners, and the giant stone slab unfolded into three parts.

She stepped aside and clasped her hands in front of her, looking expectantly at the duo.

The two of them stared back at her.

Siàu's self-satisfied smile quickly disappeared into a small frown, and she peered at the stone slab as if maybe she had done something wrong. She eyed it over from a few angles before directing her gaze at the two once more. "What's wrong?"

Fatik eyed the thing in confusion. "What is that?"

"It is a privacy divider … You change on each side so that nothing is seen. Typically, it is not often used as we change which days men and women use the hot springs."

Well. It's definitely better than changing in front of him. The stalagmite wall would also offer privacy while in the water. She shrugged. "I guess that works."

"It's not very big," she heard Fatik mutter, but Thea was already looking around and spying a wooden bench shrouded in mist. A fresh pile of cloths was neatly folded, and a few bars of plain soap accompanied them.

She turned to Siàu with big, pleading eyes. "Do you by chance think I could have a bar of soap and a rag?"

The woman nodded. "You may use them. We wash all rags after use, and a woman in our village makes a new batch of soaps weekly."

"Thank the goddess," Thea whispered and went over to get her and Fatik some. The soap was somewhat clear and had been molded around dried flower blossoms, and a mild scent wafted from the squares. She bit her lip in amusement at the fact that Fatik was going to smell like roses.

Siàu made herself scarce after it was clear she was no longer needed, though she did part with a quiet warning not to take too long since it was so hot in the cave. "I'll also be bringing fresh linen to dress in soon," the willowy woman had announced just before she left.

When they began changing behind the screen, it was terribly awkward and silent, but they agreed that Fatik would go into the water first. The divider had been angled so that Thea couldn't see his side of the hot springs from her position. She knew when he was finally in the water by the loud hiss that escaped him.

She still felt horribly exposed in an open area with a naked man only separated by a wall of rock, but she trusted Fatik enough to know he wouldn't sneak a peek at her as she rushed into the spring. She still felt safer when she was cloaked by the depths of the hottest water she'd ever stepped foot in. She let out an equally loud hiss and began rubbing at her limbs as the near-boiling heat lapped at her skin. Soon, it was more soothing than torturous, and a sigh she hadn't realized she'd been holding in escaped her as she relaxed against the rock wall. It was as if every ache in her body from the journey was washed away before she could even get to scrubbing.

After her skin was nearly pink from the heat and the vicious way she'd taken the rag to her skin, Thea placed the bar of soap and cloth on a nearby rock and settled into the water to relax for just a bit longer. She could hear gentle splashes on the other side of the wall. The soft sounds echoed off the walls around her, but other than that, the room was quiet. Tucked away from the rest of the world, Thea could almost believe a snowstorm wasn't ravaging the land outside the cave.

"How long do you think the storm will last?" She asked Fatik right before she wondered if it was good etiquette to talk to someone while they were in a bath.

Fatik didn't seem to mind. "Usually, storms in the mountains this late in the year only last a few days. I don't know if it'll still be safe to travel right after it passes, though."

Thea sighed and let her head fall back onto the wall. It was about time they got out. She could sense a headache from overheating coming on. She herself felt like a dragon for the way breathing in the hot steam burned her nostrils. Her lungs felt like they were sitting over a bubbling caldron, molten lava following through the veins within. It radiated through her entire chest, in every pore on her face, in the back of her throat. Like she was about to spew flames just by exhaling. This was a lot different than any bath she'd taken before now.

She heard the telltale signs of Fatik exiting the baths. His wings flapped about, and a quiet "Not bad" escaped him before he called out a little louder, "I'll be outside."

"Okay," she yelled back, only to wince as her voice bounced around the room. She waited a few moments before exiting the pool.

She hurriedly toweled off, but she hesitated at the fabric folded neatly in front of her. Would it fit her? Siàu was the tallest woman Thea had seen in the cave, but she was very lanky. None of the other women were as tall as Thea from what she could tell, and though few were strong with clear muscle definition, most were as willowy as their guide.

You won't know unless you put it on.

Her dirty clothes had already been taken, but thankfully, her belt pouch remained. She tried to dress quickly, but she wasn't used to the style of clothing. She had been given two robes; one was clearly an inner robe, and the other obviously belonged on the outside. The inner robe was a pale, off-white color that resembled a simple dress. The outer robe had been dyed pastel blue, but at the bottom, where the skirt was more flowy, were white silhouettes of the mountain range. A long, dark red ribbon accompanied the outfit.

She tried her best to remember how the people of the Huǒshān Clan wore the robes, but it was clear when she walked outside the hot springs and found both Siàu and Fatik waiting for her that she had missed a step or two. It didn't help that the material came up nearly to her calves.

Siàu shooed her back into the hot spring and, even though the embarrassment had her cheeks warming redder than the heat steaming off the spring, she let herself be essentially redressed. The robes had been bunched around her hips, and Siàu somehow managed to lengthen the material without magic to where it rested at her ankles. The top of the robe was more uniform in how it was tucked, and the belt around her waist was no longer sloppily tied off. It was knotted into an elegant bow with the leftover ribbon ending at the hem of her skirt. It wasn't tight in any of the places a dress would be, and as she twirled around, she felt—dare she say—elegant.

She only noticed she had been smiling when she let out a small laugh, and when she stopped spinning around, she caught Siàu also smiling.

"Come," the woman said with dimpling cheeks, "I will do your hair next. It's hot in here."

Chapter Twenty-Seven

The Children Who Ran Away

Thea stood in front of Renkilo and his longma with wariness. Beside it, a copy of the creature stood proudly. It had been clear that the only mode of transportation up to the top of the giant, floating rock was going to be on the back of the dragon-like steed. Agni had taken it upon himself to replicate the terrifying beast.

"I do hope the *qynzos* are to your liking?" the Clan Leader queried with a proud smile, for it was obvious by the way Isabel was still spinning around in her pale yellow robes that yes, they did like the outfits they were wearing. She hadn't taken a dip in the hot springs, but she had vigorously wiped herself down with a washrag until her skin was near glowing. Blue birds were the motif decorating her clothing, along with a magenta belt. It somehow all tied together with the color of her overgrown bob that Siàu had pulled up into a neat bun with a matching magenta ribbon.

Fatik was rather dashing in his outfit. It was pale like the rest of him yet complemented his fair complexion and features. Rather than a skirt, he wore loose pants that, when his legs were together, almost appeared like one. The top half of the outfit was identical to theirs, though his included gray bamboo silhouettes along the sleeves.

Thea picked at the hem of her own billowy sleeves. She'd gotten plenty of stares the more people came out of their homes to gather wood, tend to their livestock, or simply observe the moonglows. Her hair had been parted by her ears and braided over the top of her head like a headband, incorporating the smaller curls around her hairline so they wouldn't be sticking out oddly.

"Ah, yes, they're very nice." If not a little chilly now that the heat of the hot spring had left them behind.

Renkilo nodded. "We will make sure you are able to dress correctly by yourself, so when you take them home, you will not be left clueless."

Isabel stopped spinning. "Wait—you're *giving* us these?"

The Clan Leader chuckled as he hopped on top of his longma with grace he shouldn't be capable of. "Of course. Think of us fondly when you wear it, and should anyone ask where you got it, let them know of us up here in the mountains. Having guests has been more entertaining than I had imagined. Should anyone be curious enough to come up the mountain and visit us with fair intentions, we would welcome them with open arms."

"Should they survive the journey," Fatik commented with a dry smile.

Renkilo winked at the Dragonkin before helping Isabel up on the beast behind him. "Then they would have earned the right to enter the Huǒshān Clan's dwelling, no?"

Isabel raised her fist in the air and bellowed out, "Only true adventurers welcomed!"

Thea covered her face in embarrassment as fellow clansmen lingering around the rice fields turned and looked upon the group in confusion. Renkilo started cackling, drawing even more curious stares.

"Come on, Thea, the longer you stand there, the longer Isabel will attract attention."

Thea glanced up to find Fatik already atop Agni and holding out a hand. She quickly took hold, and with the help of Namara hoisting her up onto the longma-copy, she settled in behind the Dragonkin. Namara was the last to join, and she hopped up onto Agni's back without a problem.

The demon's new form spread its scaly wings, thin membrane stretching before the two longmas started running. Their wings flapped once, twice, and jostled the riders from the sheer power behind the action before launching into the air. Thea clung to Fatik as his own wings threatened to spread and catch the wind that whipped around them. Namara was completely unbothered with her superior balance, and Thea could hear the kelpie giggling behind her.

She opened her eyes to get a view of the cave, only to cling harder to Fatik as the ground below her was now *very* far away. Thank the goddess the Dragonkin was sturdy. He patted her arms in reassurance as they soared through the air, and she could see everything from up here. The forests were massive, almost junglelike. The pulley system, made up of ropes and bridges, looked even more complicated from above. She could see all of the river and how it disappeared through a small crack in the opposite side of the cave. The moonglows grew closer and closer, shining their brilliant, glittering light like twinkling stars.

When they landed, it was on a giant stone slab crowned with an ornate wooden gate to welcome them. Two circular, elaborate designs were torched across the wood, interrupted by a metal bar that kept the doors from being opened willy-nilly. A knocker was placed in the center—a ring in the mouth of a dragon that glared at them with its iron gaze.

Twin trees that were perhaps the stiffest and most ridged trees Thea had ever seen hovered over the gate on either side, tipped in dark green pine needles. They didn't look like any evergreen she had seen previously, not with how their branches all reached out in one direction as if a fierce wind had blown them over. Behind the gate, the embellished building she'd seen from below rose up like the very mountains it hid within. It was more imposing the closer they neared, and its gold, ornamental decorations stood out in stark relief against the plain backdrop.

Thea dismounted on wobbly legs. Agni was quick to transform when everyone else got off, but the form Thea had been used to seeing throughout their trip did not make an appearance. Instead, Agni disappeared in a cloud of smoke, only for a rodent to pop out and fall into Namara's waiting hands. The rat raced up her seafoam-green arm and perched itself on top of her shoulder. She giggled and scratched under its tiny jaw with her finger.

"Uh, hello? What am I, chopped kraken?" Isabel huffed and glared at the pair, crossing her arms over her chest.

Namara looked guiltily away, but Thea saw the small smile she was trying to hide behind her dripping locks of hair. Agni couldn't be bothered to offer his partner an apology squeak and continued to give tiny licks to the kelpie's face.

Isabel stomped her foot like a child, and a solid thump reverberated off the stone slab under them. How that metal leg of hers wasn't dented by now was a miracle.

The Clan Leader stepped up to the gate and grabbed hold of the knocker. He tapped thrice, enough to activate a mechanism that pulled the metal bar up and back until the wooden doors could be opened.

As they passed the gate, Renkilo instructed over his shoulder, "Please do not step off the stone path."

Thea didn't quite understand why that was so important until they passed through the doors. She hadn't been able to see much of what was on the other side of the gate while in the air, and the perimeter wall hadn't offered much of a view around it either.

There was sand. Everywhere. Unlike the sand in the desert, as golden as the sun that beat down on it, this sand was white. Linework patterns had been raked into it, broken up by islands of moss and large stones. Some stones had jagged edges, some were statement pieces, some were smooth and round like eggs, but each had been placed with a delicate attention to detail.

Isabel's dark brown eyes remained wide and curious, though she stayed on the stones that lay a curvy path to the building's front doors. The group remained quiet as they gathered under the elevated, covered porch. Thea fidgeted with the hem of her sleeves again as the possibilities of what—of *who*—was on the other side of the large double doors spun through her head.

Two of the few remaining children of Saellah, Merrjewl and Cel'dion.

The doors swung open, revealing a room similar to that of the Heavenly Temple. Large beams supported the structure, carefully carved and dressed with ribbons of varying colors, and banners hung from the rafters. Large plants draped down from their handwoven baskets and splashed the room in hints of life. Candles were everywhere, of all shapes and colors and sizes. Smoke drifted in the air. Sandalwood, borneol, saffron, and a delicately floral scent all wafted into a collective, unique smell.

In the center, on a raised platform where plenty of cushions and pillows resided, two individuals sat up straight with their legs crossed under them. One male, one female, each with identical, dark hickory skin partially hidden by the robes they wore. The female had silver-blonde hair that fell down to her lower back, straight as her spine. She gave off a luminescent light as if her soul were a beacon of magic.

The male was similar, only his hair was pitch as night as it cascaded over his shoulders in voluptuous waves. He did not glow, but upon opening his eyes at the sound of the group walking closer, Thea was met with pure starlight. He did not have normal eyes with a pupil or iris. Everything that should have been there had been replaced with the night sky.

He leaned back with a beaming, white smile, and the waves around his shoulders shifted, revealing long, pointed ears underneath.

Thea gasped, and the noise caught the attention of the female elf. Crystalline blue reflected back at her instead of the night sky, captured within an iris rather than bleeding outward.

Her smile was soft, voice softer. "Welcome, far-children and friends. We have heard much about you."

The children of Saellah … were elves.

"I shall retire for now," Renkilo announced once Thea and the others were situated in a semi-circle around the elves. "I have yet to do my own daily meditation. I will return in a bit." He gave a slight bow toward the elves before he swept across the floor, slid open a door, and disappeared behind it.

"So," Isabel started as soon as the Clan Leader was gone, "are you two really elves? Why did you call us far-children? What are you even doing here—"

"Isabel," Thea hissed, effectively shutting off the no doubt endless list of questions, though she was hopeful those first three would eventually be answered. She remembered the term "far-children" from the Skrite in the Skrittish Library, but she'd never gotten clarity on the term.

The female elf giggled behind a sleeve before she peeled back the curtain of her hair to reveal her equally long, pointed ear. "Why, yes, we are of elven blood. As to why we called you far-children, well, all humans with elven ancestry are essentially the grandchildren of the goddess. It is how humans developed the ability to practice magic, after all."

The male at her side gently laid a large hand on top of her knee, though he didn't look at her. "My beloved, we have yet to introduce ourselves."

The elf's dainty hand fell from her hair to cover a surprised "o" formed from her heart-shaped lips. A light dusting of pink brought warmth to her dark, cool-toned skin. "Oh my, you are indeed right, my love." She faced the group with a smile that could melt the most frigid of hearts. "I am known as Cel'dion. Pleased to make your acquaintance." She tipped her head in a small bow.

"I am Merrjewl," the male elf said with an easy grin. "It is a pleasure to be in your company."

After Thea and the rest's introduction passed, the Spellweaver took charge of the conversation while Fatik hung back and translated to the demons sitting next to him. Isabel was taking notes and hanging onto every word.

"We were told we would be speaking with you today, though we were not told why. Did you request us?"

Cel'dion looked to her partner, but Merrjewl had yet to look back at the female elf. "Yes," she finally answered after a moment. Once we were informed of the details of your mission, we knew we had to speak to you. You see, I was the one who placed that tablet in the temple two hundred years ago."

Thea felt her jaw unhinge. "W-Wait—what? You? You placed the tablet there?"

Cel'dion nodded and lounged back against a plush cushion. Merrjewl held out his hand, nails as dark as his hair, and her fingers slipped between his and squeezed. "Do you know why the tablets were split up and stored in the elemental shrines across Aeristria?"

Thea shook her head. "Not much was told to me by the sylphs in the western temple. They only mentioned the Light

Elf King—disdainfully, I might add—and how he split the tablets up after the Great Divide."

Merrjewl's lips twitched at the mention of the king. "The Allatari is who you're referring to, and I can understand their frustration and pain. We hail from Satviriya, the elvin city in the Black Forest, though it has been a long time since we last called that place home."

"Even longer for you," Cel'dion pointed at the male elf. She directed her gaze back at the others with a frown tugging at her lips. "You see, Merrjewl is a Dark Elf while I am a Light Elf. Once, there was no separation between our kinds. We were simply elves and nothing more."

Thea looked between them both. "Does that explain the physical differences?"

Merrjewl nodded. "Yes. I believe it was the very beginning of the Elven Era when elves first discovered a new form of magic. At the time, all the elves were Light Elves, though we did not call ourselves that. It was so long ago. Humans had not even crossed over to Aeristria yet."

Thea pulled back. "Wait, what?"

Cel'dion looked surprised. "What is it?"

Isabel clambered to sit up. "When did humans cross over? Where did we come from?"

The elves seemed shocked by the question. "You really do not know?" Merrjewl asked, scratching behind his pointed ear awkwardly.

"Our original Coven was burned down, so we don't know much of our history," Thea helpfully supplied. However, that only seemed to make the elves tense even more, and Cel'dion looked down at her lap and fiddled with the fabric.

Thea narrowed her eyes. "You know something about that, don't you?"

Merrjewl sighed. "We do. There is no point in denying this. Though we were not the ones who burned down your Coven, we owe you the truth."

"Start from the beginning, my love," Cel'dion encouraged.

The dark-haired elf did not look at his partner, but he nodded, nonetheless. He sat up straight and cleared his throat. Then he began.

"As I stated before, it was the beginning of the Elven Era when our kind first discovered a new type of magic. This new type of magic … it changed the physical appearances of those who used it. As you might have been able to guess, this new magic was later called dark magic. This magic tainted the user, though I was never able to see exactly what I was tainted with. I had to rely on others to tell me what physical attributes of mine changed as I continued to practice."

Isabel made a noise of confusion, halting Merrjewl from continuing.

"Something on your mind?" he hummed.

"Is it … is it because …?" Thea trailed off, pointing to her eyes.

Cel'dion gave her a confused frown before peering over to her lover. Understanding flitted across her face quickly. "Oh! Oh, Merrjewl, they didn't know you were blind."

A look of amusement crossed over the Dark Elf's face. "Not everyone is as observant as you are, my dear," Merrjewl said with a small smile, patting her knee. "Let it be known I was born blind. The magic may have altered my appearance, but it did not take away my sight. That is not to say I see nothing, though. With the position I am sitting at right now, and the way Raen is turned at this point in the day, I can see our neighboring galaxy quite vividly. Planets we have yet to name and stars your kind may never know about have been keeping me company since I started practicing the dark arts."

Cel'dion smiled warmly at her beloved. "One day we will rejoin the universe, and I will have the pleasure of seeing what he sees every day."

Thea was speechless. To know that magic had gifted the elf with the vision of the universe—it was incredible. Isabel was equally as fascinated, judging by the way her pen flew over the page writing down notes. She paused and looked up. "So, back up—what's the difference? Between elves? Is the tainting thing the only thing?"

Cel'dion noted that, outside of the physical differences listed, with the color black "tainting" the individual through their hair, eyes, fingernails, and more, the main difference was—"The Light Elves' ignorance. They believed that dark magic was the product of Unsoul, and they forbade it from ever being used. Then Dark Elves, Dark Elf sympathizers, and Light Elves who were neutral to the conflict but who didn't want to be restricted in any sort of way built a large ship and sailed off to discover new lands."

Isabel gasped, and her hand stopped furiously writing. "They became pirates? And sailed the seas?"

Cel'dion chuckled. "Not quite. They didn't sail very far before they came across the nation of Elidron."

"Is that where humans originate from?" the redhead guessed excitedly.

Merrjewl smiled. "Correct. The elves began families with the humans, thus bearing the first human magic users. The king of the land was kind and fair, and he gifted the elves an enchanted land as a gift for bringing this wondrous magic to his people. In return, he wanted to know more about Aeristria and where our kind had originated from. It was during a time of peace, so with the guidance of the elves, he sent a fleet of boats back to the heart of magic. This was about … how long ago, now?"

Cel'dion hummed. "You and your brethren boarded the ship about two hundred and fifty to three hundred years ago, I believe."

"That sounds about right, and it took us a few months to wash ashore. Half Heart Bay was not even a port at the time, nor was anyone settled there, so we trekked through the Black Forest—"

Isabel jumped from her seat and interrupted with a gasp. "What about the wolves?"

Cel'dion's amused smile fell. "The forest had yet to see such monsters."

"Yes, you need not worry," Merrjewl assured before continuing. "The humans set up the first Coven as a sort of settlement in the Black Forest. Most of the humans swore their hearts to the elves, but a few did not. Those who kept their bloodline magicless are how some of the humans of today remain unable to cast spells."

Thea swore Isabel was going to get a cramp in her hand with how fast the researcher was writing all this down.

Cel'dion sighed. "It was not long before the humans and the Dark Elves began meddling in the forbidden magic once more. To the Light Elves, they believed that to be, and I quote, a 'blasphemous, irrevocable sacrilege against the Highest Mother.'"

"Well … isn't dark magic … bad?" Thea hedged carefully, hoping she wouldn't offend.

Merrjewl smiled in understanding. "Not to us. Elves are the children of Saellah, the Mother of Magic. The first of our kind were born from her tears as she wept for a world where magic could flourish. The second generation came from the High Elves—the celestials, as some call them, who were born from Saellah's womb. They continued the lineage of the elves by giving birth to us. The third generation and every generation thereafter came from breeding between elves, but no later-born elf is any different from the first or second generation."

"It has been that way for a millennium up until recently. But, to answer your question, magic is magic to an elf. We *are* magic. The thought of magic being able to taint something that is already magic is ludicrous. Now, for humans, it can be more dangerous, especially for those with little to no willpower. Furthermore, the fact that the Wild Hunt spell hasn't been properly performed in two hundred years … I would dare to say tampering with the dark arts would land a person in an early grave, if not worse."

Thea shuddered at Cel'dion's words as she thought back to Cressida. Even for someone with incredible willpower, dark magic wasn't something to trifle with.

"Anyway," Merrjewl continued, "the Light Elves were incensed that the elves who returned with the humans began practicing dark magic once more. The Light Elves went to great lengths to tear rifts between families. I mentioned Unsoul earlier. Are you familiar with him?"

Thea sat up a little taller in her seat and cast a quick glance at Fatik. "I learned about him fairly recently."

The blue of Cel'dion's crystal eyes cracked like glass in the wake of her ire. "Those wolves you spoke of earlier? You have him to thank for them. My kind's blind hatred and discrimination turned them to the god, where they made the deal to give up their souls in exchange for the wolf's form."

The Spellweaver quickly rubbed her eyes as she tried to process the information being dumped upon her. "Wait, wait, wait—the Light Elves are the wolves? What? But didn't they forbid dark magic because they thought it was a product of Unsoul's? Why would they then go to him for help?"

"They thought what better to fight fire with than fire? What better way to destroy Unsoul's creation than with Unsoul's power? So, the Light Elves were irreversibly transformed into the legendary wolves."

"The radical ones, anyway," Merrjewl commented.

Cel'dion sent a sharp look her lover's way. "All of our kind were radical for how your kind was treated."

The Dark Elf's frown gentled into a sweet smile. "You never treated me badly, my beloved."

Cel'dion softened. Her cheeks pinked again as she looked away. "I-In any case," she said and lightly cleared her throat, "yes, the Light Elves became the wolves of the Black Forest."

"Why, though?" Isabel asked innocently. "Just to get rid of dark magic?"

"No. It was for one purpose and one purpose only," the female elf continued. "To kill the Dark Elves."

Thea's eyes widened. This was the first she'd heard any of this. The Coven's library held no records of anything mentioned from the elves, and if it did, she certainly wasn't aware of it.

Cel'dion nodded at Thea's disbelief. "And it was mostly that blasted Denmarius's fault. How I loathe him in particular."

Thea looked between both elves. "Who is he? What did he do?"

"He was the leader of the wolves. He was the one who emboldened the elders' hatred to new levels of animosity. He inspired their fear and disgust with long tales of untruths. He decided that the Dark Elves and the humans who came with them should be punished."

Thea was afraid to know more, yet she had the smallest inkling she already knew what the elf meant by that. Still, she asked, "How so?"

Merrjewl straightened in his seat, and his deep voice washed over them. "First, the Great Divide happened. Dark Elves were run out of the city, and the Light Elves were banned from even speaking to us. It was forbidden, and if the laws were broken, the Light Elf would be cast out with my kind."

"Or, in my case," Cel'dion cut in, "I would be killed to spare the marring of my father's reputation. Of course, my death would no doubt have been blamed on the Dark Elves and would have acted as the catalyst to lead a full-on assault."

Thea's eyes widened. Her father's reputation had been everything to him, more so than his love for his children—

and yet, it was hard to imagine even *her* parents killing her off to save face. She shivered at the vileness of it all.

"My father was a respected elder in the community, and I was his precious daughter. If I stepped out of line, it would reflect back onto him. However, this led to opportunities I will get into in a moment. First—because I was of high standing in our society—I, together with my father, the Allatari, and other trusted members, recorded all the important spells with our civilization's most vital knowledge on the tablets before breaking them up. This was just after the Great Divide. The elders and the Allatari agreed that by doing this, it would eventually stop the humans and Dark Elves from continuing to practice the dark arts."

"It did not," Merrjewl muttered under his breath.

Cel'dion huffed a laugh, but her face grew somber shortly after. "I did not anticipate it would either, so I began to formulate a plan. You see, just before the divide in elves, Merrjewl and I had begun our courtship."

"You hadn't even blossomed into a female yet," Merrjewl chuckled from the side. "You were so smitten at such a young age."

Cel'dion playfully slapped the male's shoulders. "At least I had my mind made up. I believe you changed your gender three times before you settled on the male physique."

Merrjewl's brow furrowed. "It was twice, thank you."

Thea sent a confused look Isabel's way, and the redhead shared a similar look with her as she shrugged her shoulders.

The female elf rolled her eyes. "Anyway, we were in our second week of courting when my father forbade me from having anything to do with the Dark Elves. I played along.

'Yes, father,' and 'As you wish, father,' were things I uttered often. However, I acted as reconnaissance for the Dark Elves so they could avoid the wolves' rotating patrols. If a Dark Elf even breathed near the city, they would be killed. I hated how his kind were treated, and so did a few other Light Elves. I wanted to run away with Merrjewl, but where would we have gone? The ship was too far away to reach in such a short period of time, and the wolves knew the forest like the back of their cursed paws. I would have been found and dragged back before the moon settled in for the night if not killed on the spot. Besides all that, I was the only one relaying information to the Dark Elves."

Thea nodded along, eyes flicking back and forth between the elves.

"I came to my father and sought permission to take the tablet to the northern temple. It was far enough away, yet still close enough not to automatically receive a no from him. At first, I thought it would be as easy as playing the Stroviol—walk in, bait his growing paranoia, and convince him to let me take the tablet to the northern temple. Who better to entrust the tablet to than I, after all? I'd helped write what was on them. However, I misjudged his obsessively protective nature. My plan to run away with Merrjewl depended on my taking the tablet to the mountains, so I persisted. It was only after days of negotiating that my father and I came to an agreement. I was to be sent with an envoy of Light Elves to meet with the salamanders at the temple where they had been preparing the space for the tablet's arrival. The wolves were fierce and patrolling the woods, but they were of sound mind then. They knew the difference between our kinds, so my father felt reassured of my protection."

"You said that the Light Elves knew the forest like the back of their hand, so how did you meet up with the Dark Elves?" Fatik piped up from the side. His wings shifted nervously as all eyes—except Merrjewl's—turned to the Dragonkin. "Uh … Namara wanted to know."

The kelpie had positioned herself on the wooden steps so as not to ruin the fabric of the many pillows and cushions on the dais. Her all-black eyes flitted to everyone curiously as she awaited Fatik's translated answer.

Cel'dion looked forlorn as she answered. "As much as I had wanted to, that is not what my plan consisted of. Elves live very long lives, as you well know. My plan relied on longevity. The wolves ended up escorting the envoy to the edge of the Black Forest, and I could tell Denmarius had made it a point to be there—for he was the mastermind behind the tablets after all. He cared about the plan to break them up as much as he cared about killing trespassing Dark Elves. So, I ventured on this journey so that I would gain the trust of the wolves and the elders. Along the way, I made notes of the environment—where Merrjewl and I could escape to when the time did come. I found this cave by accident when I was excusing myself to the bathroom, and I made sure to keep it that way when I went back. I had no clue it had already been occupied by the Huǒshān Clan for some time. After that, I delivered the tablet to the temple and came back to the city."

Thea leaned back. "What happened then?"

"A century or so of awkward tension," Merrjewl spoke softly. "The humans were curious folk, and while some stayed with the families they created, others broadened their horizons and explored further south. They founded Tolvade as a secondary settlement, but it was explicitly for farming and trade. The districts all around Tolvade's center were originally just comprised of farms, but after years of use, only Adalith's land remained fertile."

"That's why the farmers are so rich," Thea whispered. "They're direct descendants from Aeristria's first settlers. And that's why trade is still so prevalent today."

The elves stared at her with wide eyes, and Thea felt suddenly self-conscious about her outburst. "What is it?"

"We didn't know Tolvade was still standing," Cel'dion murmured. "Or, at the very least, we didn't think it was flourishing."

Fatik shifted in his seat. "Why wouldn't it be?"

"Well …" she sighed and looked at her lover. A gentle squeeze of her hand was all she needed before she straightened her spine. "You will know why in a moment. First, let us backtrack. After I placed the tablet in the temple, the Dark Elves and I sent messages to each other monthly during the century-long stalemate. Any more frequently would have aroused suspicion. Any less frequently could have resulted in lives taken. The wolves were not fair creatures, after all. I would overhear the elder's gripings of the Dark Elves, their concoctions to get rid of them all—the curse they summoned to try and kill off Merrjewl's people, which failed miserably as elves are immune to curses. I wrote to Merrjewl's sept about the recent barrier enacted and how the elders kept fortifying it. I feared this would backfire on us somehow, but father refused to listen to me. Time began running out, but I still hadn't found a good window of opportunity to run away. Then, near the end of the stalemate, the elders had a meeting. The humans were still practicing the dark arts and sharing information with the Dark Elves. I had already known about this for some time, but word eventually spread to the rest of Satviriya. The elders … they …"

She looked away in shame.

Thea fidgeted in her seat, and she shared a glance with Namara. The kelpie spared her a look, but her features were awash in a seriousness the Spellweaver hadn't seen in a long time. She turned back to the elf.

"What happened? What did they do?"

Cel'dion sighed, eyes closing as the truth rang out. "They agreed that … because of the humans' continuous meddling with the dark arts, your Coven was to be burned to the ground."

Thea jumped to her feet. "What?" she growled out. "You mean to tell me the elves were responsible for burning down the first Coven?"

The female elf bowed low, nearly parallel to the floor. "I apologize for all that my kind has done."

Merrjewl finally turned his head to where his partner sat, and he tugged at her hand. "Sit up, my beloved, you had no part in this war."

Cel'dion straightened, but the smile on her face was sad. "Oh, but I benefited from the Light Elves' privileged sanctity all the same."

"You had to follow along with them so that we could escape the forest," he argued.

"That doesn't change the fact that while you suffered, I was hidden away in the safety of Satviriya."

Merrjewl brought Cel'dion's hand up to his lips and delivered a soft kiss to her fingers. "I would suffer an eternity if I could spend but a second with you."

Thea sat back down and glanced away to offer what little privacy she could while Cel'dion made an embarrassed, scandalized noise before swatting playfully at her lover. "Oh, you! Even if you say that, others should not have had to fear the Light Elves. Elves who were once their brethren," she sighed, and heavy disappointment was palpable in the air. "It was that night, while so many elves would be distracted burning down the Coven, that I slipped away into the forest to meet up with Merrjewl's sept. A few other Light Elves joined me, those who thought similarly to me. I trusted them wholly …" The female elf nibbled on her lip. "Not that it mattered."

Fatik shifted in his seat again, a soft look on his pale face. "What happened?"

"We were ambushed," Merrjewl stated.

Isabel shot up. "How? You just said—"

"Denmarius," he growled. "He was a crazed elf. Sanctimonious incarnate. But he was smart. He had known all along that something was amiss. It hadn't mattered how fast we vacated the premises. He had tracked us down in his wolf form, saw Cel'dion colluding with the Dark Elves, and went into a blind rage. The betrayal of a Light Elf—of someone of such high rank in elven society—made him go completely feral." Merrjewl glared at no one in particular as he remembered the events of that day. "What followed after was nothing short of a massacre."

Cel'dion covered their conjoined hands with her palm. "I should have known I never could have gained his trust.

He trusted no one but himself. Furthermore, a Light Elf sold us out just before the ones responsible for burning down the Coven left. Reesa. They were so sweet, timid most of the time. They broke down into tears when we heard the first wolf's howl. They told us everything and then ran behind the wolves that emerged from the surrounding trees." She shook her head sadly. "I fell and broke my leg trying to flee from them, and I would have suffered a much more horrible fate had it not been for Hajun—Merrjewl's brother— mending my injury. He died right in front of me just as I was healed."

Merrjewl turned away just as a shooting star streaked through his eyes. "Some of the Dark Elves and humans who survived and fled with us either died on our perilous journey to the mountains, or they succumbed to the wounds even I could not heal. If I did not have the stars to guide me, I would have also yielded to the mountain's force. In the end, three others managed to survive, and they married into the clan. The last one died several years ago. We are all that is left."

Silence followed the statement. Thea and the others glanced at one another as the elves were swept up in their memories.

Isabel put aside her notebook and sat up straighter. "What did the Huǒshān Clan say when you arrived?"

Cel'dion looked at her lover, and he squeezed her fingers as if sensing her gaze. He sighed. "At the time, it was too painful to divulge what had happened to my kind, so we did not disclose anything to the clansmen. We instead taught them our magic and how it differed from their own. Eventually, the years bled together, and we still had not yet come to terms with the betrayal of our former brethren—so we still had not yet elaborated the importance of the tablet in the temple."

"A fact we soon came to regret," Cel'dion whispered. "One day, we woke up to hear news that one of the clansmen, Enzou, had left with only a few parting words to his mother and father. There had been no announcement, no word that he had been contemplating journeying down the mountain, no nothing. One day he was here, the next he was gone. If we had known, we would have told him to deliver a message to any civilization he managed to find."

Merrjewl sighed. "We sent someone after him, but they came back hours later reporting they had found no trace of him. We can only hope he made it down the mountain and managed to find whatever he was looking for. After his disappearance, we told Renkilo everything. Word spread quickly, but no one has come along after who has wanted to leave the mountain, so we have waited here forever since for someone to retrieve them."

You may have waited forever, but at least you were not trapped inside those temples like the salamanders and the sylphs.

Thea sighed and leaned back. For elves that had specialized in reconnaissance, their lack of communication was astounding. And it had nearly doomed the entire world. "I just don't understand why you didn't send word for us to come collect the tablet sooner. Or at all. We nearly lost everything in the fire, so we didn't know we'd been performing the Wild Hunt spell incorrectly for so long, and those who did are long dead now. Were you two just going to wait until the magic in the world dried up completely? Were you seriously going to do nothing?"

Fatik shifted uncomfortably beside her, and she briefly wondered if her questions had come across as too harsh. She couldn't help it. Someone responsible for breaking up the tablets and secreting them away was right in front of her. Someone who had had the chance to bring the tablet to Tolvade and turn the tide of the Light Elves was sitting right in front of her. Someone who hadn't done that.

Merrjewl grimaced, but it was Cel'dion who spoke up. "You have to understand," she beseeched. "We were so surprised to learn that someone had climbed the mountain and made it to this place we now call home, but we were even more stunned to know someone from the Coven had journeyed here. We thought you all had sailed back to Elidron. The last thing I heard was that the humans vowed to reinstate their loyalty to the king and carry the emblem of the phoenix with them. I see they meant that quite literally." She nodded to Thea's insignia.

She peered down at her crest and furrowed her brows. "I'm sure some may have sailed back, but humans are resilient, and after a hundred years we would have had plenty of time to recover."

"One hundred years is nothing to an elf," Merrjewl said with a shake of his head. "Sometimes it feels as if only yesterday the elves stumbled onto dark magic."

Thea's gaze was stern as she responded. "One hundred years is probably a long time for the salamanders that are still trapped in the temple, never mind the fact that they've been waiting double that time. Let's not forget the undines in the forest. I know that the sylphs in the desert have been desperately trying to reach someone to get out. As for the gnomes, the Allatari summoned the wrong ones by the way, and they destroyed the temple in the Jeweled Canopy and messed up the entire ecosystem in the process."

Cel'dion raised a delicate hand to her lips. "Even if we took the tablet out of the temple, the salamanders would have remained trapped within. They cannot leave until the ritual is completed. We thought it too cruel to have them think they would be freed so soon. We also couldn't allow the magic gathering in the tablet to warp this haven we found with the Huǒshān Clan. And the truth is that the temple was the safest place for the tablet to remain while we waited. Furthermore, we barely survived the perils of the mountains, so coming back down to find what we deemed was a broken civilization was suicide."

"Look, I understand how fear can drive a decision." She knew all too well and very recently at that. "Your actions— or lack thereof—are understandable, but they could have led to the erasure of magic itself." Both elves frowned, and a heavy guilt washed over them, but Thea carried on regardless of the uncomfortable accountability they were having to face. "You didn't know the status of the humans, but you didn't even make an attempt to reach us."

Cel'dion bowed low once more, and she gently tugged on Merrjewl's hand so that he would mirror her pose. "I do hope you can find it in yourselves to forgive us. There are a lot of things we wish we could undo. Now that you are here, we humbly ask you to take utmost care of the tablet on your journey back."

Thea eyed both elves and quickly held up a hand when Isabel looked like she was going to speak. The redhead swiveled her head around to aim an inquisitive look at the

Spellweaver, but Thea merely held up a finger as she thought over everything that had been divulged to her.

"I cannot speak for all the beings of Aeristria, but I will forgive you …" she said after a long moment, but just as Cel'dion's face lit up, Thea continued, "on one condition."

Merrjewl cast a wary gaze in the Spellweaver's general direction. "What is the condition?"

As long as she had someone indebted to her, she was going to take advantage of it. She didn't care how that made her seem. She wasn't doing this purely for herself. The elves owed the world far more than this simple request anyway.

"I want to know more about the tablets, and then I want you to teach me how to perform a spell."

Chapter Twenty-Eight

Aeristria's Lifeblood

Thea waved Namara goodbye as the rest of the group stood on the edge of the floating rock. The kelpie had given Thea a small smile when she'd laid down her conditions, but it had looked … false somehow. It worried Thea, but she would have to talk to her partner later. Everyone was about to head down, and there was no time for idle chit-chat with the elves waiting.

Isabel had had no further use for the elves' knowledge now that spells would be involved, and she wasn't exactly supposed to be privy to what the tablets contained, as she wasn't an official Coven member. Fatik wasn't either, but he hadn't minded and even mentioned checking out the hot spring once more. Agni didn't care one way or another, but he went wherever Namara went, much to Isabel's annoyance.

"It's like I feared. I've been replaced," the redhead was complaining as she was assisted onto Agni's back. The rakshasa had transformed back into the longma creature and was perfectly content to carry all of them back down to the ground. "Fifteen some-odd years with a being—ya think ya know 'em, but then they turn your back on ya," she continued to gripe in an overly exaggerated manner.

"I think you meant 'turn *their* back on you,'" Fatik corrected with a patient smile.

"Don't come at me with your logic!" she snapped. "Can't you tell I'm distraught?"

The Dragonkin patted Isabel on the head, but she only sniffed miserably. Namara gave a small smile from the back of Angi's rump.

"What are your plans for the rest of the day?" Thea asked her before the group could take flight. She was trying to gauge the kelpie's answer to see what the issue might be.

"Agni and I will probably check out the hot springs Fatik mentioned. The river is nice, but it's out in the open, and everyone stares."

Isabel whirled around on the demoness. "I wanna go to the hot springs, too!"

"There goes my chance at relaxation," Thea heard Fatik mutter under his breath.

Thea crossed her arms in exasperation, but a smile had spelled its way onto her face. "Don't stay in the water too long, Isabel. You'll overheat."

The research merely waved her off. "Yeah, yeah, I'll be fine."

Agni fluttered his wings, signaling his desire to take off.

"Have fun!" Namara called over her shoulder as they launched off the platform and into the air.

Thea waved once again, but she didn't trust herself to get too close to the edge. Major heights were a no-no in her spellbook, and she wanted to pretend for a little longer that she wasn't hundreds of feet up in the air on a giant, floating rock.

Upon entering the large residence once more, Thea found her new tutors situated on the dais still. Cel'dion aimed a smile at the Spellweaver, but it was a bit strained after their previous conversation. Merrjewl did not look as lively either, and Thea hoped this wouldn't disrupt their discussion.

She dropped to her knees and quickly folded them under her. "I appreciate you agreeing to this," she said, hoping to lighten the mood.

"Teaching others how to properly wield their magic is what we do best," Cel'dion stated. "If this is what it takes to gain your forgiveness, we would be happy to oblige."

"Why do you care so much if I forgive you or not?"

Merrjewl stirred next to his lover. "What you said earlier … it's not that we haven't ever thought of it. We did, but we still ignorantly believed we had time. That someone would come along eventually. That we wouldn't ever have to see the horrors of this world again if we just stayed on the mountain and waited."

Guilt settled in the pit of Thea's stomach. It was small, and she was just in her actions for speaking out against them … but what made her any better? She hadn't experienced their trauma. She hadn't lived a horrible life by comparison. She may constantly be assaulted by memories of voices that slithered insults into ordinary conversations, but what was that in comparison to death, betrayal, and genocide? She had run away from her problems. She had run and hadn't looked back. And she was condemning them for doing the same?

The stakes weren't the same.

Who's to say she would have acted any differently if they were? It's easy to say what you would do in any given situation until you're faced with it.

Thea looked away as the words she wanted to say got clogged in her throat. She gave a soft cough, clearing what was there before she glanced up at both elves. "I'm sorry for how my words came out. I'm … I'm not sorry for what I said, but how I said them. I heard your story, but I didn't stop to comprehend the depth of your words. I still wish you would have tried harder, but who's to say I wouldn't have done the same?"

It was as if a weight had been lifted. The tension that had remained vanished. Thea felt a lightness she couldn't describe in her chest, and the elves' shoulders slumped ever so slightly.

Cel'dion's smile was much more genuine as she said, "Thank you. We accept your criticisms. It is easy to become defensive even when you know you are in the wrong."

Thea smirked. "I do it all the time. Pride is sometimes worse than a devil."

"It is a monster all its own," Merrjewl agreed. He straightened in his seat and offered her his own broad, easy grin once more. "What was the first thing you wanted to learn?"

"Oh! Right." Thea mirrored his pose and sat up straighter. "First, I want to ask something personal, if I may?" She directed her gaze toward Cel'dion.

The female elf looked surprised. "Oh? You may."

"After all these years away from your father, you still refer to yourself as a Light Elf? Have you never practiced dark magic?"

"Ah," she murmured with a nod as if she'd been asked this question before. "You could say there is dark magic within me—the spell that kept me alive performed by Hajun. But it is a drop in the proverbial ocean. I could not, in good standing, call myself a Dark Elf—not after all they suffered just by existing while I was living the way I did in Satviriya. I have learned the magic and embraced it as another facet of Saellah, but I have not practiced."

"Why not?"

Merrjewl shifted and cast his unseeing gaze up toward the ceiling. "We have learned that performing dark magic spells attracts … attention."

Thea quirked a brow. "Attention?"

"From the dragons," Cel'dion whispered as if the very dragons she spoke of were upon them.

"The energy manifested—it calls to them," the Dark Elf continued. "We do not understand it, but we have avoided it unless we are fortifying the barrier."

Again, Thea was confused. "The barrier? Like the one over Satviriya?"

Cel'dion waved a hand at the Spellweaver. "Oh, no. Trust me, that barrier needs no help in its fortification. I would venture to say the barrier has been fortified so much that it refuses to let anyone in *or* out. No, what we do is much more meaningful. We uphold the barrier around the entire mountains' borders. Every new moon, when Unsoul is at his weakest—sky magic is his domain after all—we perform the spell to strengthen the barrier to keep the beasts from escaping the mountain range. The Huǒshān Clan's original members thought it their duty to cage the dragons within the mountains so they would not fly back down and wreak havoc. Their magic was strong for having no influence in the dark arts, but it was only fortified along the southern mountains' border. Merrjewl and I have encompassed the entire mountain range."

Thea's eyes went wide. "There's a barrier around the entire mountain range?"

Merrjewl nodded in confirmation. "It is invisible to the eye of anyone but the casters—though I suppose that just means Cel'dion is the only one who can see it. That will change over time, but we still have many years ahead of us, so we have yet to begin training anyone to take over the spell. It would be a waste as they would live the full extent of their life before we even reached our middle ages."

His lover giggled beside him. "How else did you think the dragons were staying up here? Did you never wonder why they haven't flown down to your city?"

She shook her head. "Honestly, the dragons are somewhat of a myth. Not a lot of people in Tolvade know they even exist outside of storybooks."

It was the elves' turn to look confused. "Do you not have annual blizzards, or do they not reach the lower city? They are quite disastrous here. No one is allowed to leave the caves for months until it has passed."

Thea cocked her head to the side at Cel'dion's query. "Yeah, we do, but what does that have to do with anything?"

"Oh, my!" Cel'dion giggled again. "Thea, the blizzards are caused by the dragon's mating season! They become quite volatile during the winter months. Fights to the death are quite common. They kick up so much snow and wind with their giant wings that they actually manage to alter the weather and send a massive cold front down the mountain."

The Spellweaver sat stunned at the revelation. So much information had been dropped into her lap over the past twenty-four hours, she was sure she wouldn't get any sleep tonight. It'd be keeping her up until the early morning hours for sure.

She couldn't wait to tell Isabel this.

"That sounds like a lot of dragons being born every year," was what she ended up saying after a while. "Are you sure the barrier is going to continue to hold?"

"From what we've observed, the dragons only lay one egg in the summer. As Cel'dion said, fights to the death are quite common during mating season. The winner and sometimes other dragons will feast on the corpse, and if they go long enough without large enough prey, they will often kill one another."

Thea grimaced. "Guess it evens out then. Enough about dragons, though. I think I might get sick if I learn any more. I did have another simple question." When she had both elves' undivided attention, she asked, "What's the difference between mana and magic?"

"Nothing," Merrjewl stated simply.

"… What?"

"Mana is just what we elves refer to magic as," Cel'dion clarified. "The Huǒshān Clan has adopted that terminology as well, but there is no difference."

"But I see them using mana without any reagents! They don't use wands or dusts or anything."

The elves' faces took on a confused look once more. "Wands and dusts — they just amplify the magic you already have."

Thea slouched in her seat. "Well … yeah. But no one I've ever met has had enough power to use their magic without a reagent." Even Cressida used amplifiers.

Merrjewl hummed. "Well, you should be able to use some magic without these things. It may not be as powerful, but after the Wild Hunt spell is conducted correctly, you will notice a drastic difference in your power."

"Really?"

Cel'dion nodded. "Do not forget that two hundred years' worth of magic has not been put back into the land. Although I believe it will not right everything immediately. The influx of magic will feel like so, but it will take many years before the healing is complete. I doubt that the first Wild Hunt spell will afford the humans the ability to perform magic without these reagents you use."

"Their blood must be very diluted if what you say is true, my love," Merrjewl mused.

Thea felt herself bristle at the words, but she calmed when Cel'dion placed a hand on her lover's knee. She gave the Spellweaver a scrutinizing look before speaking softly to the Dark Elf. "I do not think she is aware of how to contain her magic. Her aura is wild."

The Dark Elf leaned back and crossed his arms over his wide chest. "I thought I sensed as much."

She looked between the two in frustration. She did not like being talked about as if she weren't even there. "What are you two talking about? What aura?" Peering down at herself, she saw nothing but air around her.

"Tell me," Cel'dion said instead. "Your magic is not very strong, correct? You sometimes have difficulty channeling it when not relying on these amplifiers?"

Thea felt heat crawl into the apples of her cheeks, and she stared at the floor. She never really minded her lack of magical prowess, but she believed even as a child in the academy that Summoner status was out of the question. Rafe had always excelled at magic, whether it was his concentration skills on highly advanced incantations or simply raw power. She'd tried her luck with the alchemical aspect of magic—the formulas, the history, the comprehension of what reagents reacted with what spells. Rafe had had her beat there as well.

"It's gotten better over the years," she admitted quietly after a moment. "It's not that big of a deal, anyway. I have my amplifiers."

"Yet you are unable to do this one spell," Merrjewl countered.

She felt herself bristle all over again and snapped her vision back toward the Dark Elf.

Cel'dion touched Merrjewl's shoulder lightly. "My love, let me handle this." Aiming her gaze at the Spellweaver, she gave Thea another heartwarming smile. "Let's try something, shall we?"

Thea shifted and narrowly looked at both elves. "Okay …"

"Let's close our eyes." Then, as if to demonstrate, Cel'dion closed hers. Thea sighed and followed the request.

"What color is your magic, Thea? Surely, you've noticed everyone's is slightly different? Maybe certain spells or dusts change the color, but when it is just you calling forth your magic, what color do you see?"

Thea's brow quirked as she tried to remember. She recalled her amulet's fleeting barrier jump to her defense in swirling purple. When she was in the armory before her mission to the desert, the arrow that manifested in the automatic crossbow was a light lavender color. So too were the cords that appeared when it linked up to her magic.

"Purple."

"Correct."

Thea's nose twitched at the comment, but she still didn't open her eyes. She did wonder why she needed to close them in the first place. "How do you know? And why'd you even ask?"

"I can see it, but rather than tell you, it's important you have that basic connection with your magic. You've worked with your magic long enough to discern what its true color is."

"Okay … now what?"

She heard a giggle come from the female elf. "Now, let us imagine a flowing river in your mind. It is a wild current, splashing up onto the banks, trailing off into oblivion with no end in sight."

Thea clenched her eyes shut tight as she pictured the river in her mind. It was as loud as the waterfall in the cave as the water rushed past her.

"Okay."

"The water should be purple just like your magic. The water *is* your magic. Do you see a stick at your feet?"

"No?"

A very male snort. "*Imagine* a stick at your feet," Merrjewl instructed.

If her eyes weren't closed, Thea would have rolled them. She imagined a stick at her feet. There weren't any trees nearby—none that she'd thought up—so she didn't know how it miraculously got there, but she wasn't going to fight her tutors on logic.

He continued. "Now, place the stick in the river to block the flow of the water."

Okay, Thea was going to need a bigger stick. Her brows furrowed as she turned the twig into a large tree branch. She began dragging the limb over to the river. Of course, it was lightweight (it was in her mind after all). She could make the stick purple, too, if she wanted to—great, now the branch was actually purple.

She groaned and rubbed at her face, but she had a feeling that if she opened up her eyes, the imagery would vanish, and she would have to start all over again. Why was this so difficult?

"Take a deep breath," Cel'dion said quietly. "Relax your shoulders, relax the muscles in your neck, in your face. That's it, there you go. Inhale … exhale."

Thea breathed out as she loosened up her body. The tree branch had reverted to its natural coloration, and now she laid it in the river. Because physics didn't matter, it didn't move even though the river's water rushed up around it and over it. She stared at it.

"Now what?"

Both elves chuckled, and she saw herself glare at nothing in her mind.

"Start building a dam. Your goal is to cut off the river's flow."

Thea wanted to scoff. Build a dam? Why couldn't she just imagine one already built?

But no matter how hard she tried, the dam wouldn't materialize. After several failed attempts, she gave up as she felt real-world sweat start to grace her temples. With the Light Elf's constant reminders to breathe and relax, she walked back and forth from the dam to the banks. Grabbing large sticks one at a time, she eventually cut off the river's flow.

With a headache emerging, she studied her efforts with a proud smile. She dared not open her eyes yet for fear she'd undo everything she just did. "Okay, it's blocked off. Won't it just get backed up and flow over the sides though?"

"Don't think too much of it," Cel'dion said around an amused smile. "You just stopped your magic from flowing out carelessly. The source of your magic only pumps out continuously if there's no control over that flow. You've been wasting so much, and you've had to expel more than necessary just to bring it forth visually. Open your eyes. Do you feel any different?"

Thea hesitated for a moment before her eyelids fluttered open, and she squinted at the suddenly bright light overhead. She rubbed at her temples as she tried to calm the rising headache, but then she paused.

It was subtle. So subtle in fact that she hadn't detected it at first. Doubtful she would have at all if Cel'dion hadn't pointed out the change.

She called to her magic, concentrating it to the tips of her fingers. The pressure she'd felt before when calling her magic—as if she'd had to force it to manifest—had been her normal. She did it without thinking most days, but now … it was as easy as breathing. Lavender sparks zapped from her fingers, and a breathless laugh escaped her as she watched in pure wonder. Her magic now rushed to her fingers just as the blood in her veins did. Effortlessly. Naturally. She willed it, and it happened just as if she willed a body part to move.

She turned to the elves, broad grin near beaming. Merrjewl's glittering eyes twinkled proudly as he smiled back at her. "I can sense an improvement. Now, let's try that spell."

Chapter Twenty-Nine

A Spell Reincarnated; a Remedy Rediscovered

"Wait!" Thea called out abruptly. "First, tell me what's written on the tablets. I've been wanting to know ever since you said you helped write what's on them."

Cel'dion looked surprised. "Oh. Hmm, well, for starters, the Wild Hunt spell is broken up into four parts. Each tablet has a part of that spell. The elders were petty like that. As for the rest, the tablet in the Black Forest had the desummoning spell on it. The tablet in the mountains tells the reader who Unsoul is, how he was a master of his domain in the sky, where terrifying dragons were born. They were created to destroy and bring death to Saellah's creations on land."

Thea shivered. "How awful. Some lover."

Cel'dion's lips thinned. "I concur. Admittedly, however, he did not do this maliciously. Where there is creation and life, there must be destruction and death. Without one or the other, the cycle cannot continue."

"The tablet also contains the incantation on how to contact the god, though I'd advise against it," Merrjewl informed. "He may be Saellah's heart-sworn, but he is not the Father where she is the Mother. Not even the wolves can lay claim as the sons and daughters of the god. Those who can, fly. Or used to anyway."

At Thea's silent question, Cel'dion waved at her. "We'll be here all day divulging secrets of the world's history. The tablet in the desert also brings up the dragons, but only for their blood. A dragon's blood—"

"Cures everything," Thea finished quickly. She felt herself grow pale as her own blood rushed from her face. She cursed. Then laughed. She wiped away the exhaustion from her face and groaned into her hands. "I didn't even know. The irony."

Merrjewl cleared his throat. "What irony?"

Thea sighed and leaned back. "I traveled to the desert not for the tablet, but because there's a myth circulating among the nomadic tribes that reside out there that Draconian blood cures things thought uncurable. We found the tablet by happenstance—actually …" Now that she thought about it, it had been the wyvern that had agreed to help them as long as they retrieved the tablet in the first place. "Why would a dragon want the tablet out of the temple so badly?"

The female elf looked toward her partner, but Merrjewl also seemed to be pondering her question. "Maybe because they are a different type of magic, they could sense the tablets swelling with power. It could have made them uncomfortable or disturbed them, as the natural order of magic in the world was becoming unbalanced. They also could have heard the sylphs crying out."

Thea rested her chin on her fist as she contemplated that theory. "I wonder if their voices ever did make it out of the temple. They told me they kept trying to reach someone. They're air elementals. Their voices could have carried on the wind. Maybe … maybe that was how the myths circulated to begin with? It's too much of a coincidence otherwise."

Cel'dion nodded. "There are few true coincidences in this world. Even if the goddess hasn't had a hand in some of life's designs, there is always an explanation for something."

Thea nodded and looked up. "And the final tablet?"

"The opposite of what the tablet in the mountains has written on it," the Light Elf said. "It lists a part of the Wild Hunt spell, but mostly it talks about Saellah, how she is the mother of magic and the creator of the celestials and elves. And, yes, it does list how to contact her, but the Mother has always been, um, fickle with answering her children. You could call to her a hundred times, and she might not ever answer you directly. Only the High Elves can demand an audience with her, but only once every thousand years."

The Spellweaver sat back and nodded. Countless thoughts ran through her head, and a lot of them she couldn't wait to tell a certain Summoner back home. She hadn't really anticipated having this conversation with the elves today—she hadn't anticipated *anything* that had happened today.

"What spell were you trying to learn again?" Cel'dion prodded.

Thea thought back to the library underground. The Skrittish. How old were they? Would the elves have any knowledge of them? The water that hung from the ceiling looked a lot like Merrjewl's eyes—perhaps it was related to dark magic somehow? She shook her head.

Stay focused.

"I found it in an old text. It's a containment, regeneration, and water spell all in one. It was used by humans to stay hydrated in the desert by keeping them from losing water through sweat. They would still stay cool, though, because of the spell. I wanted to know if it was possible to use on Namara. She's a demon, but she constantly drips water onto everything and—" *I've always looked at it as a burden until recently. I see how much it affects her, even if she likes to pretend it doesn't,* she finished silently. "She holds herself back from doing a lot of things because she doesn't want to get everything wet. But if she dries off, she dies."

Merrjewl hummed as he sat back in his seat, hand on his chin. "Do you happen to remember the incantation?"

Thea nodded and recited the verbal portion of the spell. "The ingredients for the spell are gold dust and the sweat of the person being enchanted."

"But Namara doesn't sweat," Cel'dion mused. "As for the gold dust, we can nix that, but remember to use it when you go to try it later." Her eyes trailed over to something, and the elf paused. "However, I would say we have the other ingredient."

Thea glanced over and found the puddle Namara had left behind after having sat on the stairs for a while. With a wave of her tanned hand, Cel'dion brought the water over to her in the form of a wobbly bubble. Instantly, Thea was brought back to the sanctuary. Cressida had waved her hand from the second-story balcony, and Thea had found herself outside in the cold. At first, once she knew the sorceress had been dabbling in the dark arts, she'd chalked it up to a black magic spell. But Cel'dion had said she doesn't practice— neither of them could practice anymore because of the attention it calls. It was true Cressida used amplifiers ... but was that all? Cressida had never been one to give a clear answer unless she wanted to. When Thea's ignorant assessment led her to believe Cressida was using black magic to fluctuate her magic and wave things around—well, the sorceress hadn't agreed nor disagreed. Had she somehow learned how to control her magic like the elves do? Like the Huǒshān Clan can?

Thea blinked, and her vision homed in on the wavering ball of water suspended just above Cel'dion's palms. The Light Elf eyed the liquid with interest. "I believe we will need to change some of the incantation to perform the spell."

Merrjewl nodded, fingers scratching his defined jaw. "I was thinking the same thing, my beloved. Hmm. Let me think. I'll have to move around a few pieces. Let's see … what about this: Fluid of infinite shape and form, reverse the untaught flow, surround the soul like a storm, remain within forevermore."

Cel'dion stared at her partner for a few seconds. Then she shrugged. "It works, I suppose."

The Dark Elf huffed. "I'm not a poet, love."

She giggled in response. "No, I guess not."

Thea hid her smirk behind her fist. Even though Merrjewl couldn't see it either way, she didn't want it to be so obvious. Especially when he aimed an especially affronted look at the Light Elf.

"Let's test it out, shall we?" Cel'dion went on to say, ignoring her lover's ruffled feathers. She dipped her hand into the orb of liquid and, holding her other hand up under it so it would keep its shape, she recited the incantation. Slowly, she let her magic fall away from the water.

It wobbled … undulated … gravity pulled it downward and then—

"Oh, look at that!"

Cel'dion faltered, and the bubble of water popped and spilled all over her lap.

"Ugh! Renkilo, you old coot!" she cried out, throwing the elder a most stern face.

The Clan Leader gave a hearty laugh, head tipped back and hand over his belly. "Ahaha, I really got you this time! It's been ages since I've been able to do that."

"You are much too sprightful for your age, Clan Leader," the female elf said with an annoyed pout, but her lips ticked up into an exasperated smile soon after.

Merrjewl pulled the water from his lover's lap with a flick of his wrist. An easy smile lightened his features as he asked, "What brings you out of your meditation so early?"

"Oh, is it early? I feel as if a couple hours have passed."

Thea balked. Had it really been that long since she first met the elves? It was hard to tell the passing of time without the sun sending shadows scattering. Despite being so close to the cave's ceiling, she also hadn't heard the howling winds outside. The snow must have fallen onto the wooden flats, insulating the cave from the noise.

"Anyway," Renkilo went on, "I was sent a message. Something urgent is apparently going on down below. Can't do anything without my input," The last part he groused out, but Thea's attention had been caught by the former statement.

"What's going on?" she asked, climbing to her feet and dusting herself off. Her legs were a bit stiff from having sat for so long.

Renkilo shrugged. "They didn't say, just encouraged me to make haste. They always do this, though, so I would not fret. It could be that one of the pigs has escaped again, for all I know."

Still, something within tugged at Thea. "I think I'll go down with you. Just in case."

The Clan Leader didn't look bothered by this. "Of course. Shall we go then?"

Thea turned and waved at Cel'dion. "I appreciate everything you've taught me today," she directed at both elves. "I hope this isn't the last time I come and see you."

Cel'dion smiled. "I should hope not. We would very much appreciate it if you came back."

Merrjewl grinned. "Maybe next time we can be the ones asking the questions."

"I'd like that." She turned to Renkilo. "Let's go."

Nothing appeared too out of the ordinary until they were closer to the ground. The lower they descended, the more Thea could make out the swarm of clan members huddling around the temple where she and the others had been staying. Alarm swept through her, and the hair on her arms stood at attention. As soon as they gracefully landed on the ground, she jumped off and quickly stumbled to the front of the temple.

"Let me through," she barked as she pushed past the clansmen.

Once she had passed the doors, she came to a jarring halt. Fatik was pacing over a prone Isabel. The redhead was cradled in Namara's arms, where the kelpie kept her cool, watery palm to Isabel's blazing forehead. Agni was crouched in front of his partner, still as a gargoyle, yet anxiousness was evident in the lines of his weathered face. A woman of the clan was flitting between a basket of supplies and the unconscious Isabel.

"What happened?" Thea demanded, gaining everyone's attention. The nameless woman went back to her herbs and oils, but Fatik came forward to explain.

"She overheated. We weren't—" he sighed in frustrated guilt and rubbed at his brow. "We weren't paying attention. I noticed her passed out first. By the gods, she was so red. Redder than her blasted hair."

Thea breezed past the Dragonkin and crouched down next to Agni. She cast her gaze down at the redhead but directed her question at the clanswoman. "Are your remedies working?"

The woman's head jerked up, and Thea met her gaze. Her dark hair had been pulled up into a messy bun, leaving only her chin-length bangs to dangle around her oval face. She bit her at her lips and shook her head. "Most of the heat is gone," she said quietly in a deep voice that spoke of her maturity. "But she is not receptive to our medicine."

"I can ride back to the *pagoda* and retrieve Merrjewl and Cel'dion," Renkilo said from the doorway. Thea glanced over her shoulder at the man and noted his calm demeanor, though that seemed to be a farce. His hands were hidden in his sleeves, so she couldn't detect any restless twitches, but he had most likely already mastered the art of remaining calm in the face of an emergency.

"No need, I can heal her with my magic." She wasn't a doctor, but healing spells were taught to all Coven members to cover all sorts of injuries or illnesses. Not many could reattach an arm after it was severed, but something like taking the excess heat from a body could be accomplished. Though she suspected Namara had more to do with that than the woman's herbal remedies. If Isabel wasn't receptive to them, then magic could override that.

"Wait," Fatik said, his voice like steel as he hurried over to Thea.

She paused from reaching into her dust pouch and leveled him with an impatient look. "What? I need to hurry, Fatik—"

Pale, luminescent eyes met hers defiantly. "She doesn't want magic to heal her. We need to try something else."

Thea stared at the Dragonkin. Then she exploded.

"WHAT?"

All three beings flinched, and the medicine woman scurried away to Renkilo's side.

"She doesn't—"

"Are you serious?" Thea bellowed, pushing on when it looked like Fatik was going to try and continue arguing with her. "The only reason she hasn't started convulsing is because Namara has been keeping her cool, but she could still slip into a coma if we don't do something *now!*"

"Then whatever Namara is doing could work!" Fatik tried to reason. He turned toward the kelpie, who was nervously eyeing both of them. "Can you control your body temperature? Could you make the water you expel cooler?"

Namara's mouth bobbed open like a fish's. "I mean, yes, but I—"

"See?" Fatik cut her off, turning to Thea with a plea in his gaze.

"You cut her off," the Spellweaver seethed, barreling on when Fatik grimaced. "What she was about to say is that *Isabel could go into shock.* I don't have time for this. *Isabel* doesn't have time for this. If you don't sit back and let me work, I will knock *you* unconscious and *then* heal her. I will not have her die on me, do you understand?"

Fatik stood and moved away, and his wings subconsciously unfurled from behind his back in defense. "There has to be another way. Isabel made me promise not to use magic on her again."

"Well, I made no such promise." She went to stand, about to say more. There was a verbal lashing just waiting on the tip of her tongue, but then she froze. It was as if the magic curtain rose, leaving the solution in the center of the stage with a big spotlight on it. Everything that had been spoken about with the elves came rushing back to her. Magic, the gods, the tablets—one in particular. She eyed Fatik, who was now warily staring at her.

"Fatik," she called, her voice now soft once again, "I ... I want to try something."

Fatik's wings ruffled on his back, and his pearly tail swished anxiously. "What?"

She looked back at Isabel. "I want to try something. But it's going to have to involve your blood."

Alarm then confusion morphed across the Dragonkin's face. "I'm not following."

"Do you want me to go against her wishes and heal her with magic dust?"

"Well, no—"

"Then give me your arm. It's one or the other. Make a decision—*now*."

Fatik jumped and rushed forward, holding out his arm even as his expression was hesitant.

Thea grabbed his arm and brought him back down to a crouching position, unholstered her dagger, and then laid the weapon over his perfect, flawless skin. At Namara, she ordered, "Open her mouth."

Namara complied, and with a quick, horizontal slash over his upper forearm, Thea angled the limb over the redhead's open mouth. The crowd at the door gasped, but she ignored them and kept her eyes on the wound. Dark red blood welled up and beaded at the shallow cut before falling away.

He's a quarter dragon, so more is probably needed.

Just as she suspected, Isabel's ruby skin began to pale, and her temperature plummeted. Thea dropped Fatik's already healed arm and used two fingers to check for a pulse at her throat. "It's stabilized."

Agni pushed passed her and took Isabel from Namara's arms. He stood easily and carried the still unconscious woman to her room. Namara quietly followed, though she kept throwing glances back Thea's way as she departed.

Thea fell back on her bottom and gave a breathless laugh. "It worked. It—I mean, of course it—I …" She laughed again.

"So that's what dad meant," she heard Fatik murmur. Then he sighed, and it was as if the weight of the world had fallen on his shoulders. "I can't do that ever again."

Thea whipped her head around to stare incredulously at the Dragonkin. "What are you talking about? You're a walking miracle! I know the citizens of Aeristria haven't treated Dragonkin very well, but that'll change once they hear—"

"Thea," Fatik interrupted, and his voice was steel once more. "It will kill me."

Chapter Thirty

A Fault Line of Faults

Thea stared at Fatik with wide, confused eyes. "What?"

Fatik sighed and glanced at the door. She turned to find Renkilo already ushering the clansmen out of the doorway. He peered over his shoulder to find them staring at him. "I will give you some privacy, but I would appreciate a status report when your companion wakes up."

Thea nodded. "Of course."

With that, Renkilo shut the door, and the two were left alone. Thea turned back and stared up at the tall being. "Okay, they're gone. Now what do you mean it will kill you?"

Fatik walked over to one of the supporting beams in the temple and slid down to the ground. Leaning his head back to stare at the coffered ceiling above caused the wispy, white strands of his hair to fall back over his shoulders. "It's complicated. Dad didn't really elaborate. He just said that our blood—our dragon blood—is our first treasure. A dragon's nature is to hoard, but do you know why?"

Thea strolled over slowly and knelt down before him. "Honestly, I just assumed it was a greed thing. My dad hoarded stuff all the time."

Fatik leveled her with a thoughtful look before staring off at something once more. "It's not a greed thing. It's a survival thing. Our treasure, things that we own—not what we've swiped, or stolen, or pillaged, or what have you—but the things we *own* are considered our actual, real treasure. Dad's going to be just fine—maybe a little miffed that we gave the map back, but that treasure was never his. If Renkilo had come down from the mountain and demanded it back, Dad would have to give it back or risk tarnishing his soul. That's the worst that could happen, but when a dragon gives away their *real* treasure, a part of them withers and dies. That's why when someone comes to us demanding something, threatening us over it, we have so many other things to give them. The more we hoard, the safer our real treasure is."

Thea let the words sink in fully after Fatik was done speaking, and she brought her hands to cover trembling lips. "Oh, goddess, I—I just …"

Fatik smiled at her. "It's okay, you didn't kn—*ow!*"

"You idiot!" she cried, punching him in the shoulder once again. "You should have let me heal her with my magic! You dummy!" She went to swing again, but Fatik hastily blocked it before hurriedly shuffling back.

"Will you stop hitting me? I didn't know that's what dad meant until now!"

"How could you not know!"

"I don't know!"

Thea groaned and scrubbed at her face. "This wouldn't have been an issue if you had just communicated with him!"

Fatik's wings flapped, and he scowled at her. "I know you're not talking."

"Your dad's not a—" She snapped her jaw shut and glared, not so much at Fatik but at the trap she'd set for herself.

Fatik dove in for the kill as he raised an eyebrow. "Yes, go on. My dad's not a what? Scumbag? I beg to differ."

Thea huffed, and she resigned herself to losing that battle. But she still needed to have the last word. "You said yourself he wasn't a *bad* dad."

The Dragonkin snorted and sat up once he was sure he wasn't going to get socked in the arm. Again. "Yeah, well, I never looked for mugs that read 'Number 1 Dad on Raen' so …"

Thea couldn't help but smirk at that, and she idly picked at the woven mat under her. Her smile fell quickly. "It just sucks, though."

"What does?"

"The fact that Dragonkin have been conditioned to hoard as a means of survival. The fact that beings come up to you and threaten you, or hurt you, or exclude you. The fact that those in Tolvade treat the Dragonkin the way they do. The fact that if giving away your blood didn't kill you, it would be such an easy way to win over the masses. I know it would only be that way because you're doing something for them, but still …"

Fatik shook his head and leaned back against the wooden beam. "Everyone has some deeply ingrained survival tactics in them. Running away, quick reflexes, freezing up. Ours just happens to be hoarding. And I don't think it'd be as easy to win over the humans as you say. I think it would be the opposite, actually."

Her head popped up. "What?"

"Realistically, Tolvade would be split in half. Yeah, you'd have those who would rejoice. Medusa's Kiss wouldn't be any more troubling than the common cold with us Dragonkin walking around with a needle permanently stuck in our veins."

Thea winced at the visual.

"But then you'd have those who would hate us even *more*. Why? Because we—or some of us, I guess—*knew* we could cure Medusa's Kiss and we did nothing. None of us stepped forward to cure anyone. The extremists would either kill us or kidnap us and force us to give up our blood. It wouldn't matter that a Dragonkin can't be forced. Our blood just turns to ash or smoke or whatever it turns into when extracted unwillingly. They'd still try, and when it didn't work, they'd just kill us. Those of us who gave it willingly would only be useful for so long, too. Our dragon blood doesn't regenerate as your blood does. It keeps itself alive for way longer than normal red blood cells can, but once our blood is gone, there's no getting it back. Then, once we outlived our purpose, they'd kill us. That or we'd just die."

Thea chewed on her lip. "Isn't that a bit extreme?" To think some were as cruel and hateful as he said disturbed her … and that there were beings out there that would drain him dry? Not to mention that the blood that he'd lost tonight couldn't be brought back. She felt sick to her stomach knowing that she had taken that away from him.

"Is it? Do you hear what they say about us when they think no one's listening?"

She swallowed as her eyes examined the Dragonkin. She took in his expression, the wisdom in his bright eyes, his pale lips thin in his seriousness. "I—I suppose I don't."

Fatik lent her a tired smile. "Demons aren't excluded either," he muttered quietly and nodded at their room.

Thea glanced over her shoulder just in time to see Namara sliding open the door. "She's awake." The kelpie began to fidget with her hands as she peered at the exit, avoiding Thea's gaze. "And she's asking for you, Thea."

"Where is she!" yelled a very angry Isabel from within the room.

Thea's expression hardened as she stood to her full height. "Thanks, Namara. You can wait out here if you want."

The demoness nodded and rushed out of the room. Angi stepped out after her much more slowly. He aimed a stoic look the Spellweaver's way, but he laid a heavy hand on her shoulder and nodded at her before following after Namara.

Gathering herself for what she knew would be an intense reaming session, she crossed the threshold and closed the door behind her. Several lanterns had been lit to illuminate the room in a warm, orange glow. Isabel sat back against the wall with her arms crossed over a bouncing leg. A scowl rested on her face, but unlike previously, where she had merely pouted or gotten fussy, this time she was properly angry. The way she was chewing on the inside of her lip, she was likely to gnaw the whole thing off.

"How dare you," she said seriously, and it was probably the only time Thea had ever heard her sound like the adult she was. She wasn't much older than Thea, but normally it was as if maturity had skipped the redhead altogether. Until now.

Thea leaned back against the wall on the opposite side of the room and waited patiently. There would be more. When she didn't immediately cave, there would be a tidal wave of anger washing over her. Isabel was waiting for a response, but Thea wouldn't give her one. Not yet. Because whatever excuse she gave wouldn't be good enough. Isabel wouldn't hear her out—at least, not until she was done venting. So, Thea kept her face in check and stayed quiet.

Finally, after realizing she wasn't going to gain a reaction from the Spellweaver, Isabel hopped up and started pacing. "You know how I feel about magic," she started off. Thea nodded, but Isabel wasn't looking at her. "You know I don't use magic. You know this, so why did you heal me? Huh? Why?" Her voice began to rise the more worked up she got.

Thea expected this. This was not the first time she sat through a lecture, an argument, a fight where she was expected to either stay quiet or have all her defenses shot down.

"Whatever happens to me happens to me," Isabel continued. "That's how I live my life! So why do you keep trying to push your ideology onto me? Why do I have to conform to your beliefs? I—don't—like—using—magic!"

Opening her mouth to say something, Thea thought better of it and sealed her lips. Better to let Isabel get everything out first.

"It's bad enough you forced me to use this barrier oil or whatever, but now you heal me? With magic? Who asked you to do that? Who said it was okay? I don't care if you or anyone else uses magic—I've never tried to push my beliefs onto others. So, why am I the one disrespected? Huh? Answer me that, Thea?"

Isabel was huffing by the end of her rant, having nearly worn a path into the woven floormats. Her skin was still pink, but Thea couldn't discern if that was still from the heat, the orange color of the room, or her mounting frustration.

She took a breath and asked in as calm of voice as she could, "Are you done?"

Isabel sent her a scathing look. "Don't patronize me!"

Her jaw clenched. "I'm not. I'll give you my reasons, but I don't want to be interrupted when I do."

The redhead stopped pacing and angrily crossed her arms back over her chest. She was back to chewing her inner lip again, and her eyes had set in a hard stare, but she was quiet.

"I saved your life because there was no other option," she began. She straightened up from the wall and made direct eye contact with Isabel—something the redhead couldn't hold for very long. "Namara had you in her arms first to try and cool you down, but that's all it did. It wasn't stopping the heat from affecting you physically or mentally, and the medicine woman the clan brought in was trying her herbal remedies to fix the issue. Except you weren't receptive to those remedies. You were minutes away from convulsing, slipping into a coma, *dying*, Isabel. I saved your life with not even my magic, but Fatik's—" she paused and quickly debated if she could trust the redhead with such information. She looked Isabel up and down and decided *yes*, she could trust her because even if the redhead never forgave *her* for what she'd done, she wouldn't take it out on the Dragonkin in the room behind them. "I used his blood to help heal you.

Dragon's blood is still a type of magic, but it's natural—more natural than potions and powders, and I thought you would appreciate that much at least." That was a lie. She'd just been trying to get Fatik to cooperate with her. Something she still felt immensely guilty about. "Which, by the way, is something that can't get out to the general public for his safety," she added when she caught the contemplative look in the researcher's gaze.

After a few moments of silence, Isabel's quiet voice rang out in the small room. "I didn't ask you to save my life."

Flabbergasted, Thea balked. "Of course I'm going to save your life!"

"I didn't ask you to!" she shouted back, much louder than before.

"You didn't have to!"

"If I die, I die! That's how life is!"

"Not when you can prevent that from happening!"

"I would have died without the use of magic, so I wouldn't have been able to prevent it at all!"

Thea could feel her anger, her indignation rising. She had never met someone so ungrateful for being saved in her whole life. Something inside her snapped. "I don't CARE if you want to go off and die on your own! But I am NOT having you burden the team with your absolute SELFISHNESS because you hate using magic! What am I supposed to do, haul your lifeless body back to the Coven along with the tablet? Dump you at the Council's feet and go, 'Yeah, sorry about this and all. I could have saved her, but she chose death over a recovery spell. Oh well!' Really? Should I have made Agni carry you in his arms, knowing that if you hadn't been so stupidly stubborn, you would be alive? How dare *I*? How dare *you* to put all of us through that! All because you don't like magic! That much? Why? Why do you hate magic so much that you'd be willing to risk your life and haunt the rest of us for the rest of ours?"

"You know why I hate magic!" Isabel screamed.

"Because your mom couldn't use it?" Thea yelled back just as loudly. Vaguely, she was aware the rest of the clan could probably hear their argument, but she didn't care in the moment. "Did your mom hate the fact that she couldn't use magic? Is that why you don't use it? You said she saw it as a gift! So why, Isabel? Enlighten me!"

"It doesn't matter—"

"IT DOES MATTER! It matters when you almost kill yourself over it! It matters when you put me and everyone else at risk because you'd rather die than use a simple healing spell!"

Isabel shut her mouth, but flames still warmed her dark brown eyes.

Thea had passed the point of empathy. She had watched Coven members lose their lives on the battlefield. She had seen horrendous injuries that couldn't be healed take out veterans. Death wasn't a constant in the Coven, but it came with the territory, and if you could prevent it, you did. "Did your mother resent magic so much that she would prefer you dying before you used it?"

Isabel's eyes widened, and Thea would later hate herself for how she latched onto that weakness. She stalked forward, and Isabel flattened up against the back of the wall. "If your mom were alive, do you think she would have been happy with your decision? Do you think she wouldn't have felt guilty at all, knowing her own daughter let herself be killed because of some ideal that using magic was bad? Because she couldn't use magic, her daughter decided death over a simple *healing* spell was worth it?"

The fight had started to seep out of the redhead. Her gaze had drifted, no longer avoiding but seeing into the unseen. Thea backed off, but she wasn't done.

Softly, she whispered, "Is that why you have a metal leg? Because instead of saving yourself, you pushed yourself into a corner on some wild adventure and paid the price with flesh? What would your mother think?"

A tear slipped down Isabel's cheek, and the floodgates opened thereafter. With horror, Thea realized she'd pushed too far. She stepped back as the girl in front of her crumpled to the floor and sobbed. *"I'm sorry*. I'm *sorry,"* she repeated, over and over.

Thea surged forward but halted just as quickly. Her gaze darted around the room, but nothing was of use. She cursed quietly and slammed open the door behind her. She found Angi pacing near his room on the opposite side, and he quickly met her eyes.

"Go to her," she snapped, though there was no anger to her words. All the rage had been sapped from her, leaving her drained and shaky. All that mattered now was Isabel's state of being. "Just go," she said again quickly, even as Agni marched toward the room. Isabel's cries were getting louder and could be heard even as the door shut behind the demon.

Thea didn't even see Namara come to her, but when cool, wet hands grasped her by the arm, she didn't shake the kelpie off. She let herself be led to the males' room. She briefly saw Fatik shrink in on himself on the floor, but the sides of her vision were going gray.

Isabel was crying. Isabel was crying because of her. Because of what she said. She was awful. She was horrible. One moment she was standing with the sensation of wet and cool on her arms, and the next she was on the ground trying to breathe.

"Thea!" Muffled. All of it muffled. It was all her fault. All of it.

Black eyes stared at her. She was looking at black eyes. She felt wet and cool sensations on the sides of her face.

Isabel crying. Isabel was crying.

Breathe. Stay—me. Her words? No …

Her chest hurt. Her chest was hurting. Her throat was raw. Wet and cool everywhere now. Tight—too tight. Everything was too tight. Bright white flared in her vision and *shifted*. The world shifted. She was weightless. Everything was blurry, dark around the edges. She couldn't breathe—why couldn't she breathe?

"It's okay," someone was saying. Namara. Namara was holding her.

"Breathe, Thea," someone else was saying. Fatik. Fatik was in front of her. His wings were spread wide. She could see nothing else.

She hurt Fatik, too. Took something he couldn't get back. She could have killed him. She was awful. Selfish. Horrible.

Her chest hurt. With every shallow breath, a pang. With every deep, shuddering inhale, a flare of tight heat washed through her chest with a vengeance. Her face was wet, eyelashes clumped together. Cool, wet arms wrapped around her from behind. Her back was damp.

The image of Isabel crying flashed through her mind over and over and *over*, and she let out another sob. It hurt, but she couldn't stop it. She'd broken the girl. She'd yelled at her. Screamed at her. Latched onto her weakness, brought her mom into it. How dare she? How could she have done something like that? Isabel would never forgive her. She wouldn't ever forgive herself.

It's your fault! It's all your fault!

Were those her words, or her mother's? Did it matter? Did it matter when it was the truth?

"Shhh," Namara soothed from behind. She could feel gentle swipes of the kelpie's thumb go over her arms in an attempt at comfort. "It's okay. It's going to be okay." But it wasn't. It wasn't okay. It wasn't going to *be* okay.

With another sob, she settled back with a shiver into Namara's arms. Then she let unconsciousness slip over her.

It's your fault.

Chapter Thirty-One

What Makes the Magic

A magpie was staring at her from afar. There were dozens of white and black birds scattered in barren trees, echoing their repetitious calls as the sun's faraway rays fractured over their feathers and created shifting hues of turquoise and teal. But one … one was just staring at her. Frozen against the chaos of fluttering wings, it watched her.

Its beak opened, but no sound came from it. Then—

It's your fault!

Ice shocked her veins as she froze. All the birds stopped moving before snapping their necks in her direction almost violently.

She stepped back once. Twice. On the third step, they burst from the trees.

It's your fault! It's your fault! It's all your fault!

Talons outstretched, they swarmed her. They grabbed at her shirt and tore at her flailing arms. She couldn't hear herself scream over the vicious caws.

Humanoid hands yanked her back—fingers pressed bruises into her skin. Wrapped around her throat. Ripped through her curls. Nails dug into her shoulders.

It's your fault! It's your fault! It's all your fault!

Thea gasped and shot up in her bed.

Wait a moment.

Her gaze darted around, but—though similar—this wasn't her room. She looked down at her lap, finding her fingers curling in a blanket with a woven design on it. This wasn't hers either. She looked around again as her heart settled in her chest. She winced at a particular deep breath and brought a hand to massage her sternum (not that it would help). Great. That would bother her for an hour or two if she didn't get a healing spell to mend the muscles in her chest.

Healing spell ...

Her eyes widened, and she flung the covers off her legs. She stumbled to her feet but paused. What was she going to do? What was her plan? What was she supposed to say after *that?*

Images of Isabel's lip trembling right before she crumpled to the ground flashed before her eyes once more. The whole argument was a blur, as was everything after that. She remembered walking out of the room and telling Agni— something. She peered around the room again. A wet spot was still on the ground—Namara had been here. Fatik's bags were shoved up against the far wall. This was the males' room.

She crept closer to the sliding door but waited. She strained her ears, tipped her head to the side and stayed as still as she could. Nothing. There were no voices coming from the entrance room. She took a deep breath, winced at the action, and slid the door open. Her head hurt, her chest was tight, and her eyes felt strained, but she wasn't going to sit in the room all day. Or night. She didn't know what time it was.

As soon as she crossed the threshold, the door on the other side of the room slid open. Thea's breath caught in her throat, and she stiffened when her gaze clashed with Isabel's.

A pregnant silence descended, swelling the room with tension so thick that Thea found it hard to breathe again.

Isabel looked—well, Thea thought it impolite to comment even within her own mind. She was sure she wasn't looking much better. Red-rimmed eyes glanced at Thea, taking the Spellweaver in. Her posture was slumped, her lips downturned into a lifeless frown. She didn't appear hostile or even angry. She wasn't bursting into tears at the mere sight of Thea, but apathy was a more concerning state if Isabel's indifference was a form of stonewalling through her emotions. It meant she no longer cared—about anything.

Perhaps she was jumping to conclusions, though.

Isabel's mouth bobbed open for a moment, but she seemed to think better about saying anything. In pure Isabel fashion, she went back and forth with herself, and her warring emotions were easy to discern as they played out on her heart-shaped face.

Eventually, she muttered something.

All Thea could hear, though, was her heartbeat in her own ears.

"What?"

Isabel sighed, and immediately, Thea regretted her words. But, in a clearer voice, the redhead repeated, "We can talk … if you want to."

Thea found herself nodding and following behind her as they headed back into their assigned room. She contemplated shutting the door, but she thought better of it. Closing it would be claustrophobic. It wasn't like it mattered much with them being the only ones in the temple.

"Where is everyone else?" She hedged awkwardly as she stood by the door, picking at her cuticles.

Isabel slid down in the same spot where she broke down earlier, and again, Thea was hit with a barrage of images.

It's all your fault.

"I think they're talking to Renkilo," Isabel said, unaware or unaffected by the conflict going on in the Spellweaver standing across from her. In the same exact positions they were in earlier. Isabel found more interest in the pilling blankets. "I told them I wanted to be left alone."

Thea nodded. She wasn't sure what else to say, and so she was left to stand there idly. Awkwardly.

She hated this. She should apologize.

"I—"

"Sorry about earlier," Isabel rushed out, beating her to the punch. She still wasn't looking at Thea. Her attention had turned to the ceiling. "I get ... *passionate* about not using magic. I live my life every day without so much as thinking about it to solve the problems I run into, and this trip ... it feels like I've been having to compromise the whole time. So, when I woke up earlier, and I felt the same way I normally do after I use magic or have magic used on me—I just—I can tell, and I hate it. And I knew you were the only one who would have healed me. At the time, I didn't care that I could have died. I've always known that if I died, it would be on an exploration. That never stopped me from leaving to go on one, though."

Thea slid down the wall and brought her knees up. She cringed at the small flare-up in her chest as she rested her chin on her crossed arms, but the pain was fleeting. The feeling she was more focused on came from Isabel's words.

"Mom wanted me to use my magic. She wanted me to show her things she couldn't do, but I wanted to be just like her. Hattie would show off what she knew, and she studied a lot to impress mom with more and more complex stuff. When she died …" she sighed. "I know mom would have wanted me to use magic to keep myself alive. But I bypassed having to use it with Agni around."

She looked down at her lap and began rolling up her pants leg. Brass metal gleamed in the low light. It was the shape of a flesh-and-blood leg but had grooves running down the shin piece. Thin pipes ran the length of the calf while nuts and bolts kept the pieces together. Clockwork gears moved with each shift of her leg while a small chronometer ticked away on the side, each with different levels of numbers under the glass. It was the most complicated yet compact machinery Thea had ever seen.

"I lost my leg a couple years ago in Banshee Bog. I was trying to get a specimen of those glow bugs. They're only in the swamp at certain times at night. I was … stupid." She huffed a humorless laugh. "I overestimated Agni's ability to protect me. Tree snatched me up real quick-like, and the leg was already under the roots before Agni could rip me away. I could have used magic to trap the bugs. To lure them over somewhere safer. I could have flung spells to keep the monsters away. I could have used magic to stop the bleeding. But I was so against using magic, the healing took three times as long as it should have. Agni refused to go on any expeditions for a year."

She looked fond as she stared off into space, reminiscing. Thea didn't interrupt. Isabel was opening up to her. She was trusting her with *everything*. Even after everything she did to her.

"I was still as stubborn as a soot stain about not using magic, so I used a big chunk of my savings to import this bad boy from Starsheena. Had to ride all the way to Half Heart Bay to hire someone. But, I'd rather have this than some magically runed prosthetic. Plus—" she knocked on the metal, and a solid *thunk* echoed back, "this makes for a lot better weapon when kicking beings upside the head." She grimaced as she remembered something unpleasant. "Connecting the nerves though … Felt like losing the leg all over again."

She pulled her pants leg down and looked away with a sigh. It was quiet for a few moments, but Thea knew she wasn't done. After another several minutes, she smiled, and it was spun like thin glass. Fragile. "Agni got me to calm down. He's good with that kinda stuff. No one would think so lookin' at him. I remember thinking 'What would I do without you?' and … well. Suffice it to say, it made me think. 'Cause, if I think that way about him, he's gotta think that way about me, right? And then I thought about how I—" the smile wobbled. A crack in the glass. "I thought about not being here anymore and what that would mean for him and where he would go and what would he do and, and …" She took a deep breath. "It ain't right, what happens to demons when their partner dies. Yeah, they get assimilated into society, but that really just means they get swept to the side. They get forgotten. They didn't have a choice in coming here. And the common folk don't really like dealing with them, especially the scary-lookin' ones like Agni. So, they get shoved even further away or have to take up shady jobs just to survive." Another deep breath. The crack had mended. "I'm not gonna live forever, either, so … I gotta find something for him to do before I die. But I gotta be *alive* to find something. So …" She looked up at Thea and held her gaze. The smile she wore now was less fragile. Tired, but genuine. "Thanks for saving me. Even if it meant using magic. I'm not … I'm not gonna use it for everything. I manage just fine. But—in the future—if … if I *need* it, I'll use it. I got it in me, ya know. Dang bank wouldn't keep my stuff in a protected vault otherwise. Not them snobs."

Thea returned her smile, but it fell as shame gripped her. "You're welcome, but I'm sorry too. I shouldn't have said the things I did. I felt like my decision was rational, and I felt like my argument was logical, but how it was delivered was … poor. I shouldn't have yelled at you. I shouldn't have said I didn't care if you ran off on a solo mission and died. I would care. I *do* care. I," her voice cracked, and she forced herself to take a deep breath. "I shouldn't have said some of the other things. At the end. That … That was uncalled for."

Isabel gave her a wry smile. "Nobody's perfect. We all say and do stuff we later regret. Well, the reasonable ones do. Know some beings personally that think they're all that and a bag of runes."

The Spellweaver snorted. "Same. What's worse is when you're related to them."

She grimaced. "Ugh. Man, that's gotta be fun." She rolled her head back and stared at the ceiling. "Oh, full disclosure. You got my permission to heal me again should anything bad happen. Just wanted to make that clear."

Thea hummed and stood up. She made her way over to the redhead and held out her hand. When Isabel found her gaze, she gave the girl a smirk. "Let's hope it doesn't come to that. Now, let's go find the others."

Isabel took her hand and hauled herself to her feet. "I told you where they were."

"Yeah, yeah, yeah," Thea said as she waved a hand at her. "You also said you *think*, which is never a good thing."

"Oi! You take that back!"

Thea giggled, and she felt a lightness seep into her chest. She'd still need a healing spell to soothe the muscles there … but this feeling … It was nice.

Chapter Thirty-Two

A Parallel World

Isabel's words kept repeating in her head later that night. It was late evening, and they had all regrouped and dined with Renkilo once more. This time, Siàu had also joined them, bringing the food Khien had cooked them up, and there was no one to play music. No matter. Their chattering filled the room just as loudly over another different but delicious dinner.

However, Thea had been distracted from the conversation and banter as thoughts raced in her mind. Not about what she had done earlier, or Isabel's breakdown, or their apologies, or anything related to their fight at all.

It ain't right, what happens to demons when their partner dies. I'm not gonna live forever, either, so … I gotta find something for him to do before I die.

She stole glances at Namara, half hanging out of the tub with a bowl in her hands all throughout their meal, and the kelpie had met her eyes a couple of times with looks of concern. Thea dismissed there being anything wrong with a shake of her head, and Namara didn't press.

"How's the weather looking outside?" Fatik asked, and Thea blinked back to the present. She found the Dragonkin still struggling with his chopsticks, but he was at least getting the food to his mouth. Even if he had to use both hands.

"Dreadful," Renkilo said before giving a hearty chuckle. A rosy hue tinted his cheeks, but it was nothing compared to their first night here. He was still coherent at the very least. "But I do believe that in a few days it should clear up enough for your adventure to continue. Ah, all good things must come to an end."

Thea made a mental note to give Rafe a status report tomorrow. A soft tap on her shoulder had her glancing over at Siàu, who sat beside her.

"Would you like some more tea?" she asked softly. A smile graced her lips, and it was a total transformation from when they'd first arrived. What a difference a day made.

"Yes, thank you."

The woman held back her billowing sleeve, revealing her tanned arm as she elegantly poured more tea from the kettle into Thea's cup. Small scars were prominent and dark against the tawny backdrop of her forearm.

"What do you say, Thea?" someone asked.

Thea swung her head over to Isabel's direction and met expectant, brown eyes. She stared for a moment, hoping to recall what the redhead had said. Nothing came to her, though.

"Sorry, I have no idea what we're talking about."

Renkilo snorted a laugh, and Isabel groaned. "And everyone calls me absentminded. Dude, I *said* we should head out the day after tomorrow. It'll be a lot of snow and all, but we got Agni and Namara. Plus, Fatik can fly—"

Affronted, the Dragonkin snipped, "No, I can't. These wings glide. I told you guys that."

Isabel paused. Then it was like a light spell went off in her head. "*Oh yeah.* Well, anyway, we got Agni and Namara. We should be fine, right?" Again, she aimed those questioning eyes Thea's way.

She mulled the idea over in her head as she brought another bundle of smooth, stringy noodles to her lips. She'd miss these dishes when she went back. "We can at least check it out, but if it's still too dangerous, we'll have to wait." As much as she would miss the hospitable Huǒshān Clan, she had work to get back to. The Coven would need all tablets to prepare for the Wild Hunt spell, and they didn't have a lot of time left before the ritual would be performed.

"Then it's settled," Isabel announced loudly, smacking her hands together. "What should we do tomorrow for our last day?"

"That's *if* tomorrow is our last day here," she reiterated.

"Yeah, whatever, dude."

The conversation bled together once more, with Thea catching bits and pieces of unfolding plans. Her eyes wandered over to Namara a few more times, but the kelpie was absorbed in everyone's banter.

I'll talk to her tonight.

With that settled in her mind, she soon found herself incorporated into the fun and lightheartedness once more. Even Agni was smiling along. Siàu was giggling quietly. Renkilo was cackling obnoxiously the more his cup was tipped back, following alongside Isabel on her grand recount of some wild adventure she'd once found herself in. Fatik was staring in increasing worry and stress the more Isabel continued. Namara was engrossed, black eyes shiny and wide and giving rapt attention to every hand gesture Isabel made.

Once again, Thea felt a sensation in her chest. It was different than when it was just Rafe and her. This was warm, too, but easy and light and … She wasn't sure how she could describe something she'd never felt before. The closest she'd ever come to this was the night she stayed up with Blythe in the desert. She just knew she liked it, and she hoped it wouldn't change anytime soon.

"Come on, Agni! We gotta try again!" Isabel insisted as she pushed with both hands up against the immovable wall of muscle that was the rakshasa. He peered down at her in what Thea could only describe as amusement. "Ugh! Come on, ya big oaf! We gotta get a specimen of those moonglows! We can compare them to the glow bugs in Banshee Bog when we get back home—oh!" She stopped pushing and looked up at Agni with big, wide eyes. "You can turn into that dragon-horsey thing again! Let's go, let's go!"

Eventually, a bouncing Isabel managed to yank Agni out the door, and Thea might have thought about how she resembled an overly excited, small, yappy dog on a leash.

Renkilo and Siàu had left a little while ago, and Fatik had retired to his room. That meant it was only Thea and Namara left. She pivoted and found the kelpie staring at the door Isabel and Agni had just left out of with fond exasperation. Then she met Thea's gaze.

"All right, out with it. You've been staring at me all night. Are you okay?"

Caught with no out, Thea gave the kelpie a sheepish grin. "I'm fine. I wanted to talk to you about a couple of things. Also," she added, almost having completely forgotten, "after that, I want to work on the spell again."

Intrigued, Namara followed her into their room. She walked back over to her tub and settled in while Thea dropped down onto her futon. She didn't know where to start, so she began with what had been on her mind all throughout dinner. She stared up at the ceiling as she licked her suddenly dry lips.

"Isabel brought to my attention something. Something I already knew, but it wasn't something that I made a big deal of."

Namara made a curious noise.

"About what happens to Coven-issued pets after their owner—" she grimaced as soon as the word left her lips, "er, their partner dies. It got me thinking."

"What did you think about?" Namara asked after a moment of silence.

She let go of the breath she'd been holding. "About you and what will happen when I die. About what's already happening. About ..."

"Things you never had to think about before?"

"Yeah."

Namara went quiet again, and Thea turned over to watch the kelpie. She was hanging over the tub, arms crossed, and her all-black eyes were staring at something Thea couldn't see.

"It's funny," she began, but Thea didn't see amusement in her seafoam-green features at all. "I was just thinking about something similar earlier today. When we were all there, and the elves were telling us about the Great Divide and … yeah."

Thea sat up. "What do you mean?"

Namara waved a hand around lazily in the air. "The elves … The Light Elves, I should say, treated the Dark Elves so badly. They cast them out. It got me thinking, too."

After another moment of silence, Thea prompted, "About?"

"What's the difference?"

Confused, she asked, "What do you mean?"

Namara sighed. "What's the difference between then and what's happening now? What's the difference between the Light Elves and the humans? I thought at first, well, the humans don't kill us when we're done being of use. They cast us out, throw us to the side of town they like forgetting about when they're done with us, but they don't kill us. But … then I remembered the tablets. Mokana told me about the one that was taken from the Black Forest. She heard the gossip through the pets' pipeline that it had a desummoning spell on it."

"That's right. The elves confirmed it for me earlier."

She finally met Thea's gaze, and her gaze was hard as steel. "Who's to say, after the Wild Hunt spell, they won't just desummon the demons they're done with? Throw us back into the underworld without a care? And why should they? We came from there. It doesn't matter if we have morals now. That we've been gifted with intelligence. That we're no longer feral." She went quiet again, brooding once more as silence weighted the room. "I used to think that Borlimane was all I had to expect once … whenever you died. Maybe I would die if a bigger, older, more powerful demon came along. Like a devil. Or a demon prince. And then you encountered one and I … Whatever, it doesn't matter now. I didn't have much to look forward to when I thought about life after your death, but now …" She shrugged, but Thea felt the hurt Namara was trying to hide. "I wonder if all I'll have to look forward to is darkness once again. Only this time, I'll be aware of everything."

Thea slowly pressed her back against the wall. She needed something solid to ground her. Her mind was a whirlwind of thoughts, but most of them were as dim and dark as what Namara suspected. She tried pushing past that. "We don't know if that's what the Coven is going to decide."

Namara eyed her, and her dark green lips thinned. "What happens when there are more demons than humans? What happens when there are more demons in town than the magic fauna? What happens then? You don't think that will incite some kind of panic?"

"But you're not feral. You wouldn't hurt anyone—"

Namara shook her head, effectively cutting Thea off. "*You* know that. Other Coven members know that. Some non-Coven members know that, but what's happening right now, Thea? Ferals are running amok. The beings of Tolvade are scared of their own shadows even as they're trying to go back to their normal lives. They jump at the sight of a demon. It doesn't matter if a Coven member is standing right next to them. What happens when they start seeing demons on every corner, every time they turn their head? What happens when they realize they're outnumbered?"

Thea chewed her lip. She knew the truth. It would incite panic. Isabel and Agni were proof. The ogre Rafe had blasted with an intelligence spell had been the talk of the town for *weeks*. How would the city have reacted if Cressida had been discovered tethered to a demon prince? A *demon prince*.

She gasped sharply, and the water in the tub sloshed as Namara flinched back. She looked up at the kelpie, and she could feel a glow about her as the idea took root. "What if we brought back tethering stones?"

Namara's brow scrunched. "What? Why?"

Thea stood up, the excitement in her too great to have her sitting down. "The whole reason tethering stones were done away with was so beings like Cressida couldn't tether themselves to really powerful demons—but what happened?" She prompted, hoping Namara was following her.

"She tethered herself anyway?"

"She tethered herself anyway!"

"So …?"

Thea huffed. "So, if beings like Cressida are going to find a way to tether themselves regardless of it being illegal, the Coven could bring the stones back and regulate them better. Demons already here, who have already been blessed with an intelligence spell, who have already been trained, could be tethered to new Coven members. We could stop summoning altogether!"

Namara's eyes widened. "They would be able to pick their partner, too. It would put a stop to pairing Coven members with demons who don't mesh well. But wait, what would the Summoners do if their main job was taken away from them?"

Thea sat back down and brought her hand up to her chin in thought. "I'm not sure … They're going to be needed to desummon the ferals, but after that …" Her thoughts rushed through her as she tried to latch onto something, anything.

Fire danced around her. Smoke caught in her lungs. Cackling laughter sharp in her ears. Fingers grabbed at her—

"Thea?"

Thea took a deep breath and blinked a few times. She found Namara's gaze on her, concern in her shiny, dark eyes. "We could convince the Coven to increase patrols around Borlimane. The Blood Mages … they're like cockroaches. I don't think we'll ever get rid of them fully. We could also improve the escort service to Half Heart Bay. We have an outpost stationed at the port, but even I know it's lacking in its enforcement." She chewed her lip. "It's worth bringing up to the Council."

"I think that's a great alternative," Namara murmured. Her eyes shifted about as her thoughts raced through her head. A wide smile split her face, and Thea felt that same sensation as earlier during dinner. "Do you think you can convince the Council?"

Thea paused and slowly sat back against the wall once more. She began chewing her lip as she considered all the options. "I know Isabel would be on board. So would Rafe and Mokana."

"So would all the demons in the Coven, and all the demons that have had to leave the Coven," Namara added.

"Really?"

She nodded. "Every demon's thought about it. Maybe not being re-tethered, but the ones Mokana talks to … they all want to come back. Not because the Coven went out of their way to be overly kind to them, but it gave them a purpose."

"Then I'll bring this up to the Coven. I might not be able to when we first get back." She sighed and realized the weight of this mission and everything that she had learned since embarking on it. "I have so much to report. But I promise I'll bring it to their attention. They're going to ask me about what I want to do when we get back anyway. If I want to stay a Spellweaver or become a Summoner. I'll give them my answer and then bring it up then."

Namara perked up. "Do you have an answer yet?"

She sighed. "No … I don't know what I want to do. Especially if I'm about to bring up all the stuff that could potentially throw all the Summoners' duties into the nearest bin."

The demoness snorted. "I guess it's a good thing your future-gazing partner is getting promoted."

Thea felt her face color. "Yeah, well, don't think I don't see how close you and Agni are getting. Are you guys …?"

It was Namara's turn to color, and she slipped down into the tub until only her eyes peered over the edge. Even then, Thea could see how soft they became at the mention of the demon. "He's so sweet. I finally got him to say more than a couple of words to me the other day." She giggled as she remembered. "I love his deep, raspy voice. He usually tries to communicate without having to talk, and it's sweet, but I …" she sighed dreamily, and the rest was lost to her imagination.

Thea laughed and stood up. "Well, what do you say we surprise him?"

That got a reaction out of her. "What do you mean?"

"It's time to try out the spell."

Namara squinted at the Spellweaver and lifted herself out of the tub. "You're more confident this time. What changed? Did you figure it out?" Her eyes lit up. "Oh! That's right, you asked the elves to help you."

Thea nodded, and she couldn't help the large grin that spread out over her face. "I did. We had to reword the spell, and we were going to test it out, but …" Her smile fell. "Well, it was about Isabel."

"Ah," the kelpie said in understanding. She peered curiously up at her partner. "So … you don't actually know if it will work this time?"

Thea took a deep breath and released it. She didn't need all this extra tension in her chest right now. "No —*but*, I have a feeling." She reached around for her dust pouch on the ground and dipped her fingers into her gold powder. She then straightened up and held out her hand. "Give me your hand. This, uh, this might take a while for me to concentrate, so just bear with me and don't interrupt."

Namara gave her a curious look but only nodded and stepped out of the tub. She held out her palms, and Thea closed her eyes and grabbed onto both of them. Only when she could feel the water running over her fingers did she begin.

The river in her mind was still held back by the dam that she had painstakingly built up. However, a few pieces had slipped away, and the lavender-colored water was seeping through the cracks. One by one, she began to haul large tree limbs over to it and placed them on top. She didn't know how long she had taken, but her concentration hadn't broken once from Namara pestering her.

She wasn't exactly sure what to do next, but she let her thoughts guide her. Slowly, she sat down with her legs crossed just in front of the dam. She held out her hands and took a deep breath. The rest of the world was numbed out, but—distantly—she could still feel a cool, wet sensation around her physical fingers.

Fluid of infinite shape and form, reverse the untaught flow, surround the soul like a storm, remain within forevermore.

She said it again. And again. And again. She could feel the water behind her churning, pushing and pulling as she chanted the spell. She wanted this with every fiber of her being, not for herself, but for Namara. She could feel the magic surge against the dam, but she would need to control it better before it would work for her. It was something she just *knew*. She couldn't break down the dam with her hands. She couldn't do anything but sit there and will her magic to flow over, to work in her favor.

She repeated it again, and again, and again, and with each chant the water grew stronger, fiercer, battering against the dam in her mind as it tried to come forth at her beck and call.

Fluid of infinite shape and form, reverse the untaught flow, surround the soul like a storm, remain within forevermore!

The water surged over the dam and spilled onto her. She could feel the cold, thrilling sensation *ping* through her chest as it raced up her arms and through her fingertips. She heard Namara gasp, and when she opened her eyes, the kelpie was stumbling back. Slowly, she wiped her hands off onto her pants until they were dry. Then she held her arm out, palm raised.

Namara was looking down at herself in confusion, but when she glanced up at Thea and her gaze caught on the Spellweaver's outstretched hand, she crept forward. Her fingers reached out, hesitated. Every emotion Thea had ever seen flickered across her pale green face. Her eyes danced around, focusing on every point of Thea's face, the hand waiting for her, her own hand.

Years of silent turmoil, annoyance, apprehension, uncertainty, inconvenience … could all be gone with one spell.

Her palm graced Thea's, but that was only half the battle. Thea looked down at where they touched. She could feel Namara's cool skin against her own, but when the kelpie pulled back, Thea couldn't feel any wetness left behind.

Both of their eyes were glued to Thea's palm, and Thea even whipped it around to inspect it up close.

Nothing.

No water. No dampness. No slime.

They stared up at each other for a silent, tense second. Namara's eyes shone with a new layer of wetness, and her next breath was as watery as she was. "Do it again," she whispered.

So, they did.

Thea held out her hand, taking Namara's in her grasp and squeezing. She pulled away, and her hand was bone dry.

Namara laughed, but it morphed into a sob halfway through. Thea's eyes felt hot, and her own laugh bubbled up from her chest as she stared at her dry palm.

"We did it," she breathed out, but even then her voice cracked.

Before she could even say anything else, arms were wrapping around her neck and tugging her close. Namara's sobs grew loud in her ear as she pressed closer, nose stuffed into the side of Thea's neck. Thea laughed, but a blazing hot tear slipped down her cheek as she pulled the kelpie closer to her.

"Thank you. Thank you, thank you, thank you, thank you," Namara whispered over and over, her body racking as she cried.

Thea sniffed before burying her face in Namara's wet locks. "Of course," was all she could manage to say.

When they pulled away from each other some time later, Thea was still dry.

Chapter Thirty-Three

A Feast of Farewells

The next two days were a blur of celebration and goodbyes. They couldn't leave on the second day like Isabel suggested, but when they checked outside, they were pleased to see it had stopped snowing. Giving it an extra day would allow the snow to settle in place. Isabel wasn't too upset, though. Especially when it meant another joyous day asking questions and learning more and more about the culture that had embraced them.

The clansmen hadn't understood Namara's excitement about her newfound ability not to drench anything and everything around her, but they were swept up in the good mood, nonetheless. She was even fitted with her own qynzo of pale blue with sloping swirls of waves dyed onto the material. The sleeves were more translucent at the elbows, as were the frills that had been added near the bottom of the skirt. The robes remained perfectly dry despite her water-beaded skin and drenched hair.

The first day had been a busy one. They had all been taught how to dress in their qynzos. Agni and Isabel tried once again to collect the moonglows from the ceiling, and they successfully came back to show off their catch to the Huǒshān children. Lastly, Thea had visited the elves for a proper goodbye.

"You must pass on what we've shown you," Merrjewl stated afterward.

"Yes," Cel'dion concurred. "Many waste their magic by not mastering their control. They will see an increase in their power and concentration."

"I'm sure the Wild Hunt spell will help out in that regard," Thea added.

The female elf had nodded. "Oh, most definitely. However, waste is still waste."

On the second day, Renkilo ordered lunch to be brought to the Bamboo Pavilion. The slats that had acted as shutters were taken down, allowing the brisk air from the mountain to flood into the cave and disrupt the rising humidity (something that Thea and her frizzed out curls had rejoiced in). Excess snow had been removed, and the moonglows slowly faded as the afternoon's light breached the shadows.

They were afforded the breathtaking view of the mountainside once again as they ate one of their last meals with the Huŏshān Clan. Tonight would be a feast worthy enough to invite the goddess herself to, and then they would leave out early the next morning before the frigid mountain air could get the chance to warm up.

Thea stayed behind at the pavilion as everyone left after lunch. Thea watched the frozen forest sway in the breeze, ice still clinging on despite the sun high in the sky. She sighed and rubbed at her arms. The qynzo was much thinner than her coat and winter gear. She didn't understand how the people of the mountain did it.

The sudden feeling of homesickness washed over her. Rafe popped into her mind, and she sighed. She hadn't gotten to report to him yesterday like she intended to, too busy exploring more of the cave at Isabel's insistence. Siàu had, of course, been their guide and gave intentionally as little information as possible until Isabel got frustrated. With a laugh that surprised everyone, the willowy-limbed woman elaborated more in depth. Thea even had to hand over her small notepad when Isabel ran out of paper in her own.

She pulled out her crystal ball and brought Rafe up in her mind. Within seconds, he was connected to her. She'd caught him hovering over some more paperwork, and already his hair was getting in his eyes. She felt a certain fondness take over her as he picked up his crystal ball and tried fixing his locks with his other hand.

"Well, well, if it isn't my most favorite Spellweaver," he said with a boyish grin.

Without reason, her eyes grew hot. She sniffed as discreetly as she could and prayed it wasn't obvious she was being emotional.

Rafe's face fell. "What's wrong? Are you okay?"

Double-dip a candlestick.

She rubbed at her eyes and laughed. "Yeah, I'm fine. It's just been …" She wanted to say a few days, but honestly, it had been longer than just that. This whole mission had kicked her to the ground and kicked her more when she was down. "It's just been." And she left it at that with another chuckle.

"Wanna talk about it?"

"Do you have the time? I don't want to take you away from such important duties."

Rafe rolled his eyes. "Most of these just need a signature. Per usual. I wish Mokana could forge my signature, but her penmanship is terrible. My ninety-year-old great grandma has fewer tremors in her hands."

"I can hear you!" Mokana yelled distantly in the background. A book was flung at the Summoner's head, which he dodged all too easily.

He aimed a dashing smile Thea's way. "You're not here to tease, so she's been getting the brunt of it. Yeah, how's it feel to be the butt of the joke all the time?" He aimed the last bit back at the rusalka, and Mokana could be heard groaning from somewhere farther back in the room.

Thea laughed. "Rafe, I can't believe you're shirking your duties to mess with Mokana."

"I can multitask, thank you," he snipped proudly, and Thea laughed again. "It's not my fault you can't. Don't project onto me."

She rolled her eyes. Another wave of fondness washed over her, and she may have gotten lost staring at the large, goofy man on the other side of the glass for longer than she realized.

When she blinked back into awareness, she caught him doing the same. The tips of his ears were red as he looked away, and Thea felt her own face heating up from being caught. Goddess above, what was she, a pre-teen?

Get it together, Thea.

"So, tell me about the last couple of days. What's the status on the delay?" He tried to ask casually, and Thea thanked him silently for the wonderful distraction.

She told him about everything that had happened since they got to the caves. All the trials and tribulations, all the history that had been uncovered, and what they would do when the sun rose tomorrow. The only thing she didn't mention was Fatik's blood and its abilities. Not that she didn't trust Rafe with said information, but she wanted a much more secure location for the both of them before she disclosed that.

At some point during their conversation, Mokana had joined in, and the rusalka's pale face reacted to every high and every low. Her jaw dropped at the spell Thea was able to cast onto Namara, and the demoness began jumping up and down in glee whilst clapping her hands.

"That's wonderful! She must be so happy!" she had cheered.

Thea had only smirked and mentioned one of the more recent reasons she was so happy about the spell working. How close she and Agni had gotten over the last few days, and how they would no doubt stay in close contact after they all got back to Tolvade. To which again, Mokana's jaw dropped.

"Tomorrow's the big day?" Rafe asked later, just before they were to say their goodbyes.

"Yeah. As soon as I get my hands on the tablet, I'm teleporting back to HQ. So, I'll be able to see you tomorrow." It felt like forever would pass by before then, but maybe it was just the two weeks catching up with her.

"I'll be there as soon as you teleport in," he promised.

Mokana popped her head into the crystal ball's view and grinned a secretive little smile. "He'll probably be so worried and stressed he'll want me stationed at the telepads waiting for you."

Thea snorted a laugh at Rafe's offended look. "Don't do that," she said before he could cut in with what would inevitably be a lie. "I don't know what time we'll make it to the temple, and there's the whole time warp thing to take into consideration. It could mess with time so badly, it might take a couple of days to get out. Last time we were …" Well, *lucky* wasn't exactly the right word. "Last time wasn't so long."

Rafe grimaced before he sighed in resignation. "You're right. I'll keep an ear out, but I won't expect you back by a certain time."

She nodded. She could deal with that.

"I love you," she said before she could stop herself. She felt embarrassed knowing Mokana was right there listening to everything, but the smile she received from Rafe was worth it.

"I love you, too."

Later that night, they feasted, laughed, cried, and said their goodbyes for the final time. Once again, that feeling Thea had found around that long table with everyone came back to her. Fatik had finally mastered chopsticks, Isabel was trying to eat a devastatingly hot dumpling and looked like a mini dragon huffing out steam from her mouth, and Namara was cuddled up next to Agni and feeding him all sorts of foods from the menagerie of plates spread before them. Music was being played for them once again, Renkilo was deep in his cups as was the norm, giggling like a schoolgirl at some tall tale Isabel was spinning around the mouthful of pork dumpling, and Siàu was settled by Thea's side.

"I will miss you," the woman said quietly at some point during dinner. When Thea looked at her in surprise, she continued. "I have not known you all for very long, but you have brought a very interesting livelihood with you that I think I will miss when you are gone."

Boisterous laughter erupted around the table, but Thea only swirled her drink in her small cup. "Do you not like living up here?"

Siàu shrugged and quickly refilled Fatik's drink. "It is all I know," she said after she sat back down. "I would not say I dislike it. It is just … routine."

Thea thought back to the conversation with the elves. Was that how Enzou felt? Was that why he left? Did he ever find what he was looking for? Thea wasn't going to ask Siàu if she planned on leaving, but a part of her was curious. If she pressed, would Siàu want to come with them back to Tolvade?

She opened her mouth to do the very thing she said she wouldn't do, but Siàu was already talking.

"I think I will miss this disruption more than anything. My life is here. It always has been."

Thea nodded. Far be it from her to remove someone from their home. She took a bite out of her dumpling and looked down at the meat within. The food, the people who made it, the atmosphere of those enjoying said food with friends and family … When she looked back up, she caught Siàu's soft, dark eyes.

"I'll miss this, too."

What Thea did not miss was how cold the mountains could be. Out of the safety of the gorge and thus the cave, the bitter wind sliced like knives through her thick clothing as if making up for all the time she'd been hiding away. The snow was too thick and the ground too unpredictable to trust Namara and Agni in horse form, and there was simply no room for all of them to squeeze onto Agni's longma form. So, they were left only with the dreadful decision to hike.

The path narrowed between the snow-capped pine trees that declined down the mountain, surrounded on both sides by sloping hills as white and bright as the Dragonkin who came up to stand beside her. In the distance, the mountains appeared bluer than anything else, almost camouflaged against the sky. Somewhere along the horizon, the snowy tops blended in with the clouds, and Thea couldn't tell which was which anymore.

"It's going to be a long way down," she commented and peered over her shoulder as the rest of the group caught up with them. "Wish we would have gotten here before all the snow."

"Then we wouldn't have met the Huǒshān Clan."

Thea sighed. Their meeting with the clan had been beneficial information-wise and survival-wise, but the emotional bond they'd all come to have made leaving all the more difficult.

Their departure that morning had been a quiet affair. Siàu had looked especially distraught to see them off as they gathered at the entrance tunnel, and the sight of her tears had almost made Thea and Isabel both cry too. They had all hugged and wished each other well in their future endeavors. Renkilo was the only one outside the morning guard who had walked with them all the way to bid them the final farewell.

"If you ever find yourself on the mountain again, consider it a given that you are welcomed by the Huǒshān Clan," he had said in parting.

It felt too fast, too soon before they were heading out, but the retrieval of the tablets was their top priority. However, splitting up from the clan left them with a certain hollowness. Thea sighed against the feeling and pressed on, moving down the steep, slanted path caked in fresh snow.

"Agni and Namara are a little ways behind still," Fatik warned from his spot on the ledge.

Thea stopped and groaned quietly. "I bet they're doing this on purpose."

Fatik chuckled at her impatience. "There's no need to rush, Thea. We have a long way to go, so we'll have to reserve our strength."

He had gotten the mental landscape down within seconds of coming out of the gorge (a testament to what a few days' break could do), and with a few pointers from Renkilo that morning, they at least knew where their destination was.

She turned back around to find the Dragonkin's wings ruffling in the icy blast of wind that blew past them. "We should get there in a few hours' time," he added.

"Great," Thea snarked. She hoped the farther up the sun got in the sky, the warmer it would get. Her fingers already felt like icicles.

"We just have to be very careful about avalanches. Giving the snow a day to fuse together was a good decision, but we still need to be cautious," he continued. "One wrong move could have it coming down on us without us even knowing until it's too late."

"Double great," Thea muttered and wiped at her freezing cheeks. Thank the goddess for facemasks at the very least.

"All right, guys, that means no horsing around," Isabel stated with some underlying joke in her tone as she popped up over the ledge and into view. She pointed at Namara, who had come up behind her with Agni by her side. "So that means *you* gotta go, missy."

It was too early in the morning for jokes to land in Thea's mind, and she was going to question what Isabel meant when Namara's gaze grew sharp.

"I'm a kelpie, *not* a horse!"

"Shh!" Fatik hissed. His tail slashed angrily at the air as he snipped, "Both of you knock it off!"

Namara crossed her arms over her chest. "I didn't even do anything!"

Thea sighed once again as the bickering continued. It was going to be a long couple of hours. She was about to snap at them when a moving figure in the corner of her eye caught her attention. She raised and pointed her arrow launcher at the object that kept disappearing behind the dipping snow ledges.

Her stance caught the group's attention, and everyone turned in defense.

"What is it?" Fatik whispered.

"I don't know," she replied quietly, eyeing the spot where the figure should pop back up at any moment. "It was as big as a person, though, so—What the?"

It *was* a person.

Namara brought a hand over her eyes to block out the sun. "Is that …?"

"Looks like one of the clansmen," Fatik finished, squinting in the glaring sun.

The person was wearing a huge fur coat that dwarfed their body. Once they noticed they had caught up with the group, they started waving their hands and trudging through the snow at a quicker rate.

Thea had lowered her arm and glanced around at the others. "Did we forget something?"

"Not anything worth them coming all the way out here for," Isabel said, a confused expression on her heart-shaped face. "I definitely remembered to grab the moonglows."

Namara gave a snort. "I doubt they'd come all the way out here just to bring you your jar of bugs even if you did forget it."

Thea brought her fingers to her covered lips and thought aloud, "At least using the barrier breaker oil this morning wasn't a total waste of product."

The figure grew larger and larger as it approached, but none of them had a clue as to who was under all that fur until the clansman was right in front of them and slipping off their large hood. They pulled down their face mask, and a familiar, out-of-breath woman stood panting before them.

Thea gaped. "Siàu?"

"What are you doing all the way out here?" Fatik shot out.

"Did we really forget something?" Namara asked the group, rather than the clanswoman who couldn't understand her.

"More importantly, did something happen?" Isabel wondered.

Siàu's face was tinged red, but whether from embarrassment or the cold, Thea wasn't sure. She did appear to grow more anxious the more everyone crowded around her.

"Okay, okay, back up, let her breathe," Thea snapped, waving off the others and bringing the taller woman away from everyone. She then stepped away and aimed an expectant look her way.

"I …" Siàu looked between everyone. "I wanted out," she finally said after a few moments. With her breath coming back to her, she continued. "My parents and siblings have always known I have wanted to journey beyond the confines of the cave, but it has always been too dangerous." She gazed into each of their eyes with an imploring expression. "I will do my best to assist you in your travels, so please allow me to join you. I have thought about this since the day you came to the caves, so do not believe I am acting rashly. I want … I want something more than the everyday life I've been living."

Thea's brow furrowed. "But last night, you said—"

Siàu winced. "Yes, I was still debating with myself even up until last night. It was only when you left, and I thought I might never get this chance again, did the decision come to me. Please, allow me to accompany you. I will make my own way in the world when we get back to your hometown."

Thea glanced at Fatik before looking over at Isabel. Fatik shrugged, but Isabel looked excited at the prospect. She peered over at Namara, who seemed surprised at being included.

"What do you think?"

The kelpie smiled. "I don't mind. What's one more?"

"Yeah, the more the merrier!" cheered Isabel, who was thusly shushed by Fatik once again.

She turned back to Siàu and gave the woman a wide smile. "Welcome to the team."

"We will reach the Pools of Time first," Fatik stated to the group as they trudged through the thick snow. The path was becoming steeper, and they regularly had to grab onto branches to keep themselves from slipping and rolling down the mountain.

Isabel was grumbling as she brushed white powder from her hair after a branch she had grabbed plopped the stuff all over her. "When is that, exactly?"

Fatik paused and peered through the trees, but only the sloping path was truly visible. "I can't see them, but I can smell them."

"That's what that smell is?" Namara asked with a pinched face.

Siàu looked between the two of them with confusion scrolled over her face. "I have never been to the pools, but I have heard there is no detectable scent."

Fatik tapped his nose. "Our senses are a lot keener than a human's."

"Unfortunately," the kelpie griped.

Thea scanned the landscape, but she couldn't see anything outside of snow and tall pines. Still … "If you can smell them, they must be close. We're buffered on either side by trees, so not much wind is going to be able to be carried through."

Fatik rubbed his fingers over his forehead. "If they're close, they're at the edge of my perimeter."

"Ugh, I'm tired of standing around here," Isabel complained and began marching down the slope once more. "They're like some kind of hot springs, right? I want to dive in as soon as we get there. I'm freezing!"

Siàu froze up, and a frown tugged at her oval face. "You must not go into the Pools of Time!"

The redhead whipped around. "Look, I overheated once, and now all you guys wanna—"

"Isabel, listen to us: they're called the Pools of *Time*. What do you think that means?" Thea asked with a roll of her eyes.

She shrugged. "I dunno, they're old?"

Siàu shook her head. "They are quite old, yes, but that is not why beings should not go near them. The myth that has been passed down since before Clan Leader Renkilo's father was even born is that they age whatever enters. No one knows by how much, but it is a terrifying thought."

It was clear that a million thoughts were racing through the redhead's mind at the new information. *"I've got to get a sample,"* Thea thought she heard her whisper. Then she aimed a wide-eyed expression at Huǒshān woman. "What if I put my hand in there? Would the rest of me age, or just the hand?"

Siàu looked at Isabel with a strange, blank look as if she were trying to assess if the redhead was serious or not.

Thea trudged past and lightly pushed at the researcher's shoulder. "Knock it off, Isabel, you're not getting close to the Pools of Time. They're magic, after all."

Isabel blanched and chased after the Spellweaver. "But my sample!"

"I can get it for you," Namara called after her, and the rest of the group began moving once more. "The water probably won't do anything to me, especially if I'm just dipping a jar in it."

Isabel turned big, beaming, chocolate-brown eyes the kelpie's way. "You would do that for me?" she sniffed and wiped a fake tear away.

"Only if you stop being so dramatic."

She *tsk*ed. "You're just like Thea sometimes, ya know? No fun at all."

"Oi, don't drag me into this."

"Oi, 'oi' is *my* thing, thank you very much!"

Chapter Thirty-Four

The Mountains Are Alive

After reaching the bottom of the slope, the forest on their right broke up into a clearing. Waters that reminded her of a certain Summoner's eyes were encapsulated into travertine pools created from the buildup of mineral deposits—according to Isabel. Not even the beauty of Lake Lorvo could compare to the unusually shaped pools that varied in size and color of blue. Some were aquamarine, some were teal, and others were almost as green as the trees around them. All layered into separate terraces that formed up the gentle incline of another mountain.

The Pools of Time were, simply, spectacular.

"This is so cool!" Isabel cheered, spinning around with a wild look in her eyes. "I've never seen rock formations like this—especially on such a grand scale!"

Thea hadn't either. The warm, humid air was dense around the clearing and had them all shucking their jackets. Thea had unbuckled her weapon first, and as she was strapping it back onto her arm, she noticed Namara making a face as if she smelled something horrible.

"Can you really smell the pools? It can't be that bad. I can't smell anything."

Namara relaxed the face she had on and sighed, waving at the air. "It's not super strong, and it's not *that* horrible. It mostly comes in waves. I won't smell anything, and then I'll get a big lungful of this rotten egg smell."

Thea wrinkled her own nose. "Sorry. As soon as Isabel gets her sample, we'll head off."

"If I figure out where the temple is supposed to be," Fatik interjected as he came up to the two, Siàu trailing behind him. He placed his hands on his hips and sighed. "I was told it was close by the Pools of Time from Renkilo, but I can't get a mental map of it. The layout of the land—it's like it's warped. I wonder if that was what was messing with me earlier when I couldn't sense this place. It was a lot closer than I expected."

Thea turned to Siàu. "Do you happen to know where the temple could be?"

The woman's shoulders slumped slightly. "No, we were never allowed near the temple, and only trusted members of our community could come this far. The dragons do not make it safe to travel far."

"Which is funny," Thea began and pursed her lips. "Aside from that one that took out that giant salamander, I haven't seen a single dragon. Not even in the air."

"They soar very high, above the clouds. Their mating season has also passed, so many are either licking their wounds and holed up in a cave or are building their nests. However, we should be careful regardless," Siàu informed. "I heard they're excellent at camouflaging their presence. It is why they are so dangerous."

Thea nodded. "We never did see that one dive out of the sky. Well, should we go ahead, take the risk, and set up for an early lunch since we're already here? That way, we won't have to set up later."

Fatik and Namara made a face. With a grimace, the Dragonkin shrugged. "We can. I don't think I'll have much of an appetite, though."

"Shouldn't we keep looking for the temple?" Namara pressed as she looked around. "It has to be somewhere close."

"We could split up to look for it?" Siàu offered.

Thea hummed and scanned the area. Isabel was standing next to Agni, one arm waving about as she held several empty jars in her other arm close to her chest. Beyond her were several small pathways through the sea of evergreens that could lead just about anywhere. It would take them forever if they all tried aimlessly wandering about.

"That's a good idea. We can do that while Isabel's busy with her samples. Agni's with her too, so she'll at least be safer than if she were alone."

"I'll take that direction," Namara said and pointed west of their location.

Thea took southwest, Fatik chose south, and Siàu picked the southeast path. Every other direction was blocked by a mountain.

"I'll go tell Isabel what we're doing. You guys head out," Thea ordered, and then she jogged over to the researcher.

"Thea, the pools are different colors! That means they have to hold different properties, different minerals—or at least more of one type than the other!" Isabel babbled in greeting. She spun to hand Agni another jar, who dipped the glass into the pools. The ones she took back, she dropped into her bottomless bag before moving on to the next pool.

"That's cool," Thea said with a nod. "Bet you can't wait to get them under a microscope."

Isabel shrugged, but her grin didn't disappear. "I don't really do anything with them once they get to the lab, but I do find out the results and if it helps progress Tolvade any. I just get this rush that makes me wanna do more, find more cool things like this. But sometimes I get to go into the lab if it's like, *super* cool."

Thea would label water from *the* Pools of Time as something super cool. "Well, the others and I are going to split up and try and locate the temple. We'll regroup here, so stay close."

She gave a goofy salute that nearly had her dropping the glass jars in her arms. "Aye, aye!"

The Spellweaver rolled her eyes and turned toward Agni. "I just learned dragons are pretty adept at cloaking themselves, so be on the lookout. We know Isabel won't be paying attention."

"Nope," she stated shamelessly.

Agni nodded before he got back to work dipping another glass jar into one of the larger, greener pools.

With that done, Thea trotted up the soft incline and around the layered pools to get back to her chosen path. Everyone had already left, so she picked up her pace and jogged through the trees. The snow wasn't as thick around the pools, but it was slick, so she had to slow down to a brisk walk after she slipped for a second time. Tread could only do so much on ice, after all.

The trail was hilly but didn't require too much endurance, thankfully. She could peek through the trees and see bits of blue and green water, but other than that, the trail was endlessly winding through nothing but more trees. She scoured the thick forest around her, but she saw nothing out of the ordinary. The temple couldn't be *that* hidden. After fifteen minutes or so, she turned back with a sigh and hoped one of the others had been more successful.

They weren't.

"That's *impossible*," she groaned and ran her gloves through her hair.

Fatik had a pinched expression as he seemed to be thinking about something. "It doesn't make sense, that's for sure. There's no way we missed it on the way up here."

"I searched high and low on my trail," Namara said with a frown.

"I wish I could be of more help," Siàu sighed dejectedly.

"Hey, guys!" Isabel called. "I found something!"

They all glanced up at Isabel waving her arms in the air before sharing a look with each other.

"It's worth checking out," Thea said with a shrug and made her way over to the bouncing researcher.

Fatik didn't move, and it was clear he was still thinking heavily. "I wonder if we should split up again and check one more time."

"I think I found the source of all the water!" Isabel kept calling out and pointing.

Thea was the only one who joined up, and that was all Isabel needed in encouragement as she began climbing up the sandy-colored boulders. She kept pointing and looking over her shoulder at the Spellweaver below.

"Look, look! See? It's like a tiny waterfall! I wanna check it out!" She yelled down, cupping her mouth so her already obnoxiously loud voice would carry.

Thea shared an exasperated look with Agni, who stood beside her. She should have known Isabel hadn't found anything useful. Her curiosity had just gotten the best of her.

"It's probably coming off a lake or something!" Thea yelled back up at the slowly shrinking Isabel.

"I still wanna check it out!"

Thea sighed and rubbed at the bridge of her nose. She turned to head back to the others still huddled up—

—But her blood froze in her veins.

A big, yellow eye was staring at her. Spikes of blood red and fiery orange projected out of a slitted pupil the size of Thea.

It all happened so fast. The *mountain* came alive. Crimson bloomed like a field of thorned roses over what she had thought were the boulders of the foothills. An avalanche of snow came crashing down around them as the dragon stood up.

She stumbled back.

A blur of motion lunged at her.

Unimaginable heat spread over her skin.

Agni was suddenly there, pushing her out of the way—

Straight into the Pools of Time.

"AGNI!"

Chapter Thirty-Five

Time of Your Life

The Pools of Time were deeper than they appeared. The surface drifted further and further away, no matter how hard Thea kicked and paddled her arms through the water. Her weapon was weighing her down. Her boots and heavy clothing all dragged her further from the surface. Her fingers were clumsy against the straps on her crossbow, and bubbles began to escape as she thrashed in frustrated panic.

Her chest spasmed, lungs on fire as she tried to hold her breath and swim up. More bubbles escaped as she fought through the fear of drowning. She was going to die in the Pools of Time. So close to the temple. So close to coming back home. What if she were aging right now? Would there be nothing but bones when—*if*—someone even did come to save her?

She ripped her weapon off her arm and tried propelling herself further, but the surface was so far away now. She reached out her hand just as her lungs gave out, and all air escaped her in a swarm of bubbles.

Water filled her mouth, and it *hurt* to swallow. She flailed, and her body lurched against itself as she tried to cough out the water, only for more to flood her mouth and nose.

She was sinking again.

Her vision went in and out.

Pain punched through her body over and over as she swallowed more and more water.

Sinking, sinking …

Sinking but … not … dying?

Her head swam as if the water had invaded her mind as well. Her limbs felt as heavy as logs. Her lungs were like lead weights in her chest. Everything was blurred, dark, but … something darker was swimming toward her.

A dragon? Just as the idea broke the bubble on the surface of her thoughts, she could see it wasn't a dragon at all.

Giant, hulking shadows lumbered through the water without purpose. For a brief, transient moment, Thea was teleported back to the library, where she stood under the loch that shimmered like the night sky and the enormous shadow that swam within. She blinked, and the memory was gone, and as the dying light of the surface filtered through, she caught glimpses of massive, hairy creatures trudging past her. Almost as big as the salamander, the beasts were gentle and ignored her as they meandered past. Long, moss-slicked hair clung to their entire body and floated loosely about them. Monstrous, curved tusks jutted out of their faces and framed two thick trunks. One of the long, hose-like snouts acted as a snorkel and grazed the surface of the water while the other felt around like a sentient walking stick.

It brushed up against her, and she couldn't even jerk away, only feel the force of the powerful, limber nose push her gently away. As the beast passed by, she could make out the milkiness of its eyes. The creatures were blind. That, or they couldn't see all that well.

There were so many of them, but as the last of the herd swam around her, she noticed the sparkle and shimmer of magic left behind. The water stirred up from their meandering forms began to ripple and bend. Images started to fill the darkness, and Thea blinked slowly as the memories of her mind took physical form in front of her. They surrounded her on all sides, all of them nothing but moving pictures of her life that flashed before her eyes. Maybe she really was dying?

Her eyes followed one changing memory after another and then realized with slow clarity … that they weren't memories at all. They were visions. She was present in each of them. She focused on one that was of her as a baby, staring up at a cheap toy that was supposed to keep her busy. Her mom was also there.

Younger, less harsh. Big, soft, poofy curls that had been blown out in the style of the time were pinned back on one side by long clips. A smile tugged at her face as she tickled under the younger Thea's chin. A smile that disappeared when her husband entered the room, cussing and throwing a fit about some business proposal gone wrong.

"They made a mockery of me!" he was yelling. The sound was distorted under the water. *"I'll show them! One day, the Bauer Empire will crush them under its foot!"*

The image changed, teleporting her to when she and Arabella were playing together as little girls. Colleen was pacing back and forth in a slim, black dress and messing with the jewelry decked out on her fingers. Her curls had been tamed and lay back slick against her head, making her cheeks appear gaunter and her features more model-esque.

She kept checking on her daughters playing dress-up in her closet, and a small smile played out on her blood-red lips.

Her father once again entered the picture, and that small smile disappeared. *"This meeting will make or break us. Do you have your lines memorized?"* At her mother's nod, he sneered and motioned for her to join him. *"Don't mess this up. And make sure they stay quiet."* He sent an indifferent look at his daughters before he stormed out of the room, his wife trailing after him like his lifeless shadow.

Thea then saw mostly images of herself like when she was trying to cheat off Rafe's paper during a test (and how he had subtly helped her), the time she first summoned Namara and the chaos that ensued in the summoning room, her sitting next to Blythe in the desert, the battle in the village with the soul eater and hellhound, her moving Rafe's couch into his duplex.

Then the images shuddered, darkened, and a new one began playing out. Her mother and father were screaming at each other. The time period was more modern—they looked nearly the same as the last time she'd seen them. Arabella was the same age, standing frightened in their mansion's hall as she looked between both parents. Colleen grabbed the nearest chair and hurled it at her father—which he only narrowly dodged—before she broke down into tears. The words of what was being said were lost on her. Everything was murmured, muffled, underwater.

More images of herself came after: her and Rafe's first kiss, her anxiety attack in the jungle, her first mission and how proud she'd been back then, the day she received her silver Spellweaver insignia, and her graduating school and looking out into the crowd where only a genial applause awaited her—then right after being startled by Rafe's booming claps. He had already graduated the year before.

The next image had her squinting as it shuddered into existence. A lone woman, skinny and frail, sat in a chair by a window. The white paint on the window's frame was thickly layered and chipped in several places. The walls were dingy and gray and as lifeless as the person in the vision. Loose, unkempt curls swayed as she turned and peered in a direction Thea couldn't see. A younger woman swept forward in a beautiful gown. She dropped before the older woman and looked up with imploring, cobalt eyes. Her dark curls had been pinned up in an elaborate bun, decked out with sparkling jewels.

Arabella? Then … that means …

She looked at the frail woman by the window with new eyes. The loose, blonde curls, the hollow eyes of dusty amber.

Mama?

A sharp, longing ache panged in her chest just as the image disappeared. She hadn't uttered that word in over a decade. Colleen Bauer had been dubbed the less affectionate title of *mom* since before she was a teenager.

The images rippled and vanished as if someone had splashed the surface of a still pool. Darkness engulfed her, but Thea had watched her life play out before her eyes. She could die in peace now. Her eyes closed, and she drifted.

Time was an illusion in the pools, but, even so, not long had passed before she heard a noise. Thea opened her eyes, but she couldn't see anything but the flickering light filtering through the water. The noise repeated—it was sharp, piercing, distant. Oh, so distant.

A shadow came into view, and Thea slowly blinked as it took form. It was far smaller than the massive beasts from before. This shadow was slimmer, faster, fluid in movement, as the water around it. The same noise from before penetrated the pool's depths, ringing in her ears and causing her to flinch.

A horse … a horse?

Her eyes flew open just as the shadow passed through the beam of light above. Namara was in full kelpie form and diving straight for the Spellweaver. Her emerald skin glowed in the dark waters, and her kelp-like mane swayed loosely with every movement. Her horse tail had been replaced with a peduncle and two flukes at the end to powerfully propel herself forward as her two front legs kicked.

Thea's limbs worked in slow motion as she reached out toward Namara. The kelpie swam by, just close enough for her to grasp a handful of slimy, slick strands of her hair, and Namara's glowing, slippery skin turned gelatinous around her fingers. That glue-like substance anchored her, and the demoness used her powerful tail to send them soaring through the water toward the surface.

Thea felt the sun on her face and pain in her lungs. Everything was too bright and too much. She was grabbed by several hands and hauled over the edge of the pool until she was positioned on her side. Her throat spasmed, her stomach heaved, her lungs flared—and all at once she couldn't get enough air in her lungs as she coughed and hacked and wheezed as more and more water left her. Her lungs burned, and water dribbled out of her mouth and nose until she couldn't stand the pain, but the hands holding her down kept her from thrashing. Everything was a blur of color, and the drowsiness in her limbs was nauseating.

Someone kept smacking her on the back, and all it was really doing was creating a hand-shaped bruise. She managed to wave them away as she spat the last bit of water out. She was so exhausted that she could barely stop the drool that escaped her lips. Her mouth tasted like she had just sucked on a wet rock, her throat was raw and stung every time she breathed, and her lungs felt like someone had reached past the protective cage of her ribs and knocked the organs around like they were their personal punching bags.

It was cold. So cold. Despite the warmth around the Pools of Time, it was still way too cold for someone who had just been dunked in water. She shivered, and she could feel her teeth chattering.

She registered someone talking to her, but her head was still a bit fuzzy. She blinked slowly as she sat back on her calves and found Namara's worried face inches from her own. It took her another moment to realize Namara was back in her humanoid form.

"Thea? Thea, say something," she pleaded, her light green hands gripping so tight onto the Spellweaver's jacket that her claws had already punctured the material.

Thea blinked again. "What d-d-do you want me to-to sa-say?" came her strained, chattering reply.

Namara slumped, and a rush of exhales was heard all around her. Her surroundings came back with more clarity, and she noted that Isabel was standing hunched over Namara with her own look of relief. Fatik was to her side beside Siàu, who both gave her thankful smiles. Only one was missing …

"Where's Agni?" She jerked around and began frantically looking for him. "Is he okay? Where is he?" She locked onto Isabel's gaze. "I thought I heard you scream just before I was pushed into the pools—"

"Thea, breathe," Namara soothed, pulling the Spellweaver's attention back to her. "He's okay, he went to check out the temple and make sure it was okay."

Thea's brow scrunched up in confusion. "What? Wait … what? What happened afterward? How long was I down there?"

Namara swallowed nervously and looked around at the others before she made eye contact again. "It's been … It's been an hour, Thea …"

Her eyes blew wide, and she nearly fell back at the declaration. She looked around at the others, but they all nodded.

"I was …" she swallowed, and the action hurt, "I was down there for an hour?"

Namara's eyes were shiny, and her lip began to tremble. "I don't know how, but, Thea, I felt our bond going faint in the beginning—I felt you dying. I was panicking, trying to get to you, but the dragon was still fighting Agni and—"

Agni fought a dragon?

"—before I knew it—*Yes*, Agni fought the dragon— anyway, before I knew it, several minutes had passed by and you—you were still alive. I didn't know how long you could hold your breath, but surely the average human wouldn't have been able to hold it for *that* long."

Thea stared at her partner for several seconds. "I … I didn't ask if Agni fought a dragon …"

Namara leaned back with a confused expression on her face. "What are you talking about? I just heard you—"

Thea shook her head. "Not out loud."

They stared at one another for several seconds as they let that information settle between them. Thea had heard of partners becoming so close they could practically read each other's thoughts, but she and Namara had never been able to do it. In the beginning of their relationship, Thea had barely been able to feel the cord that tied them together. Over time, she'd gotten used to it being there. A physical link of their bond that she'd only really thought about when … when it began to vanish as Namara lay dying.

Don't think about that.

"You said," she began and licked her dry, cracked lips. "You said I was down there for an hour. But I wasn't dying?"

Namara nodded. "I felt our bond stabilize, and I don't know how it was happening, but it was reassuring to say the least. Agni was able to lead the dragon away while the rest of us hid, and then he must have transformed into something even the dragon couldn't find or sniff out. We all watched it climb up the mountain before it took flight. The gust of wind from its wings knocked a couple of trees over, and that's how we found the trail to the temple."

"Remember that water source I found," Isabel piped up, and Thea swung her still fuzzy head in the researcher's direction and nodded slowly.

"Turns out it was worth investigating after all. When the trees got knocked over, more of the water came forward, and I was able to climb over the wreckage and see the temple from the vantage point."

Namara placed her hand on Thea's knee. "We can get that tablet and then get you checked out with Dr. Snow once we teleport back to HQ."

That sounded nice. She'd be able to see Rafe again. She could rest in her own bed. She could sleep for days without interruption. She nodded again and pushed to her feet with the aid of Namara. She smirked at her partner as a thought bubbled up in her tired mind.

"It's funny," she said and allowed the kelpie to pull Thea's arm over her shoulders.

"What's funny?"

"That out of the two of us, I'm the one dripping water all over the place."

Namara snorted and began dragging the Spellweaver over toward the mountain. "You definitely got knocked around. Don't worry, we'll have Dr. Snow take care of you soon."

Thea shivered and cursed. "Wait, let me apply a warming spell. I won't be able to dry my clothes, but at least I won't catch hypothermia. That'll kill me quicker than anything else out here."

Only once the spell was applied and warmth spread through her did she begin walking again. Movement in the trees stole her attention before she could take more than a few steps, though. Her sore eyes squinted as she focused on where the movement came from, and she almost tripped over her feet when she saw it. Namara and the others assumed it was just her still recovering, but Thea couldn't tear her eyes away from the trees.

On a pine branch that hung over the pool—the very one that had trapped her within it—sat a magpie. And it was staring right back at her.

Chapter Thirty-Six

Temple on the Rocks

"So, how exactly did Agni take on a dragon?" Thea asked as they neared the temple. She couldn't see the structure yet, but Isabel was adamant that they were going in the right direction because of the trail of water. The small stream (if one could even call it that) trickled down the slope they were climbing up and was their only sense of direction currently.

The appearance of the magpie had disturbed her on some spiritual level, but the bird hadn't followed them, so she let it be. It didn't stop the paranoia from creeping in, nor did it stop her from constantly checking over her shoulder. The foreboding dream she had in the temple kept coming back to her. Wasn't the bird in that dream a magpie as well? She shook her head and tuned into the incessant ramblings of the researcher beside her.

Isabel had instantly started gushing at her question and was beaming like a proud mother. "Dude, you should have seen him! I was all scared at first—I mean, it's a freakin' *dragon* after all, but I've never seen Agni fight like he did before! He was a force to be reckoned with, that's for sure! He was all like *whoosh* into a bird, flying around and around the dragon's head—and then *boom*—he's a bear slicing and dicing the dragon's eyeballs! And then all of a sudden he's a mouse, diving under the beast spewing molten, hot lava everywhere, and then he's a unicorn and stabs right through the soft skin of its throat, then *whoosh*, he's a bird again! Flying higher than the dragon could spout his flames, and then all of a sudden, Agni's in his normal form, and he's blasting the thing with his *own* fire! Right in its stupid face!"

Thea watched the energetic researcher retell the story with flailing hand movements and vivid reenactments. No wonder Renkilo laughed so hard when he was deep in his cups. She heard Namara snickering beside her, but there was also a proud gleam in her eye as Isabel continued describing how Agni was able to outsmart and frustrate a dragon so badly that it ended up flying off after only receiving superficial wounds.

"It was truly magnificent," Fatik commented when Isabel was done babbling.

"I have never seen a dragon so close," Siàu remarked, and a touch of wonder glinted in her dark eyes as she recalled the scene. "I can say with such confidence that I never wish to be that close again."

"Ditto," Thea said with a tired nod. "And if I never see the Pools of Time again, I'll be an even happier witch."

Namara stopped suddenly, and the Spellweaver glanced up and around, but the temple was still not in view. A surprised noise escaped her when Namara jerked her around and began looking her up and down.

"What are you doing?" she complained.

"You just spent the last hour in the Pools of Time. I can't believe I didn't think of it as soon as you came out, but I don't see any noticeable changes."

Thea quirked a brow, but her exhausted brain finally caught up to what Namara was going on about. She looked down at herself before tearing off her gloves. She flipped her hands over and back, but there weren't any wrinkles. Her fingers flew to her sopping curls and began combing through the dripping locks. "Do you see any silver or gray strands?"

Namara quickly began picking through her hair, but she stood back shortly after and shook her head. "Your hair's too wet. We'll have to wait for it to dry and lighten back up to be able to tell."

Fatik stepped forward and bent slightly, peering into Thea's eyes for a moment. His gaze flicked all over her face, but he stood back and shook his head. "I can't tell if you aged any, but you do look a little thinner."

"I lost weight?" Thea felt her anxiety spike, and her jaw unhinged at what that could possibly mean.

Isabel pulled out her notebook and jotted down a few notes. "What about your scar? The one you got from your stab wound?"

Thea blinked. Her eyes widened, and she scrambled to lift up her soaking wet jacket and undershirt. How could she have forgotten her stab wound? Sure, the pain had lessened to that of a bruise, but how could it have completely slipped her mind? The healing spells had helped, but a scar would inevitably be left because of how deep the cut ran.

She managed to work the wet clothing up high enough without embarrassing Fatik, but she couldn't see the wound for herself.

"Well?" she asked after a moment of silence in which the others simply stared at her exposed midriff. "What's it look like?"

"Dude," Isabel breathed before she immediately started taking more notes.

That was probably not a good sign.

"You …" Fatik began but paused, eyes raking over her stomach. "You really have lost a lot of weight."

She felt the blood drain from her face. She aimed a pleading look at her partner, but her voice only came out as a whisper. "Namara?"

Like a spell was broken, Namara looked up with a wide-eyed expression. "Your scar … it's healed …"

"And?"

Namara hesitated. "It's completely faded. Like … how it would look after a year or two …"

Thea slowly let go of her clothing. She did lose time. *Again*. This time by a *year*, at the very least. Nausea rocked through her like a tidal wave, and she swayed on her feet as her hand flew to her mouth.

Namara lurched forward and caught her before she could fall on her backside. Again, her arm was looped over the kelpie's shoulders, and they started walking. No one dared speak a word, and if they did, Thea couldn't hear them over her roaring thoughts.

An hour in the Pools of Time was close to a year in the real world? Maybe two? Three? And then there were still the strange events that happened while she was under those magic waters. She hadn't drowned, despite being down there for so long. The images that played out were visions of her entire life … yet her mom and dad weren't the same people she remembered them as.

Her dad had come off callous and mean-spirited, but she only remembered him as the sniveling businessman who would have done anything for a bit of coin—including marrying off his teen daughter for the chance at a merger. Her mom … Thea shook her head. She didn't want to think about her mom and… who that other woman she saw in those dream-like images was. They weren't the same person. Her mom was mean. Cold. Cruel. She only cared about herself and her image and … and she wasn't worth thinking about right now.

"Thea," someone called softly, and she looked up. Namara pointed with her head toward something in front of them. When she turned, she understood.

They had made it. The northern temple stood before them. The square structure stood stiff against the elements, its color as dark as the rock that made up the mountain. Its angled roof was buried under several feet of snow, and it was clear that the whole building was … crooked.

Agni was waiting for them with the two temple guardians at his feet. They were covered in thick, white fur and lay in an unconscious heap.

"Yo! Look at this!" Isabel shouted suddenly, and everyone turned to find the researcher pointing.

The trickle of water that they had been following was coming right out from under the temple. Namara's arm fell away as Thea straightened up and walked over to get a closer look. The fact that the leak was escaping the house of a powerful relic had her mind reeling. Something big must have damaged the building, but what could be strong enough to crack a temple spelled to survive the harsh elements?

"Did an avalanche damage the structural integrity?" Fatik wondered aloud, seemingly of the same thought as her.

"Hmm …" Isabel jumped up to her feet and jogged back toward the treeline. She turned her head one way and then the other as she examined the temple. "Either that or the tectonic plates shifting over the last couple hundred years caused the foundation to list to one side. Pressure could have built up and formed a crack in the base. Whatever water is coming from inside there could have further weathered away the stone, exacerbated the damage, and caused the leak."

Thea turned back and studied the pitiful trickle of water leaking out of the temple. It was true that tiny, hairline fractures shot up from the base of the structure and branched out along the uniform stone. If the temple hadn't been magically imbued to withstand a beating, the building would have crumbled long ago.

She shivered at the absolute destruction the malign gnomes must have caused to bust out of the southern temple.

"What *are* these things?" she heard Namara ask. She peered over and found the kelpie prodding one of the guardians Agni had knocked unconscious. Thea and the others gathered around the beings, and it was only when Agni nudged one onto its back that Siàu had the answer.

She jumped back with a look of shock. "It's a yeti!"

"A yeti?" Thea parroted curiously. She stared at the creature in wonder. The beings were as tall as Agni and looked pound-for-pound just as powerful with their muscular builds. However, rakshasas were terrifying for a reason, and it wasn't just because they were big and brawny.

These beings, the yetis, were almost completely covered in hair. Alabaster skin bleached of all color and calloused enough to feel like Thea was holding a brick rather than flesh made up their hands, feet, ears, and faces.

"They're very skittish beings," Fatik murmured, and Siàu nodded next to him. "However, they have a huge set of teeth they'll use on you if you mess with them."

Thea set down the yeti's hand she'd picked up and stood to her feet. "These two must have been summoned to guard this place for the centuries the tablet was here. When all this is over, all the guardians and elemental beings inside the temples can be set free."

"Let's do what we came here to do then," Namara said.

She nodded and moved briskly for the temple's entrance. The stairs were cracked and slick with ice, and the obsidian double doors looked frozen shut from the thin layer of frost coating them. The dark, stone building looked unwelcoming against the stark-white backdrop, but even from outside, Thea felt a sense of power *thrum* through the air as if alive. She reached out and hesitated for only a moment. She really hoped the giant salamanders from the valley weren't lumbering inside, waiting to ambush her. She didn't know how they'd fit—unless it was just one waiting to ambush them all.

Breathe, Thea. You're going to go in and get that tablet and go home! There's no point standing out here and working yourself up.

She felt the others congregate at her back, and with a surge of confidence, she pushed open the doors and stepped inside.

Immediately, everyone's feet were drenched as water surged out to greet them. The force blasting against her shins almost had her falling back. Her lips pressed into a thin line at the surprise, but it wasn't like she wasn't still soaked from earlier. She heard the others react a little less graciously, but she trudged on into the building.

The layout was like that of the desert temple, but that was where the similarities ended. Where the wind temple was as arid as the desert around it, this temple was a lot muggier. Thea felt how the humidity had her skin feeling positively clammy in the suffocating heat and grimaced.

Metal torches hung from the ceiling and held flickering fire that lit the temple aglow. A long, slithering dragon snaked its way around the room at the decorative border where the brick-red ceiling met the black, stone walls. Water had filled the sunken level of the humid building, and giant, bright green lily pads floated in the tepid water. She didn't know how the water had reached them all the way at the doors, but it was most likely a last-ditch effort to drive out anyone coming for the tablet.

On the upper level of the temple, swampy mud caked the ground. Charred tree logs leaning up against large rocks acted as the perfect sunning spots despite there being no sun. Already, Thea could spot a few wary salamanders perched on them. They were ten times smaller than the salamander from the valley—thankfully—but the same orange and black coloring flared up in threat display. One creature slipped off a log and into the water, and a giant steam cloud erupted. Bubbles dances on the surface of the pond where the salamander came up to peer out at them.

Her eyes found the tablet in the back of the temple, displayed over bright yellow flames on a pedestal so as not to be submerged. Not that it mattered. The magic pulsing off the tablet had affected the water in the temple, which inevitably found its way outside and into the Pools of Time. Possibly even the cause of the pools' creation. Above the tablet, the symbol for the temple of fire was carved into the black stone: a circle with a dot in the center.

She stepped forward but stopped just as abruptly and eyed the pool at the bottom. "I'm here to join the tablets with the others. You will be set free soon," she announced, and all the salamanders in the temple tipped their heads up at her. As big as a large dog, they were still fairly intimidating. More appeared after her statement, coming up from the water to have a look at her. Some came out of hiding from within the hollow tree trunks and out from behind the boulders.

All at once, they started bobbing their bodies up and down. Their bright orange and black colors pulsed.

"Take the tablet," they ordered telepathically in croaky voices. *"Take the tablet. Free us. Take the tablet. Free us."*

The chanting grew louder and louder in her head. She grimaced at the sheer volume but managed to turn back around and point at the others—who looked as if they were hearing the voices as well, judging by the winces they all shared.

"Don't close those doors!" she shouted over the cacophony. "I'm not losing any more time!"

"Take the tablet. Free us. Take the tablet. Free us."

Thea marched down the stairs and through the pond, avoiding the salamanders swimming and bobbing their heads as best she could. The weight of the water dragged at her clothing, and each step felt as if she were trudging through molasses. She pulled herself out of the water with a gasp and grabbed the stone tablet cradled between a wreath of thorny branches from which flickering flames danced. A *zing* raced through her fingertips, and she shivered at the sheer power the object possessed.

She cradled it close and waded slowly through the waters back to the exit. When she and everyone else were outside, the doors shut with a powerful slam, cutting off the last *Free us*. It felt like her ears were ringing despite the chants all being in her head.

Her head finally cleared, and she was left to stare at the tablet in her hands. She couldn't read the words written in the ancient language, but she knew the importance of each letter and what it meant for her country. For the world. For magic itself.

It was finally over. She could go home now.

"We did it," Isabel giggled breathlessly.

"It's over," Fatik sighed, a laugh of his own working its way out.

"Hang on to me, everyone," Thea said quietly.

Everyone silently grabbed hold of her. She closed her eyes and placed her hand over the silver phoenix emblem clipped to her jacket. With only a brief thought and the image of the telepads in her mind, Thea felt the world fall away from her.

When she felt her feet touch solid ground again, the first thing she registered was whispers. She opened her eyes, and she was met with the stunned faces of her peers surrounding her.

I did it. She felt a bubble of laughter escape her as she sagged toward Ell's desk. She was finally back in HQ.

She was *finally* home.

Chapter Thirty-Seven

Projection vs Reflection

Ell jumped up from her desk, sending the chair she'd been sitting in careening onto the floor. She shot around her desk in a flurry of flying papers and wild hair that had, at some point, escaped her messy bun. The room around them burst into life. Thea went dizzy keeping up with all the buzzing gossip now that pure relief had settled into her bones.

"Is that Spellweaver Bauer?"

"… heard she took out those blood mages …"

"… was told to alert the Council as soon as she returned …"

"Someone notify the Council!"

"… something about a high-class mission. Not even the Summoners know …"

Someone tried to take the tablet, and only on instinct did Thea reel back with the object clutched tight to her chest. She had constantly been on high alert throughout her journey, but when her gaze focused on just who stood in front of her, she relaxed.

She met kind, green eyes and a sweet smile. Ell stood before her with her hand outstretched. "I'll take the tablet, Thea. We can get you over to Dr. Snow and into some dry clothes."

Thea blinked slowly. It was so hard to think straight now that she was out of danger, now that her adrenaline didn't have to keep her moving forward or die. Even in the caves, she had remained ever vigilant. A new area. New beings all around. Complacency had nearly killed them so many times. But this was HQ. She was surrounded by the Coven's safe walls, protected by her peers. She didn't know some of the members here any more than she did the people of the mountain, but trusted camaraderie came with the phoenix badge each being wore.

She knew she could trust Ell. The woman had taken the last tablet Thea and Rafe had nabbed. She'd led them to the Skrittish Library, was part of the Secret Society. She probably knew the inner workings of the Coven better than the blue cloaks.

She handed Ell the tablet, and her fingers tingled as the blonde took it from her. Warmth was returning to her despite the wet clothes rubbing uncomfortably against her skin.

"Take care of it," she sighed quietly, and her knees almost buckled. She felt Namara latch onto her, and she once again pulled her arm over her shoulders.

Ell beamed at her and brought the tablet close to her chest. "I will! Get some rest, Thea, and don't worry about writing up a report right now." The blonde whirled around and pointed at a nearby Hunter. "Anya! Come look after my desk, pretty please! Oh, pfft, don't worry, Pristine is right here. She'll help you!" Then the blonde was scurrying around the desk and up the spiral staircase in a blur.

Thea didn't have the mental capacity to follow Ell past the first stair, nor did she see the preppy Hunter that popped up next to her until she was right in her face. She was wearing a huge, floppy, pointed hat the same color as her black cape. She wrung her hands around a knotted staff with a glowing, green, glass bulb at the top as if nervous. The freckles splattered all over her round face matched her chestnut hair, and her green eyes were shining in youthful eagerness as she excitedly announced, "I already let Second Chosen MacBain know of your arrival, Spellweaver Bauer!"

Thea's heart lurched, and she couldn't stop the tired smile that spread over her face. "Thanks ... uh?"

If possible, the Hunter grew even more enthusiastic. "I'm Hunter Katz! I'm a big fan!"

Thea's brow quirked. *A big fan? Of what?* Namara, chuckling next to her, snapped her out of her thoughts. She looked around when she noticed the others were no longer around her, and when she went to assess where everyone was, she noted Isabel and Agni (now perched on the redhead's shoulder as a small rodent) were surrounded on all sides by peers. The researcher was grandly gesturing, no doubt about their adventures. Thea rolled her eyes and looked about the room, landing on Fatik and Siàu hanging back away from the action. Now that her hands were loose, she fished around in her pouch until she could pull out the barrier breaker oil.

Namara helped her walk over to the two, which would have been embarrassing if walking now hadn't seemed harder than marching through snow. It was finally catching up to her how much of a strain she'd had to put on her body the last two weeks. Even with the rest they'd gotten in the caves, it hadn't been enough.

She handed the bottle over to Siàu, who took it curiously. "Apply this to your lips and ears once a day for now. Just a drop. It'll help you talk to the beings of Tolvade—with the exception of demons. The Coven can help you assimilate into the city if you want to stick around. You'll be able to find either Isabel or me here, and if we're not, you can leave a message with Ell," she said and thumbed over to the front desk. "She's gone right now, but that's her desk."

The blonde had no doubt already made it to the Council by now, judging from the way she'd peeled out of the room—which, in hindsight, might have been a miscalculation of trust in the very clumsy receptionist.

Siàu smiled gratefully at Thea as she applied the oil and then pocketed the bottle. "Thank you very much. Fatik has offered to tour me around town for now."

Thea glanced between the two. "You're not tired?"

Fatik chuckled. "Part dragon, remember? I have a lot more stamina than normal beings."

She found herself nodding and let go of a sigh. "All right. I'll swing by Tasgall's to properly thank you again for everything. My superiors will be in contact with you about the other half of your payment. I'm definitely about to pass out in the medical wing now."

"Thea!" a deep voice shouted behind her, startling her.

Fatik looked over her shoulder and gave her a knowing smirk. "I doubt that."

She whipped around to find Rafe halted halfway down the spiral staircase. Mokana was leaning over the railing with a wide grin and a wildly waving arm. She felt that familiar pang in her chest, and that dumb smile of hers was back, but she couldn't care less. In a blur, the Summoner was before her and sweeping her off her feet and twirling her around like a princess in a children's storybook.

A new wave of dizziness overtook her, but laughter escaped her regardless. She wrapped her arms around his neck and met him in a breathless kiss.

Now *this* was home.

Despite Thea's half-hearted protests, Rafe carried her all the way to the medical ward. She gave up whining halfway there and instead listened to Mokana and Namara excitedly catch up—mostly about Namara's new, dryer condition— over the racing *thump, thump, thumps* of Rafe's heartbeat under her ear. It was fast-paced but probably matched her own.

Dr. Snow had been expecting them, and the young doctor ushered everyone into the large, empty non-intensive care unit. She was dressed in a dark blue corset that matched the color of her eyes over a white, ruffled blouse. Her lab coat had been hung up on a coatrack, but her red insignia was still pinned to her breast. Her white-blonde hair had been pulled up into a high ponytail with some side curls framing her face.

"Here, take this and go change." Savanna motioned to the private bathroom, handing the Spellweaver a hospital robe. Rafe sat her down gently, and she took the garment without a fuss.

As soon as the door closed behind her, she shucked the wet clothing off and sighed in relief. The cotton gown given to her wasn't the best quality by any means, but it felt so much better than the damp, irritating fabric of her clothes. She glanced at herself in the mirror and watched her expression grow shocked. There were large, dark bruises under her eyes, matching the few scattered over her arms and shins. Hesitantly, she opened up her cotton robe and grimaced.

It was true. She'd lost weight. A lot of weight. Her muscle mass had almost completely disappeared. She was leaner than anything else. Still in shape, but not as large as she used to be.

She *hated* it.

It was funny, almost. Here she was, skinnier, and she wasn't even happy about it. Maybe it had to do with all the bruises and scars all over her body, but the satisfaction she thought she'd feel to not be as … as …

Manly, Arabella whispered in her mind.

The satisfaction wasn't there, being skinnier. Her mother would have cried tears of joy. Her sister would have floundered to come up with a new insult. Her father would have plastered her face all across Adalith to try and marry her off as fast as possible. Suiters who would never suit her would be lined up around the block, sniffing at the scent of old money in the air.

It was a surreal feeling, knowing she'd been chasing an image she could never seem to obtain—and now that she had it, she didn't like what she saw in her reflection any more than she previously did. She peered down at her arms and grimaced. Once she recovered, she wanted to hit the gym. Gain back what she lost.

Someone knocked on the door, startling her out of her thoughts. "Thea, you okay?" Rafe called from the other side.

"Yeah, I'll be out in a minute!" She hurriedly tied the robe over herself and grabbed a spare trash bag under the sink to load her dirty clothes into. When she came back into the room, the red imps were jumping all over the bed she was led to. It was only when a swift *whack* on one's backside from Savanna did they all scurry away.

"Yeeowch!" the red imp screeched and shot up and off the bed, holding their bottom. The others laughed and ducked under the bed when their master (mother more like) cast them a look. She pulled her pocket watch out of her white slacks and hummed at the time.

"I can do a quick routine checkup before I have to rush back to the lab. Anything pressing I should know about?"

Namara took the bag of wet clothes from Thea as she sat on the lumpy cot and reclined back. She was about to confess to being stabbed, but there was hardly anything to worry about now. The wound technically had had over a year to heal.

"Besides being tired from all my adrenaline leaving me," she groused and closed her eyes when Dr. Snow put the blood pressure cuff around her left arm.

The blonde doctor nodded without a word as her sapphire eyes focused on the ticking needle of the meter gauge while she squeezed the hand pump. She leaned back with another small nod. "That explains your blood pressure still being a little high. It should stabilize soon. Okay, now take deep breaths," she instructed and unlooped the stethoscope from around her neck.

After the physical exam, she was ordered to rest for a little while. Savanna would return to retrieve her for the meeting with the Council, but for now, Thea could lean back and unwind.

It was harder than she thought. When she first got back to HQ, her body had wanted nothing more than to sag into the nearest chair and sleep for a couple of days. Now it was fighting to stay awake as Rafe sat next to her.

He was studying her with a worried look, and Thea could practically hear the lecture he was reciting in his head. "Why didn't you tell her about the stab wound? Has it healed? I just noticed how thin you are. I thought something was off when I picked you up, but it's been a few weeks since I've seen you. When's the last time you ate?"

Her eyes drooped, but she blinked them open. She was too tired to get into the specifics, especially concerning the news that she had lost time yet again. It was like she had been drugged, but the good doctor hadn't stuck her with a needle. Not even a saline drip. The imps—for the most part—left her alone, having found interest in a trespassing horned beetle on the floor. They were loud and obnoxious, but Thea couldn't find it within herself to care.

She nodded at Rafe's series of questions. "Don't worry, I'm fine. I have so much to tell yo—" she cut herself off with a yawn, and the contagious action jumped to Rafe, who she could tell wasn't getting much sleep either.

His gaze softened. "You can tell me all about it later. Just rest for now."

She patted the small space next to her. "Hop on, you're going to rest too."

He eyed the short bed skeptically and straightened up in his chair. "I have to get back to work," he protested, albeit weakly.

Thea stared at him, eyes narrowed and waiting. She patted the bed again.

With a sigh that caused the two watchful demonesses behind him to giggle, Rafe resigned himself to his fate and walked over to the other side of the cot. Again, that skeptical look of his was back. One would think hospital beds could come in more sizes than the standard "one size fits all." Thea scooted over a smidge.

"I can just take another bed, Thea," he tried once again, hands on his hips as he stared down at her. She stared right back up at him, unblinking, and patted the bed once more in demand.

"You're incorrigible," he groaned and shuffled awkwardly onto the cot. She was too exhausted for a rebuttal and grinned drowsily as she pillowed her head on his chest. She closed her eyes and sighed.

"Ooooooh," the imps cooed at the foot of their bed, and Thea snorted in amusement as one cried out, "Yuckie!" before Namara and Mokana chased the little scamps away. Before long, Rafe's breathing evened out, and sleep came for both of them, pulling them under its waves and stealing them from the waking world.

Mokana snickered at the two humans on the bed and found Namara's gaze. "Now that they're asleep, I want to know *all* about this Agni of yours."

When Thea woke, she found the medical ward's ceiling tiles staring back at her. She closed her eyes again and groaned, rolling over onto her side. Her arm flopped about, and it took only a moment before her sleep-addled mind realized she was alone. Rafe must have returned to work while she was sleeping.

"What *is* that?" one of the imps asked curiously from somewhere. She attempted to ignore them and go back to sleep.

"I wanna touch it!" another whisper-yelled.

"*Don't* touch me," someone said. Probably another patient.

"Preeeeetty," a third murmured.

"Grab it, grab it!"

"Hey, don't grab at me, you little devils!"

"It's gonna bite meeee!"

Thea growled and shot up in bed, pillow in hand to aim at the annoying creatures. Her eyes widened, and the pillow dropped from her grasp as she stared at the foot of her bed. On the metal railing, a magpie was perched and watching her.

She screamed.

The commotion caused the imps to flail back and fall onto each other like bowling pins, and the bird jumped back and began flapping its wings. She grabbed the fallen pillow from her lap and reared her arm back—

"Wait!" the bird cried, flapping its wings in fear once more.

She froze, but this time she kept the pillow cocked back and ready to launch. She narrowed her eyes at the magpie. Nothing was out of the ordinary with the bird. It was mostly black with splotches of white along its back and beak, and its eyes were the color of terracotta pots. After a tense moment, she demanded an answer. "What are you?"

The black and white bird twisted its head one way then the other as it peered at her curiously. Then it straightened up and ruffled its feather. "What? Seriously, you don't know? Out of all the ignorant, stupid …"

Slowly, Thea let her arm fall to her lap as she squinted at the bird as it continued to ramble. "I saw you in the mountains," she said after a moment, cutting off its tirade.

The bird nodded in an exaggerated fashion. "Yes, yes! That's it!" it acknowledged. "And before that, too! Surely, you remember now?"

Thea racked her brain, but she didn't recall any other time she'd seen the bird. "Well, whatever, you didn't answer my question. What are you? Are you a familiar?" Why would someone's familiar be trying to reach her?

Once again, the bird nodded with hard up and down motions. "Yes, yes," it repeated in that raspy voice. "You may address me as Kelvin."

Several curious, red heads all popped up over the railing of Thea's cot, startling the bird into flapping about and complaining again. She glanced over at the chair next to her bed and noticed a new pair of clothes for her to slip into. Namara must have swung by the house to grab her some. She briefly wondered where everyone had run off to. She looked back at the bird defending itself against the tiny masses, pecking at curious fingers that reached up to touch its glossy feathers. She'd better wrap this up quick lest Kelvin leave with a few less feathers than when he arrived.

She swung her legs over the edge of the cot and hopped up, gathering her clothes. "Okay, well, what do you want? I assume your owner sent you my way for something important. Although I don't know why you didn't try to talk to me up in the mountains."

The imps giggled as they took turns poking the familiar, causing it to hop back and forth and gripe like an old man. The last poke sent the magpie lifting off into the air and landing roughly on Thea's shoulder. She flinched with a yelp and turned to glare at the bird.

"Hey! Get off me!"

"I cannot believe this," it squawked, spreading its wings in its attempt to balance itself as Thea straightened up. "You made the call for me, and you don't even remember! I am gravely offended! I shall not even call you master."

Thea's eyes widened. "What?" She jerked back, again causing the bird to flail on her shoulder. "*I* made the call? When did I make the call? You're saying you're *my* familiar?"

The magpie nodded. "Yes, yes. You reached out to me weeks ago! At first, I wasn't strong enough, so I tried connecting with you in dreams, but your dreams would morph into terrible nightmares. Truly tragic. And then, to make matters worse, you'd always forget when you woke up! Only after you fell into the Pools of Time did I gain enough power through our bond. You're welcome, by the way! I'm what kept you alive. Also," he hopped about continuously, "the water from the Pools of Time kept you from losing any more time in the temple! Imagine if you hadn't fallen in. I would have been stuck outside waiting for days!"

Thea's unsteady legs forced her to sit back down on the cot. Kelvin fluttered off her shoulder and landed on the chair by her now crumpled shirt. Her thoughts became a jumbled mess, and she let her head fall into her hands when it became too much. She rubbed at her temples, but that didn't help any.

"I don't understand," she mumbled after a moment. "What do the Pools of Time have to do with anything? And how exactly did you keep me alive?"

Kelvin was peering down at her eggshell-colored blouse with its shiny, brass buttons. He hopped away from the polished fasteners as if nervous of them.

"The Pools of Time—" he began, but a knock interrupted him. Thea glanced up to watch three red imps all scramble for the door. One fell over itself in its haste to open it up. When they couldn't reach, one jumped onto the other's back, and together they swayed closer toward the handle. They quickly managed to pull down the lever.

Dr. Snow swept in and gave the imp on top of the other a gentle pat on the head. "Thank you, Prudence," she murmured. She aimed a small smile Thea's way, though it faltered slightly when she saw the magpie sitting in the guest's chair. With an eyebrow raised high on her forehead, she silently asked what was going on.

Thea shrugged. "I guess I have a familiar."

If possible, the eyebrow raised higher. "You guess?"

She could only shrug again. She wasn't going to tell the good doctor the whole story—she was way too mentally exhausted for that. Decent nap or not, she still felt like she'd been run over by a speeding oxcart.

Savanna didn't look too interested anyway, and she waved the subject away. "No matter, it's time you get dressed and head over to the Council room. I've never seen the blue cloaks so antsy. From what I hear, Isabel hasn't even had an audience with them yet. Too busy writing up reports."

A flash of panic flooded her, but she let loose a slow exhale. She'd have to trust Isabel not to write up a report on Fatik's blood. The Council might already suspect something, but she doubted the High One would be cruel enough to force a Dragonkin to give up their life for the sake of another. Especially if Savanna had made any progress in replicating the blood she'd brought back from the desert. Still, she wanted to pull Isabel aside before they had council with the blue cloaks to make sure she didn't accidentally slip up in front of them.

"I'll get dressed then," she said and grabbed her clothes. She could hear Kelvin's explanation later. The bird hopped about as she stood to gather her stuff and head to the bathroom. When she came out, her eyes widened as he flew over and landed on her shoulder. She sent him an annoyed look. "Are you coming with me?"

He gave another exaggerated nod. "Yes, yes. Where you go, I go. Don't seem so upset!"

She sighed. "This is just great. I hope you know how to feed yourself. I didn't sign up for a pet."

Kelvin pecked at her ear, and she flinched and growled out a pained exclamation. "I am the knowledge of the universe that will help you bridge your pathetic magical capabilities to a higher realm! I should think myself capable of finding food for myself! And I am not a pet, though technically you *did* sign up for the responsibility of a familiar."

Thea glowered at the bird. "Peck my ear again and see how useful all that information is to a dead bird."

If anything, Kelvin only appeared more miffed. "I can't believe I'm stuck with you."

"Ditto."

Chapter Thirty-Eight

Judge, Jury, and the Verdict

Thea was still rubbing her ear as she followed Dr. Snow down the hall. Savanna walked with confidence, yet she was hardly looking at where she was going, what with her eyes glued to the clipboard in her hand and all. She was curious what the doctor's findings were after two weeks away.

She cleared her throat awkwardly. "Um, so have you made any progress with the—uh, blood?" She didn't know how classified the dragon's blood was, so she just settled for that.

Dr. Snow peered over her shoulder with that same dry smile. "That's right, you were the one who brought back such a generous sample. The Council already knows, so I don't see much reason not to tell you since you know about its existence. The lab was able to completely copy the specimen, so Medusa's Kiss won't be a problem for much longer."

Thea couldn't help the relieved smile that slipped onto her face. However, images of a certain redheaded sorceress flickered through her mind. She eyed the doctor once more. "So, *all* the patients have been cured? They get to go back to their lives?"

If Thea hadn't been looking, she wouldn't have seen the change in the doctor's expression. Savanna's lips thinned for only a moment. Her eyes took on a glassy appearance for a mere second, but then she was looking over at Thea again with that same bland, fake smile. "They were all cured."

Thea's heart squeezed in her chest. She knew what that meant. If she hadn't known the truth, she would have assumed that all the patients with the cursed disease were happy and free. She aimed her own bland smile back at the doctor. "That's good."

"Thea!" someone called, and the Spellweaver turned to find Isabel waving her down from the lobby with a stack of papers under her other arm. Around her stood Namara, Mokana, and Rafe. A familiar-looking rodent sat perched on the kelpie's shoulder.

Rafe noticed Kelvin first, and he stared down at the magpie with a look of confusion. "What's with the bird?"

She sighed. This was going to be a common question for a while. "I'll explain more later, but this is Kelvin … my familiar."

The whole group stared at her with wide eyes, and she grimaced when they all collectively yelled, "What!" Even Kelvin jerked back from the noise. Thank the goddess they were some of the only few beings in the lobby at the moment, though the two Hunters walking by jumped at the noise.

"I said I'd explain later," she griped and rubbed at her face in exasperation.

Dr. Snow cleared her throat and aimed a pointed look at the group. "I don't have all day, guys. Are we ready?"

"I need to speak to Isabel for a moment, but we won't be far behind," Thea piped up before the group could move on.

Savanna sent her a questioning look but shrugged. "Don't take too long. I won't be the one in trouble if you don't show up promptly."

Ignoring the puzzled expressions coming from the others, she nodded. "It'll only take a moment."

When they began ascending the stairs, Thea dropped her voice so no one else could hear her. "You didn't write anything in your reports about Fatik's blood, did you?"

The confusion cleared instantly on the redhead's face. "Ah, that's what this is about. Don't worry. I didn't mention a thing. Savanna also said she was able to copy the blood you brought back, so it won't matter anyway. I won't say anything either."

She nodded. "Good. Ready to go talk to the blue cloaks?"

Isabel groaned. "Goddess above, this is gonna take forever. They're gonna wanna hear about *everything*."

"Yeah," she agreed reluctantly. "Let's get it over with, though."

Thea was already exhausted, and the meeting had barely begun. Where had all her energy gone? She felt like she'd gotten plenty of time to rest and recover in the caves, but ever since the Pools of Time incident that morning, she'd been sapped dry.

Goddess help me, that had been this morning? It felt like she'd gotten dunked and nearly drowned forever ago.

Regardless, she tried to keep her exhaustion to herself and hoped her face remained neutral as the High Priests went back and forth between her and Isabel's recounts of the mission. Rafe stood on the side with a notepad and quill floating in the air beside him, transcribing everything that was said. As the Second Chosen over the case, it wasn't out of place to see him there. She just hoped he kept his professionalism when he heard some of the more ... *chaotic* moments in the mission.

Namara and Mokana stood beside him, out of the way, but if the kelpie needed to be called to corroborate with anything, she was still in earshot.

Thea let Isabel do most of the talking, though her input was necessary to align with Isabel's side of the story. With everything that happened to them, Isabel would already have a report in hand waiting to be handed over to Rafe. Thea was impressed with her efficiency and promptness.

"When she fell, Thea used a spell to glide down the mountain to retrieve her," Isabel said.

Mia turned to Thea and gestured for Thea to continue. She brought out her crystal ball and tapped on an icon on the glass. "Yes, she is correct. Along with our guide, Fatik, we descended the mountain. However, I did not use a spell. I used Feather Fall on Namara so she would not injure herself from falling, and that is the same spell we used to climb the mountain. I glided down on Fatik's back. However, at the bottom of the mountain, we stumbled upon a trashed encampment. I understand blood mages and feral demons are gathering in the outskirts of the Black Forest, and I believe this was one of their campsites. I didn't know how to send these images to anyone in the Coven …" She ended awkwardly and rubbed at the back of her neck.

The Celestial held out their hand, and Thea ascended the elevated platform and placed the crystal ball onto the pedestal before the High Priests. With a flick of their wrist, the High One brought the images to life. They popped into existence in the air before them, and the Celestial made a spreading out motion with their hands that caused the images to lay out before the blue cloaks. It was eerily similar to what happened to her during the Pools of Time. How images seemed to appear out of nowhere.

Once the blue cloaks had looked at the still shots, the Celestial scooped up their fingers, and the images vanished. Still cupping their hand, they made the motion of dumping whatever they were holding onto a piece of paper. The paper then floated up and over to a stunned Rafe. He grabbed the parchment and stared down at it, blinking in confusion.

"Please file that along with the reports," the High One instructed gently.

"Yes, of course, High One," he returned with a dip of his head.

Thea was asked to retrieve her crystal ball, but when she looked back at where the images should have been, they were gone.

The rest of the meeting dragged on, and Thea wasn't even allowed to zone out as Isabel dragged on with all of her findings, notes, theories, and reports. She was forced to weigh in unless the subject specifically dealt with researcher particulars.

They spoke about every detail of their journey—every long, boring detail. Thea knew the Celestial, a High Elf, could read what was on the tablets, so she didn't bother mentioning what each one contained. Information wasn't being withheld if they already knew, right? The only hiccup that had Thea's heart in her throat was when she was recounting Isabel's ailment in the caves. She'd been too busy dancing around the subject of Fatik's blood that she hadn't noticed the particularly dark look on Leto and Lilith's faces until she was finished with her story.

Silence blanketed the Council room as if the others could sense the anger radiating off the twins. Even Isabel looked nervous, and she looked everywhere but in their direction.

"All that matters is that you are safe, though we would caution you to be more careful in the future," the Celestial said after a moment, and the tenseness settled down in the room. For now. Isabel had better find somewhere to hide after the meeting because it looked as if the twins (Leto especially) were still ready to strangle her.

Thea couldn't speak much for herself, though, when Isabel went on about the Pools of Time, then the source of the pools that she'd originally found, then the dragon, and then the fact that Thea was knocked into the water … for an hour.

She placed her head in her hand and sighed, not bothering to look over at Rafe and his no doubt ice-blue eyes. She could feel how furious he was with her at the moment. Furious and confused, which was never a good combination for his overprotective nature.

"And how is it that you managed to survive underwater for over an hour?" Torro questioned adamantly, and Thea was saved from focusing on the angry Second Chosen on the sidelines. However, she now had to speak to her least favorite High Priest, and she didn't even know the answer herself.

She looked at her familiar still perched on her shoulder. The Council members hadn't questioned the bird, but she had seen a few of them giving Kelvin curious looks.

The magpie shuffled his feathers and looked back at his new master. "Oh, you want me to answer?"

High Priest Mia hid her smile behind her fist and pretended to clear her throat. "Is it that you do not know, Spellweaver Bauer?"

Thea directed her gaze back at the Council panel and shook her head hesitantly. "I don't. Kelvin—my, uh, familiar—says he is the reason I survived. I never received an answer out of him before I was summoned."

"It would seem that you two are connected in a way that is very much different than the bond between your demonic partner and yourself," the Celestial stated. They held out their pale hand, and Kelvin immediately fluttered over to his new perch, landing delicately onto their long fingers.

Thea didn't understand what the Celestial meant and aimed a short glance over at Namara. The kelpie shrugged, looking just as lost.

"I'm afraid I don't know what you mean," Thea hedged quietly.

The High Elf hummed as they studied Kelvin's feathers. Without looking Thea's way, they asked, "How long did it feel like you were under the water, Spellweaver Bauer?"

Thea glanced up at the ceiling as she mentally counted, but her sense of time had been turned on its head while under the constant assault of water choking her and drowning her in its depths. If she had to guess, "Fifteen minutes? Give or take a few …"

"And do you know exactly how much time actually passed while in the water? Anything that changed about you physically?"

Thea really didn't want to answer that question. She didn't know what the point of this interrogation was about, but she really, *really* didn't want to answer that question.

"I sense that you know, yet you hesitate," the High One said.

Thea's fingers tightened into fists behind her back, and she let go of a calming breath. One that did not help whatsoever when she glanced over at Rafe. "Based on the stab wound I received at the beginning of the trip … the wound appears to have had a year or more to heal."

Quiet murmuring broke out around the Council members. She peeked over at Rafe through her bangs, but he wasn't looking at her anymore. He was staring off at something, face closed off against the world. His arms were crossed, and his fingers were biting into his other arm fiercely. She could see him tremble, willing himself to hold everything in. She looked back at the Celestial, who was gazing down at her. The being was way too bright to maintain eye contact, but Thea tried.

"And yet only an hour above the water passed," they said and peered down at the bird on their hand. "Did you know of your familiar before you entered the water?"

Thea shook her head once. "No."

"Not for lack of trying on my part!" Kelvin crowed.

The Celestial hummed again and sent the bird back to its master with a gentle wave. "Your familiar had already been contacted, yet you were not aware of this. This is quite rare, but not unheard of. Sometimes a being's subconscious can wander without their knowing. With one foot in the natural world and another in the Pools of Time, your connection is essentially what kept you alive. Yet, while in the Pools of Time, your connection grew so solidly that— even though an hour had passed—it was as if a year had gone by between you two. Tell me, your familiar gained a corporal form after this, didn't he? When before he was nothing but a dream away?"

Thea stared at the Celestial in awe.

The being nodded, the Spellweaver's shock being enough of an answer. "I assumed so. Your connection was weak because you were unaware you had reached out to your familiar, and only when your bond grew over the time frame of a year, thanks to the pools, was he able to gain a physical body."

Thea let the information process in her mind, and it made sense. It did, really, but it was still a lot.

With that out of the way, Thea let Isabel go on about Agni fighting off the dragon. In true Isabel fashion, her storytelling enraptured the blue cloaks. As the rest of the meeting dragged on and on, Thea began to wonder if the High Priests really had nothing better to do for the day or if she was just exceptionally tired.

"Ms. Thomas, we thank you for your time today and all of your prompt reports," The newest High Priest, Rebecca Livingston, stated once all the blue cloaks had been brought up to speed. "Dr. Snow, what is your verdict?"

Thea's brow pinched as she turned to the young doctor on the sidelines. Dr. Snow hadn't said anything throughout the entire meeting, and Thea had nearly forgotten about her several times. Now the woman was going to enact judgment on them? For what?

Savanna pushed back a strand of hair behind her ear and cleared her throat. "Based on her last physical exam, overall behavior, ease of mobility, and mental capacity, I will say a day's rest is all that is needed."

Rebecca nodded. "Then it shall be done. Ms. Thomas, you will adhere to Dr. Snow's recommended rest period and remain in the city at all times until after the Wild Hunt spell is performed. Is that in any way unclear?"

Isabel looked like she wanted to put up a fuss, but one look at the twins had her lips thinning. "Nope, all clear over here, boss. So … I can go now?"

Lilith covered her face with her palm, and Leto sighed quietly, eyeing the heavens for assistance. Rebecca paid no attention to either of the Remes siblings and had yet to be charmed by the redhead, so she merely nodded and said bluntly, "You're dismissed."

"Great," she clapped and gave a sloppy salute to Thea with a wide smile. "See you when I see you, Thea. Let's catch lunch sometime. I'll invite Fatik and Siàu," she called over her shoulder as she practically skipped out of the Council room.

Thea was impressed with her nerve to act so childishly in front of the blue cloaks, but at the same time, Isabel wouldn't be Isabel otherwise. She waved silently at the redhead as she left. She felt a wave of dizziness wash over her as she did, and she had to plant her feet a tad further apart to keep her balance. She really hoped this meeting would adjourn soon.

When Rebecca sat down, Lilith stood from her shared chair. Her deep frown softened when she glanced down at the Spellweaver, but her voice remained neutral when she asked, "Spellweaver Bauer, we would also like to thank you for your time and your verbal report. Second Chosen MacBain will be writing up the full report, so there is no need for you to do so. Before we release you here today, do you have an answer for the Council?"

Thea felt her mouth go dry. Her gaze drifted between each Coven member, but she knew she did not have the answer they were seeking. In truth, she did not want to become a Summoner, and a smaller, quieter part of her had started to nag, tug, pull at the thoughts that raced through her mind and asked her if she still wanted to be part of the Coven at all.

There was still the matter of Namara, Mokana, Agni, and all the other demons' fates after their human partners passed away. She hadn't been able to think up a more reasonable, more persuasive argument besides her initial thought process in the Huǒshān Clan's temple room. If she said no to the High Priests now, she may not get to have an audience with them again so close to the Wild Hunt spell. And, for whatever reason, she wanted the thought of her partner's fate to be embedded in their minds. Not for it to be swept aside by distractions such as the massive spell about to take place.

So, with a deep breath and a feeling like this had all happened before, she said, "I do not, High Priest Remes."

More murmuring broke out around the panel of blue cloaks, and Thea felt apprehension run over the fine hairs on her skin. She hoped her answer, or lack thereof, did not offend. She felt it was too late to try and explain that she really hadn't had the time to think, so she kept her mouth shut and waited for them to address her once again.

The Celestial stood, and silence reigned in the room once more. Lilith quickly found her seat as the High Elf aimed a calm, reassuring look Thea's way. "I understand your mission has been perilous. This has taken a toll on your physical, mental, and, I would presume, emotional well-being. Is that not correct, Dr. Snow?"

Savanna stepped forward and nodded sharply. "Yes, High One. I would suspect that after the initial physical exam and a thorough analysis of her overall demeanor today, a three-day rest would be sufficient to bring her back to normal levels. A week of light duty on top of that would also be beneficial."

Thea's eye bulged at the doctor's words. She'd never had three days off in her entire career, excluding her week-long comatose healing. And light duty on top of that? What would she even do?

The Celestial nodded and then turned toward a stunned Thea. "Then it shall be done. You are to rest within the comforts of your home for the next three days. After that, report to the Coven for your light-duty briefing. I expect your answer after the Wild Hunt spell has been fully conducted, Spellweaver Bauer. That is sufficient enough time to clearly think about your future. You will not be allowed to delay any further. Is that in any way unclear?"

Thea felt as if the world had just fallen on her shoulders. A part of her wanted to cry. A part of her wanted to rejoice. A part of her didn't know what to do with the knowledge that she would have three whole days to do nothing. Another part of her was relieved she would have until after the Wild Hunt spell to not only give her answer but convey her, Isabel's, Namara's, and every other demons' concerns for their future. But first, she would be stuck at the house with Rafe no doubt overdoing it on the doting.

She swallowed the hard pill she was being forced to take and answered as calmly as she could. "Yes, High One."

Chapter Thirty-Nine

Breaks and Breaking

Somehow, the prospect of a three-day break felt longer than the two-week hike she'd endured. Every day she had been working toward a goal, a destination. She had a purpose every morning waking up on the stiff, frozen ground. Now, in the comfort of Rafe's duplex, she didn't know what to do.

Rest, they said. No one even wanted her to leave the house, but like hellfire that was going to happen. She'd go stir-crazy if she didn't feel the sun on her face or the wind in her hair—as bitter as it still was some days.

Kelvin had made himself scarce when she'd arrived home. Told her he'd peck at her window if he wanted her attention, but she was going to be "useless" for the next couple of days. Namara had walked with her home, but she was right back out into the thick of the city as soon as the door closed on Thea's bedroom. Now, she stood in the middle of the room, not knowing what to do.

She stared at her bed and knew it was too soft. Lumpy. She swiped her pillow off the bed and retreated to another room in the house. The room filled with assorted candles, a desk toppled with paperwork, a bookshelf collecting more dust than books, and a bed that was a bit bigger, a bit firmer, and smelled like a certain someone.

She fell asleep instantly.

"I'm going," she snapped.

"You are not," he countered, eyes narrowing. "You are supposed to be *resting*."

Thea and Rafe stared at one another stubbornly. Neither was budging, but Rafe couldn't stay with her all day and make sure she was behaving. He had to get back to the Coven soon.

"I was resting when I came home yesterday and most of this morning," she insisted. She had barely woken up when Rafe came storming into his room, thinking she had gone off somewhere. She remembered him settling down next to her, a hand in her hair, and the rest was a blur. That morning, she stirred at the smell of breakfast, and her stomach had nearly caved in on itself at the thought of a home-cooked meal.

Rafe crossed his arms over his chest. "You still need to recover. That was what Dr. Snow said. I was there, remember?"

Thea scoffed and rolled her eyes. "She didn't say I needed to be bedridden, Rafe. I'm just going to the sanctuary. I need to talk to Blythe."

She couldn't put it off anymore. It'd been a constant, nagging thought in the back of her mind ever since she came back from the desert. She knew Cressida hadn't made it. Even without proof, she knew. She'd known since she read that one passage from the book in the Skrittish Library. She knew, and she hadn't warned Blythe. Blythe, who remained positive and optimistic in the face of her suffering, withering oathbound, deserved to know the truth. Even if it meant the end of their friendship.

It would never be a true friendship if she kept that secret.

Blythe, sweet and bubbly Blythe, would no doubt hate her. For giving her false hope. For not warning her. For not preparing her for some of the worst pain she would likely ever feel. For not being there for her in her time of need. For allowing her to be all alone with Cressida, no longer anything more than a husk, a shell of the soul once tied to her own.

Thea swallowed as a *pang* echoed throughout her chest, and she looked away toward the door. She was dressed lightly. A thick, dark green, drawstring shirt over a cream corset would be enough for Tolvade's sunny weather. She'd lost her arrow launcher to the Pools of Time, but she still had her sickle strapped to her back, and that was all that mattered.

Namara stepped forward, hands up to ease the tense situation. "We can always go another day, Thea. You should really lie down and rest—"

Thea groaned and slid off the stool under the island counter. "Not you too." She grabbed her dust pouch from the hall tree and secured it to her person. "I'm going to talk to her. I know ferals are still a concern, so Namara, if you don't mind coming with me, that would be a big help. Otherwise, I *will* be going alone."

Rafe threw his hands up in the air. "Why is it so important that you go now? You can't wait until after the

Wild Hunt spell? Your health is important, Thea. So is your safety."

"I don't want to hear that from you. You've got more bags under your eyes than a purse shop."

"Thea—"

"*I have to, Rafe!*" she lashed out, and she immediately felt regret hit her for letting her anger flare like that. She took a deep breath and met his startled expression. "I have to. I—I know what happened to Cressida."

Rafe's brow pinched, and he leaned back. "What? What do you mean you know? How could you have known?"

Thea swallowed. "I've known since the start that … that Cressida wouldn't make it. I knew the night before we set out for the desert. One of the books in the library—it pretty much told me what would happen. And I kept it a secret because we needed to have Blythe escort us, and I didn't think she would if she knew it was a lost cause." She couldn't look at Rafe anymore. She didn't want to see his disgust. "It was selfish, I know. I knew it was selfish when I made the decision not to tell her. But I have to tell her the truth. It's the only thing I regret not doing. So, I'm going to the sanctuary, and I'm going to make things right even if that means she'll hate me for it."

She turned, ripped open the door, and marched out. She kept walking even after she heard her name being called, and she kept walking when Namara came bounding up beside her. She was thankful the kelpie quietly trekked alongside her. She needed the silence to figure out what she was going to say.

She noticed a small shadow flying overhead and knew it was Kelvin trailing after her. He must have sensed her mood because he kept to the buildings, street signs, and eventually the trees. There was still some snow dusting the woodland path to Srbeveara, but only in the shade of the now blooming trees.

Namara had mostly been silent, but she kept looking north before hurrying after Thea. After the third pause, Thea turned to her and crossed her arms over her chest. "What's the matter?"

Namara appeared conflicted, but her dark eyes flicked to the woods around them before narrowing on a particular direction. "I can sense ferals, but they're far away. They're not headed for us, but … Thea, this isn't good. There's a lot of them."

Thea felt a chill sweep over her. "You think the Coven …?"

"They know. Moka said so. I know we're headed to a sanctuary, but I'm pretty sure we're not allowed to be out this far from the city center."

"I can scout them if you would like," called Kelvin from a low-hanging branch.

Thea immediately shook her head. "No, the blood mages will know they're being scouted. The Coven's got a plan, so we're not instigating anything. The only thing we can do now is ignore them. You say they're not headed for us?"

Namara shook her head. "They're just camping out in an area right now. They're far enough away that I don't even think the hellhounds could sniff us out."

Thea nodded and continued onward. "Then we have nothing to worry about. Right now, anyway."

Namara rushed after her. "That doesn't mean one or two can't break away from the group and find us, Thea. I can't sense them unless they're really powerful or—like now—shoved together into one large grouping. I couldn't sense that soul eater, or the hellhound in that village, remember?"

Thea sighed but kept marching. "All the more reason to check on Blythe. She's out here all alone. I know she's got a barrier up, but even Cressida couldn't keep out an army of ferals if she wanted to. Maybe if she was tethered to that … *thing*, but not on her own."

"I don't know, she kept them out when they were running loose."

"Yeah, but all at once? An army attacking the barrier all at once? If nothing else, I've got to get her out before the Wild Hunt spell goes off. I don't know what's about to happen, but I know that spell will be the catalyst for *something*. They're lying in wait, and that's never a good sign."

She heard Namara sigh. "Okay, but we'll hear what she has to say, and then we're leaving. With or without her. I promised Rafe I'd haul you out of here at the first sign of danger and that we wouldn't take too long."

Thea snorted. "Sensing the ferals a few miles out wasn't the first sign of danger?"

"Do you *want* me to haul you out of here?"

"I'd like to see you try."

"You think I can't?"

"What a quaint little abode," Kelvin interjected, and both Thea and Namara turned from their argument to find they had come across Srbeveara without noticing.

"Well, we're already here," Thea said with a smirk in the kelpie's direction. Namara stuck her tongue out at her.

The sanctuary was a tad different than she remembered. She did recall that the two-story cottage was no longer encased in an orange defensive barrier but rather a baby blue one that nearly blended in with the sky. But now there were a lot more flowers growing around Srbeveara. They'd taken over the wrought iron staircases, and blossoming vines curled up the warm, stone sides. Flowerbeds of roses, lavender, and—more than anything else—tulips in all colors hugged the sanctuary like a moat. The wrought iron doors with their heavy knockers had also been replaced with thick, dark wood. The structure looked untouched by the forest's clinging chill as bright green grass swayed in the clearing.

"She's done a lot to the place," Namara commented quietly.

You tend to throw yourself into anything you can when you're trying to distract yourself.

Thea sighed and walked through the barrier. A welcoming embrace caressed her skin for the briefest of moments, and she felt a surge of emotion hit her that made her eyes hot. Blinking rapidly, she wiped at her eye as nonchalantly as she could and grabbed the new, wooden knocker to announce her presence. She felt Kelvin land on her shoulder and cock his head curiously.

Within moments, the door opened, and Blythe came into view. As exuberant as ever, Blythe was wearing a bright yellow dress that belled out at her hips. A sheer, mauve wrap graced her shoulders with an owl cameo pinning the fabric together in the front. Her hair had been smoothed all the way to the right, where it had been styled into a bouquet of knots and twists. Flowers from the garden accented the hairstyle and complemented the color of her outfit.

One eye was painted a dark rose color with tiny jewels above the lashes, but the other eye was left bare. It appeared they'd interrupted her in the middle of completing her look.

Blythe blinked owlishly at Thea, who stared back in equal shock. "Thea?" She shook herself and allowed a bright smile to grace her features. "What a surprise. And Namara, too? Oh! You have a little friend! How sweet! Come in, come in. I was just in the middle of doing my makeup!"

Much like the first time she met Blythe, she was hauled inside with more strength than she gave the sorceress credit for. There was a nice breeze that skimmed through Thea's curls, and the scent of fresh linen was prevalent. That same haunting, melodic voice that sang through the halls of the sanctuary was still there, but the tune was different. Airy, more upbeat notes carried throughout the cottage that paired well with the spring feeling.

The waterfall was back to flowing with vigor, and she could feel a *thrum* of magic in the air, but other than that, the sanctuary wasn't too much different on the inside. Thea spun around to find Blythe marveling at Namara's new, dryer existence.

"*Zermenelo!* I never would have thought this was possible!" she exclaimed with a beaming smile. "The last time you were this dry—" a dark look suddenly crossed over her half-painted face, and her bubbliness subdued itself. "Ah, well, those times are behind us now, *eau?*"

Thea cleared her throat and gazed down at the floor. "Blythe, I uh … I need to talk to you about something."

It must have been the way she said it because the sorceress gave her a strange look. One that wasn't confused or intrigued. One that looked like she *knew* what Thea wanted to talk about. It unnerved her, but she stood her ground regardless. Each of them was silent as they walked into Blythe's personal room.

Blythe put down her long, pencil-like brush and took a soft breath into her lungs. She held it for a long moment before slowly releasing it into the air. She hadn't interrupted Thea once. Didn't even look at her as she applied the same rose color to her other eye. Didn't even flinch at the truth when she applied the tiny jewels to the tacky surface of her lid.

She turned to Thea, who sat on the daybed in her overly eclectic room. Namara sat with her with Kelvin perched on her damp shoulder, but neither had said a word since they were ushered in. Blythe situated the tulle of her skirts over her crossed knees and said, in a very calm voice, "I know."

The words held such weight behind them that, for a long moment, Thea was left staring at the sorceress. She knew. She knew? How could she have known? Rafe hadn't even known. He'd talked to her the night before they left for the desert. Had she slipped up somewhere? When did she even find out?

As she went to question how, the sorceress continued.

"Well, I did not *know*. I ..." she sighed and looked off to the side. "I had my doubts after the night Asmo found me in the desert. He is the one who told me she would die if we gave her the wyvern blood. I did not want to believe him. How could I, when all he had ever done was lie? He had deceived me and deceived Cressida. Yet, there was the morning after when I told you and Rafe what happened. The look of surprise on your face ... well, it gave you away in the end. I know you must mask your emotions for your work, but something about your expression ... It nagged at me."

Thea swallowed, and she felt her eyes grow hot, but thankfully, the tears did not fall. She straightened up and tried to build up that same wall that she always built. She'd told Blythe once it was okay to cry, but she ate those words every time she put up one brick at a time to keep others at bay, to keep them from seeing what she was feeling, to keep them from knowing how their words affected her.

"I still did not want to believe it could be true. I thought to myself, 'how could she know? She would not know something like that,' and yet, here you are, telling me that you knew all along."

The bricks began to crumble. Thea felt her lip tremble, and she bit down on it before it could give her away.

"I made Cressida into something she was not. I made her invincible in my mind. I thought she would survive anything. She was so strong even in the end. She—" she cut herself off and began fanning at her eyes. "She was going to be okay. I knew it, I—"

Blythe sobbed suddenly, and the bricks disintegrated.

Thea raked her fingers through her curls and ducked down so Blythe couldn't see the tears that escaped, but she knew she wasn't fooling anyone. She choked the noises that desperately wanted to escape down as she let Blythe finish.

After a few shaky breaths, she continued. "Even in the end, when I wanted to believe that the cure would save her, and she would be able to live the life she wanted—that *we* wanted—I held back. I thought, 'this will take her from me. This cure will kill her,' but it was in my hands. I could not stop myself because another part of me wondered if those thoughts were even true at all. The cure … it *does* cure, but it does not stop death from taking what it is owed. And Cressida … Cressida owed. She had ever since *that* night."

Thea cupped her hands over her mouth and hoped her hair covered her face. She didn't want Blythe to see her when the sorceress told her to get out and never come back. She wanted to know if Blythe would be safe out here all alone, but she would not get the chance to. Rafe would have to come by later. Blythe wouldn't be vindictive toward someone who had nothing to do with her plan, right? She could only hope.

"I want you to know …" Blythe took another deep breath, and Thea stiffened. "I want you to know that I … I forgive you, Thea."

Silence descended in the room, and she felt like her ears were ringing. She hastily wiped at her face and leaned back, staring at the sorceress in front of her.

"… What?" she asked quietly after a tense moment to see if her mind had played a cruel trick on her. There was no way … She was forgiven? No. She couldn't even forgive herself!

Blythe wasn't looking at her, but she managed a small smile. "I do not hate you, Thea. I am upset with you for withholding the truth from me. But I have dealt with my emotions over the last few weeks. I do not fully excuse your actions, and I admit that they do hurt me, but I do not have it in me to hate. I cannot *not* forgive someone. If I do not, I hold onto that sadness for longer than is healthy for me. I must admit, though, I am glad you did not bring Rafe and Mokana. I could hardly look into her eyes the last time I met them. It would be much too painful right now."

Thea had been staring at her fingers, idly picking at the cuticles while she absorbed every word Blythe said. She was forgiven … She was truly forgiven. She knew Blythe was not a hateful person … but to go so far as to forgive her? She didn't know what to do with that information.

Wait … what did she mean by looking into Mokana's eyes?

Thea found Blythe's tired gaze, painted up in spring colors and dazzling jewels, and frowned. "What do you mean about not being able to look Mokana in the eye?"

Blythe giggled, but there wasn't much joy in the sound. "It is silly, but surely you must see the resemblance between Cressida's eyes and Mokana's? It is uncanny."

Thea's frown deepened, and her brow pinched. "Mokana's eyes are like … blue-green at best."

It was Blythe's turn to look confused. "No, I am sure I am not mistaken. I distinctly remember them being green with gold flecks in them just like Cressida's."

Thea looked over at Namara in bewilderment. "Her eyes don't change color, do they?"

The kelpie was rubbing at her face and finally groaned, startling both women. "When are you going to connect the dots, Thea? It's been obvious since forever now."

Thea glanced questioningly at Blythe before returning Namara's gaze. "What are you talking about?"

The kelpie crossed her arms over her chest and sent her partner an unimpressed look. "Mokana's eye color changes based on the person's preference. And if that person is particularly smitten with someone, it takes on that color—but Moka says that only happens if she sees that person's eyes first. She's not a mind reader."

Blythe lunged forward in her seat with a look of surprise. "What!"

Thea was equally as stunned.

"Yeah, I mean …" Namara shrugged. "That's how she was able to lure men to their deaths so often back in her feral days."

Thea's brows furrowed. "How was *that* obvious? How were we supposed to know?"

Blythe began laughing as if she couldn't believe what she was hearing. Thea might have laughed, too, any other time.

Namara shrugged, a touch defensive. "You've known her for years! I thought it would have clicked *eventually*."

Blythe laughed again. "*Beryt'ayn*, I am glad to know it was not just my imagination. I thought I was going mad."

Thea shook her head and finally allowed a small smile to grace her features. She wanted to change the subject away from what it could fall back to. "You are mad for staying all the way out here by yourself. Didn't you get the message on your crystal ball a week or so ago? I know we're still in the city limits, but you need to be careful out here in the woods."

Blythe was fanning at her eyes and checking in the mirror to make sure her makeup hadn't creased. She hummed in thought. "Oh, yes, I did get that message. You do not have to worry, though. The sanctuaries are well protected."

Thea crossed her arms over her chest. "Blythe, I'm not …" she groaned and raked her fingers through her curls again. "I'm really not allowed to tell you this, but the 'dangerous conditions' they were talking about are groupings of ferals and blood mages. With the Wild Hunt spell going to happen soon, I just know they're going to pull something, and I don't want you getting caught in the crossfire."

Blythe finally looked away from the mirror, and it was clear that just the mention of the blood mages was enough for the shadows on her face to grow as a seriousness came over her. "Ah, that is troublesome." She sighed and closed her folding mirror and began putting away her makeup. "As I said, the sanctuaries are well protected. In fact, they're capable of protecting the entire city."

Thea was about to go on another rant, but she stopped herself short. "What? What do you mean by that?"

Blythe closed her vanity drawer and aimed a secretive smile Thea's way. "Well, if you must know, it is a sanctuary secret. I did not even know about it until I spoke with Branwen. She runs the sanctuary in Adalith. She is the one who told me how to properly control the amplifiers and how to better manage the magic in Srbeveara. The Coven alerted her about the possibility of having to use the Aegis Alliance spell here soon. She was crystal ball called directly by the Celestial themself."

Thea'd never heard of such a spell, and it must have shown on her face, for Blythe continued. "The spell is completed when all sanctuaries link up with each other through the flow of the Keepers' magic. When that happens, a giant defensive barrier covers the city. It has never been performed because it was never needed after the creation of the sanctuaries, but there were some instances of similar spells being performed in the last few eras."

Thea nodded and sat back on the daybed to think. It was both unfortunate and fortunate that the spell had not been performed before. That meant the safety of Tolvade's citizens had not been grievously endangered—on a scale so massive the spell hadn't warranted being activated during the ferals' peak activity.

"So, how do you," she waved her hand in the air, "you know, connect with all the sanctuaries if they're all scattered across Tolvade's districts?"

Blythe's secretive smile was back. "Let me tell you all about the tunnels under the city."

Chapter Forty

Meeting Legends

The week that followed was quiet. Life had returned to normalcy, yet Thea still felt the anticipation in the air. The Wild Hunt spell. The ball following it. The ferals and the blood mages. It all still felt too up in the air for her.

And it all came to a head the day of the ritual.

Thea woke to the sounds of chaos. Sirens wailed in the dim morning light, loud enough to rattle her windows. Rafe was barging into her room at the same time she was flinging herself out of bed and running for the window. Already she could see smoke billowing dark funnels into the sky, and she yelped as a flash of black and white nearly slammed into her window. Kelvin began pecking furiously at the glass.

Rafe was behind her instantly. "The ferals being kept in Zaraltrac Prison have broken free. The city's in an uproar. There's no word from the Coven—I haven't even been summoned yet."

Thea threw open the window and let Kelvin in. She could hear distant screaming, and her mind was already working into overdrive as she began listing everything she needed to do. Without bothering with modesty, she ripped off her nightshirt and grabbed the nearest, tightest blouse she could find and slipped it on. Loose, snaggable clothing would kill her out there. Rafe was already looking away by the time she was slipping on her flexible, fireproof leggings and leather boots. She snatched up her dust pouch and followed him out of the room.

They didn't speak—they knew what to do. Namara and Mokana stood anxiously waiting as they suited up with their weapon holsters. Thea shoved a protein bar in her mouth and nearly ate the wrapper in her hurry. Tasted like powder and chocolate.

An alarm blared from Rafe's crystal ball just as they stormed out the door. Outside, beings were racing out of their homes in a panic. The distant screams were louder here.

"Get back inside!" she shouted as she marched down the road, pointing and directing others back into their homes.

"Got it," Rafe said in a clipped, harsh tone and ended the call. His gait picked up speed, and he strode toward the town's center. "We're to meet Riker in the town square as quickly as we can."

Thea nodded and didn't ask questions. She wasn't friendly with the stoic Summoner, but there was no one else she'd want at her back in the middle of a battle. In normal circumstances, Rafe would have now outranked him—but this was not normal circumstances. Riker's sheer battle experience propelled him to the front lines as the man in charge. During war, only a few outranked the Summoner.

They'd barely made it into town when a massive, golden orb ascended into the sky with a high-pitched ringing noise before exploding. From its core, light hung suspended in the air while the disembodied voice of the Celestial called out to all of Tolvade.

"Code Pandora. This is not a drill. All residents of Tolvade are to seek shelter. If you cannot stay at your own home, or fear it is too dangerous, go to a friend or relative's home. There are shelters near the town square and within the Coven for those to seek shelter in as well. All homes, businesses, and hospitals are to accept wayward souls inside for safety. Code Pandora. If you live along the edge of the city, be advised you are to IMMEDIATELY move further into the city. Code Pandora. Seek shelter now. This is not a drill."

Thea cursed. One shared look with Rafe had them both breaking out into a run toward the center of town. The message continued to repeat itself, competing with the sirens still wailing through the air. All around her, in the far distance where the prison was located, smoke billowed and tainted the sky with its long, inky tendrils. She hoped whoever was fending off the ferals would make it out of this alive.

But she doubted they would.

A cluster of other Coven members had already descended in the city center, and it was easy enough to find Riker doing what he did best: barking orders and scaring others into listening to him. His partner, Aurora, a vampiress standing by his side was just as intimidating.

"Riker," Rafe's deep voice called over the swelling noise, gaining the scarred man's attention.

"Rafe, Thea," he greeted briskly. "Everyone is splitting up into teams to deal with the crisis. Blasted Coven's flying by the seat of their broomsticks on this one."

"You're with us, then?" Thea asked, surveying the other groups. So far, there were only six of them, including their demon partners. While each of them had either gone up against ferals or blood mages before (or both), she didn't like the thought of going up against an entire faction with so few numbers.

Riker peered over his shoulders in both directions. "I've got two more coming with their pets, and they've got a wild card up their sleeves."

Thea studied the crowd with fingers twitching. She could be doing something right now. "Wild card?"

"Yeah—there they are," he said and pointed at a Spellweaver and Summoner duo. Thea immediately recognized the giant ogre trailing them, accompanied by a succubus and two beings not belonging to the Coven. Thea's eyes widened at one of the being's dark skin and twilight eyes.

Dark Elf.

The other being was an azbanonite, but the creature did not belong to the Yama Clan but rather the Sleekit Clan. They were bipedal foxes with gold eyes, sharp teeth, and a long, fluffy tail. They were also as mischievous as imps.

Riker quickly went through the introductions. "Thea and Rafe, say hello to your team members for the day, Vanessa and Leon. This is their pets, Namara and Mokana, and this is Lyx and Bobo."

The Sleekit stepped forward with his chest puffed up. "Yo, I'm Malachi."

The Dark Elf nodded in their direction and simply gave her name. "Raven."

Rafe eyed them suspiciously and raked his scrutinizing gaze up and down them. "You're not Coven members."

Thea was about to speak up and defend the Dark Elf (though she couldn't speak for the azbanonite), but the dark-haired female Spellweaver beat her to it.

"Raven is my last living relative and can aid in magic casting." She glanced down at the Sleekit beside her and made a face. "I've made an oath to protect Malachi." It looked as if it pained her to say as much.

Thea's mind reeled at the news of her being directly related to an *elf*, but she was snapped out of her musings at Riker's thunderous tone. "You and I will have a chat after we survive this mess, Spellweaver Peterson."

She and Rafe shared a look with one another. This was *the* Spellweaver Peterson. Thea glanced over at the blond Summoner by Vanessa's side, and it clicked exactly who the man was. Leon Zvěrokruh. She could hardly recognize him, but his typical good looks and demeanor had her instantly pinning him. He looked so different now than he had back when she'd first seen him attending a gala in the past. She supposed that after several years and being away from a certain societal circle would transform anyone.

She caught the retreating back of Malachi being escorted away, and she didn't hesitate to get down the business. "What are our orders?"

Riker met her gaze, and his slate-gray eyes were like steel. "We're instructed to head to the northern borders of Tolvade to reinforce our weak point," he informed.

Vanessa balked. "Just us?"

"This is what the Coven has ordered," Aurora said for the first time, and her voice was like velvet.

The massive ogre beside Vanessa said in a most refined voice, "It would appear we are the smallest team."

That was true. They were the smallest team, even now, but Thea was much less worried. She'd fought multiple blood mages all at once, Rafe had thrown himself into their fray, Riker had killed many in his day, single-handedly, and they had *the* Vanessa in their squad. Add in the towering ogre that was *made* for squashing ferals, along with their demon partners, another Summoner, *and* a Dark Elf?

They would be fine.

Rafe pulled out a small booklet with a teleportation seal burned across the leather cover. It was almost exactly like what Ma had pulled out before their desert mission. He had all the ingredients for the teleportation spell ready. They quickly moved away from the diminishing crowd to make enough room for the circle, and so the back-and-forth conversation wouldn't bog down Thea's concentration. Mokana and Namara hurried to set everything up while Rafe uncorked the bottled unicorn blood.

As Riker's orb began chiming, he pointed and barked at them to keep working on the spell before he snapped at the being on the other side of the crystal ball call. They didn't argue, working quickly as Rafe's upgraded reagents allowed them to cut out the fat and use less overall. They were nearly done when Riker ended his call, and the news he reiterated to them had Thea's skin prickling.

The Great Orb was going to go down, and they would lose their ability to freely communicate with one another and teleport throughout the city. Thea had to hand it to the blood mages for striking their weak points and targeting vital infrastructure. She glanced at Rafe beside her and noticed his iced-over blue eyes.

"We're ready!" he announced.

Just then, a ground-rumbling explosion detonated not far from the Borlimane district, and Thea steeled herself. She took a deep breath, caged up that tender heart inside of her, and shielded her emotions. This was war.

She glanced at Vanessa as the Spellweaver blanched. A part of her envied the younger witch. A part of her was happy she wasn't so green, that she'd had a couple kills under her belt, but a softer part of her wanted to be in Vanessa's shoes again. A world with less bloodshed and death was a world she wanted to live in.

She hoped the girl would be able to hold her own in battle, but above all, she hoped this war wouldn't scar her too badly.

Chapter Forty-One

When Hell Breaks Loose

As Thea surveyed the farmland they now stood on, she realized one thing. It was quiet. Too quiet. And she wasn't the only one who thought so. Namara hovered near her, and she welcomed the kelpie so close to her back. Mokana flanked her other side, and Rafe stepped up to Riker as they both glanced around the fresh, green fields of crop. The mountains that had changed her life forever rose up in the distance, taller than the clouds dared to be.

They were to reinforce the protective barrier that the blue cloaks were supposed to throw over the city, but just as Thea felt a surge of confidence, Namara gripped her arm with bruising strength. She whipped around, finding the kelpie pale and her dark eyes wide.

"What? What's wrong?" she whispered.

"Something isn't right," Aurora announced, and Thea glanced at the vampiress before snapping her gaze to their surroundings. She couldn't see anything.

The hum of powerful magic being performed grabbed her attention next, and the magic resonated deep inside her down to her core. Immediately, a cloudy barrier fell down just before them. The Wild Hunt spell would be underway soon.

Thea looked back at Namara and placed her hand over the seafoam-green one still clutching at her. The kelpie was looking around, confusion warping her features. She patted her hand so she could step away and prepare the chalk lines for the reinforcement spell. Namara hesitated but eventually let go.

They got to work as the others talked amongst themselves, but Thea tuned them out. She didn't like speaking much during tense situations. She feared she'd miss something—a sound, a blur of movement, the change of the breeze grazing her skin. She needed to soak it all in, and Rafe was much the same way, but she didn't quite know why. The man could concentrate through a concert.

When they were done, she let Riker know and held out her hands toward the forcefield. One by one, the others joined her and lined up to begin the incantation.

"What was made, strengthen, from foes of our nation, keep them back, keep us safe, may the wards know your grace. Goddess reach down, touch that which is spelled, and ensure the enemy is repelled," they all chanted. Over and over again.

The chalk under their feet pulsed with power and skittered along their bones, whispering in the air around them before it solidified into a wall over the barrier. It grew slowly, reinforcing itself each time they repeated the chant. Thea dug deep, and with every utterance of the incantation, she felt within her the push and pull of the river in her mind. It surged, battering against the dam as she repeated the words.

Namara's soft gasp next to her ripped her from the inner place in her mind, and she felt her magic wobble from the jolt. She then felt the blood drain from her face as dark, smoky masses rose up from the ground at the edge of the forest. One by one, they took form.

Banshees.

Thea cursed just as Namara grabbed her by her shoulders and yelled out, "Keep your masters protected!"

The horde of banshees brought back their heads and screeched.

Thea felt like she'd been punched through her chest as the sensation of fire licked up every inch of her skin. She shivered, and Namara braced her from behind. The screams were the sounds of nightmares, and from them dark beings were borne. Coming up from the ground just as the banshees had, sinister shadows burst into existence.

The screams raced over the fields and battered against the barrier with physical force, and Thea again felt as if she had been shot through with a blazing arrow. She grunted as Namara kept her from toppling over. She shut her eyes and concentrated on the incantation, willing the river in her mind to surge over the dam.

"By the goddess, no," Rafe rasped out close to her, and she opened her eyes again only to wish she hadn't.

An army of blood mages, demons, and towering, monstrous wolves from the Black Forest stood against the backdrop of soaring, black clouds of smoke.

This wasn't supposed to happen!

Thea squinted at the massive army before them, and it clicked in her mind just as Riker said, "They fooled us."

It was all a diversion. The blood mages had orchestrated everything and pulled the wool over all their eyes. They—the smallest group in the entire Coven—were to keep the entire main army at bay. She was impressed. She was also furious.

Riker barked out for them to disconnect from the spell. They were going to hold off the numbers manually. The barrier wouldn't hold up. It was up to them and them alone. She was going to do everything it took to keep them back, to keep them from reaching the city, to keep them from reaching the sanctu—

She froze. She snapped her gaze in Riker's direction, and her wide-eyed expression was enough to gain his attention. "The defense system!" He had to know exactly what she was talking about. That aegis whatever spell Blythe had told her about a week ago. If Blythe was fending off ferals, she might not be able to perform it, but if she could— it could save the entire city!

Riker gave her a feral grin. "Indeed. I'll need you to activate it. Take Rafe with you. You'll need help with battling your way through the city. Activate the defense system and then report to Lorvo Lake. No matter what, we need that ritual to be completed."

Thea and Namara shared a look before the kelpie stood back. Thea watched in wonder as the spell she had placed over the creature seemed to quit working—water spilled around her feet and dripped off her freely before it was abruptly sucked back into her pores and shriveled the green grass under her as it stole that water too. She transformed quickly, quicker than Thea had ever seen her do so previously. She reared back in her horse form and slammed her razor-sharp hooves onto the ground with a scream that rivaled the banshees.

With a quick parting, Thea hoisted herself onto the demon's back. Her skin became gelatinous and stuck to her thighs for maximum grip. Namara was about to fly. She pulled Rafe up behind her, and Mokana eagerly bounced from foot to foot beside them.

When Thea barked the order, Namara took off.

She gritted her teeth at the jarring, breath-snatching pace Namara set. Her thighs were practically swallowed up in the creature's back, but her upper body was taking a beating as she tried to adjust to the breakneck speed. When she found her rhythm, she gripped the kelpie's slimy mane with one hand and reached behind her for her sickle. Mokana's long, leaping strides kept her in pace with the galloping demon beside her, and her long, white hair whipped behind her like a sheet in the wind. Overhead, Thea could see Kelvin soaring above them.

She had to backtrack and race through the paved roads of Adalith, and she watched as panicking citizens rushed about. Some were taking to the street, screaming and hollering like fools, and they were already clogging up the only way out.

An overturned oxcart stood in their path with no room on either side. The owner of the car had already abandoned the frightened cow, and Thea sucked at her teeth in annoyance.

"Brace yourself," she called out, the wind trying to rip the words from her throat.

She felt Rafe grab her around her waist just as Namara leaped into the air with all the power of a demon. Mokana vaulted through the air beside them, twisting and landing on the axle connecting the ox to the cart. The impact crushed it, and the ox raced off with the sides of the cart still attached to it. In no time, the rusalka had caught up to them as they flew over the border of Cascades and into the center city.

Tolvade was in just as much chaos, but more beings were out in the streets fighting for their lives. Some branded pickaxes and metal shovels, others waved burning torches and wands in the faces of lesser demons such as shrieking harpies and vile, horrible abyzous. A group of merchants from far-off lands fended off a hissing lamia while beings soared through the air on brooms and shot down a wailing banshee.

Never thought I'd be on the same side as broom gang members, Thea thought in bemusement as they raced past the fried demon.

Coven members of every rank were in the streets as well. Cleansers were blasting a naga into a brick building while someone else was fighting off a man-eating dakini by quickly jabbing at debilitating pressure points, causing the female creature to fall at their feet. Hunters were fighting alongside their tethered partners, striking ferals and blood mages with all their power.

There were too many monsters. Thea's mind raced as she tried to think just how *this* many had slipped past the borders, but it all came screeching to a halt when a Coven member shot a fireball at a blood mage, and the woman combusted into black smoke.

She cursed. It all made sense. No wonder the northern border had had so many dark beings on that side. The army didn't have the massive numbers they feared they did. The scale had just been tipped to the northern border, while most of the monsters in the city were illusions!

"Did you catch that?" she yelled over her shoulder, and she pointed at a hellhound just in time for it to burst into smoke and leave a merchant standing confused and relieved in the street. The man raised the pitchfork up in the air and started bellowing in triumph before plunging into the masses.

"That only means the sentient ones are back at the northern border," he stated by her ear, and she could only nod as they passed a screeching banshee surrounded on all sides by civilians and Coven members alike. She would have to get to the sanctuary as quickly as she could and make sure Blythe was focusing solely on the defense system spell.

Suddenly, the ground exploded close to them, sending rubble and debris flinging into the air and pelting everything in the nearest vicinity. Thea gasped as a giant tree root sprang up out from the busted pavers, but instead of pulling anyone on their side underground, the massive root wrapped around the ankle of a scythe-wielding redcap and drug it screaming through the hole it created.

"What the—?"

"I'll tell you later," Rafe shouted over the noise.

Another explosion cut off her response, but this time it came from overhead as a giant, flaming boulder struck the thin barrier around the city. It wouldn't hold out for long. They had to hurry.

They hooked left and took the path out to the woods, and immediately, Thea spotted a blood mage pulling the bloody strings of a civilian, cackling like the maniac they were.

Her blood ran cold. She knew what that felt like. She knew the horror, the nauseating fear, the anger that pumped through her faster than the blood in her veins that had turned against her. She gripped the bone handle on her sickle, but before she could slice the dark-haired mage from his victim, Namara reached out and snagged the distracted caster up from the ground with her teeth and dragged him under her racing feet. His scream tore through the air before it was abruptly cut short, and Thea dared not turn back to see what was left. Namara spit out the cloth that had been torn from the body.

The kelpie weaved through the streets and alleys, Mokana by her side the whole time. The rusalka managed to dodge sprinting civilians and was able to parkour off the walls of buildings when the path narrowed. Smoke was heavy in the air, stinging Thea's eyes and making it hard to breathe from the fires scattered around town. The eerie cackles of blood mages and monsters rang through the city. Kelvin followed them overhead all the while.

Thea's thoughts raced on what to do. She had to get a message out to bring backup to the northern border. The spell Blythe needed to perform would help, but she knew nothing about it. She didn't know how well it would hold up against black magic users.

Just as they passed the treeline of the Vemeese district, a monstrous wolf barreled out of the woods. Namara barely had any time to dodge, and Thea watched in horror as its giant paw swiped over her head. She whipped around to follow it, but just as her eyes landed on the house-sized monster, a ball of fire exploded across its snout.

Namara skidded to a halt and whinnied shrilly into the air. She spun around, and Thea found the source of her excitement. Sprinting toward them was the terrifying rakshasa they'd come to know. In his dark gray arms, Isabel clung for dear life. He slid to a stop just as the wolf recovered, angrily swiping at its face with its paws, and Isabel jumped from his arms.

"We'll hold it off!" she yelled. "Just go, Agni will catch up to you later!"

She then did something Thea thought she'd never see the redhead do: she dipped into a dust pouch, and her hands began to glow. Namara was already turning, cutting off Thea's vision, but she could hear the explosion of high-powered magic hit its target and the resounding howl of pain that followed after.

They raced through the woods at breakneck speeds, and Thea reacted too slowly to a chupacabra pouncing from the underbrush. Mokana was there before she could blink, slamming bodily into the large, hairless creature and raking her claws through its eyes, effectively blinding it. The bear-dog beast roared in pain, swiping heedlessly in the air. Pound for pound, she'd lose in a fight, even with her opponent handicapped, so she turned and fled the scene as quickly as she could.

Kelvin warbled from high above, and Thea looked to her right just as a wendigo prowled out from behind a tree. Standing on two legs with its impressive antlers atop its deer-skull head, it stood taller than Agni. Its skin was mottled ash and blotchy red, and wiry fur grew in patches along its malnourished body. Before she could think of a spell to cast, Rafe's staff came into her peripheral and blasted the feral demon back into the woods. It landed with a sickening crash, and the tree that took the impact cracked and splintered before falling onto the monster.

Just a little further to go!

When they finally reached the clearing around Srbeveara, it was just as Thea feared. Ferals were slamming their bodies into the sanctuary's barrier, blood mages were blasting the forcefield with spell after spell, and banshees were screaming their earsplitting wails in waves to attract more and more monsters to the scene. They would be fighting these creatures back for hours at best, and the others at the northern border needed help now. Thea's mind raced.

"I can distract them," Rafe announced in a gruff voice. Already, Thea could feel the power resonating off his staff.

"No," she shot down. "That's suicide. We do this together."

"Someone has to send word to HQ. I can send Mokana—"

Kelvin chirped in rapid succession as he flew down and landed on Namara's head, and Thea's gaze latched onto the bird.

"Kelvin!" she snapped, and the bird fluttered at her sharp tone. "I need you to deliver a message. Ugh! I'm so stupid, why didn't I—ugh, it doesn't matter. Go deliver a message to HQ! Go get backup and send them to the northern border! Half the ferals in the city are illusions, and I'm betting half the ones here are too, but Riker and the others need help, *now!*"

"I'll be a quick as I can," the magpie promised.

"Find Winona!" Rafe shouted as the bird took flight. "I was told she's taken over HQ! She'll know what to do!"

Kelvin circled the air above them once more before flying off. Thea prayed he wouldn't take too long, but as her gaze shifted to the demons in front of her, it was clear they had already attracted some undesired attention.

Chapter Forty-Two

The Gates to Hell

Kelvin surveyed the land below him as he flew high in the sky. The city was dotted with fires and littered with debris, broken support beams, shattered glass, and twisted metal. Smoke billowed up in white-gray and pitch-black tendrils. And he was tasked with finding one person amongst thousands.

They didn't bother to tell me who this Winona is, he thought angrily. He was stressed enough to be molting over this. His specialty was brewing up potions and sharing the knowledge of the universe. Not battles. Not dodging demons and trying not to get eaten alive.

He supposed HQ was that big building his master had woken up in last week, and it was coming up into view quickly. He swooped down, flew past a powerful beam of magic, and fluttered through the front doors. Already, he could see beings laid out in slapdash cots throughout the lobby. Some went as far as the hallways while the medical team—they all appeared to be wearing shiny, red insignias—rushed back-and-forth between patients. The front desks had been transformed into med stations where equipment, boxes of gloves, and cases of medicine had shoved paperwork and office supplies out of the way.

One woman was commanding the scene with a scary-looking Ghul by her side. It was humanoid, deathly pale, and had long black hair that touched its shoulders and fell into its blood-red eyes. Black markings spiked out and away from its flashing gaze like cracks in stone. The demon was a type of jinn, specifically one that feasted on human corpses. Kelvin cocked his head and wondered who thought putting a Ghul in an infirmary was a good idea, but he didn't quite understand why these humans tied themselves to demons in the first place.

A woman rushed by, bringing his focus back to the crisis, and he tried to stop her. "Hello, can you tell me who—" but she was gone in a blur.

"Wait, please tell me—" he tried with the next being who hurried through.

He hopped along the desk, trying to catch up to a little red imp. "Excuse me—" but the creature whizzed by without even looking up at him.

Growing aggravated, he fluttered over to the woman barking orders and blasting anything that tried getting past the front doors.

A Coven member was panicking by her side. "Winona, we're running out of supplies!"

Kelvin cocked his head to the side. This was the woman he was looking for. He should have known.

"I'm a little busy!" she snarled out. She was on both knees, hands splayed out over a circle with chalk lines hastily drawn within. A wand lay in the center, while candles sat at each point the chalk lines came to. The flames danced wildly as she reached for her dust pouch—which he now realized contained herbs rather than dusts—and grabbed some shiny stones, placing them in a specific pattern across the circle. "Where is Snow!" she demanded, and the other person scurried off to find the doctor.

Kelvin watched her, entranced by her nimble fingers working so effortlessly with the craft he loved above all: apothecary.

Her silver eyes snapped over to find him staring at her, and he was dragged out of the haze her work had placed him under. "Who are you?" she demanded, not even wincing when a hellhound battered against the small forcefield she had erected between the Coven's open doors. Innocent beings could flood in, but foes would be kept out. It was a highly advanced spell.

"My master comes to warn you that the northern border is under siege by the full might of the army. The ferals and blood mages you see in town are mostly illusions. My master has arrived at a sanctuary to ward off the ferals there so that a defense system spell can be activated."

Winona squinted at the magpie, directed her gaze at the hellhound battering her barrier and snarling in its frustration, and cursed creatively enough to fry feathers. "Who is your master?" she snapped at him.

"Thea Bauer."

For a fraction of a second, Winona's silver eyes widened. Her expression stonewalled, and it was all business once again. With an infuriated groan, she craned her head over her shoulder and yelled out, "Lahlou!"

The Ghul rushed over and said in a whisper-soft voice, "You called?"

"Take over for me. Something's come up, and you're the only one I trust to keep this barrier going." Just as she stood up, Lahlou took her place, and the chalk markings on the floor glowed with new power. "All right, listen up!" She shouted into the room, and abruptly, everyone stopped running about. They stared at her with clipboards clutched to their chests and blood splattering their garbs. "Lahlou is taking over the barrier! Any questions, find Snow! Do not let anyone die, is that clear?" Her words bounced off the walls of the lobby and brooked no room for argument.

"Yes, ma'am!" a chorus of voices rang out.

She turned toward the bird and nodded. "First, I need to make a stop. My teleportation magic differs from normal methods. It can only get me so far, and I can only use it every so often."

With no time to waste, she then pulled out something from her pouch and held it to her chest. It was long, thin—like a porcupine quill?—but thinner. Kelvin cocked his head in confusion at the object in her hands. She closed her eyes, whispered a small chant in a language so dead that Kelvin mistook it for gibberish at first, and the whisker-looking strand in her peculiarly curled hands began to smoke up before it was immediately engulfed in white flames. Dark brown, bubbling liquid began to form around her feet. It expanded to the size of a small puddle, and instantly, Winona was sucked in.

Kelvin frantically hopped around, cawing in amazement and confusion. *What kind of alchemic-apothecary blend of magic was that!*

The bubbling puddle of goo began to slowly shrink, and Kelvin flitted about the edge as he frantically wondered what to do. As it got smaller and smaller, he made the decision to dive in.

Kelvin flew out of the hole that opened up from a ceiling and nearly collided with the woman who made such a confounding portal. He flapped his wings just in time to catch enough air to let him land on Winona's shoulder. She eyed him, and there was a certain look in her silver gaze.

"Took you long enough. You almost didn't make it."

The magpie peered around, but the room they were in was small, dim, and entirely made of brick. "It's a good thing I did. I can't stand being spat back out when a spell rebounds."

Winona placed her hand onto the brick wall in front of her and pressed her fingertips into separate bricks. She gave a soft chuckle. "You wouldn't have been spat back out." The bricks pushed in, and a click sound went off. The wall divided into two and opened up like a gate, revealing the other side. "If you hadn't made it in time, you would have been severed in half."

She walked past the bricks without another word.

Kelvin felt cold as the realization that he'd almost *died*—again in this blasted war he wanted no part of—set in.

A long corridor went as far as his eyes could see, but in the middle of it was a large being in hooded robes. At its side, a much smaller imp was whispering up at it. Both paused and glanced at Winona, and the woman hummed.

"You got here fast," she stated with a question lingering in her voice. Then, directing her attention at the tall being—

who Kelvin now recognized as a rarely seen Skrite—she said, "Will you take us to the teleportation room?"

The being dipped its head, turned, and began to walk in a certain direction. The imp at its side grinned, and there was a glint to her eye before she reached into her pocket and held out an old, silver key. Her hand was adorned with gaudy, shiny rings. Kelvin ducked away. He hated shiny things. "Topside ain't gonna know what hit 'em, Winny."

The woman huffed and took the key, giving it a disdainful look. "We can only hope, Ma."

They arrived shortly in a small room, and a blue, stone table with an iridescent sheen stood in the middle. The hooded alchemist reached out and grabbed a corked potion bottle before it swept over to a spot in the floor that was well-worn. As it poured the contents onto the ground, Winona and the imp shared a look.

"Meet you at the Hell Hub soon, toots. Don't be too afraid of Tiny now," she snickered and produced her own key. She inserted it into thin air, and an outline of a short, black, iron door appeared out of nowhere. When the imp opened the door, hellish wails bled into the room. All Kelvin could see on the other side was smoke and fire and sand.

Winona scoffed. "Your *Tiny* could make Cerberus look like nothing more than a playful pup. Chain it up for me, would you?"

The imp only laughed and let the door slam shut behind her, effectively cutting off the anguished screams on the other side. The door disappeared as if it were nothing more than a sheet of paper being slowly eaten by flames.

The Skrite made a chittering noise, and Winona and Kelvin both looked over to find the being standing next to a colorless portal. The outsides swirled off like fog, and Kelvin detected the hum of the magic that resonated throughout the room. Winona sniffed and made a face, waving at the air as if she smelled something she didn't like. She then aimed a sincere look the being's way and dipped her head.

"Your assistance has been most helpful, Kishnar. I have one more request for you, and only you or another Skrite will be able to pull it off."

The alchemist cocked its head, and Winona didn't waste any more time. She pulled out a tiny purse from her pocket and pulled at the string keeping it synced together. She reached her hand in—all of it—and pulled out something that defied the laws of non-magic physics. A large, stone tablet was given over to the Skrite, and the being's thin, furry, claw-tipped hands reached out and grasped it.

"This has the desummoning spell on it. The Celestial has already memorized the part of the Wild Hunt needed, and you are the only one who can read the spell. I was to give it back after the Wild Hunt if all went smoothly, but I was entrusted to give it to you should an emergency arise. This qualifies."

The tall, hooded being made a noise somewhere between a chittering sigh and grunt, but it bowed its head regardless.

"Thank you," she said again and stepped through the portal without delay.

Kelvin cawed at the feeling of magic caressing his feathers, and when he blinked, they were …

Back at the lobby! What—

Winona whistled loudly, and again, everyone in the makeshift infirmary froze and turned toward her. "Change

of plans! You four, you two over there, you three, and you—
yes, you, you're with me! Red Pins, grab your medical
supplies. Everyone else, have your wands at the ready!"

The ten Coven members (and those tethered to them) all
came rushing up to her, nervous expressions on most of their
faces.

"We're portaling out of here, so don't lose your
breakfast."

"But we can't teleport right now!" A tethered harpy
squawked out.

A human raised his hand anxiously. "Do you even have
the proper ingredients to teleport?"

Instead of replying, Winona turned and took out the
silver key the imp gave to her. "No, but I have a key."

"A key?" someone queried.

"Listen up," she barked. "You are about to go to a place
that is neither Hell nor not-Hell. I ask that you do not ask
questions when we get there, trust in me, and stay together.
When I open this door, you will be ripped away from the
fabric of reality you all know, but it is important that you do
not panic. I will be waiting for you on the other side, and
then we will again portal out to the northern border through
a shortcut that is only accessible this way. Does anyone have
any questions?" When silence met her ears, she looked down
at the key in her hands and stuck it in the air. The same door
from before appeared, taller now, and Winona grabbed the
bone handle.

Kelvin fluttered off her shoulder and onto the ground.
"I will head back to my master now that my purpose has
been served."

Winona aimed a nod at the bird. "Tell your master to forget about the northern border. Send her to assist Kishnar in the center of town." She then straightened up and stated over her shoulder, "We need to make this quick. Follow me and stay close together!"

Kelvin flew out the doors just as the hellish sounds ripped through the lobby.

No way am I getting dragged through Hell—literally!

Chapter Forty-Three

Aegis Alliance Activate!

Thea slammed her fist into the face of a blood mage, sending the man careening back into a kappa. The frog demon burst into a cloud of black smoke. They had been battling for what felt like ages, and the spell Blythe was supposed to perform still had not gone off yet. They had weeded out most of the illusions and were now fighting off the real things. Thank the goddess above Isabel and Agni had joined up with them, and—much to everyone's surprise—they hadn't been alone. Fatik, Tasgall, the pixies, and even Siàu had entered the fray and were giving it all they got to a cleave a path to the sanctuary.

Fatik's winged back hit hers, and she heaved for breath as he covered her long enough for her to dip into her dust pouches. She'd already used up her amulet for the day, dodging an arcane spear that would have taken her head clean off. She was covered almost head to toe in blood—none of it hers, thanks to the healing spell she kept applying to herself. Fatik was similarly stained pink, and the Dragonkin was putting up a fight that rivaled Agni.

Mokana grabbed a hellhound by the shoulders and hurled it into the nearest tree. Namara slammed a Light Elf wolf in the knee and caused it to buckle while Agni set ablaze its white fur all along its legs. Rafe was slashing and countering two banshees, and Isabel was holding her own with impressive, quick moves that mirrored Siàu's. The redhead was imbuing her punches and kicks with magic that sent the enemies further. Tasgall was wielding dual wands and striking down opponents left and right, while the pixies used their incredible strength to throw the ferals into the nearest tree trunks.

"I have an idea," Fatik panted and grunted as he swung his bloody fist into the throat of a snapping manticore.

"I'd love to hear it!" she yelled back over the screams of the banshees.

"Isabel's been working on her—" he grunted, and the sound of something snapping reached Thea's ears just as she pelted another blood mage with fire magic, "on her magic, and she's perfected this one spell Tasgall taught her. I think it would hold off these dark beings until the desummoning spell goes off!"

Thea sank her sickle into the hind leg of the Black Forest wolf that had backed up into her reach and rolled out of the way when it whipped around and snapped its teeth at her. Agni was there in seconds and was shooting giant flames at its snout. The fire sprang onto the creature's nose and consumed the fur of its muzzle. It reared back and snarled in pain before jumping away and rubbing its paw over its nose. It couldn't move freely with all the fighting going on, and the trees weren't as large and spaced far enough apart like the ones in its homeland. It tipped the scales in their favor, but it didn't mean the battle had been easy or was going to be. If only Agni could transform into one of the wolves—but no, apparently that wasn't in the realm of possibilities, and Thea wanted to give Unsoul a piece of her mind for gatekeeping cursed forms.

"Agni!" Fatik cried out, and Thea and the rakshasa exchanged glances before she jumped in his spot and reared back her arm. The wolf snapped its jaws and growled, and Thea flung her sickle at the beast with all her might. It hooked into the wolf's jaw, and she yanked down hard enough for it to sink through its tongue, straight down to the jawbone.

The wolf howled and flung its head back, and Thea was lifted off the ground. She gritted her teeth and growled as she held on as best she could, using her weight to propel her toward the coarse, white fur. She grabbed two handfuls and latched on even as the beast jumped around.

"Rafe!" she screamed, and within seconds a blast of magic shot through the wolf's shoulder. It howled again and slammed back into the thick tree trunks around it. She groaned as her fingers strained to keep holding onto the fur.

Blood welled up and leaked out of the beast's new wound. Another blast was narrowly thwarted by the wolf's sidestepping, giving it enough time to focus on Thea. She screamed when it snapped its drooling jaws at her, but she was just out of reach. However, she could still smell the beast's breath from how close it had gotten.

Something struck the back of its head, and it whipped around and snarled so fiercely that Thea could feel the vibrations under the fur she clutched at. She bared her teeth and growled out a *"Climb, girl, climb!"* Her bloodied, dirty fingers gripped the wolf harshly, and she began scaling the beast as quickly as she could with the chain still tight in her grasp. Before the wolf could thrash and jostle her off its body, she clambered up until she had gotten up between its shoulder blades. It shook itself furiously in an attempt to dislodge her, but another blast of magic had it howling and bucking like Namara on a bad day.

She rode it out until it was distracted enough, and then she grabbed a handful of dust and placed both palms on the back of its skull. "Mind be free, soul be purged, sleep come to me, let the calm surge," she whispered, and the wolf stumbled. She chanted it again and again, the river slamming against the dam in her mind until the water rushed over it. It was instant, like her magic was used to the force needed to come forward, and immediately the wolf collapsed to the ground. She was nearly thrown off it from the force, but she managed to stay on as it crashed to the ground.

She was panting from the exertion as she slid down, but the battle was still waiting for her. She dodged a blast of magic from a blood mage, but her movements were slowing, growing lethargic. She couldn't keep this up.

Then Mokana was there and ended the blood mage's life. The dark-haired woman crumpled to the ground, and Thea nearly fell forward in relief. Long, thin arms wrapped around her and held her up.

"Come on, Thea, they're leading the ferals away."

What?

It was then she heard it.

The sound of a baby wailing in the distance had every feral bounding toward the treeline. She whipped her head around, but she couldn't see half of their party.

"Where—"

"Agni is luring them with the power of a mafu's cries. Isabel and Tasgall are going to secure them with a binding spell until the desummoning spell goes off. Rafe chased a blood mage through the trees, and Namara went to back him up. I'll stay here and make sure nothing else comes through."

"I'll be here too," Fatik jogged up to them to say. He was also out of breath and covered from head to toe in dirt and other, more gruesome things.

Siàu had caught up to them as well and nodded her agreement. "I am here as well."

She looked between them. "Won't they need help?"

Fatik shook his head. "Mom and auntie are grounding them. They'll be fine."

Thea nodded and turned her attention to the sanctuary. "I'm going to see how Blythe is doing with the spell. The ones at the northern border can't afford a delay any longer."

She staggered forward until she could right her footing and pass through the barrier. She shoved the doors open and heaved a sigh when she felt the welcoming magic greet her. Hurriedly, she whirled around, but she couldn't find Blythe anywhere. With only her instincts guiding her, she rushed past the waterfall and kept going until she was past the pool Namara once had to use. The door to the basement cellar was bricked up, so Thea backpedaled and looked for other tunnels Cressida could have hidden from her.

It was dead end after dead end. She felt dizziness take over her until she stumbled across a tunnel lined with fat, white candles. It was the only lead she had, so, despite the twinge of fear settling in her chest, she marched on through the dim, cramped passage. When she finally found Blythe, the sorceress was in a hollowed-out cave deep under the sanctuary. She was drenched in sweat and surrounded by burning candles that highlighted her damp skin. Her hair had collapsed into a tangled bun half hanging by her shoulder, her pearl and sapphire dress clung to her as if she'd swam in it, and her arms trembled in their outstretched position.

She was a sight for sore eyes, yet Thea could cry from the sheer relief. "Blythe," she croaked, and her throat protested.

Blythe's dark brown eyes snapped open, and she made a noise somewhere between a sob and a wail. "Thea! Thank you for coming. Please, I need assistance. I cannot keep doing this." Her voice wobbled as if all the strength she had was just keeping her standing. "We have been trying, but as soon as I am ready, the Lorvo sanctuary is under heavy attack, and when they are ready, the dark beings are hammering against my barrier outside and disrupting my concentration. I am still new to this, and Dulce's magic is waning. I cannot do it alone, and if we don't do it soon—"

Thea rushed over to her and grabbed her hands. She could feel the woman's fingers shivering in her palms. "You've got this," she assured. "I'm here now, and I'm going to give you everything I have in order to ground you. Just take a deep breath for me. We're taking care of everything outside. Now, I need you to clear your mind and imagine a river …"

It felt like forever had passed when Thea finally felt the explosion under her feet, and the sheer amount of magic that shot through her left her feeling cold, then burning hot, then cold all over again. Her hair whipped back like a giant gust of wind had been summoned, and she clutched at Blythe like a lifeline.

The sorceress sighed, and it was as if bliss had laid claim to her soul. Her arms stopped trembling, her magic a comforter around her, and she let go of Thea's hands.

"I have it from here," she breathed out in a sigh. "Thank you." The last part was a whisper, and Blythe went as still as a statue. In that moment, she resembled the goddess Saellah from the carvings in the Huǒshān caves.

Born without magic, and now she embodied the mother of it all. Thea stepped back and watched in amazement at how ethereal the goofy, silly, loud woman she'd come to know now was. She stepped back again, and Blythe remained as still as stone.

All was done. On Blythe's part, at least. Thea still had a job to do. She turned and stumbled out of the cave.

She tried to hurry. Really, she did, but when she told Blythe she'd give her everything, she had she meant it. She tripped over the uneven stone flooring and caught herself on the rough walls. She heaved in air, but it settled into her lungs like a fire. Her fingers gripped the wall beside her, but she could hardly feel them.

I can't give up. Isabel and Tasgall are holding ferals down with a simple binding spell. We have to …

She couldn't finish her thought before her mind dissolved into mush. Instead, she put one foot in front of the other despite the ache in her legs, the dizziness that threatened to trip her up again, and her vision darkening around her.

"Thea!" someone called, and she looked up toward what she hoped was the waterfall. Everything was blurry, but she could see someone tall making their way toward her.

"Thea!" That was Namara's voice, but Namara's arms weren't that tan—or hairy.

A bottle was shoved into her face, and it was already tipping past her lips and spilling its contents onto her dry tongue. Horrid bitterness nearly had her spitting it back out, but she swallowed it down with a cringe. Hands were lightly running up and down her arms, torso, legs, and then her head.

Her eyesight cleared almost immediately, and the aches in her legs vanished. When her hands stopped trembling, she wiped her lips and made a face.

"Ugh," she complained, and aimed a weak glare at the one who had forced a Blood and Peppermint potion on her. Basilisk blood she could deal with—it was mind over matter as the blood didn't exactly have a taste, but *mugwort*. It was so *bitter*, and it left a fuzzy film on her tongue that stayed for hours.

Rafe grinned back at her, grabbed her by the arms, and yanked her to him. She fell against him with a "Oof!" and he laughed heartily.

"You're absolutely crazy, Thea," he said with exasperated fondness. "I can't believe you *climbed* a *wolf!* Not just any wolf, a wolf from the *Black Forest*."

She peered up at him and found his soft, blue-green gaze. "Well, it'd be a little difficult to climb a regular wolf with how small they are."

Someone snorted behind them, and Thea peered past the large Second Chosen to find Namara with her fists propped on her hips and her own wide grin spread across her face. "Come on, smart aleck, the war's not over. You can tell us all how you not only scaled a mountain but also a legendary wolf later. Mokana's waiting outside."

Thea sobered immediately and stepped back from Rafe's embrace. "Right, we've got to get back to the northern border. They need our help."

Namara shook her head. "Actually, Kelvin arrived about ten minutes ago while we were all busy corralling the last of the ferals into the redheads' binding trap. He said we're to head to the center of town to help a Skrite perform the desummoning spell."

Thea sent Rafe a wide-eyed look. "A Skrite? Above ground?"

Rafe nodded. "I know, but desperate times call for desperate measures."

They briskly headed out and shook themselves after dashing through the waterfall. "What about the others?" Thea asked as Rafe pushed the doors to the sanctuary open. Mokana was standing in the blood-stained clearing, looking up at the double barrier. Already, Thea could see a difference in the color of the sky as the second barrier she'd helped Blythe with protected the city. Nothing special, just a warmer hue to indicate it was up. Physically seeing it with her own eyes had a sense of relief sweeping through and nearly bowling her over. That mugwort potion was the only thing keeping that from happening.

"Agni, Fatik, the pixies, and Siàu are all standing guard and protecting Isabel and Tasgall so that they can concentrate on keeping the ferals bound down," Rafe reported.

Thea nodded. "Good, that makes me feel a lot better. Namara, are you good to transform?"

The kelpie was already stretching her limbs above her head. "Yep. Let's get this magic show on the road."

Chapter Forty-Four

The Hunt is On

They rode like the underworld itself was nipping at their feet. Thankfully, the healing spell she'd gotten had her feeling better than when they started. She was running low on magic dusts, but it would be enough. She'd make it enough.

They raced through the trees, and Namara and Mokana barely dodged the wendigo that came stumbling out of the bush. Its antlers were broken and fractured in some places, and a large crack ran up the front of its skull-head. Rafe twisted around and, with another resounding *boom!* from his staff, he sent the creature back into the neighboring trees. Thea kept her eyes on the path before her, but she could hear another resounding crack from several other trees splintering and collapsing.

They could see the smoke from the city, and the buildings of Tolvade came into view. Some were nothing more than piles of rubble, and others were missing giant chunks of bricks or metal. Just as Namara's hooves hit the cobblestone streets, the ground exploded underfoot. They were showered in bits of rock and clumps of dirt, and the kelpie reared back and roared out a deep, resonating sound as a huge vine shot out from the debris. It zipped right between Namara and Mokana, though, and sailed through the air and grabbed the impundulu that had been diving at them so silently they hadn't noticed. The human-sized bird cried out from its raptorial beak, and the sound was like thunder booming in the sky above them. It flapped its massive, azure wings as it was ripped from the air, and Namara backed away even further when small sparks of lightning zapped out from its feathers while it continued to struggle. Within moments, it was yanked toward the hole, its wide wings snapping and folding unnaturally. In a blink, it was gone. Only the hole in front of them and one last thunderous cry that echoed out were the only signs of what had just happened.

"You are seriously going to tell me about that later," Thea said over her shoulder, but she gasped when her eyes caught sight of the sky above her.

Mokana was pointing up and shouting, "Look!" Rafe turned to find what his partner was yelling about, and even Namara was craning her head up and around so she didn't miss anything.

A huge boulder slammed into the double-layered protection barrier, but it was what was beyond that which held Thea's attention. The sky was transforming. The fluffy, white clouds dotting the sky began to shift and take form. The hooves of an army of horses and unicorns soon became discernible, and at their feet, the clouds morphed into the hunting hounds. All the souls of Aeristria, borne of magic or not, came rushing down from the sky with a battle cry that rocked the city.

"You! Shall! Be! Judged!" came a voice so thunderous that Thea felt her heart slam against her ribcage as lightning cracked through the sky like the storm of the season was upon them. The ground under them began to tremble, and Namara shifted around from hoof to hoof with the reverberations rising in force. The buildings that had barely been holding on started to collapse in on themselves, shooting out giant plumes of brown dust and ash. Namara shot off into town when the leaning tower of brick and mortar beside them began to groan and crumble.

Thea continued to watch the sky, entranced, and saw the Wild Hunt split. She couldn't see where each half went, but the second one began to flood the city with speed so fast, Thea couldn't keep track.

A golden light flared in the center of the city and snatched her attention. It flared again, and Namara redirected and headed straight for it. A large mountain of bricks, twisted metal, and broken glass blocked the path, but Namara only sped up and launched herself into the air. Thea gritted her teeth as they soared over the rubble and landed hard on the other side. Mokana landed with a flip and nearly tripped over a stray brick.

"Be careful," Rafe admonished, but the rusalka only peered over her shoulder with a cheeky expression and her tongue sticking out.

Thea sat up straighter. "Where did that light come fr—oh."

The fountain in the very center of Tolvade still stood above the wreckage like a beacon. The figures that held no definitive shape struck a chord in Thea that hadn't been there before, but she was quickly distracted. Around the fountain was a giant circle with intricate linework. Small words Thea had no hope of reading scrawled out around the perimeter of the circle and along some of the chalk lines.

Beside the fountain, finishing it up was a Skrite. It continued to work diligently despite the group of Coven members pointing weapons at it warily.

Rafe pivoted and shoved off Namara, marching over to the scene with purpose behind his steps. "Stand down!" He ordered, and the group of Summoners, Spellweavers, and their pets looked at each other in confusion. "Lay a wand on one of our great alchemists, and I will bring down the full extent of the Coven on you. Stand! Down!"

Instantly, the group of beings flinched and took several steps back, their weapons hanging limply beside them. Thea raced over while Namara transformed and knelt just outside the circle. A far-off caw had her looking up and finding Kelvin circling above her. Right. They had to assist this Skrite in some way.

"How can we help?" She asked, but the Skrite ignored her just as he had ignored the others. She waited patiently, watching his every move as he completed the last of the circle. His hood was pulled up further, and Thea knew the sun had to be painful for him. They had no time to fetch an umbrella, especially when he stood to his full height. The same yellow glow pulsed around the circle, signaling that the section was completed. Some of the beings around them gasped at how tall the Skrite was, but Thea wasn't intimidated. He turned in her direction, and even though she couldn't see past his furry snout, she knew he was looking at her.

"If you wish to be of assistance, then take my hand. You do not need to repeat this incantation, as you cannot fathom the words I am about to use. All I ask for is your power. Are you able?" He

turned to look at Rafe, and she could tell the same words had been transmitted to him as well.

"Yes," the Second Chosen replied without hesitation.

Thea nodded, but she needed to make sure of something before she dove in without thinking. "Yes. But I have one question first."

The alchemist cocked his head to the side, signally he was listening.

"Is this going to desummon every demon, or just the ferals? What about the demons that used to be tied—" Her words were silenced when the being raised up a large, rat-looking hand adorned in tiny claws.

"You need not worry, far-child. Only the demons without purpose in their hearts and wisdom in their minds will be sent back to where they belong."

Thea took a deep breath and let it out. She never would have forgiven herself if she had had a hand in sending Agni—or any other demon previously tied to the Coven— back to Hell simply because they were no longer tethered. "Then, yes, we'll help you."

Rafe turned toward the group of Coven members who had been watching—some now performing healing spells and drinking potions—and bellowed loud enough for the whole city center to hear, "All those who are magically capable and wish to assist in the desummoning spell and finally rid the city of its feral demons, please step forward! Everyone else who is injured, on the brink of magic fatigue, or has other orders, please vacate the area! HQ's main lobby has been converted into an infirmary!"

Immediately, several Coven members from the group and most of the citizens in the surrounding area all rushed forward. The Skrite turned toward the circle, facing the statue in the fountain, and held out his palms pointed toward the sky. Thea came up on one side, Rafe the other, and together they took the Skrite's offered hands. They were surprisingly soft, narrow without the bridge of a thumb in the way, and the back of his hand was dusted in wiry fur. Beside her, Namara took her other hand, and on Rafe's other side, Mokana stepped up. The circle filled up with Coven members, their demonic partners, and non-Coven members alike. All of Tolvade's residents wanted to participate. Thea felt hands on the back of her shoulders and noticed those who couldn't stand in the circle were grounding the ones who could.

Soon, the Skrite began to recite the ancient spell, and bits and pieces of the words floated through her mind with syllables and sounds she'd never heard together before. The circle she stood over began to glow, and the statue in the center of the fountain crumbled into nothing more than a pile of dust. The splaying, golden light reached up and out so brilliantly that Thea was forced to finally close her eyes. She concentrated on her magic, and the dam she'd built up started to crumble. She didn't have to push or pull. The magic within her came naturally. The dam gave way, and the lavender water behind it came flooding out. She could feel the surge course through her entire body. She could feel the way the cool sensation washed over her shoulders, her arms, all the way down to her fingertips. How it reached down to her legs, tingling when it met her toes.

A small, tiny, childish voice she'd kept locked up for so, so long escaped her in that soft, blissful moment.

Is he calling out to you, Mother?

A whispering breeze brushed against her skin, and an equally soft, blissful voice murmured back.

"Yes, my child."

Thea felt the tears coming in the way her lip trembled and the way her chest was heavy with emotion. She could feel the wetness slip down her cheeks, but she didn't stop them from falling. Not this time.

In every corner of Tolvade, where monsters of the abyss ran for cover, golden portals appeared to illuminate the darkness. In the center of town, down forgotten alleys, in the farm fields of Adalith, and everywhere in between, ferals froze like time itself had stopped. Rays of blinding light lit the city aglow as if the goddess herself had made an appearance, and every demon caught in the desummoning spell's grasp cried out in rage and fear as the ground under them opened up. The citizens, beaten and bruised, watched in awe as the monsters that had terrorized their lives and killed their loved ones were sucked back down to Hell in plumes of dusty clouds. As the clouds dissipated, the only trace ferals had ever run amok was the dilapidated ruins of the city and the scars that had been left on the hearts of its people.

But, with time, even that would be mended.

Chapter Forty-Five

Dance the Night Away

Thea stared at herself in the mirror, but—this time—she was admiring herself rather than criticizing. She was wearing the gifted qynzo and, despite being a paler color, the blue complemented her cobalt eyes nicely. The white silhouettes of the mountain range at the bottom of her swishing skirt had a *pang* of longing thrumming through her chest, but she took a deep breath and let the feeling wash over her with a silent promise to return one day. The dark red ribbon was tied just the same way Siàu showed her—mostly because it was Siàu that had tied it.

Thea had run around the city for a good hour trying to find her and hoping she hadn't left yet. Thankfully, Isabel had let her crash on her couch, and together they both had had Siàu happily dress them up. She wouldn't be attending the ball, but she would be sticking around town for a little while longer. Her next destination was Half Heart Bay, no doubt because Isabel had hyped it up the way she usually did when recounting things. A simple warning of caution was given to her before Thea left for the sanctuary.

Speaking of the sanctuary, her gaze found her eyes in the mirror. Each time she looked at herself, it was quite the shock. The color of her belt now matched the scarlet eyeshadow decorating her lids. Blythe had done that part, and she'd been so excited to have someone to do makeup with. She'd even done up Thea's hair as well—with no input from Thea whatsoever—but had managed to have the updo suit Thea's tastes rather than Blythe's own wilder ones. Her curls had been tamed into a gentle swoop over one shoulder and secured by a tight knot in the dark blue scarf Chaska had given her.

Blythe had shoes for days, but Thea's feet were a bit bigger than the petite woman's heels could handle. So, she splurged and got some pearl-white ones that she could reuse … at some point. Thea'd asked what Blythe was going to wear for the ball, but the sorceress had gone very quiet. She felt like kicking herself, but Blythe's cheerful expression was back before she could chastise herself too harshly. It was a touch forced, though.

Someone knocked at the door, and Thea called for them to enter. Rafe opened up and peeked into the room, and when he found her, he gave her a beaming smile.

"You look stunning," he said as he stepped fully into the room. He wore a burgundy tunic with gold, spiraling designs embroidered around the neckline and sleeve cuffs. His charcoal cloak had been fastened to the side and hung off one shoulder, where it nearly grazed the floor. His black trousers were tucked into knee-high boots, and the black leather belt around his waist was encrusted with small garnets. Gold buckles and eyelets tied the whole look together. The ensemble was a tad tight in some areas, but it seemed to fit him really well. His hair had been freshly washed and styled, and it was now reaching past his ears.

She could feel heat in her cheeks at the compliment, but she aimed him a wide smile. "So do you. Are we ready to leave?"

He nodded and stepped over to her and found her gaze in the mirror. "Mokana and Namara are just about done." It was clear his mind wasn't on the two water-based demons, though, as he looked her over with a small smile. His arm reached over and tugged her closer. They didn't match. His clothes were more noble-like, and hers were straight out of a time and place forgotten, but she felt like they made it work.

This was the second day of the ball, technically. Yesterday, after the massive desummoning spell went off, they'd stuck around and helped clean up some of the mess of the city. The cleansers would have their work cut out for them over the next several months. She and Rafe, and everyone else for the most part, had worked well into the evening hours, then they had placed their offerings at the temple—correctly this time, as they learned that every other year that step also hadn't been performed correctly. Neither of them had lost anyone especially close, so they headed home to rest for the remainder of the night instead of dancing under the stars and admiring the painted ceiling of the Domus Mortuorum. They hadn't seen the others who'd helped them at Srbeveara either, but Thea knew she'd be seeing them tonight.

"Are you excited about dancing again?" he asked after a moment. He was referring to the fact that she hadn't danced since she was a young teenager. A child, even. Was she excited?

She hummed. "I don't know. I guess I'll find out when I'm on the dance floor. I'll tell you what I'm not looking forward to, though."

Rafe peered down at her. "What's that?"

"You're stepping on my toes," she giggled.

The Second Chosen looked offended. "I'll have you know that for the past two weeks I've been taking lessons, thank you very much."

She gaped at him. "You've been taking lessons?"

"After my work at the Coven is done. Sometimes I had to switch to morning classes if I knew my day was going to end late."

She gasped and slapped at his shoulder. "No wonder you looked so exhausted! Rafe, I can't believe—I wouldn't have minded you stepping on my toes if it meant you getting some sleep!"

He laughed and caught her wrist from delivering another purposefully weak hit. He then brought it to his lips and kissed the back of her hand. "I wanted to surprise you."

Her face flooded with heat once more, but the words melted her from the inside. She averted her gaze and mumbled out quietly, "Well … thank you."

"Break it up, ya love-goblins!" Mokana shouted from the hallway. "You can gaze longingly into each other's eyes on the dance floor!"

Namara sighed dreamily beside her. "I hope Agni wants to dance."

The rusalka wrinkled her nose at them all. "Gah, I'm never getting with anybeing if *this* is how I'm going to act."

Thea snorted a laugh. "Come on, Mokana, we'll find someone willing to dance with you."

"Oh, no! I'm going for the snacks and the snacks only! Bring on the food!"

Domus Mortuorum was, essentially, the house of the dead. A dome ceiling crowned a cylindrical building with rounded windows carved out from the stone. Inside, the ceiling and walls were decorated in murals depicting scenes from the Wild Hunt. Thea had thought for the longest time that the paintings were nothing more than grandeur and exaggerations from children's tales, for no one had actually seen the Wild Hunt—the real Wild Hunt—in two hundred years.

It had truly been a sight to behold when the clouds descended and took form after all the offerings were made. The lake was lit up with thousands of lights and suspended orbs. The stars in the sky were out in full force, and on the horizon, one couldn't tell what light was gifted from space or magic. Beings of all kinds were dancing away the night, sitting at white-clothed tables spread out across the lawn, or catching up with their lost loved ones at the Domus Mortuorum.

Under the crystal chandelier that floated over the outside dance floor and the glowing candles it held, Thea danced with grace with Leon Zvěrokruh. The Summoner was just as fluid in his movements as she was, but it was cold and business-like just as all the other dances in her life had been. That wasn't to say the Summoner was anything like the sleazy men who'd wanted her young attentions back in the day, but there was no connection between the two other than a cordial understanding of one another.

"I'm glad you guys were able to survive the battle," she stated awkwardly halfway through the song.

A shadow seemed to cross through his eyes, and Thea wondered if she'd been wrong about that. Many beings had lost their life during the war, so perhaps she'd misspoken. "Um, I mean—"

Leon nodded and offered her a bland smile. "Yeah, we're glad you guys made it out, too. Thanks to you, the northern border was quickly secured."

She let out the breath she'd been holding and nodded as well. She twirled out at the next step in the dance, held onto by a calloused hand, before she was twirled back in place. "That's good to hear."

The conversation died after that, and the song couldn't end quickly enough. They parted with a nod to each other, and she called out for him to enjoy the rest of the night before rushing off the dance floor. The next song started playing, but she wasn't about to get trapped in another awkward situation like that again. She found Rafe's tall form by the table loaded with foods of all kinds and stepped up quietly by his side. He offered a small plate with a sliver of cake and some sandwiches.

"I'm about to glamour myself," he complained. "I almost got pulled away by someone else just now. I see you also bailed on the next song. I swear if I get dragged away for one more thing—"

Thea laughed and took a bite of her sandwich. "I guess that means you don't care for a dance? We haven't gotten to share one yet," she said after she swallowed down her food.

His shoulders relaxed, and he held out his hand. No one would mind them cutting in a little late. Thea set down her plate, knowing she would forget where she put it later but not caring in the moment, and took his offered hand. They swept out across the dance floor, and it felt like all eyes were on her. She recognized many were looking at Rafe, but he was looking at her, and that was all that mattered.

The song was playing a calm melody, and she got lost in the lilting, hauntingly beautiful notes. Rafe whirled her around gently, and she let a laugh bubble up from her chest as he so effortlessly lifted her. His eyes were soft, his smile softer. He winced when he stepped on her heel, but she only laughed again.

She twirled out of his embrace, landed in the arms of Leto Remes, and her eyes nearly popped out of her skull. The blue cloak laughed at her expression and whirled her back into Rafe's arms. She looked back and found the High Priest with a giggling Isabel dancing away with him. She was wearing the pale yellow qynzo, and together the four of them swirled around each other in perfect rhythm.

"It must be his and Lilith's turn to step away from the spell," Rafe commented, easily dipping Thea close to the floor.

She sprang back up and peered over her shoulder. "I wonder if he's the one …"

"Yeah, he's definitely the one. I'm just glad they've decided to stop tiptoeing around each other. Isabel never thinking she was good enough was really getting in the way of Leto's courting."

Thea's brow quirked. "Isabel always came off as so confident. Why does she feel that way?"

"You should know better than anyone how someone's insecurities don't necessarily match their personality."

Thea's lips thinned, and she nodded. She remembered the redhead's words on the mountaintop. *"It's complicated."* She shook her head and let it go. It wasn't any of her business. She was just glad the researcher was happy and laughing away. But a blue cloak? She never saw it coming, not from the magic-hating woman she'd been dragged through the mountains with.

"Oh, that must mean my brother is around here somewhere," Rafe said suddenly, dragging Thea out of her thoughts. She glanced up and found him searching the crowd before giving up. "He usually hates these types of events, but Lilith would have dragged him out here."

She could picture the strong-willed woman doing exactly that and yanking a big Rafe look-alike by the ear. She chuckled at the thought.

"Speaking of blue cloaks," Rafe continued, and paused only to twirl Thea out one last time. She spun back into his waiting arms and aimed a questioning look up at him. "What's your decision? You have until the Wild Hunt is over. One more day after this is all that's left."

She sighed and curtsied as the song ended. They stayed on the dance floor and waited for the next one to continue. "Would you believe me if I said I still don't know?"

The next song was another slow one, which she welcomed. She took his hands again. "What's troubling you?"

He stepped on her toe once more, and she snickered. It didn't hurt all that much if she was being honest, but she should have known better than to buy *white* shoes. "Well, I love my field work, but Namara brought something to my attention. I want to bring it up to the High Priests, and depending on their answer depends on if I stay."

Rafe quirked a brow at her. "Stay a Spellweaver?"

She shook her head. "Stay with the Coven."

The song continued to play, but Rafe froze on the dance floor. "What?" He gaped at her and shook himself when he realized he was in the way of the other dancers. They quickly reclaimed their rhythm. "You've been working for the Coven for years. Your goals, all of your dreams began with the Coven. Why would you want to leave?"

She looked out over the sea of beings, both of the physical and spiritual realms clustered around tables, and then out beyond the glittering lake. "The Coven's helped me so much. It's gotten me to this point in my life, and I'll always be grateful. But that doesn't mean it can't change for the better. I know a lot of beings who would be on my side on this. I think I can do this, Rafe. I want to help demons like Namara and Mokana and Agni and—all of them. We're part of the governing force of our nation, yet we can't even guarantee the fates of those we employ? I want them to have a plan for the future we can't be a part of. I want them to always have a purpose and a sense of belonging. Same with the Dragonkin. I didn't realize how bad they have it, and I blame my ignorance for that. They're citizens just like the rest of us, and they should be able to call Tolvade home just as much as we do. And—And the beings of Herbon deserve peace of mind too. The blood mages need to be dealt with for good—as well as the Dark Market." She took a deep breath, realizing she'd been rambling.

Rafe stared down at her for several minutes as he assessed her. He then slowly leaned down and placed a kiss on her forehead. As soft as a butterfly's wings, he pulled back and gave her a smile that wove itself into every corner of her heart. "Whatever you choose to do, know that I'll do everything in my power to support you." He spun her around before she could respond, and when the song ended, he held up a finger. "On one condition."

"What's that?"

"Move in with me."

Her eyes widened, and then confusion twisted her features. "But I'm already—"

"You're still paying for your old place. After everything, are you really planning on moving back in?"

She forgot to bow at the end of the song, but it didn't matter. She was led out to the lawn, where she sat down at a dimly lit table. Her thoughts raced all the while.

It was true. Ever since the beginning of this all, she'd been staying with Rafe with the idea of leaving when it all came to an end. Yet, as the weeks stretched by, and more and more dangerous missions were stacked on top of their shoulders, she'd come back to Rafe's duplex with the thought of home on her mind. And it wasn't just the comforts of the duplex, of the memories that they'd shared under the one roof, but it was the man himself that she'd come home to.

"Okay," she said quietly. She glanced up at him and his wide eyes. "I'll move in. Completely. Namara deserves a bigger room than your small office anyway."

Rafe quirked a brow before the implications of what she'd said got through his thick skull. His cheeks warmed slightly, and he looked away. "I'm going to need to get a bigger bed. You kick when you sleep."

She tossed back her head and laughed, and it was like a floodgate of happy, glowing emotions bursting from within her. She then sent the Summoner an impish grin. "You know … if we're going to be moving around all this furniture, we could look into a new place? Namara likes the view of the waterfall from those houses in Vemeese …"

Rafe gave her a thoughtful look before a warm smile overtook his face. "I think we can arrange that. I'm sure I can get all my siblings to help us move, too."

Thea's jaw dropped. "Wait, really?"

"Oh yeah. Leto actually told me what I could expect on my next check, and … we'll be able to afford that nice house, Thea."

As if a weight had been lifted off her shoulders, she found herself laughing all over again. They could enjoy the rest of the night and begin thinking of the future tomorrow. The demons were gone, the tablets had been reunited, and the magic in the land was no longer dying. She could feel it in the air, in her blood, in every breath she took, and in the lightness in which everyone carried themselves.

She looked over at the dance floor and found Namara and Agni, in his full demonic form, dancing away without a care in the world. Beings stared, but the two carried on with laughter.

She was going to preserve their happiness any way she could. She didn't know what the future held, but she was going to make sure changes happened. If the Coven didn't help her after everything she's done for them, she'd find something else that would.

She eyed Rafe, who was looking out over the sea of beings with a content look on his handsome face. "Come on," she said and slapped the table lightly. "Let's dance some more. I want to fall into bed tonight exhausted and sleep in tomorrow. No waking up before the sun," she ordered, and Rafe stood up with a chuckle.

"But then how will I make you breakfast in bed?"

She aimed a weak glare at him, but it melted into a lazy grin. "You won't. We'll make it together."

"I like the sound of that."

She hummed and took his hand in hers. "Me too."

Chapter Forty-Six

The Last Goodbye

Blythe waited until the last few beings made their offerings before she crossed the lit-up lake. She'd been dreading this all week. It'd been a losing battle between her and her thoughts ever since she heard about the Wild Hunt. She kept thinking about the offerings that were to be made … and how today was the last day she'd have the chance to make those offerings.

On the first day of the Wild Hunt, she had wanted to make her offerings and be done with it. But Aegis Alliance had taken all her strength from her when it finally went down. She remembered waking up on the cold, cave floor, and her memory of what had transpired that day had been spotty the rest of the evening. She'd gone to bed that night staring at the empty side of her bed, but the tears refused to come to her anymore.

On the second day of the Wild Hunt, she had been fully prepared to march across the lake, give Cressida a piece of her mind for how she'd lied to her, deceived her, *left* her. She'd picked out her best dress to show Cressida exactly what she was missing. Her dark blue ballgown had glittered like the midnight sky, and her hair had been tied up in several knots and decorated in small, navy, silk scarves. She would have outshone even the Celestial. But she'd gotten as far as the lake's shore, saw the dome-shaped building full of beings wanting to speak to their lost loved ones, and turned around and left without a word. Only briefly did she catch a glimpse of Thea and Rafe in the crowd, and a part of her resented her cowardice. She could have had the two of them supporting her through this, but now she had only herself.

Now it was the third night of the Wild Hunt, and she was out of chances if she didn't go make her offerings. Yet … she still wasn't ready. Not when an offering also meant goodbye. The *final* goodbye. She knew that she would see Cressida. She had saved Cressida's soul, after all. The dragon blood her oathbound had consumed had killed her, stolen her away, but it had cleansed the darkness from within. She'd been saved, and so there was no doubt that she had been part of the Wild Hunt that crashed down onto the city with a vengeance.

She watched from within Domus Mortuorum as a few beings made their offerings, and she busied her hands by wiping at the invisible wrinkles of her periwinkle, mermaid gown. She wouldn't be dancing tonight, so the form-fitting outfit wasn't a concern. As she looked out the many windows of the building and watched the stars twinkle from beyond, she thought she might never dance again.

When those making their offerings finally left, she made her way over. Her movements were slow, stiff as she lit the incense stick, placed the tulip she'd been holding close to her chest down on the altar, and knelt to the ground.

"I offer this tulip as a symbol of our love, my oathbound. Please, *please* do not hide from me. I wish to speak to you one last time." She swept her arms out and whispered, "May the goddess bless your passing from this world to the next." The words were hollow and didn't mean much to her, but the cultural significance would be important to Cressida, who had been born in this city. Or maybe it wouldn't be. It was Cressida she was making an offering to after all.

She stepped back and turned away. She walked with her head held high through the doors of the old building, past the lake, and over the grass lawn. She passed through rushing crowds and floating orbs and heard the trumpets begin to belt out into the night as she found a table near the back. She sat down while everyone standing just outside Domus Mortuorum pointed up at the sky. The clouds high in the air came down in a wave and settled over the lake like fog, and those lost to the war began to take form and meet with their loved ones. There were still plenty of beings milling about on the final night of the Wild Hunt Ball, but she still didn't see anyone she recognized. She was all alone in this.

"Is this seat taken?" a familiar voice spoke softly.

Blythe looked up and felt as if the air had been punched from her lungs.

Cressida was bathed in a milky-white light as she stood by the table. Her sharp, green eyes were gentler now, pale in the ethereal glow she was bathed in. Mutely, Blythe shook her head. The ex-sorceress pulled out the chair in front of her and sat down. They simply stared at each other for a moment, and Blythe couldn't find the words she had angrily latched onto all day.

"I'm sorry," Cressida finally said. She peered down at her ghostly hands messing with the wrinkles in the linen before finding Blythe's gaze once more. "I can't tell you how sorry I am, Blythe. I never meant for any of this to happen."

Blythe felt her lips tremble, and she whispered out, "*Dy ondz khebits'or.*"

Cressida looked away. "I didn't mean to *lie* to you. I didn't want you to see that side of me. I didn't want you to see how weak I was. The curse made me sick, the dark magic made it worse, but I had been weak all along. I …" Tears glistened in her pale green eyes, and she swept a ginger lock behind her ear. "I had finally found happiness after all these years. You … You made me so happy, Blythe. Everyone I ever cared about left me or died, and then you come along, and it's like everything is perfect. But then I find out I'm Medusa Kiss's next victim." She laughed around a wet sob, and the sound struck Blythe through the heart. "I wanted to do everything in my power to stop it from taking me. Even if that meant losing a part of myself in the process … Looking back now, I see that piece of me that I lost was a lot bigger than I realized. I … I hope you can forgive me."

Blythe carefully wiped at her eyes and sniffed. She didn't know why she had bothered putting on makeup for this. Maybe she thought she wasn't going to cry. That she was going to be angry. That she had already moved on. That she had left all her tears behind her. What a fool she could be at times.

"Of course, I forgive you. I am just so …" She took a shuddering breath and locked eyes with her lost oathbound. "I am still so *mad* at you. I wish you could have trusted me. I wish you would have believed in me. I wish you would have confided in me. I am your *oathbound*. I deserved to know what you were going through. I could have gone back to my homeland—" She cut herself off and took another deep breath. There was no point discussing what-ifs. Cressida was dead now. She stared out across the lake and watched beings she didn't know dance and laugh and have the time of their lives.

"Just answer one question for me," she pleaded softly after a moment, but she didn't turn to look at the woman she loved.

"Anything, my heart."

"Why didn't you come back to me?" She finally met her eyes and watched as sadness filled the gem-like irises she loved so much.

"I couldn't bear to be with you in the form of a familiar. I couldn't watch you find someone else, love them as you did me, and know I would be nothing more than an animal through it all."

Blythe shook her head, and she felt her chest close to bursting. The tears slipped down her cheeks as she sobbed out, "There won't ever be anyone else!"

Cressida flinched, but her expression didn't change. "You say that now, Blythe, but one day—"

"Who else can compare? *You* are my oathbound. *You* are the only one I will ever love, Cressi. How could you decide something so selfish and leave me all alone? I'm all alone, Cressida!"

She broke down into tears and brought her trembling hands to hide her face. She hated this. She hated all of this. Why couldn't life let her be happy? Why couldn't life have let Cressida be happy? Why did Medusa's Kiss have to choose her of all beings? No, that wasn't quite right—why did Medusa's Kiss have to exist at all? Why couldn't

Cressida have had one consistent thing in her life, a person she could trust that hadn't been ripped away from her, so that when the time came, she could have trusted Blythe with the truth? Why? *Why, why why—*

She felt gentle fingers pulling at her, and she sniffed and looked into her love's soft gaze. Those same, gentle fingers swiped at her running makeup with a tenderness that made her chest ache all over again.

"That's not true," Cressida cooed to her. "I've been watching you, my love. You are not alone. You have become the mother to all those at the sanctuary, a dear friend to many in the city, and I know you will be loved by many more in the future. And I will always be there with you as well." She smiled at her and curled a strand of hair behind her ear. "I don't know if I should be impressed or saddened by your conviction to never love another again. A part of me is happy. I want you to always love me like I love you, but I want you to be happy, too, Blythe."

Blythe sniffed and watched miserably as her oathbound messed with the fine hairs she'd gelled down by her ear. "I can be happy all by myself, though. I can be happy with the creatures in the sanctuary and the friends that I have made."

Cressida nodded. "Yes, you can, but promise me one thing, my little peacock griffon."

She made a small noise, and Cressida's hand found her own. It was cool to the touch, and a fresh wave of sadness crashed into her as the reality that she was truly, *truly* gone settled over her. Cressida tipped her chin up so that she would meet her eyes.

"Promise me that if love ever does find you again, that you will give it a chance. I don't want you settling for just anyone, but if someone comes along and offers you the world, grab it with both hands, my darling. Promise me."

Blythe felt cold fingers slip between her own, and the vision in front of her wavered as more tears slipped down her cheeks. Memories of their life together flitted by in the back of her mind, but as she stared into Cressida's milky-green eyes, none of them mattered as much as this moment right now. Because this moment, this final goodbye, would live on with her in Cressida's place. The coolness of her fingers on her chin, the light that shone around her, the soft notes of the Wild Hunt Ball's orchestra playing across the dewy lawn. She would remember every detail. She would engrave it upon her soul. She would—

Her lips trembled as she opened them to speak, but her words were lost to the breeze. She tried once more, but her heart squeezed, and whatever she wanted to say was stolen as Cressida's lips found hers. A sob tore through her throat, muffled only by their kiss. She flung her arms around her oathbound's shoulders and hung on as if she could keep Cressida here with strength alone. The soft press of her lips was cold, but it was everything her heart had wanted for weeks. A kiss to wipe away her tears. A kiss to make everything better. A kiss to forget everything that's happened to them … A kiss to go back to the way they used to be.

Cressida drew back despite Blythe's quiet protest, but she soon felt those soft lips caress her tear-stained cheeks. "Promise me," her love whispered in her ear.

Blythe steeled herself and closed her eyes. She could make this one last promise. She could shoulder all this pain by herself. She wouldn't ever need anyone ever again. But for Cressida, she would assure her. She would make this promise not for herself, but for the woman she loved. What was one, little, tiny white lie in the face of all that Cressida had done to her?

She took a deep breath, but her voice was nothing more than a quiet whisper. "I promise."

A tear slipped down Cressida's cheek. "Then—"

"But you have to promise me something, too."

Blythe felt the tremors in her fingers as they dug into the illustrious material Cressida was wrapped in. It was the outfit she was burned in. Seeing it clinging to her love's slender frame broke one more thing within her, but she needed to say this. If these were the last words she would ever get to say to Cressida, she'd rather it be this than even "I love you." Because this meant more.

Cressida's brow furrowed. "What is it?"

Blythe found her gaze, and her fingers cupped the woman's cool cheeks. "When it is my time to leave this world … please … please come find me. I will walk this life alone for however long I have to, but promise me right now that this is not the end for us. Come find me, and let us live the life we were supposed to have together in the stars. Promise me."

Cressida's eyes shone as if touched by the goddess herself, and her tears reflected like glass from the floating orbs over the crystal lake. She lifted her hand and extended one slender pinky, and she smiled the most beautiful smile Blythe would only ever see again in her dreams.

"I promise."

Epilogue

A Lifetime Swallowed by the Stars

Kishnar could hear the mad giggles coming down the hallway, and he heaved a silent sigh as he stepped away from the reference rotary. The large wooden wheel was designed to keep several books open at once. Seven flat, wooden slats each allowed a heavy tome to stay open on the desired page while the scholar rotated through whichever reference was needed in searching for the answers to life's many mysteries.

Whoever was behind the giggles nearing the door was *not* one of such mysteries. It had been many centuries since he'd had to perform the massive desummoning spell on that fateful day, yet it had been a few centuries before that when the Celestial had last taken the elixir to keep from going mad indefinitely.

It was time once again.

He swept across the glittering tiles and waved a hand in the air. The arched door before him opened up, and the High Elf in charge of the country he resided under came stumbling in. They took one look at him, and their giggles stopped, and immediately tears began overflowing from their iridescent gaze. Kishnar sighed again. They were apparently like this almost every time and would probably be like this the next time as well. The price to pay for a life so long lived. He would not be around to see them the next time, but this did not sadden him. His life was vast in comparison to a mortal's, and all that time allowed him to gain all the knowledge in the universe.

Come along, he instructed, and the Celestial sniffed and followed him.

Their emotions had been described as chaotic and ranging from one extreme to the other. Their equilibrium—as he found out after having to catch them when they stumbled—was also affected by their descent into madness. They flinched out of his hold, and their eyes were wide as they frantically began looking around the room.

"They're coming, they're coming," they began to mumble beside him.

He had been instructed by the others to play along with the High Elf's ramblings, so he quietly asked, *Who is coming?*

"The dragons, the dragons, the—" they broke off into a sob so loud it pierced his sensitive ears. He sighed quietly again.

That, too, had happened hundreds of years ago. He recalled it was not too long after his day in the sun. Disaster had fallen onto the city once more, but he had not been called to go above ground. He did not know the specifics, but it did not matter to him. The world above could burn to ashes, and it would slowly be rebuilt as was the mother and father's design.

Maybe that was what had happened after all.

"It's okay, it's okay," the Celestial cooed in a childlike voice, tears having suddenly evaporated. "Mother gained another star in the sky that day. She was so young though …"

He nodded along and led them to the entrance of the library, and immediately they began to twirl around under the nebulous waters hanging over the many shelves. They both walked—or, as to say, *he* walked, *they* spun about and danced and skipped and frolicked and nearly tripped over their feet—past the cradle of fire that would burn away their memories.

He procured a goblet from his robes and held out his hand high in the air. A massive, dark shape moved through the water above him. Slowly, a creature's trunk of immense length slipped through the surface. It grabbed ahold of the goblet and retreated up to the rippling water. With a quick motion, it flipped the cup over and dipped it into the loch. It flipped it again and brought it back to Kishnar's waiting hand.

The Celestial stared in awe as the creature's trunk disappeared back into the water and the shadow moved away. The Skrite handed the drink to the High Elf, and they bounded over and peered inside.

"Oooh, pretty," they murmured.

Drink, he ordered softly.

They downed the contents in one gulp, yet the face they made told him it must not have tasted very good. Immediately afterward, a trace fell over them. They blinked in a daze, and their mind numbed out.

Spread your arms and call to the Mother. He moved them around and positioned them in front of the cradle of fire and kept their wobbly arms raised as they called—very softly— up to the goddess.

The fire in the cradle crackled, and sparks flew up into the ceiling. Rather than being snuffed out, the embers were captured in the water and immortalized as bits of memory. They sparked with life from the depths, and Kishnar peered up as he watched a thousand years of the Celestial's life flash before him. The following images emerged:

An open book full of poems next to a note.

Countless faces coming and going, standing before thirteen chairs. Coven members in blue cloaks sitting on either side of them, some who look away too fast.

Coven members in those same blue cloaks warring amongst one another. A mass of golden light, and all that was wrong was made right by a raven-haired girl. Hellhounds caged within spelled bars.

A tablet centuries old and full of this world's magic cradled in hands of light. Then, darkness, and a prince of shadow and sin standing proud just before that darkness gave way to the white light that spilled forth. A second tablet. A third. A Fourth.

A dome that protected all those who dwelled within. A spelled seal that brought the clouds in the sky together to form an army.

A sea of thankful faces. Towns rebuilt. Roads that had once not been there were now paved. A mountain of snow and ice and friendly faces. A desert with a sea of sand and beings protected by the subjects of the goddess. A harbor filled with ships from those who sailed the seas.

A butterfly flapping its wings before landing on an outstretched finger.

More, countless meetings. Peaceful smiles. Peaceful blessings.

Then, abruptly, the memories changed.

The image of a dragon flashed in the water. Many dragons. Sharp teeth and flapping wings—

An explosion of light—

Ah, so that is what transpired that day.

The Celestial kept calling, and the fire in the cradle roared until it drowned out their voice. As the memories engraved themselves into the suspended loch, the High Elf waved on their feet. Kishnar was there as they collapsed into his waiting arms. The last of this lifetime fizzled away from them, but the embers …

The embers would always remember.

The End
Or is it?

From the author:

The story of Thea and Rafe (and Blythe) is over, but the world of Raen is just getting started. There are many more stories in and out of Aeristria that have yet to be told. Look forward to more cameo appearances from your favorite characters, more magic, and more adventures in the future!

If you've enjoyed this series, please tell us so in an honest review. The feelings we bring out in you, you bring out in us when you tell us what you loved, what you wish could have happened, and what you can't wait for. Thank you all for accompanying us on this amazing journey. I can't tell you all how much you've helped us grow as authors and as beings ourselves.

May you forever find the right books in your time of need.

Octavia J. Riley

Glossary

<u>Places:</u>

Adalith: add-ah-lith

Aeristria: air-ist-tree-ah

Borlimane: boar-lih-main

Satviriya: sat-veer-ee-ah

Tolvade: toll-vade

Vemeese: veh-meese (rhymes with geese)

<u>Beings:</u>

Cel'dion: cell-dee-on

Chhêu: che-oo

Cleatus: klee-tus

Denmarius: den-mar-ee-us

Dulce Maina: dull-say my-nuh

Enzou: en-zo

Eurytus: eu-ry-tus

Fatik: fay-tick

Fông: fong

Hajun: hah-june

Huǒshān: hu-oh-shen

Khien: key-en

Kishnar: kish-nar

Lahlou: la-loo

Malachi: mal-uh-kai (rhymes with sky)

Me'Glach: meh-glock

Merrjewl: mer-jewel

Molionids: Mole-ee-an-ids (the singular name of Cleatus and Eurytus)

O'Glach: oh-glock

Phú: Foo

Reesa: ree-sah

Renkilo: ren-key-low

Siàu: s-yao

Tasgall: tass (rhymes with grass)-gul

Tiōng: tea-oh-ng

Demons/Creatures:

abyzou: ap-bee-zoo

Azbanonite: as-ban-oh-night

dakini: dah-key-knee

cecaelia: seh-sail-ee-ah

Fae: fay

Ghul: ghoul

impundulu: im-pun-doo-loo

jötunn: joe-ton

longma: long-muh

nandi (bear): nahn-dee (bear)

rakshasa: rock-sha-sah

rok: roh-ck

rusalka: roo-sal-kuh

Skrite: s-cry-t

Skrittish: sk-rit-tish (rhymes with dish)

Remember, folks, skrit is a derogatory word and should not be used!

Other:

Ernimoen: air-knee-mow-en

Hondonese: hon-done (rhymes with clone)-eze (like easy)

Hondonis: hon-done (rhymes with clone)-iss

pagoda: puh-go-duh

qynzo: chin-dzo ("d" is hardly pronounced just like the "t" in tsunami)

Blythe and Dulce's Phrases and Words:

Irnomuin: Ernimoen

bibi: papa/dad (informal for father)

emmi: mama/mom (informal for mother)

Eltom Dimoz: Golden Sea

Gaygha: village (shorted name for Gaygha Peshtpenvets i Estvetsyt'aynniruv)

Gaygha Peshtpenvets i Estvetsyt'aynniruv: The Village Protected by Deities

Zermenelo: Amazing

Dy ondz khebits'or: You lied to me